The Loveless Brothers

Enemies With Benefits

Best Fake Fiancé

Break the Rules

The Hookup Equation

One Last Time

Wildwood Society

The One Month Boyfriend

The Two Week Roommate

Dirtshine Series

Never Enough

Always You

Ever After

Standalone Romances

Ride

Reign

Torch

Safekeeping

The Savage Wild

Convict

the Hookup Equation

USA TODAY BESTSELLING AUTHOR
ROXIE NOIR

Copyright © 2020 by Roxie Noir

All rights reserved.

No part of this book may be reproduced in any form or by any electronic or mechanical means, including information storage and retrieval systems, without written permission from the author, except for the use of brief quotations in a book review.

Cover: Najla Qamber Designs

For all the women who use the men's room sometimes.

Fuck the patriarchy.

CHAPTER ONE
THALIA

I put my head down on my arms and groan.

"Come on," commands Victoria from across the table. "You got this. You can do it."

"We believe in you!" Harper adds, on my right. "Go, Thalia! Go! Go! Chug!"

"Chug?" asks Margaret, cool, calm, and collected on my left.

"Chug… knowledge?" Harper says. "Look, I'm just getting into the spirit of the thing."

"You know, *chug knowledge*," Victoria deadpans. "The common phrase that people say all the time?"

"See?" says Harper.

I lift my head, rest my chin on my arms, and look at Margaret again. She's holding six fingers up in front of her face, the answer sheet in front of her, and trying not to laugh at Harper.

"Which ones do we have?" I ask.

Margaret clears her throat and looks down at our answer sheet.

"Chastity," she starts. "The easy one."

"Is it?" asks Victoria, and Margaret just grins.

"Charity," she goes on. "Temperance."

Harper snorts.

"Kindness, patience, and humility. Props to Victoria for coming up with that last one."

"Thank you."

Margaret and Victoria clink their glasses together, then each drink.

"I don't know," I tell them, carefully resting my forehead against my fist. "Fortitude? Is that a virtue?"

"It sounds like it could be," Margaret says.

"Filling up the gas tank in a borrowed car," I say, still staring at the tabletop, willing my brain to work better. "Picking up litter that isn't even yours? Making more coffee if you take the last cup? Remembering to wipe the stove down after you do the dishes."

"Pretty sure it's gonna be one word," Margaret says.

"I like fortitude," Harper says. "It sounds right."

"It's not," I say. "Arrrrrgh."

Victoria puts her elbows down on the table, silver bracelets clanking, then leans toward me, her red lipstick bright against her ebony skin, her hair bouncing gently with the motion.

"Thalia," she says, very, very seriously. "You attended twelve years of Catholic school."

"Thirteen," I correct.

"Thirteen years of Catholic school," she says, not missing a beat. "Thirteen years of itchy wool skirts, ugly sweaters, and nuns. Thirteen years of getting your knuckles smacked by rulers. Thirteen years of no boys. And you know why?"

Victoria pauses dramatically. She's got a flair for this sort of thing.

"Why?" I ask, totally drawn in.

"For this moment," she goes on. "I don't believe in coincidences, Thalia. You went to Catholic school for a reason, and that reason is this very bar trivia question."

Victoria can sometimes get kind of intense after she's had a few drinks, and that means she's taking this bar trivia night *really* seriously.

"You have it in you," she goes on. "I know you've got that seventh virtue knocking around somewhere in that brain of yours. Come on, Catholic school. Come on."

"Come on, Catholic school!" Harper hoots, pumping one fist in the air.

She's had a few more drinks than the rest of us. She's the birthday girl, after all.

"Cath. Lick. School!" Harper says, slowly, pumping that fist. "Cath. Lick school! Come on!"

"Oh God," I mutter.

"Ask for all the intercessions you want," Victoria says, sitting back, spreading her hands wide. "Francis? Christopher? Mary, you up there? Help a girl out!"

Right above us, the speaker crackles.

"All right, you've got another sixty seconds to name as many of the seven virtues as you can for our free drink round!" the trivia host says. "Then it's on to pop culture. Hope you've been paying attention to the movies this year!"

"Cath-lick school!" Harper says again, motioning for Margaret and Victoria to join in. "Come on! CATH-LICK SCHOOL!"

"CATH-LICK SCHOOL! CATH-LICK SCHOOL!"

Now all three are chanting. Margaret's banging the table. I squeeze my eyes shut, fingers pinching the bridge of my nose.

Nothing.

I *know* I know it, but I can't think of the seventh virtue to save my life.

Instead, I take a drink of my whiskey ginger.

Still nothing. I take another sip.

Maybe six is enough, I think. *Do the other teams even know six virtues?*

Six virtues are plenty, right?

I put my glass back down on the table.

As I do, the name of the seventh virtue hits me so hard I practically fall out of my chair, and I grab Margaret's arm dramatically.

"DILIGENCE!" I whisper-shout, trying to keep the other trivia teams from overhearing me. "IT'S DILIGENCE. D-I-L-I—"

She's already written it, because a pre-med college senior with a 3.9 GPA knows how to spell *diligence*.

Margaret jumps off her chair without another word, pen still in hand, waving our answer sheet as she makes her way toward the trivia night moderator.

"Go!" Harper shouts, unnecessarily.

"Is that it? You're sure?" Victoria asks. "You're totally sure?"

"I'm totally super sure," I say, and drain my whiskey ginger in excitement. "Once I wrote a paper for tenth grade English and somehow only spell-checked the first half, and Sister Agatha called me in and lectured me about the virtue diligence, and God, she *loved* reminding me that a young lady could never have enough virtue —"

"Of course you can," Harper says. She's blue-eyed, blonde, and looks like she'd be hard-pressed to understand a complicated traffic light.

But looks can be deceiving, because she knows five languages, three of which are dead, and once spent an entire evening explaining the economics of the late Roman Empire to me.

"I've got plenty of virtue," she says. "Victoria's got

plenty. Margaret, I dunno. Thalia, God knows you've got more than enough and could probably stand to offload a little."

"What's Thalia offloading?" Margaret asks, sitting again.

"My virtue," I say, maintaining a perfectly straight face. "I was thinking of dumping it in the river down by the old railroad bridge, since Harper thinks I've got too much."

Margaret laughs and takes another drink from her gin and tonic.

"Well, I think you should dump your virtue whenever you want and into whatever receptacle, so long as everyone involved is an enthusiastically consenting adult," she says. "And don't forget to be safe."

The four of us have been friends since we were freshman and roommates since we were sophomores, so by now, the fact that I'm still a virgin is a running joke. It's not like I have some strong attachment to my virginity, I just happen to still have it.

"Allllll right, the scores are tallied up!" the trivia host says over the speaker.

All four of us sit bolt upright, hanging onto every word, especially Harper. After all, this was her idea of a fun twenty-first birthday party — some people do twenty-one shots and get blitzed, she's had considerably less than that and is determined to utterly destroy the trivia night competition.

"Turns out you all aren't up to snuff on your virtues," the guy goes on. "Last week the drink round question was the seven deadly sins, and let me tell you, those teams…"

"You're running trivia night, you're not a stand-up," Harper mutters. "Get to the question."

"Down, girl," Victoria says, patting her arm.

"I'm just saying."

"Anyway, there's no coin toss tonight because only one team managed to name all seven heavenly virtues!"

Harper punches me excitedly in the shoulder. Victoria bounces her palms on the table.

"Tell us," Margaret hisses.

I'd say that my friends can be a little competitive and intense, but I'm also leaning over the table, both hands clenched into fists, waiting to see if we won even though I'm ninety percent sure we did.

"And those are, of course, Patience, Charity, Chastity, Kindness, Humility, Diligence —"

"Yessssss," hisses Margaret.

"—and a virtue that nobody here tonight is celebrating, Temperance!"

That gets a mild laugh from the various tables around the bar.

"Congrats to the winners of tonight's drink round, Tequila Mockingbird! The bartender will be around with your shots in just a few minutes. The next round starts in ten."

"Shots?" I ask the table, frowning. "Can't I just get another whiskey ginger? What's it a shot *of*? What if I don't want a shot, can I —"

"You could go ask someone who knows," Harper says. "Or you could have some fun and do a shot with us."

"No peer pressuring," Margaret admonishes her.

"Yeah, no peer pressuring," I add, laughing.

"I wasn't peer pressuring," Harper protests, picking up her own glass. I think it's her third drink, but since it's finally her twenty-first birthday — she skipped the third grade, so she's a year younger than the rest of us — no judgement from me.

"Are you kidding? That was a textbook example of peer pressure," Victoria adds in.

"No, a textbook example would be, like, hey kid, have some marijuana because all the cool kids are doing it and also your friends are doing marijuana, and you won't be fun if you don't do drugs," Harper says. "I didn't say that, I just said shots are fun."

The three of us all give her separate quizzical looks.

"Is everything you know about drugs from *D.A.R.E.* in the fifth grade?" Margaret finally asks.

Harper shrugs dramatically and finishes off her drink while Victoria catches Margaret's eye and simply nods.

"Right," Margaret says. "Anyway, don't — oh, *wow*."

I follow her gaze over Harper's shoulder.

Wow is right, because the curly-haired, no-nonsense, tattooed female bartender is standing there, holding a tray with four shots on it.

They're not regular-sized shots. They're in those tall shot glasses.

And they are *bright* blue.

"Here you go," she says, stepping forward and depositing the glasses on the table in front of us. Margaret moves our pencils and answer sheets out of the way. "Four Smurfs' Vacations. Enjoy!"

Just like that, she's gone. Delicately, Victoria picks up a shot glass.

"No!" Harper says, waving one hand. "We have to do it together!"

"I'm just smelling it," Victoria says, laughing at Harper. "I think it's... coconut rum and blue curacao?"

"It's something blue for sure," I say, picking up a shot glass as well and watching the liquid suspiciously, wondering if this is a good idea.

On one hand, I don't really do shots. I'm a total lightweight, and it only takes a couple of drinks before I'm that embarrassing girl who's vomiting in someone's bushes while sobbing that squirrels are too precious for this world.

Just a random example of something that could, in theory, happen to a lightweight. It's certainly not an actual incident from freshman year.

On the other hand, I've only had two drinks so far, it's Harper's twenty-first birthday, and this is basically my last chance to party before diving headfirst into my senior year of college.

"Is the idea that this is what Smurfs drink when they're on vacation?" Victoria asks, looking deep into her shot glass. "Or is this made of Smurfs?"

"This just got dark," I say.

"You're overthinking this," Harper tells her. "Stop it. It's my birthday. No thinking. Cheers!"

We clink our glasses together over the center of the table. We all shout, "Wooo!" We all drink.

The Smurf's Vacation isn't as bad as it looks. True, it's so sweet I feel like a sugar bomb went off in my mouth, and yes, fake coconut and fake banana are both horrible flavors, and yeah, there's an unappealing and stringent aftertaste, but I've definitely had way worse.

There are four distinct *clonks* as we each put our shot glasses back on the table, each of us making a noise of surprise at what we just put into our mouths.

"Smurf jizz," Harper says.

"Stop it," says Victoria.

"At least you waited until after we drank to say that," I tell them.

"It was an experience," says Victoria, taking a gulp of her Guinness.

I glance down at the floor to my right as I feel the Smurf's Vacation start to take effect. If I was tipsy before, I'm definitely headed toward *kinda drunk* now, and I'm trying to calculate the best course of action to get off this barstool with my dignity intact.

Difficulty level: short-ish skirt and three-inch heeled boots.

Good thing alcohol makes me brave. I swing my legs around and hop off, and I only wobble a little bit when I land.

"Be right back," I tell my friends, and then I head for the bathroom at the back of the bar, winding between other trivia teams and past pool tables.

The Tipsy Cavalier is... sort of a dignified dive bar, if that makes sense. Even though Marysburg is a college town, it's far enough from campus that it's not frequented by undergrads. It's quieter than an undergrad bar. It's a little bit civilized, never mind that it's in the basement of a former warehouse that's probably been standing since the mid-1800s.

That's one thing about Virginia I still haven't quite gotten used to, even though my family moved to the state seven years ago now. How *old* everything can be. The walls in the back of the bar, where the hall with the bathrooms are, are made of raw stone and I swear they've got hundred-year-old graffiti on them.

As soon as I turn the corner, I see the line.

"Crap," I mutter to myself, stopping short.

Against the wall there are five — wait, no, six — women, all either chatting with each other or looking at their phones, all clearly waiting to use the single-stall women's bathroom.

I sigh and get in the line, hoping I don't miss the beginning of the next round. The woman next to me is scrolling Instagram, and I wish I hadn't left my phone in my purse back at the table as I wait.

And wait.

And *wait*.

I wonder what on earth the woman in the bathroom is even doing. Is she pooping? Taking a bath? Looking at Facebook on her phone?

Giving birth?

Actually, I'd cut her some slack for that last one.

Meanwhile, the men's room? Ghost town. Every so often a guy will breeze in and then, thirty seconds later, breeze out. Like they haven't a care in the world, which they probably haven't, since they don't have a bathroom line and aren't standing in a hallway in heels with their legs crossed.

At last, a woman comes out of the bathroom. She doesn't seem to have a newborn with her. I try not to glare as the next person in line enters, and now I'm only five people away.

In heels. Legs crossed, now a little tighter. Ghost town of a men's room across the hallway. The girl next to me sighs and mutters "Come *on*," under her breath.

And I make a slightly-drunk snap decision.

I push myself off the wall where I was leaning. I walk across the hall to the men's room, head held high, shoulders back, determination in every step.

But still, in front of the men's room, I pause for half a second, a shudder working its way down my spine as every molecule in my body screams *no! No! Wrong door!*

"Do it!" someone shouts behind me.

It's all the encouragement I need, and I push the door open, holding my breath.

I step into the men's room.

And then I whisper, "What the hell?"

It has a urinal *and* a stall. Twice as many peeing opportunities for men, while across the way, the women's has only a toilet. No wonder they're breezing in and out of here while we're stuck staring at concrete walls in uncomfortable shoes.

Sometimes, it's hard not to hate men.

But I really have to pee, so I put my bathroom grievances aside, enter the stall, and get down to business.

Just as I flush, the bathroom door opens.

Footsteps enter.

I freeze. My heart leaps into my throat, and for a long moment, I stare blankly at the beige metal wall because I have no idea what to do. I didn't think this far ahead. I didn't think ahead at all, thanks to the Smurf's Vacation.

It didn't even occur to me that I might get caught.

So I do nothing. I stand stock-still in the bathroom stall, staring wide-eyed at the back of the metal door, and hold my breath.

The footsteps enter. They come right up to the stall, then pause.

He can't be more than a foot away from me.

My palms start sweating, all my alcohol-induced bravado gone.

What if it's a cop? I think.

Can I get arrested for this?

I think I can get arrested for this. I've never been arrested before. They'll send me to jail, and I can't go to jail, I can't handle those social dynamics —

I, Thalia Lopez, am many things.

A daughter. A sister. A college senior. A Madison Scholar.

I am not a rule breaker.

I'm a rule follower, neatly and to the letter. I love toeing a good line. I love staying within boundaries. I delight in abiding by the law, and right now, I wish with every ounce of my being that I were outside, in the hallway, standing in heels with a full bladder.

Finally, the steps move again. A moment later, there's the sound of a urinal being used, then flushed. The water in the sink goes on. Paper towels crinkle.

At last, the bathroom door opens and swings shut.

I exhale and, without thinking, lean my forehead against the cool metal door.

Then I remember where I am and jerk upright again, because I'm sure this door is crawling with germs.

Thank you, Jesus, I think. *I promise not to commit any bathroom crimes ever again.*

I slide back the lock on the door, double-check that my skirt is pulled down properly and covering everything it's supposed to cover, and then push the door open and stride forward confidently.

I nearly walk into him.

"Aughfwoo!" I yelp, and stop suddenly, and the sudden stop makes my heel catch on a piece of broken tile and have I mentioned that I am, technically, somewhat inebriated? And anyway, now I'm flailing in the general direction of the urinal.

"Whoa," he says, and catches me, one hand on my upper arm, holding me until I've properly found my footing again.

"You left," I gasp, the only thing I can think of because I'm medium-drunk and also medium-stunned and more-than-medium confused.

"Really? Seems like I'm still here," he says, one eyebrow slightly raised, the ghost of a smile flickering across his face.

His very, very handsome face.

For a second, my brain simply switches off because this bathroom stranger might be the most handsome man I've seen in my life. He's probably the most handsome man I've ever seen in person, and absolutely the most handsome one I've seen in a men's bathroom.

Tall. Wide. Green eyes. Brown hair, tending to gold in spots. Slight stubble. Square jaw. Forest-green t-shirt stretched over thick shoulders and biceps that must be Photoshopped or something.

I feel like someone must be playing a trick on me. Did my roommates somehow hire someone to come flirt with me in the bathroom? Is this some kind of setup?

Am I being catfished? Are they the ones catfishing me, or do they think they're doing something nice by hiring an excessively attractive man to follow me in here?

I stop gawping, clear my throat, and look directly into a sea of green.

"This is the women's restroom, right?" I ask.

CHAPTER TWO

THALIA

Single eyebrow still raised, he casually looks to his left, then his right, as if he's searching for something, and even *that* is attractive.

Good Lord, what is *in* a Smurf's Vacation?

"It's not," he says, his smile widening a few millimeters and giving me heart palpitations. "And I have to say, I was under the impression that women's restrooms didn't have urinals."

I rub my hands together, palms slightly sweaty, and glance over at the urinal.

"Though since I've never been in a women's restroom, I can't say I know for sure," he goes on. "If there's a line for the men's, I just wait."

"I'm sure you also only cross the street at crosswalks and never exceed the speed limit," I say, my mouth running ahead of my brain. "Since you love following rules so much."

I press my lips together, because I need to stop talking. I'm nervous and slightly drunk, and that's making me be an asshole to this very handsome man who's clearly just teasing me.

Flirting? Is he flirting?
Oh no. Oh crap. Oh no.
How do people flirt?!

"If you opened the door and then shut it just so I'd come out and you could bust me, that's entrapment," I inform him, heart hammering away in my chest, mouth still several steps ahead of brain. "And entrapment is unconstitutional and also illegal."

He smiles, his green eyes crinkling.

For Pete's sake, he has *dimples*.

Send help.

"And mean," I add because I can't stop myself.

"Then it's a good thing I'm not a cop, just a concerned citizen," he says, still dimpling.

I pause. I make myself take a deep breath and think for half a second before I respond.

"And you find me concerning?" I finally ask, tilting my head to one side.

He takes a moment to answer, his eyes narrowing even though his smile doesn't dim. If I didn't know better, I'd think he was checking me out, but obviously that's just the Smurf's Vacation talking.

"It's a position I'm coming around to," he says. His voice is low, relaxing, with just a hint of a rasp and a dollop of Southern twang.

Must be a townie, because there's no way on God's green earth that he's a student. I know a whole lot of students, and zero of them are anything like this.

"How, exactly, do I concern you?" I ask.

My chest feels like it's filled with jello. My palms are damp. I can hear my pulse roaring through my ears.

Some people are born flirts. It comes naturally to them. Talking to an attractive member of the opposite sex doesn't freak them out. The thought that someone might be interested in them doesn't invoke a flight-or-fight reaction.

I, on the other hand, am a born not-flirt. Every single time I find a guy attractive or interesting, I wind up sticking my foot in my mouth so hard I leave teeth marks on my knee.

"For one thing, I'm terribly worried over your inability to read simple door signs," he says. "The one on this door *does* indicate that it's for men."

"Does it?" I ask, opening my eyes wider. "Is that what that funny little picture meant? I thought it was some sort of ancient pictogram, carved by the Paleolithic humans who dwelled here. I was about to report my findings to the Smithsonian."

Too sarcastic?

Too sarcastic. Crap.

"Thank God I spared you that embarrassment," he deadpans.

"And yet, you just couldn't leave well enough alone?" I ask, raising my eyebrows. "I'm just trying to live my life and skip the women's bathroom line."

Now he's grinning. The dimples are very deep, and I force myself to resist the urge to stick a finger into one.

"I've always been too curious for my own good," he says, still smiling, shrugging. "And I've never liked letting people get away with things."

"Things like using a restroom in peace?"

"Things like taking the law into their own hands and skipping a line," he teases.

I finally break away from his gaze and head for the sink to wash my hands, watching him over my shoulder in the mirror.

"Bathroom lines are the result of misogynistic architecture," I say. "Meaning that bathroom design is awful for women and fine for men."

I've got a whole thesis to back up this statement, but right now I need to concentrate on getting soap out of this dispenser. It's trickier than it looks, I swear.

"So you weren't just skipping a line, you were subverting the patriarchy," he says.

My chest feels even wobblier, and something tightens in my stomach. It's not fair of me, but I'm definitely surprised that a man this handsome just said *subverting the patriarchy* in casual conversation.

"Exactly," I say, shutting off the water. "When we finally elect a female president, it'll be because of this moment."

"So I shouldn't go through with my citizens' arrest?" he asks. "I was all set to try and remember the Miranda rights so I could do it properly."

"And we've established that you do things properly," I say, grabbing a paper towel and drying my hands. "Crosswalks, speed limits, and now Miranda rights."

I ball up the paper towel and toss it at the trash can.

I miss by about a mile, and of course he picks it up and tosses it in.

Then he rests one hand on the door handle and gives me a brief, up-and-down look that makes me unspeakably nervous.

"What if instead of arresting you, I bought you a drink?" he asks.

I swear there's a herd of buffalo stampeding through my chest and right over my brain.

"That's your move?" I say. "You trap a girl in a bathroom and give her an either-or proposition?"

Then I snap my mouth shut because that's not what I

meant to say, that's nothing like what I meant to say, but I'm nervous and terrible at this.

I'm going to die a virgin, aren't I?

For the record, I *meant* to say something like *yes, you're very handsome and also kinda funny and I think I'd like to continue our acquaintance*.

His smile fades.

"Sorry," he says, voice suddenly serious, the smile disappearing from his face. "It's not a move and you're not trapped."

He pulls on the door handle.

The door doesn't open. It catches with a quiet *clunk*, and he frowns at it.

Nerves and alcohol swirl through me, and before I know it, I'm talking again.

"Yeah," I say. "I'm sure this isn't page forty-three of some pick-up artist handbook."

Then I laugh, so he knows I'm teasing. Flirtatiously. That's what I'm doing, right?

"If I were following the handbook I'd have already shown you a couple card tricks and started touching you without your consent," he says, half to himself, as he turns the lock on the door, then pulls it again.

Another *clunk*. The door is still shut, and now we're both staring at it.

I'm nervous for a whole new reason.

"Card tricks?" I ask, still staring at the lock.

"Yeah, it's a big thing with pick-up artists," he says, tugging at the door again.

Nothing. He flips the lock, but it's clearly not doing anything, just rasping uselessly around in a circle.

"You know, they wear some ridiculous hat and a loud shirt and carry around a deck of cards so they can go up to cute girls and tell them to pick one?" he says, still talking mostly to the door. "It's a way for them to get within physical proximity of a target without seeming threatening."

He grabs the handle with both hands and pulls, the muscles in his arms knotting in a very pleasing fashion.

The door doesn't open, just bangs back and forth against the door frame.

"Don't, you're gonna break it," I say.

"It's already broken," he says, though he steps back from it. "Shit. *Shit*."

I approach the door and, mindful of my above-the-knee skirt, crouch in front of it even as I don't entirely believe the situation.

This is not really happening, right?

The door's just stuck and if we kinda nudge it the right way, we'll be free to go, right?

I jiggle the lock, but the lever just spins freely, obviously not connected to anything any more.

"Hold on," he says, and his voice is closer than I thought it would be, close enough that it sends a prickle down my spine and I hold my breath, tense. I don't know if it's the alcohol or his proximity that makes me suddenly warmer, blood rushing to my face as I'm intensely, acutely aware of the inches between us.

The stampede is back.

Then a bright light shines over my shoulder, into the crack between the door and the frame, the deadbolt gleaming in the phone flashlight as it spans the gap.

This door is very locked, and the lock mechanism is very much not working.

I flick the lock's lever one more time, just to make sure. It spins and then hangs straight down, completely useless.

"Well, that's answered," he says, his voice not far from my ear. My spine prickles again and I swallow hard, closing my eyes, honestly not sure if I'm excited or nervous or both or neither.

We stand. He takes a step away, then holds his phone up to his ear. I take a deep breath, look around, try to maintain control of my faculties despite the ginger whiskeys and the Smurf's Vacation.

It's a challenge. He sighs, fixes his eyes on the ceiling light, shoves one hand through his light brown hair.

"Come on, answer," he mutters.

I rub my hands together, then intertwine my fingers. They feel distant, like they're further away from my body than they should be, and I'm trying to anchor them back to myself, keep my body parts from drifting off on a sea of bright blue booze.

I'm never, ever taking a shot again.

"Steve, for fuck's sake," he says, lowering his phone, hitting a button, then listening again.

My phone is, of course, in my purse and my purse is back at the table.

My roommates must have noticed my absence.

Surely, rescue is imminent.

I take a detailed inventory of the bathroom anyway.

One sink with a smudged mirror and soap dispenser. One beige stall, made of standard-issue bathroom stall material, containing one toilet. One urinal. One ancient-looking paper towel dispenser. One nearly-full trash can under a smallish window, set back into the wall, made of those blurry glass panes.

"Put the beer down and answer your phone, you idiot," the man says behind me growls. "Jesus."

I stand under the window and look up at it, hands against the concrete wall, balancing on my toes. For a moment I have to close my eyes and take a deep breath as everything sways slightly, and then I open them again.

I'm pretty sure the window opens. I think I see a crank.

Now he's pacing, phone still pressed to his ear, even though the bathroom isn't big enough for him to take more than two steps.

Step, step, turn. Step, step, turn. Even here, and even despite his size — I'm pretty sure he's north of six feet — he's oddly lithe and graceful, his whole body smooth clockwork.

Step, step, turn. Like some sort of caged animal.

I'm staring. Am I staring?

I'm for sure staring and... no. No, I'm not stopping. Everything about him is *delicious* and I think that even if I tried to, I couldn't tear my eyes away.

Finally, he takes the phone away from his ear and shoves it back into his pocket, shaking his head.

"No dice," he says, that edge back in his voice. "You?"

"My phone's out there," I say, and turn to the door.

One option left. I cross the bathroom, raise my fist and pound on the wood.

"HELP!" I shout, still banging. "WE'RE STUCK!"

I'm rewarded almost immediately with footsteps.

"HEY!" a woman's voice shouts.

"HEY, THE LOCK'S BROKEN!" I shout back.

"WHAT?"

"THE LOCK! IS BROKEN!"

"OH SHIT! CAN YOU GET OUT?"

I take a deep breath and close my eyes, because this clearly isn't going to be simple.

"NO! WE'RE TRAPPED!"

Behind me, he's pacing again, both hands jammed into his pockets, jaw clenched.

"I'M GONNA GET HELP!" the woman on the other side shouts. "STAY STRONG!"

"Fuck," he mutters.

Step, step, turn. Step, step, turn. I watch as he goes back and forth, back and forth.

"Are you claustrophobic?" I finally ask, leaning against the door.

"No," he says. "But I don't exactly love being trapped in small spaces. No one does."

"Some people do," I point out. "It's a whole fetish. People build themselves pods and lockers and — uh, I saw a documentary once."

That was the Vacation talking.

"A documentary?" he asks, still pacing.

"You're the one who knows what page forty-three of the pickup artist handbook says," I point out.

"I saw a documentary."

"Wiseass."

That, at last, gets a smile.

"I was curious, so I picked up a manual," he says. Step, step, turn. "It was like reading a car crash. I couldn't look away."

"Did they work?" I ask.

"HEY, ARE YOU OKAY IN THERE?!"

The woman on the other side of the door is back.

"YEAH," I shout.

"I GOT THE BARTENDER!"

"DON'T USE THAT LOCK, IT'S BUSTED!" the bartender hollers. "I GOTTA GO CALL THE LOCKSMITH."

"IT'S SUNDAY NIGHT!"

That's my new bathroom friend, shouting from behind me.

"WHAT?"

"IT'S SUNDAY NIGHT!"

"WHAT?"

"THALIA!" shouts Margaret's voice. "ARE YOU OKAY?"

I want to shout *no, I'm trapped in a men's bathroom with a very handsome stranger and I've been making a damn fool of myself for at least ten minutes now*, but that's too many words to shout.

"I'M FINE!" I holler.

"WE GOT SECOND PLACE!" she shouts. "WE WERE IN FIRST BUT THEN THERE WAS A SPORTS ROUND."

The handsome man and I look at each other.

"Congratulations," he says.

"Thanks," I say, then turn back to the door. "GOOD JOB! YOU GUYS CAN LEAVE IF YOU WANT, YOU DON'T HAVE TO WAIT HERE FOR ME."

"LET ME TALK TO VICTORIA AND HARPER," she shouts, and then I hear footsteps heading away from the door.

"What was that about Sunday night?" I ask the man, because it seemed important at the time but we skipped past it.

"Only emergency locksmiths are open," he says, one hand on his hip, the other running through his hair again in what's clearly a stress-related gesture. "It's gonna take hours. Shit. Why the hell haven't they replaced the lock if they know it's busted? Can't they chop the door down with a fire axe or something? Give me an axe, I'll do it."

"Heeere's Johnny," I say. It gets a smile.

"Point taken," he says, then turns slowly, looking around the bathroom.

When he gets to the window, he pauses, then glances over at me.

I shake my head.

"Too small," I tell him.

"It's not."

"It's too high."

"I can get you up there."

Now the buffalo are tap-dancing in my ribcage.

"You can go," I say.

He looks at me like I've just casually suggested he light his own pants on fire.

"I can't leave you here alone," he says.

"Just toss my phone back through," I say, shrugging. "And maybe a burger. I'll be fine."

"Okay, I was unclear," he says, folding his arms over his chest. "I'm *not* leaving you trapped in a men's bathroom."

There's that jello-in-my-chest feeling again.

He strides to the window and reaches up. His fingers find the crank, and after a few seconds of pushing, he turns it.

The tiny window starts moving, dislodging dirt and dust as it opens inward.

"See?" he says.

I flatten my hands against the front of my skirt. My not-indecent-but-definitely-on-the-short-side skirt.

"If you lift me who'll lift you?" I ask.

The window's all the way open and he steps back, brushing his hands against his jeans and giving me a relieved grin.

Hello, dimples. Hi. I missed you. You're nice.

"I can manage," he says. "Come on."

My palms are sweating again, and I'm tempted to say something like *oh really it's fine, it's so high up can you even lift me* but that's not really a question. He can definitely lift me.

Will I manage to keep my dignity while being hoisted through a window and wearing a skirt? Unclear.

"All right," I say, and walk to the window.

He's already standing there and he pushes away the

garbage can, crouches, laces his hands together, and holds them out.

"Grab onto my shoulder for stability," he says. "Don't worry, I've done this before."

I raise one foot to put it into his hands, then frown, bend down, and take my heeled boots off.

"Thanks," he says as I put my slightly damp bare foot into his warm, strong hands and try not to think about how gross I am. "On three. One. Two —"

"Eeeee!"

I don't mean to make that sound as he lifts me, but I do. I grab onto the concrete ledge of the rather small window and, without thinking too much, stick my head through and my upper body follows until half of me is sticking out, into the alleyway behind The Tipsy Cavalier, and half of me is still in the men's bathroom.

I could think about the fact that Mister Handsome Dimpleface might be looking up my skirt, but I choose not to. Instead I put all thoughts of dignity aside and very, very carefully scootch until I've got one knee through the window, then the other, my whole body balanced sideways in this precarious position.

Then I take a deep breath and flail toward the ground, feet-first.

By God, I almost make it, only I stumble a little as I land and wind up on the asphalt, one knee roughed up but otherwise fine.

"You all right?" he calls.

"Fine!" I call back, getting to my feet.

"I'm tossing your shoes over," he says, and a moment later, my boots come out.

As I'm putting them back on, he appears, head first, then maneuvers himself around properly and drops lightly to the ground like it's nothing.

Then he looks at me and grins.

"That was something," he says, and I can hear the relief in his voice. "God, I thought we'd be in there for — your knee is bleeding."

I look down at it. I'm scratched up, but it's no big deal. There's, like, one drop of blood.

"My landing sucked," I say. "I'm fine."

"Shit, I'm sorry," he says, and before I know it, he's on one knee in front of me, two light fingers on my shin as he examines the scrape.

I bite my lip as nervousness spikes through me. Nervousness and something else that spikes as I look down at the top of his head, watch his big, gentle hands as his fingers just barely graze my skin.

Without warning, I wonder what it would be like to kiss him. Whether he'd be gentle like this or a little rough, what his stubble would feel like on my face, whether he'd pull away early and leave me breathless, wanting more —

"I didn't think it was that far down," he says, apologetically.

"It wasn't," I say, with a quick laugh. "It's no big deal. Really."

"Still, I'm sorry," he says, and then he stands.

Right in front of me.

Like, eight inches away. The buffalo stampede in my chest is going over a cliff.

"Listen, it was a trying time," I say, trying to make a joke. "We're lucky we made it out alive."

That gets a smile and the smile gets dimples and the dimples get a skipped heartbeat from yours truly.

"You're right, we've been through a lot together," he says. "Thalia, right?"

I blink in surprise, then frown slightly.

"Is that some pickup artist trick?" I ask, breathless.

"You somehow find out a girl's name without asking her and then you use it in some kind of neurolinguistic —"

"Your friend shouted it through the door," he says.

I close my eyes and take a deep breath, feeling like an idiot.

"Of course," I say. "I'm sorry."

He just looks at me, half amused and half expectant, and I find myself staring at his lips, his jaw, the way that his hair is just a little too long and curls against his neck —

"If you want, I could tell you mine," he says.

I'm not having a smart day, am I?

"I think this story's better if I simply refer to you as *my mysterious bathroom stranger*," I tease.

"It might be," he concedes. "But we're out of the bathroom now, and I'd rather ruin the *mysterious stranger* part."

"Don't tell me you're about to hand me a copy of your memoir."

"No, just ask you on a date," he says, and the smile is back and the dimples are back. "I've got tickets to the sculpture show at the Botanic Gardens for tonight, and my brother just backed out."

"*Light Cantatas?*" I ask, surprised. I tried to get tickets last week, but it closes tonight and everything was sold out.

"That's it," he says. "If you really want, you can keep calling me a mysterious stranger, but it seems like that could get burdensome when you're telling your friends what a great time we had."

I laugh despite myself.

"Hold on," I say. "You're making a lot of assumptions. What if I have a terrible time?"

"So you're saying yes."

"That was a trap," I say, still laughing.

"No, that bathroom was a trap," he says. "This is me

asking you on a date where I may or may not tell you my name, according to your wishes."

"Even if my wishes are —"

"YOU'RE ALIVE!"

I whirl, mid-sentence, at Harper's voice echoing through the alley, and half a second later she emerges into the orange light of the street lamp at a half-run.

"You stopped answering through the door and we thought you'd drowned in the urinal!" she goes on, practically falling on me to wrap me in a drunk bear hug.

"The urinal?" I ask.

"We didn't really think that," Victoria calls from behind her, walking like a normal person. "Obviously, we deduced that you escaped."

"She was worried," Harper whispers into my ear. "Though not actually about the urinal. We all know you're much more likely to drown in a toilet, there's more water. Or maybe the sink, though that probably depends on what kind of sink the men's bathroom has. I wasn't brave enough to go in there when I had to pee."

"Can you let me go? I can't breathe," I whisper back.

"Sorry," she says, and releases the hug as Margaret and Victoria walk up, and even though they're both also drunk, they're managing to play it cool a little better.

Sort of. All three of them are very obviously checking out my bathroom friend while trying to act like they're not checking him out, and while I can't blame them I'm the tiniest bit annoyed.

"Hi, guys!" I say, probably sounding a little too perky. "Check it out, I'm alive!"

"Did you go through that window?" Victoria asks, eyeing the window I just went through.

"I was getting claustrophobic, so I talked her into it," Mysterious Handsome Stranger says.

It's like he's giving them permission to finally look at him, because three sets of eyes simultaneously swivel in his direction.

Harper's the first one to find her voice.

"Well, thank you for your service, my good sir," she says. Her voice takes on a haughty, formal tone that she only ever uses when she's drunk and trying to hide it by sounding like she's conversing with the Queen of England. "Clearly, Thalia here is deeply in your debt. My name is Harper, by the way, and I am her friend."

She reaches out one hand, and Handsome Bathroom Man takes it.

"Pleasure to meet you, Thalia's friend Harper," he says, and in the low orange light, I can see one dimple sink halfway in a smile as Harper continues to shake his hand.

Then she clears her throat.

"And you are?" she finally asks.

Behind her, Margaret sighs.

Bathroom stranger cocks his head in my direction, eyebrows raised, teasing half-smile on his face, and looks at me.

Now they're all looking at me: Handsome Stranger laughing, like we've got a secret, my friends just puzzled.

"All right," I finally tell him. "I guess the mystery is over."

CHAPTER THREE

CALEB

The corners of Thalia's lips quirk, then pucker slightly, like she's trying not to laugh and failing, and even in the ugly orange streetlight, I find it nearly impossible not to stare at that single, tiny motion.

I'm starting to wonder if there was something in the cherry coke I drank. Maybe the bartender used moonshine cherries by accident or slipped in a shot of everclear or something, *anything* to explain what's happening.

Her friend tightens the handshake slightly, and I remember that there are others present.

"You could always cover your ears," I tell Thalia. "If you like it better this way."

"But what if you're eaten by a giant carnivorous plant at the gardens?" she asks, her lips quirking again. *Jesus*. "I can't just tell the cops that a mysterious stranger went missing near the Venus Flytraps."

"Venus Flytraps don't get nearly big enough to eat people," says the white friend with sideswept dark bangs and shoulder-length hair.

"Read the room!" the black friend with a huge silver necklace hisses to her.

"But they don't," the first girl says defensively.

"We're all in a great deal of suspense," says the third friend — the blond still hanging onto my hand — in a very official tone of voice. "And this situation also seems steeped in sexual tension, which is certainly odd because Thalia's never —"

"Just tell me your name," Thalia interrupts her, stepping forward. "Also, Jesus, Harper, you can stop shaking his hand now, he gets it."

Harper clears her throat, gives my hand one more jiggle, then lets go.

"Caleb," I tell Thalia.

She laughs. I don't know why, but she does, and I like it.

"All that for two syllables that aren't even weird?" she says. "I thought you were going to say your name was Dinglehopper or Spacecraft or Egbert or something."

"Spacecraft is my middle name," I say.

"And yet, you choose to go by Caleb?"

She's still laughing, her head slightly tilted, her hair draping over one bare shoulder, black strands against bronze skin.

"I've made a lot of puzzling life choices," I tell her.

It's true. I have a Ph.D. in mathematics. No one in their right mind goes to grad school.

"Like jumping through a bathroom window instead of waiting sensibly for rescue?"

"Like going to bar trivia when I barely drink and don't watch sports or follow pop culture," I say.

"Fucking sports questions," mutters the white friend with the bangs.

The blond who shook my hand for too long pets her head.

"I already subscribed to the SportsCenter newsletter so we can study for next time," she says, soothingly.

"We'll make flashcards," says the black friend with the necklace.

"Nerds," says the first girl, lovingly, then looks over at Thalia. "Are you going to introduce us to your new hot flirt partner or do we all have to do awkward handshakes?"

"My handshake was fine," mutters the blond one.

"Right, sorry," says Thalia, standing up a little straighter.

The movement pushes her breasts out, against her tank top, and as hard as I try not to notice, I do. I think I notice every single movement she makes, like I'm tuned to her frequency.

"Harper, Victoria, and Margaret," she says, pointing to the blond white girl, the black girl with the necklace, and the white girl with the bangs. "This is Caleb Spacecraft."

"Pleasure, Mr. Spacecraft," says Victoria.

"That's his middle name, dumbass," whispers Harper. "We just established that."

"No, the pleasure is all mine," I insist, matching Victoria's tone.

"Thank you," says Harper, and curtsies.

Thalia and I look at each other, her lips quirking again like she's trying not to laugh.

"You never did answer me," I tell her.

"Certainly not, and I'm offended you even asked," she says, folding her arms in front of her.

It catches me completely off-guard, and I hesitate for a moment.

"All right," I say, nodding. "Well, it's been —"

"That was a really bad joke! Sorry," she says, unfurling her arms and stepping toward me, then stopping. "Shit. I'm sorry, it was funnier in my head but it was just awkward in person, which happens kind of a lot."

Fuck it, I'm charmed. There's something about this girl, sweet and prickly and guileless and clever all at once. She's beautiful. She's unexpected. She's *interesting*.

"And also, I forgot the question," she admits, her voice softer now.

"I wouldn't want to offend you," I tease.

"I'm harder to offend than you might think."

"Then asking you on this date probably doesn't move the needle," I say, moving another step toward her.

"Oh! Yes," she says, and laughs. "I mean, no, it doesn't offend me. I thought I already answered you."

"You didn't."

"*Go on the date*," one of her friends stage-whispers, and both of us turn our heads at the same time.

I'd forgotten we had an audience, even though they're standing a couple of feet away. If they could, I think they'd be munching popcorn.

"I'm going!" she hisses back. "I just said yes, chill out."

"Woohoo!"

"Atta girl."

Victoria just grins and gives Thalia a thumbs-up.

Thalia turns back to me.

"I'm sorry about my comrades," she says.

· · · · ★ ★ ★ ★ ★ · · · ·

THALIA'S WATCHING a glowing purple flower as it moves up the trellis. The paper blossom is tentative, hesitant, its petals slowly unfurling under the power of the heat lamp above, the light inside it pulsing in answer as it climbs upward.

"How is this working?" she whispers, her eyes still glued to the art, her face glowing with the violet of the flower's inner light and the re-orange of the heat lamp above, striking her like a low desert sun.

She's entranced by the flower, one hand halfway extended and then halted, fingertips touching lightly, lips parted, her whole body paused like she wants to touch it and knows she can't.

I'm entranced by her, by her rapture, by the way her face moves as she looks over the art like she's asking for its secrets. If I were that flower, I'd tell her. How could I do anything else?

I step closer to her, bend low, like we're conspiring.

"There's a sealed pocket of air inside each flower," I say. Her hair smells sharp and sweet, citrus and rose. "They rise when the heat lamp goes on, lower when it's off. The lamp rotates, so they eventually all wind through the trellis. They're kinda like mini hot air balloons."

I'm pretty sure it's more complicated, but that's the gist of it.

"That's it?" she breathes.

"That's the basic premise," I say, forcing myself to straighten up.

I want to touch her. I want to run my hands through her hair, want to put my hand on her back, want to bend down and kiss her full lips and all this want makes me feel like I'm going mad because I've known this girl for all of two hours.

It's lust. I know full well that it's lust. What else could it be?

"Do you know that because you cheated and read the plaque?" she asks, still watching the flowers, now sinking, heads turning downward, long woven stems resting against the trellis as they fall in slow motion.

"Reading the plaque isn't cheating," I say. "That's what it's there for."

"Too much information can take the wonder out of a thing, though," she says, her face still dreamy, her eyes still wide and captivated by the flowers, her hair falling over one cheekbone.

I want to tuck it behind her ear but I resist, make myself look away because I don't know what will happen if I touch her. I don't know if I'll be able to stop. Earlier, in the alleyway, I nearly kissed her knee while examining her wound, the urge so powerful it felt like an arrow to the chest, pinning me in place.

I didn't. I don't do that. I'm not a man who kisses women without permission, definitely not on knees, absolutely not in alleyways. There's a progression to these things: a conversation, a drink, a date, a second date, a kiss, maybe more.

Life has patterns, systems, a proper order, and up until tonight, I've had no problem keeping that order but Thalia is a sudden bolt from the blue and I'm jumbled, disarranged.

"You don't think there's beauty and wonder in knowing how things work?" I ask, concentrating all my willpower on not moving her hair from her face.

"I think there's something to be said for believing in magic," she says.

Above the trellis, the heat lamp goes on again and a dozen heads turn upward, faces toward the heat, like so many sunflowers.

"Do you?" I ask as the flowers start to unfurl again, lifting themselves.

"Of course not," Thalia says, her lips quirking again, like they're about to move into a smile. "Not in magic. In magical, yes. I believe in a space between seeing and understanding, where what's in front of you seems impossible until suddenly, it isn't."

"You like not knowing?" I ask, still looking down at her.

"I like feeling as if there's more to this world than I could comprehend," she says, slowly, her eyes following a flower. "I like that moment before logic and reason kick in, where you see something astonishing and you think, maybe there really is magic in the world and maybe anything is possible."

I laugh, softly, and she looks over at me, a half-smile on her lips.

"I don't actually believe in magic," she says, a little defensively, and I shake my head.

"No," I say. "What you call magic I call anxiety."

Thalia lifts one eyebrow. The heat lamps switch off, and her face goes from desert sunset to moonlight. A couple behind us wanders off, and although we're right by the entrance to the gardens — we haven't gotten far — suddenly I feel like we're alone, somewhere private.

I want to kiss her. I want her to tell me about magic and the spaces between things and I want to kiss her, taste her, sift her hair through my fingers.

"I can't stand not knowing," I admit. "I never could. I live for that moment when things fall into place, when the mechanism's revealed. When everything makes sense again."

"So you read the plaques," she says, finally brushing the strand of hair from her cheek.

"When I was a kid, my mom took my older brother and I to see a magic show," I say. "It was the usual stuff, card tricks, rabbit out of a hat, you know. And it drove me completely insane."

She laughs. It feels like the sun just turned on.

"I hated not knowing how it worked," I go on. "I hated that there was this guy, on stage, lying to all of us about what he was doing, telling us it was magic when it was just sleight-of-hand that he wouldn't explain, and I hated that I couldn't figure it out. So I went home and learned a bunch of magic tricks so I could understand what was really happening."

"Did it work?" she asks.

"The magic tricks?"

"I mean, did knowing soothe you?" she asks. "Once you knew that it was just a flick of the wrist here, a misdirection there, did you feel better?"

We're facing each other now, her dark eyes searching mine, and I have the sensation that I'm a cipher being unscrambled, my numbers and letters and symbols rearranged into a message that makes sense to the right reader.

I feel like this girl I don't even know is undoing me.

"I did," I tell her, thinking back to me, nine years old, shuffling a deck of cards again and again. "I revel in the pieces falling together the way that you revel in not knowing."

She's smiling. Still giving me that look, like she's decoding me.

"Is that the real reason?" she asks, head tilted.

"I knew card tricks well before I ever touched a book about how to be a pickup artist, thanks," I say, one eyebrow raised.

"Okay, defensive," she says, but she's laughing again. "I meant was needing to know how it worked the real reason you learned all those tricks?"

I stay quiet, gently unraveling.

"Or did you hate that some guy in a sweaty tux was trying to pull the wool over your eyes?" Thalia goes on. "I hear you can't stand that."

"If you're fishing for an apology that I pretended to leave the bathroom and didn't, I don't have one to give," I tell her. More people come up to the morning glory sculpture. Someone bumps my arm and apologizes, but I barely notice.

"I wouldn't take an apology if you tried to offer one," she says, and her gaze is finally wrested from mine by a big family with three kids, the smallest of whom wedges her way between us. The father apologizes. "I've been wanting to go to this for weeks. Should we go look at the rest of the exhibit? You can read the plaques and I can marvel."

"I promise not to tell you what they say," I tell her, and we turn away from the paper flowers and the heat lamp.

"You can tell me," she says as we enter the tunnel, light glinting from her eyes, her hair. "Just let me wonder for a few moments first."

There's a family coming from the opposite end of the arched tunnel with a stroller and a little kid, and as Thalia moves right to make space, her knuckles bump into mine.

"Sorry," she murmurs, then looks up at me as I slide my hand into hers.

"Don't be," I say, simply, and we walk along hand in hand.

CHAPTER FOUR

THALIA

Caleb takes my hand and the strangest thing happens: I'm not nervous. Not even a little.

I'm excited, and I'm giddy. My heart is thumping and my pulse is raised and I can feel the adrenaline coursing through my veins, adrenaline and oxytocin and buckets and buckets of hormones, and that all lights up a lot of the same neural pathways as anxiety, but it's not the same.

Anxiety is a kind of fear. Excitement is a kind of happiness. Close but different, mirror reflections of one another.

"What next?" he asks, giving my hand a slight squeeze, maybe unconscious. "*The Serpent's Orchard* or *Moondial*?"

He looks down at me as he talks, his voice sending a shiver down my back.

Which one is the most secluded? I want to ask.

"The orchard," I say, and we exit the long arched pathway, emerge into a colonnaded path, the only lights wrapped around the base of each column. It makes the garden feel like a spaceship.

"Then I think we go right, if memory serves," Caleb says. "I've only been here a few —"

"LEVI!" a voice hollers, breaking through the quiet murmurs of art appreciation.

"Oh, come on," Caleb mutters, mostly to himself.

I wonder, for a moment, if I'm in some sort of wacky comedy where my date has lied about who he is and his true identity is about to be revealed by accident.

"Levi!" says the voice, closer now. "Oh, thank fuck you're here. Levi, I am in a damn pickle because it's Sunday night and none of the rednecks in this town —"

Caleb closes his eyes and sighs deeply.

"I'm sorry about this," he tells me, quietly.

" — Just goes to voicemail and I ask you, how does anyone do business —"

The shouter stomps up along side us. We all stop walking, lit from below by an unearthly purple.

"Hello, Vivian," Caleb says.

" — ah, shit," she answers, frowning, looking him over. Her face is lined and she's got an unruly black mane, streaked with gray. She's standing there rigidly, feet firmly planted, like she's ready to fight or lift something heavy. The work boots and coveralls she's wearing, the latter splashed with paint, suggest that the latter is more likely.

Then: "Maybe you'll do. Can you swing a hammer?"

His hand tightens on mine, just for a moment.

"It's nice to see you," he says, with more than an edge of irritation to his voice. "This is my date, Thalia. We were just enjoying your show."

"Lovely. Charmed," she says, pushing huge, thick glasses up her nose, barely glancing at me. "You helped him build that house, right?"

"Caleb," he says, still irritated, pointing to himself.

I'm looking back and forth between the two of them, and I've got the strange feeling that I'm watching two completely different conversations. It's been long enough since the Smurf's Vacation that I'm pretty much sober by now, but this sure doesn't make me feel like it.

"Yes, I know which one you are," she says, sounding annoyed as she pushes huge, thick glasses further up her nose. "And I also know that the sea monster just broke yet again because the original builders ignored my detailed design notes and now the jaw's hanging off and it's not much more than a slack-jawed snake."

"This is Vivian Atwell, the artist," Caleb says to me, still having a different conversation from the woman in front of us.

I have no idea which one to respond to.

"Nice to meet you," I tell her as she glances over her shoulder. "The morning glories were lovely."

"Yes, they're nice," she says, distracted. "But they're not broken, are they?"

"Nope," I say flippantly, well aware that the question is rhetorical.

"Well, the sea monster is and you're the only person I've found so far with a chance in hell of righting it," she says, now talking to Caleb again. "Come on."

With that, she turns and starts walking.

"I'm on a date, Vivian," he calls after her.

She turns back, ten feet away, and looks at Caleb like she's just told him that an avalanche is coming and he doesn't believe her.

"The art. Is. *Broken*," she says, astonished.

I've now moved past feeling awkward about this interaction and into being sort of entertained by it. Clearly, Caleb has dealt with this woman before, and just as clearly, nothing is expected of me.

Caleb just sighs, then waits. Vivian shifts her stance slightly, though she's still firmly rooted like she's about to lift something.

There's a long, long pause. She clears her throat and looks like she's concentrating.

"I would be ever so grateful if you would pause your nightly cavortation and assist me with repairs," she calls, sounding like Harper when she's drunk. "Perhaps your date would appreciate a glimpse behind the scenes. I'm told it's very interesting."

Not for the first time, I have the sensation that I've followed a rabbit down a hole and found myself in Wonderland. Is Vivian the red queen? Is she going to insist that my head come off? Where's the caterpillar?

Another couple strolls past us on the walkway, and all three of us watch them as they pass Vivian, very obviously ignoring whatever's going on here.

"Please?" Vivian finally calls.

Caleb looks down at me.

"She's a good friend of my mom's," he explains, voice low. "Probably because my mom is the only one with enough patience to stand her when she gets like this."

"Let's do it," I tell him, giving his hand a quick squeeze, my pulse ticking up at the same time.

Caleb raises one eyebrow.

"I don't like to give into terrorists' demands," he says, voice still low, the tiniest bit rough, like ruffled velvet.

"But the art is *broken*," I say, fighting back a smile. "It'll be a good story. Someday she'll be famous and you'll have a good story about how this well-known artist chased you down in a garden and called you the wrong name."

"I'll be incredible at cocktail parties," he deadpans.

"Exactly."

Still hand-in-hand, we walk forward.

"All right," he says to Vivian, in a normal voice, when we're close enough that we don't have to shout. "Take us to the sea monster."

"It's in the sea," she says, pointing down the spaceship path, as if it's obvious.

· · · * * ★ * * · · ·

THE SEA MONSTER isn't in the sea. We're a four-and-a-half hour drive from the nearest sea, at Virginia Beach, a distance and journey I know pretty well because my family's lived in Norfolk, right next door, for the past seven years.

It's more of a pond monster, stationed on a platform between lily pads. The pond partially surrounds a small Thai-style building, the points and turrets of its roof outlined in golden light.

Vivian may have zero social skills, but she's good at what she does.

"There," she says, pointing, though we didn't need the help. "Slack-jawed, like some sort of inbred yokel. The jaw is supposed to move with the breeze but the idiots who actually built the thing decided on their own that it didn't need that amount of bracing, so obviously the strain snapped the joint and now my beauty looks like it's about to spit chaw into the sea."

Pond, I think but don't say out loud.

"Are there materials?" Caleb asks.

"Behind the temple," she says. "Small supply shed. Five-twenty-seventeen. Rowboat's right there. Fix her up good, I'm supposed to be at a damn Q&A talking to art students who want to talk about intersectional multimedia semantic bullshit."

With that, she turns and stomps away, her heavy boots vibrating the wooden bridge that we're standing on.

"Sorry about her," Caleb says, probably before she's even out of earshot. "She and my mom have been friends for a while, and she's really not this bad most of the time. I think she's stressed."

"She has friends?" I ask, looking after her, and Caleb laughs.

"At least one," he confirms. "My mom's got a habit of taking on odd ducks, though."

We walk over the bridge, through the lit temple where the northern lights are being projected on the ceiling above us, and behind it we find a small, locked storage shed that opens to the combination she gave us.

"This is gonna be pretty slapdash," Caleb says, looking at what's inside.

"Well, you're no Levi," I tell him, and he just snorts. "Whoever that is."

"Levi is my eldest brother, and we look nothing alike," he says. "Nothing."

"You sure about that?"

"Of course," he says, grabbing some wood, a box of nails, and a hammer, a smile playing around his lips.

"Not even a tiny family resemblance," I go on, leaning against the temple and grinning.

He leans into the shed, disappearing for a moment.

"Maybe a little," he admits.

"You know that the more you claim you don't look like someone, the better chance that you could practically be twins," I tell him. "My brothers swear up and down that they don't look a thing alike, but seeing them together is like seeing double."

Or at least it used to be, I think, then push that thought aside.

He backs out of the shed, arms full, and nudges the door shut with one foot.

"I can carry some of that," I say.

"I've got it."

"Let me help."

"The artist didn't ask you, she asked me," he says, teasing. "And I can't have you getting splinters on our first date, this is already going off the rails."

First, I think.

"Technically, I think she asked your brother who canceled," I say, walking beside him to the rowboat at the edge of the water, wedged between lily pads.

Caleb just laughs and puts the materials into the bottom of the metal boat, which rocks slightly.

"That would've been a real mistake," he says, straightening. He stands at the edge of the water, holds out his hand. I take it. "Seth couldn't fix this to save his life."

I step carefully into the boat, my hand held tightly in his as I sit on one of the bench seats, careful to keep my knees together. I didn't exactly pick my outfit with a pond construction outing in mind, but I'm not mad about it.

"So the brother who was supposed to come couldn't fix it and the one who could fix it wasn't supposed to come," I say as he grabs the single oar from the bottom of the rowboat and looks around, like he's trying to get his bearings.

"This is starting to sound like one of those logic puzzles you do in elementary school to teach rational thinking or something," he says. "If Ben has a red ball and Dave is late for class on Tuesday, which student likes dinosaurs the best?"

"I always liked those," I admit as Caleb looks over the side of the rowboat and carefully plunges the oar into the water, a lily pad sinking beneath it. "My favorite second grade teacher had a whole book of them for when I'd finish worksheets and quizzes early."

"They're satisfying," he agrees, glancing over his

shoulder at the dark frame of the sea monster, looming over us. "You had a favorite second grade teacher?"

It takes me a moment to understand what he's asking.

"We moved twice that year," I explain. "I had Mrs. Ferguson for a month, then Mrs. Gonzalez for six, then Miss Clampett for two."

"Army brat?" he asks, both his hands clenched around the wooden oar, his muscles tightening as he draws it back, facing me.

For a moment, I'm rendered completely dumb at nothing more than an attractive man rowing a boat. In the moonlight and the cast-off neon from the Thai pavilion, the yellow and red and white all catching the curves of his muscles, his arms, his shoulders, his smile and all at once, something deep inside me awakens and yawns.

Suddenly, I understand why lust is so dangerous. I want to reach out and touch him, kiss him, climb on top of him and the sheer force of the wanting is so strong that I have to hold onto my seat with both hands to keep myself back.

I've thought I was in lust before. When I was thirteen and kissed a boy for the first time, then wanted to do it again. When I was seventeen and let my high school boyfriend touch my breasts underneath my bra for the first time. Last year, when I got to third base with a guy I was seeing.

Growing up very Catholic can do that to you, make you think that every little desire is lust.

They weren't. This is.

"Navy," I finally say, two oar strokes later, remembering that we were having a conversation and what it was about. I clear my throat, press my knees together, tear my eyes from his body. "We got stationed somewhere new every time my dad got promoted."

"Was it hard?" he asks, glancing over my shoulder.

I turn. The monster is there, looming, unlit, jaw hanging at a strange angle.

"Yes and no," I say, gazing up. "It meant that if I didn't like somewhere, we wouldn't stay too long, but same if we were somewhere I liked. I usually adapted all right. I think my younger brother actually preferred getting to start over fresh again and again."

I stop short, not sure how much to say, how much to put off for later dates.

I'm oddly certain there will be later dates, the knowledge a warm, fuzzy comfort in my chest instead of the spiky panic that usually lives there during an outing with the opposite sex.

"But?" Caleb prompts. He's stopped rowing and now the boat is gliding, gently, right past the monster's gaping, ragged jaw. I glance in as we drift past, silent, and can see the splintered edges of the broken beam inside.

"But I think it was hard on my older brother," I finish, still looking into the maw. "Javier…"

Wanted nothing more than to finally get my father's approval?
Sometimes fell in too easily with the wrong crowd?
Lived under the shadow of my father's expectations?

"…my older brother needed structure," I finally say. "Consistency. Stability. More than Bastien or I did, I guess."

The sea monster is perched on a concrete slab, out in the middle of the pond, and Caleb kneels in the boat, then grasps the edge of the slab and leans in, carefully, his head now in the monster's mouth.

Even though I know the power to the monster is cut — even though I know that it's not a real monster, that there are no real monsters — a shard of anxiety works its way into my chest at the sight.

"I lived in the same house from the time I was born

until the time I went to college," Caleb says. "My mom still lives there. I went to the same schools as all my brothers. Had most of the same teachers. Vivian Atwell is far from the first person to call me by the incorrect name."

I laugh and he reaches out, runs his fingers along the fractured wood.

"It was a rural school in a rural county and I guess we do all look a little bit alike," he says, then turns back to me. "I'm gonna see if I can't rotate this head so I can crawl in there a little better, but you should hold on because it's likely to rock the boat."

I move my hands from the bench to the sides, knees still firmly together — half because I don't want him to see my underwear, half in the hopes that it'll quell the fire rising inside me.

"Is all more than two?"

Caleb pulls back, kneels on the bottom of the rowboat, takes the jaw in his outstretched hands, muscles bunching and knotting, light playing over them.

I press my knees together even harder.

"Brothers?" he asks, then shakes the head. The boat rocks.

"Yeah."

"*All* with respect to brothers is four. All older."

Rock, rock, rock. I hold on.

"You have four older brothers? How are you alive? I barely survived one," I say.

Do they all look like you? Lord have mercy if they do.

"I'm very resilient," he says easily, pulling and pushing and rocking one more time, the monster's head slowly turning. "To their credit, they were never cruel on purpose. Only by accident. Mostly."

"I had two and I sometimes thought they'd do me in," I say, my eyes still glued to his arms, his hands, the power and gentleness he's putting into this, all at once. "And only one was older. I could beat Bastien up until he hit puberty."

The monster's head is sideways, upper and lower jaws resting on the concrete, and Caleb lets it go, leans inside, his head briefly disappearing into the monster's mouth.

Even in the low light I can see the muscles in his back, through his t-shirt.

God. God. *God*.

"I think I can cobble something together, especially since it's only gotta last through tonight," he says, then pulls his head out, sits back in the boat, and looks at me. "Won't ruin the magic, will it?"

"The magic of a broken art piece?" I tease.

"The magic of believing in sea monsters," he says, dimples sinking into his cheeks. "Say the word and I'll leave it broken."

CHAPTER FIVE
CALEB

I'm saying it like a joke, to tease her, but only because I like to hear her laugh. If Thalia said the word I'd row this boat away right now and leave the sculpture dark and broken in the middle of this pond, Vivian's unhappiness be damned.

"Most people think sea monsters were probably oarfish," she says.

I select some wood, some nails, a hammer, and bungee cord, tossing them all onto the concrete in front of me.

"Most people?"

"Most people who are interested in figuring out what sailors in the seventeen hundreds were actually seeing when they reported sea monsters," Thalia amends herself. "Which amounts to… several people."

"So several people think that sea monsters were actually oarfish," I say. "Hold on."

Carefully, I pull myself onto the concrete pad in the middle of the pond, right into the monster's mouth, its wooden teeth grazing my torso on either side.

Especially in the dark, it's a little unsettling.

"Several well-respected people," Thalia says. "Oarfish are these huge, snake-looking fish that get to be thirty feet long, and they mostly live down pretty deep so people never see them on the surface."

For a moment, I look around and contemplate a thirty-foot snake-looking fish.

I think I might prefer the sea monster.

"I thought you wanted to believe," I say, carefully opening the jaws wider around myself.

"I want to believe briefly and reasonably," Thalia says.

Over the monster's upper jaw I can see her shift in her seat, hands behind her now, leaning back. Her skirt rides up another half an inch and for a moment, just a moment, that half inch of soft bronze skin is all I can see.

"Saying that I want to believe makes it sound like I'm fixing to picket Area 51 and demand answers," she goes on, clearly oblivious to the effect she has on me. "I want to believe for a moment, and then I want to know that there's a perfectly rational explanation for sea monsters and mermaids and ghosts and bigfoot, et cetera."

I shift again, lift the monster's head up, then lie down beneath it, bend one knee, and prop it up on that. The monster is designed to shift and glimmer with the wind, and it's pretty clear that at some point tonight, there was a little too much breeze and it cracked a weak point in the hinge of the jaw.

My plan, as I said, isn't to fix it forever. Levi could probably manage that, but he also built himself an entire house and all I did was help.

Also? I'm very, very distracted.

"What's Bigfoot, then?" I ask her, grabbing a length of wood.

"Bears, probably," she says. "People who have no nature experience go into the forest, see one standing on its hind legs from far away, and think they've discovered a new species."

I lay the new piece of wood alongside the broken one, then try to bend it back. It's not fully snapped, just splintered, but that's enough.

"Except that one famous picture," she calls. "That's a guy in a costume. He admitted it later. Same with the Loch Ness Monster."

"Nessie is a guy in a costume?"

"The famous picture was also faked," she says, laughing.

I get the splintered piece bent back, let it go carefully, then hammer two nails into the new piece of wood.

"My hometown's also got a lake monster," I tell her. "Deepwood Dave."

That gets a long, long pause from Thalia.

"Does it lives in Deepwood Lake or Lake Dave?" she finally asks.

"It lives in Deepwood Lake," I tell her, getting back under the jaw, lining up the new wood with the old. "And his name is Dave. Or her name, I guess. I'm not sure anyone's ever asked Dave how they identify. Someone would have to find them first, though my niece spent about a year trying."

"No sightings?" Thalia asks.

I hook one end of the bungee cable to a nail, pull it tight, and start wrapping it around both pieces.

"None confirmed," I tell her. "There were several possible sightings but they didn't stand up to her rigorous scientific standards once she investigated them further."

"Rigorous standards?" Thalia says, thoughtfully. "I like this kid."

I finish binding the wood together and hook the cord on the other nail, then gently lift the monster's jaw. It's not a great fix, and it shifts slightly as I move, but I think it'll last a few more hours.

"I think she's done," I say, carefully sitting up between the jaws, the wooden teeth scraping my torso again. "Should we go light her up again?"

I hand the remaining wood and tools to Thalia, who puts them into the boat, then carefully lower myself onto the bench seat. She's sitting upright, rigid, feet apart and knees locked together, hands gripping the sides of the metal rowboat, black hair spilling over her shoulders.

It's a little off-balance, slightly undone. My gaze drifts to the scratch on her knee, where she stumbled coming out of the window. It's barely visible in the dark but already I'm thinking of her skin warm and soft beneath my fingers, the fact that I nearly kissed her knee.

I wonder what she'd do if I did that right here, right now. In the boat. On the pond, with no one else here. I wonder if she'd unclench her thighs and let her skirt ride up a little bit higher, whether she'd say *no we shouldn't do this here* or simply *no*.

"You okay?" she asks, and I realize that I've been holding the oar in my hands without moving for several seconds, so I smile at her, pretend my thoughts are G-rated.

"You look like you're ready to hold on through a storm," I tell her, taking the oar. "Am I that bad of a captain?"

"Who says you're the captain?" she asks as I push the oar into the water, pull it forward. I'm rowing backwards, but it's only ten feet to the shore.

"Clearly, I'm the one guiding the ship," I say.

"Captains don't row."

"Captains don't pilot rowboats in ponds that are three feet deep at most," I say, and the boat bumps into the shore. Carefully, I get out, pull it parallel to the ground, offer Thalia my hand.

She takes it, disembarks. I don't let go and neither does she: strong and delicate all at once, long fingers with short nails, neat dark polish on all ten.

Then she holds up our joined hands, pulls them toward her, my forearm stretched out in the low light.

"What is it?" she asks, nodding at the tattoo. "A kite?"

"A constellation," I tell her.

"A constellation of a kite?"

"A constellation of a sextant," I say, even though she's right and it does look a little like a kite, especially in the low light. "It's a navigational instrument that measures latitude."

"Can I touch it?" she asks.

"Yes," I say, though I want to scream it, shout it, beg her with that one single word: *yes, yes, yes you can touch me.*

Thalia reaches out with her other hand, sinks her four fingers into the four points of the constellation, one over each star, her touch just as heated .

"Is it a tattoo with a story?" she asks, taking all but one finger off, using that one to trace the lines.

"I got it when I turned eighteen," I say. "All five of us went together. I forget whose idea it was. We all got constellations. My mom's an astronomer."

It's not the whole story, but this is a first date and even though I find myself wanting to unveil myself to her completely, take off my skin and let her see inside, I stop myself.

I don't say, *my brothers wanted to get something for Dad, and I talked them out of it.*

I don't say, *I'd just found out the truth.*

It wasn't hard. I pointed out that he was gone and she'd

done the work of raising us all for the last nine years and that if we commemorated someone, it should be her.

If we did it again, I'd feel differently. Now, I'd get his tattoo. I'd ink him into the flesh that's half his. But back then, I couldn't. Not yet.

"Your mom who's friends with Vivian?" she asks, still tracing.

"They went to college together, at the VSU satellite campus in Blythe, both in their thirties," I say. "I think it was a real bonding experience."

Finally she covers it with her palm, cool against my arm, and her touch sends a shiver through me. The fingers of her other hand are still intertwined with mine, and to an outside observer it probably looks like we're in the middle of some strange mating dance or ancient ritual.

Maybe we are.

"Do you have any others?" she asks.

"Just this one," I say, but for the first time ever, I wish I did. I wish fervently, desperately, that I had a reason for her to touch me somewhere else.

"You?" I ask.

Thalia laughs, shaking her head, black hair gleaming in the light of the moon and the neon of the Thai pavilion, swishing over her shoulders. She takes her palm from my forearm and the spot suddenly feels too cool, like something is missing.

"My parents would kill me," she says.

"I thought your dad was in the Navy."

We're still holding hands and she turns toward me, fingers interlaced, bringing our hands to shoulder level, waving them slowly up and down like we're half-dancing to a waltz that only we can hear.

"He is," she says.

"He doesn't even have a Navy tattoo? Most military guys I know have at least that."

"He's *very* traditional," she says, raising her eyebrows, her eyes still on our interlocked hands. "Tattoos are for drug addicts, lowlifes, and whores, didn't you know?"

"Which of those am I?" I tease, and she looks up at me, eyebrows still raised, mouth moving into a smile.

She's close. So close I think I can feel her body heat, though it's impossible for me to tell if that's true or just my imagination.

"That's a trick question and I'm not answering it," she says. "They've only ever gotten me into trouble."

"Good trouble or bad trouble?" I ask, shifting closer to her.

She's looking up at me, dark eyes wide, laughing. I put two fingertips on her bare shoulder and slide them, gently, down her arm.

"All trouble is bad," she says. "That's what makes it trouble."

"You've just never gotten into good trouble," I say, still sliding. My heart feels like it's in a marching band, blood crackling through my veins.

"But you're about to offer to show me some?" she says, eyes dancing, head slightly tilted. "Is that your next line?"

"It's not a line if you're going to follow through," I tell her, skating my fingers back up her arm. "But since you don't seem to want trouble of any kind, I'll insist we stay on the straight and narrow."

"I didn't know we'd gotten off it," she says, and now her voice is quiet, melodious, musical over the hum of art patrons in the distance. "Unless I'm really wrong, we're both consenting adults behaving themselves."

I don't want to behave myself. Thalia makes me feel

wild and untamed in a way I'm not sure I've ever felt before.

It's lust, pure and simple, and I know it's lust but the knowledge doesn't make it any easier to bear. It's beating through my whole body like a timpani drum, vibrating my skin, reverberating through the air between us.

I shift forward, and now we're touching, and I take my hand off her arm and slide it, slowly, around her waist and she rocks forward almost imperceptibly, but I feel it. I feel everything she does.

"And what exactly are you consenting to?" I ask her, feeling my own voice dip dangerously low.

Her lips move, half-pucker, the face I've already learned she makes sometimes when she's thinking.

"The art show," she murmurs, her eyes flicking to my lips. "The sea monster."

I tighten my fingers around hers.

"Holding hands?" I ask.

"Yes," Thalia says.

"Tracing my tattoo with your fingers?"

"Yes."

I hold our clasped hands up in front of my face.

"A kiss here?" I ask, lips brushing her knuckles.

"Yes," she says, the word a little more than a whisper.

I press my lips to her fingertips, my eyes locked on hers, my pulse thrumming.

"A touch here?" I ask, pressing my fingertips into her spine.

"Yes," she murmurs.

I leave her hand on my shoulder, run my fingers up her arm.

"Here?" I ask.

"Yes."

To her collarbone, her neck, her pulse hot and racing

just beneath her skin until my thumb is skimming along her jaw, my own blood hammering at my veins.

I watch her face for a long moment. Not because I'm unsure, but because I'm sure, and I want to remember this.

"A kiss here?" I finally murmur, and I brush my thumb along her full, lush lips.

"Yes," she whispers.

So I kiss her.

CHAPTER SIX
THALIA

I feel like I've been waiting years for this kiss.

It's a ridiculous way to feel, and I know it. I met Caleb a couple of hours ago, so logic dictates that I can't have been waiting any longer than that.

But when he touches my lip with his thumb and then with his mouth, when his fingers dig into my back but his lips stay gentle and warm, when I press myself against him without even meaning to, I feel like I've been waiting years.

I step forward, into him. I slide my hand to his neck, into his hair, feel his warmth between my fingers. I move my lips against his and he responds, pressing harder, his thumb now on my cheekbone.

We kiss. We kiss and time passes, the world spins, and I've got no sense of it. Could be seconds, could be hours. I don't know.

Then, he pulls away. A fraction of an inch.

"Don't," I say, virtually a growl.

"Don't what?"

"Stop."

He kisses me again. Now, harder. Now, needier. Now he

works his fingers into my hair and I open my mouth under his and the kiss deepens. He digs his fingers into my spine and I press forward, standing on my toes. His slight stubble is rough against my face, his body muscled and hard against mine, and even though the keys in his pocket are digging into my hip, I don't stop.

Then the sea monster lights up, and we both pull back in surprise, still half-wound around each other, and I look across the pond at the glimmering, glowing beast.

"Oh," I exhale, still panting for breath.

Caleb takes a deep breath, clears his throat.

"Thanks," he calls out, and I finally look over his shoulder to see Vivian, standing by the breaker box where she just plugged the monster back in, gazing across the pond with her hands on her hips, the same ready-to-challenge stance she had before.

"We were working on that part," he mutters, low enough that only I can hear him.

Beyond Vivian, the monster shines. It glows. I have no idea what its scales are made of — up close it looked like some kind of film — but it moves loosely in the breeze, shuddering this way and that, the lights in the scales designed to look like they're rippling with the wind.

The effect is that it looks strangely alive, alive enough that I find myself gripping Caleb's shirt in one hand, holding my breath as the monster seems to come up for air, gently shake itself off.

"It'll do," Vivian calls. "How's it fixed?"

If she's noticed what we're doing, she doesn't show the first sign of it.

Caleb takes a deep breath, clears his throat, takes my hand, walks to the edge of the pond where Vivian's standing.

"Rigged it with a bungee cord and a two-by-four," he says. "It'll hold for a few hours."

"Huh," Vivian says. "Well, it's better than it was."

Caleb slides his thumb over my knuckles, and I swallow hard at the friction.

Leave, I think at Vivian. *Please leave, we were very busy...*

"DRAGON!" a kid shouts from somewhere far, far closer than I want. "Cool!"

"Oh, wow," an adult voice says. Moments later, there are steps on the bridge and then four figures are coming across: two small, two full-size, and my toes curl with sheer irritation, like I'm a teenager on a movie date and my mom just sat down in front of me.

Then Vivian walks away without another word, just marching off.

"Thank you, Caleb," he says, lightly, as if he's making a suggestion. "What a nice favor you did me."

"She's always like this?" I ask, as the two kids practically run into the Thai building, then stand there and stare up at the light projected on the ceiling. I shoot a glare in their direction, because they are *really* getting in the way of my good time.

"More or less," he says, his thumb still rubbing over my knuckles. "Usually not this bad. I think she's one of those artists who just gets... really absorbed, you know? And forgets about everything else."

"Such as manners," I say, just as another family makes their way toward us, across the bridge with a chorus of *wow!* And *cool!*

I look at Caleb. He looks at me.

I'm still trying to catch my breath from before. I'm still trying to process that I'm here, that I keep saying *yes* to this near-total stranger who feels like anything but. I'm still half-convinced that I'm dreaming, or down the rabbit hole.

"I should put the tools away," he says, turning to me, in a voice that feels like lava trickling down my spine. "Would you mind giving me a hand?"

Some kids shout. A parent chastises. I'm pretty sure someone screams at a sibling.

"Away in the shed behind the building?" I ask, catching on.

"The very one," Caleb says, already walking toward the rowboat. "Irresponsible to leave them in the boat like this. They could be taken, used as weapons…"

He hands me a hammer and a bungee cord, then grabs an armful of wood himself, and with every step toward the dark back of the Thai building my pulse gets faster and faster.

I haven't exactly had a ton of boyfriends, but when I was a high school senior, I dated Mark Muncie for three months. I don't think we spoke more than fifty sentences total to each other because pretty much all we did was try to find dark places to make out where we wouldn't get caught. And sometimes, he touched my boobs, though I never let him take my shirt off.

Mark wasn't memorable, but for a long time I remembered the thrill of getting my boobs touched in the darkened parking lot of an elementary school. For a few years afterward, sneaking around with Mark was the baddest thing I'd ever done.

This feels like that times one hundred. I know we're adults. I know that we've got better places than this to make out, but I sincerely think that I might implode if I have to wait long enough to get to any of them.

We turn the corner of the pavilion, and suddenly, it's dark. We're on the edge of the botanical garden here, marked by a fence and then the deep, dense Virginia forest.

There are no lights on this side of the building but the silhouette is outlined in bright neon.

He opens the shed, puts his armful of wood in. On the other side of this wall, kids are shouting and lights are blinking. Caleb holds out one hand for the hammer and as I hand it over, the silence between us finally becomes too much.

"You're not a serial killer, are you?" I tease.

Caleb looks at me like I've suddenly started speaking Japanese.

"This would be a good setup is all," I say, already wishing I'd said nothing. "You know, you lure a girl out here, behind a building, with the hammer…"

He just looks at me, hammer in one hand, hips slightly cocked and even in the dark his shirt clings to his chest in ways that make my mouth go dry, my pulse speed up.

Then he tosses the hammer end over end, catches it neatly.

"Is there anything else you'd like to accuse me of while we're out here?" he says, and in the dark I can't tell if he's smiling or not.

This. This is why I'm still a virgin.

"Sorry," I say, shaking my head. "It was a dumb joke."

He tosses the hammer again, then places it neatly into the shed. Swings the doors shut.

"First a pickup artist, which, all right," he says. "Then a serial killer, which you've got to admit was a bit much."

"Unless you were actually a serial killer," my mouth says without brain approval.

"Which I'm not," he says, grabbing the combination lock from the top of the shed where he left it, spinning it around one finger. "Anything else, Thalia?"

He whirls the dial on the lock, holding it up to catch the

light, and shoots me a teasing, challenging look. I relax, just a little.

Don't say something mean or dumb, I tell myself. *Just be slightly normal this once.*

"A sea monster medic?" I say.

"All right," Caleb says, pulling the lock open and fitting it through the door.

"A renowned rowboat captain?" I lean my shoulder against the door of the shed, a foot away from him, hoping I look casual and knowing that I probably don't.

He snaps the lock shut, spins the dial. My heart pounds.

"What else?" he asks, his voice low, teasing, as he closes the distance between us. "Come on, Thalia, one more."

I feel like the sea monster, as if my skin is rippling with light, as if I'm unfurling at the slightest breeze.

"You're a good kisser," I murmur.

With that, he pushes me against the shed door and proves me right.

This time he's rougher. Less restrained. He works his fingers through my hair, his other hand planted on the wall next to my head, and I open my mouth under his, the kiss already deep.

I have two fistfuls of his shirt, pulling him toward me, and he lets me do it. He growls and kisses me harder and his fingers leave my hair, brush down my neck. His hand finds my hip, pins it against the wall, the wood digging into my back.

There's another noise. A tiny groan, a gasp, and after a moment I realize that it's me, and Caleb chuckles.

"Shh," he teases. "There's kids out there."

"This is still PG-13," I murmur back. "Perfectly tasteful."

He kisses me again. Deep, hard, and as he pulls away I catch his bottom lip in my teeth.

"What's it take to get an R rating?" he asks, his lips already on mine again.

"Lots of bloodshed or one nipple," I answer into his mouth.

He kisses me slowly, thoroughly. He shifts his hips and now they're pressed against mine, pinning me to the wall behind me.

"Just one?" he asks, and now his hand is at my shoulder, fingers toying with the thin fabric of my tank top strap.

"I didn't make the rules," I tease.

Our hips shift again, still pressing me against the wall, and the words *please God just tear this tank top right off of my body* are on the tip of my tongue but I kiss him again to stop myself.

He pushes himself against me, harder, and I push back, drinking in the beautiful heat of his body, even as I wriggle a little bit because he's got something in his pocket that's pressing into me, and I swear it feels like a TV remote or something —

My eyes pop open in realization mid-kiss. Luckily, his stay shut.

Dick.

That's his dick.

I freeze, suddenly unsure of how to proceed. It's not the first time this has happened — I'm an accidental virgin, not a nun — but I didn't handle the other instances with grace, either.

Is there boner etiquette when you're frantically making out with an incredibly hot man behind a building at an art show? Should I pretend I don't notice? Grab it?

Grab it and say, *hey, big boy, is that a cucumber in your pocket or are you just happy to see me?*

Okay, clearly not that last one.

Suddenly he pulls back, our faces an inch apart. He

swallows hard, panting for breath, his fingers still tangled in the strap of my tank top.

"You okay?" he murmurs.

"Fine," I whisper back. "Very fine."

I close my eyes again, kiss him harder, and don't grab it. Another sigh escapes me as he shifts again, pressing me harder against the wall, and I can't help but roll my hips, my fingers grabbing his belt loop without my brain's permission.

My body's pretty clear on what it wants. It's my mind that's wondering what's polite in this circumstance.

"We shouldn't be doing this here," he says, his lips barely leaving mine.

"No one's watching," I murmur.

His hand skims down my hip to the outside of my thigh, warm through the fabric of my skirt. My heart skips another beat.

"But are they listening?" he asks, and I nip softly at his lower lip.

"What is there to hear?" I say.

My hips roll again, his erection like iron against my lower belly, and the sensation sends a shockwave through me: lust and surprise and excitement and nervousness, a little bit of trepidation and did I mention lust? That one for sure.

"Nothing yet," he says, his fingers under the shoulder of my tank top, tracing my collarbone. "But the more we do this the more tempted I am to see what you sound like when you come."

"Oh," I squeak out, my spine going rigid and my eyes going wide.

Hello, full-body blush.

Hello, warmth flooding my entire body. Hello, getting so wet that it's actually the tiniest bit uncomfortable.

Clearly, my body is fine with this turn of events, but I have absolutely no idea what to say to that. Literally none.

I just stare at Caleb for several long, long seconds, confused as hell and *wildly* turned on.

"Nothing," I finally say. "I don't sound like anything."

He looks at me for another second, his beautiful green eyes studying my face like he's memorizing me.

Then he smiles, looks down, pulls away a little more.

"I'm sorry," he says, dimples deep. "Too much."

"Kinda," I admit. "I think you're supposed to save that for the second date."

"The second date," he says, one eyebrow lifting. "All right. What are you doing tomorrow night?"

I'll probably have lots of homework, there's a meeting for my work-study project at six, and I think I'm supposed to meet someone for a group project at the library after that, but right now I couldn't care less about any of that.

"I'm free," I whisper.

"A friend of mine who works in the film department is putting on a free outdoor showing of *The Philadelphia Story* in Lafayette Park," he says. "I'll bring the picnic. You bring yourself."

"Deal," I say, and he leans in again, kisses me one more time.

It's slow. It's long. His body moves against mine with a grace and restrained force that I can feel vibrating through his muscles, desire radiating from every inch of his skin.

There's no question what he wants. What I want, I think, even though it's terrifying and insane to want it of someone I met hours ago.

Finally, we separate. He laces his fingers through mine, takes a deep breath, leans our foreheads together.

"Come on," Caleb says. "Let's go look at some art."

CHAPTER SEVEN
CALEB

CALEB LOVELESS
ASSISTANT PROFESSOR
MATHEMATICS

It doesn't look right.

I read it again, slowly this time. I double-check the spelling, the kerning between the letters, the capitalization. All fine.

But it still doesn't look right. The problem must be with me, still not completely convinced that I've somehow landed here, in an assistant professor position.

It still feels strange. There were points in the past six years when I seriously contemplated dropping out of graduate school. I thought I'd become a rock climbing instructor, or a whitewater rafting guide or something, anything, that let me be outdoors and never deal with academia again.

Once, after a particularly intense round of backstabbing and drama, I'd even filled out the paperwork but my mom and brother Levi talked me out of quitting.

And now, I've got this brand-new sign on my brand-new office in the brand-new Mathematics Department building. Last week I moved out of my grad student apartment that I shared with two other students and into my own place, a renovated carriage house that I'm renting.

Last night, I met a girl. That part's not unusual. I go on a perfectly average number of dates, but I've never been on a date like that. I've never been on a date with someone like Thalia.

Long after I got home and went to bed I laid there, staring at the ceiling. Thinking of Thalia's voice saying *I believe in magical, not magic*, of her scraped knee outside in the alleyway, of how kissing her made my bones shake.

Of how I wanted her there, then, wanted so desperately to push her skirt up and slide my hand between her legs, make her come just like I told her I would.

But instead I stopped. Not because I thought we'd be caught or because I gave a damn about that, but because I want more from her.

In short, I want to know her before we fuck. It's probably old-fashioned, and as I laid in bed, watching the ceiling with what felt like the world's hardest cock, I wasn't thrilled with myself for my own decision.

My phone dings softly in my pocket, and I pull it out.

Thalia: 7 sounds perfect.
Thalia: What do I bring?
Me: Just yourself.

But there she was, standing in the stall, all bright red lips and winged eyeliner, wearing high heels and a short skirt, black hair tumbling around her shoulders, and I've been laser-focused ever since.

Thalia's not my type. My type tends to wear a lot of

flannel and torn jeans, not neat skirts and heeled boots. My type doesn't wear red lipstick or winged eyeliner. They usually come with a nose ring, at least one tattoo, and tend to look like they could participate in a drum circle at any moment.

Thalia doesn't look like she attends many drum circles. Instead, she looks like she has a favorite pen and strong opinions about day planners, and somehow, I find that irresistible.

The door to the stairs at the end of the hall opens, and a middle-aged Asian man in jeans and a cowboy shirt steps through.

"Good thing they finally finished the new building," Oliver calls to me, down the tiled hallway. "You were all set to get the haunted office in the old department."

"You say that like only one of those offices was haunted," I call back.

The closer he gets, the more interesting Oliver's fashion choices become. I don't have my contacts in or my glasses on right now, so what looked like a gray shirt with embellishments from far away is actually a paisley pattern in various shades of pink, embroidered swirls and stars over the pockets.

"Well, I'm sure that entire building was haunted by the forgotten souls and crushed dreams of those who walked its halls and yet were denied tenure," he says dryly, coming up and standing next to me. "But we were going to put you in the office where a visiting professor swore up and down that a ghostly little girl used to show up and ask if she could help her find her dolly."

"Did she help?" I ask, the only logical question.

"I believe instead she called Gerald at three a.m. in hysterics," he says.

"I'm sure he took that well," I say, keeping my voice low, and Oliver just sighs.

"We didn't have another female visiting professor for quite a while after that," he admits. "No matter how many the rest of us recommended."

"Gerald nursed a grudge against an entire class of people for the actions of one? Doesn't sound anything like him," I mutter, glancing over at Oliver.

My advisor — no, my *former* advisor, we're now colleagues — gives me a conspiratorial look.

"Even in a brand new building, the walls here have ears," he says, one eyebrow raised. "And you don't want *your* soul to join the ghosts of the un-tenured, do you?"

I just shudder.

"Perish the thought," I say, and I'm not being sarcastic.

Being denied tenure is the worst thing that can happen to a professor, barring death of disfigurement, though frankly I might opt to lose a finger, given the choice.

It's not like getting fired. If you get fired, you can still get a job in your field — get denied tenure and not only do you lose your current job, you stand a zero percent chance of getting hired anywhere else, either.

In other words, if you get denied tenure, you'd better have a backup career in mind. It's hell.

"Thought not," Oliver says, lightheartedly. "I, on the other hand, have had tenure for a number of years, so I'm free to call Gerald a total dinosaur who wouldn't know what to do with a new idea if it bit him on the ass, and who hasn't had a single original thought go through his head since the first Bush administration."

I just laugh, and Oliver raises one eyebrow.

"His dinner parties are incredibly dull," he declares. "The drinks are weak, the food is bad, and he only invites other ancient white men. And me, to prove that he's open-minded and knows someone who isn't an old white man."

"Well, I find Dr. Comstock to be a lovely, wise, generous, dignified, and…"

I trail off, thinking.

"…informative individual," I say, just a little too loudly, glancing down the hall toward the rest of the offices.

Oliver grins.

"You'll be a full professor in no time," he says. "I've got a class at two, are you heading to campus?"

"Honors Calc in Keyes," I say, and we walk down the hall toward a set of glass double doors.

I'm pretty sure I owe my job to Oliver Nguyen. He was my advisor while I was getting my doctorate here, and when this position suddenly opened up last year, he's the one who practically forced me to apply.

I later found out that there were nearly a thousand applicants, many of whom were probably more qualified than me. It's a miracle that I got it.

"I hope they've fixed the AC," he says. "No one can learn in a sauna. Last semester it got so out of control —"

"Professor Loveless?" a voice asks, right as we pass the main Mathematics office.

It takes me half a second to remember that that's me.

"Yes?"

"Dr. Comstock has asked to see you," says Karen, his Executive Assistant — not secretary, *never* secretary — calls through an open doorway, framed by heavy wooden doors.

She's looking at me expectantly from behind a massive wooden desk, her dyed-blond hair practically a helmet.

"Of course," I tell her, and nod at Oliver.

"Good luck. We'll talk later," he says, clapping me quickly on the shoulder, then walking away. Karen gives a single nod, then points to an office door.

"You can go ahead in, Dr. Comstock is expecting you," Karen says, already looking back at her computer through reading glasses.

"Thanks," I say, and push open the door.

Behind a huge wooden desk, surrounded by bookshelves, is Dr. Comstock, as he prefers to be called. I've never called him Gerald to his face and never will. The only person I've heard get away with it was Ezekiel Thurston, an emeritus professor who just turned ninety-three and who's been around for so long that he could probably get away with burning the place down.

"Professor Loveless," he says, waving a hand at me while still looking through his glasses at his computer monitor. "Have a seat."

I sit, crossing one ankle over the opposite knee, and wait. In academia, almost everything is some kind of psychological power play — all about who can make someone else wait the longest, who can inconvenience someone else the most, who has to call who *professor* and who can get away with first names.

It's my Achilles heel. I'm straightforward to a fault and have never been able to shake the notion that everyone else is, as well. I'm an awful liar. I hate saying what I don't mean, even when I know it's good for my career.

So I wait for Dr. Comstock to acknowledge me. I've still got plenty of time to get to campus, so I don't mind watching the sun stream in through the big windows at the front of the office, scanning the titles of the books on the bookshelves.

"All right, sorry about that," Dr. Comstock finally says, even though I'm at least savvy enough to know he's not sorry. "Had to respond quickly to the Vice Provost, you know how *she* is."

"Of course," I say, even though I don't know.

"Well," he says, bringing his hands together over the desk. "Normally this is where I like to give new hires a quick welcome, introduce myself properly, let them know that my door is always open, that sort of thing, but naturally you know all that already."

"Yes," I agree.

His door is *not* always open, but we can both pretend.

"Therefore, let me just say that the whole department is extremely pleased to witness your transition from doctoral student to assistant professor," he says. "On behalf of the Virginia Southern University, welcome to the faculty."

He stands, holding out one hand. The whole thing has an air of showmanship about it, but that's part of the job. I stand, shake his hand, thank him for the formal welcome. We exchange a few more pleasantries, and then I turn to leave.

"By the way, Caleb," he says, just as I reach the door. "I need you to attend the Madison Scholars welcome reception next Friday night. I'm supposed to go, but I'm afraid something's come up. Could you?"

It's not really a question. It's more of a test to see how much I want this, because we both know full well that what's come up is that he doesn't want to go to a banquet populated by undergraduates.

"Of course," I say with a smile. "I'd be happy to."

"Thank you," he says, and I leave his office, nod to Karen, and finally make my way to campus to teach my first class as a real professor.

* * * * * ★ * * * * * *

TRUTH BE TOLD, it's a little anticlimactic. Even though this time I get to write *Professor Caleb Loveless* on the whiteboard, this is now my seventh year teaching Calculus I. Even though it's Honors Calculus, all that really means is that we cover more material and the final is a little harder.

In fact, I'm pretty sure I've taught in this exact room before. The view from the narrow, vertical window looks familiar, and I think I remember the strange orange spot on the tile floor in the corner behind the computer.

The first student arrives a full seven minutes before class, puts her things down at a desk in the front row, and walks up to me. Before she opens her mouth, I know exactly how this is going to go.

"Hi, Professor Loveless, I'm Angela Gillard," she says, holding out a manicured hand. "I just had a few questions before class starts."

There's always one. VSU is one of the top-ranked public universities in the U.S., so there's no shortage of intensely motivated, high-achieving students. Angela's blond, not a hair out of place, wearing slacks and a button-down shirt despite the heat.

She'll probably be Secretary of State in twenty years.

"Welcome to Calculus," I answer her, and she nods, then pulls my syllabus from a neatly-labeled folder. I notice that it's already highlighted in several colors.

"I wanted to talk to you about the class schedule," she says, and flips pages until she lands on November. "I have some travel planned that I can't miss..."

Behind her, the other students start filtering in, one by one. Most of them are dressed like regular college students on a hot late-August day — shorts, t-shirts, flip-flops. It's close to ninety degrees out. I'd be wearing shorts if I weren't teaching the class.

"...so I'd like to schedule some one-on-one time to discuss what I've missed before Thanksgiving," Angela is saying.

"My office hours are on the first page," I say.

She gives me a smile like I didn't understand her. I did.

"I'd really prefer to schedule a time," she says.

"If my office hours aren't enough, we can certainly discuss that come November," I offer. "Did you have any other concerns?"

Her lips flatten into a line, and she gives me an irritated look, but accepts my answer.

"Yes, about the final," she says. "Can you tell me..."

I check the clock while she grills me about the timing of the final. Three more minutes until my first class starts, and the room is nearly full.

Despite myself, despite the fact that I've done this again and again, I get a little bit nervous. I always do. I'm sure it's only natural.

"I'm afraid the rooms aren't assigned until later in the semester," I tell Angela. She's not pleased.

"I ask because my finals schedule is going to be very complex, and I'd like to know as soon as possible whether I need to request an alternate exam period," she says, not backing down an inch.

"Rooms are determined by lottery in mid-November," I say.

"Surely, some can be arranged earlier?" she says. "It doesn't seem like it's so much to ask —"

I hold up one hand, stopping her.

"I have nothing to do with the process," I say. "When I find out when and where your exam will be, I'll tell you. Now, I need to start class."

"Who do I talk to about this?" she asks, not moving.

"That sounds like an excellent question for your advisor," I tell her. "Please take your seat."

Angela's not happy with that answer either, but she sits, neatly arranging a pen and four highlighters next to the syllabus she's already pulled out.

I straighten the stack of syllabi on the table up front, take one, walk to the lectern, center it, adjust the glasses I usually wear for the first few weeks of class, since they make me feel more professorial.

"Welcome to Honors Calculus 102," I begin. "I'm Professor Loveless. If you're supposed to be in Modern Dance, you've got the wrong classroom."

It gets a ripple of polite laughter, as usual.

"Today will be a fairly short class," I say, launching into my usual spiel. "I'll just be going over the syllabus, policies, and expectations, and we'll begin instruction on Wednesday. If you've got any questions…"

As I talk, I look over the students, who I swear get younger every year. They're sitting in neat rows, some watching me, some reading along in the syllabus. It's the first day, so no one is looking at their phone during class yet.

At this point in the semester, they're still bright-eyed, bushy-tailed, optimistic, even the ones who are required to take this class for their major. That'll probably change in a few weeks, as things get increasingly complex.

"…will count for forty percent of your grade," I'm saying, the same thing I say every semester. "Your midterm will count for thirty percent, and the final for —"

I stop short, frozen. My voice sticks in my throat. I can't even draw a breath.

For a long, long moment, silence reigns in the classroom. Papers shuffle. Pens click.

I stare, disbelieving.

From the back row, spine ramrod straight, eyes wide as saucers, Thalia's staring right back at me.

CHAPTER EIGHT

THALIA

I want to melt into the floor and disappear into the cracks between the ugly tiles.

I should have left the second I saw him at the front of the classroom. Yes, I need this class to graduate, and yes, this is the only section that works with the rest of my schedule, but taking five years to graduate suddenly doesn't sound so bad.

Not when my math professor is the same man who pushed me against a wall last night, kissed me like our lives depended on it, and told me he wanted to make me orgasm.

Just the memory of it makes the heat rush to my face again, my hand squeezing my pen so hard it's a miracle that it hasn't —

Crack.

— And there my pen goes. I drop it quickly and it lands on my Honors Calculus syllabus, deep blue ink oozing out thickly.

I just stare at it. Caleb — no, *Professor Loveless*, oh God — is talking again, and now he's moved on to his absence policy. At least I didn't get too much ink on my hand, though now I can't follow along on the syllabus, as if I was doing that in the first place.

He's my professor.

Last night, I felt my professor's dick. When it was hard. While his tongue was in my mouth.

And it got me very, very turned on.

I want to disappear.

I glance at the doorway, and contemplate making a run for it. It's not far. I took a seat in the back row on purpose, for no other reason than I simply could not stand the thought of my peers looking at me in my current state of agony.

But I don't. I stay put, because making some sort of ruckus would be worse than staying quiet, right? Maybe if I stare at my ink-stained syllabus for long enough, when I look back up that won't be Caleb any more, it'll be some other hot professor with glasses —

Nope. Nope, it's still him.

I don't look up for the rest of the class period, not until everyone else is shoving papers into their bags and standing.

That's when I hear, loud and clear: "Thalia Lopez, could I see you for a moment? Everyone else, I'll see you Wednesday."

I wait for everyone else to leave before I make my way to the front, tossing my ruined syllabus into the trash, along with my busted pen, rubbing the ink on my palm into a big smear. Two other students are asking him about something — grading policy, it sounds like — so I stand back and try to think about literally anything but last night.

Finally, the last one leaves. Caleb — nope, Professor Loveless, God in heaven I can't believe this is happening — and I both watch him go.

Then we look at each other. He takes off his glasses, puts them on the lectern, stares at them for a moment.

Then he walks around the table at the front of the room and leans against it, facing me, arms folded over his chest, sleeves rolled up to his elbow.

There's the tattoo. The sextant. His forearms are even nicer in the daylight, thick and muscled —

"I didn't realize you were a student," he says.

I swallow, my mouth dry as the desert, and shift the messenger bag I've got slung over one shoulder.

"I didn't realize you were a professor," I say.

"That makes what happened last night wildly inappropriate," he goes on, voice low.

We lock eyes.

"Not if we didn't know," I murmur, quietly, so anyone in the hall outside can't possibly hear.

"Even so," he says, his voice matching mine. "Ethically, last night is murky at best. And going forward —"

"Is black and white?" I ask, before he can say it, tumbling over the words in my need to get them out first.

I don't want to hear him say it. It feels easier if it's me.

"Yes," he agrees, then pauses. Looks at me, and for one single millisecond I think of holding hands in the botanical garden, following Vivian down the lit path.

"I unequivocally cannot date a student," he says, his voice low, soft, gentle. Secret. "University policy is crystal clear on that point."

It hurts.

I knew it was coming from the first second I stepped into this classroom and saw him, but it still hurts.

"Of course," I agree, holding my body upright, rigid. "It would be wildly inappropriate."

"It would," he says.

And then, so quietly I barely hear him: "I'm sorry."

THE HOOKUP EQUATION

"I am, too," I whisper, and then I wait.

I don't know what I'm waiting for. Something else, some grain of hope. *Call me when you graduate*, maybe.

But he doesn't. Right now, he's probably wishing that he could go back in time and delete yesterday, delete me as anything but one of eighteen students in a calculus class.

So I nod once, gather my wits, and leave the classroom.

· · · * * ★ ★ ★ * * · · ·

I SWEAR to god they're mocking me.

The moment I open my bedroom door, there they are: brightly colored and vibrant in the late afternoon sunlight. Each one tall, proud, and thick, and a reminder I don't fucking want right now.

"Margaret!" I shout, practically throwing my bag to the floor. "Your dicks are on my desk! Again!"

"Sorry!" she calls, her voice echoing across the small apartment. "Don't worry, they're the social media dicks."

"Yeah, they'd goddamn better be!" I shout back, and now I hear the creak of a desk chair, some rustling.

"Sorry," she says again, and two seconds later she comes through my bedroom door. "Your room has the best lighting at magic hour and I was doing some stuff for the store's Instagram —"

"Could you please not leave a bunch of dildos on my desk?" I snap. "It doesn't feel like a lot to ask. No giant blue dicks on my desk. Too much?"

"Okay, okay," she says, scooping all four into her arms in one swoop, holding three against her body and the biggest one, which is purple and quite frankly alarming, in her right hand. "I swear, they're brand new."

"I don't care if they're brand new or a dick you found

excavating King Tut," I say. "I don't want them on my desk. I don't need them in my room."

I grab my messenger bag off the floor, dump it on my twin bed, wrest my laptop out of it and put it on the scarred wooden desk. Margaret's still standing there, holding a bunch of dildos, watching me.

"What?" I ask, the word coming out about five times bitchier than I mean it to.

"Are you okay?" she asks.

I pull my desk chair out and sit, staring at my unopened laptop.

It's been a shitty afternoon, but getting unceremoniously dumped by your calculus professor will do that to you, I guess. I'm angry and hurt and upset, and I don't even have anyone to be angry *at*.

At Caleb? What else was he supposed to do? At myself, for not screening him properly last night?

No, I'm just angry / hurt / upset / everything at the universe in general, and it's really unsatisfying.

"Thalia," she says again. "What's wrong?"

For a moment, I don't even know if I should tell her the truth. Can we get in trouble for accidentally going on a date?

Fuck it, I think.

"You know the guy from last night?"

She tosses the dildos onto my bed and sits beside them, facing me, cross-legged, eyes narrowed.

"Did something already happen?" she asks, astonished.

Last night, when they got home from the bars at one in the morning, I was still awake and may have waxed rhapsodic about my date. I may have waxed a *lot*.

"Yeah," I say, resting my forehead on one hand. "He's my calculus professor."

Total silence. After long enough, I turn and look over at Margaret.

She's staring at me in surprise, her mouth a little O.

"*That* guy is a professor?" she finally says. "Professor. Not a TA or a grad student or something."

"Pro-fucking-fessor," I say, a word that I'm not sure makes sense, as I open my laptop.

"And he took an undergrad out? That's shady," she says, and now she sounds concerned. "And a serious ethics violation —"

I turn in my chair, holding up the laptop that I've opened to the VSU Mathematics Faculty page. She leans in, reading.

"His current research specialty is Diplodean Number Regression Theory and he's hiked all three major long-distance trails in the US. Someday, he hopes to complete the Great Himalayan Trail," she reads, then looks at me. "And he *dates students* —"

"I didn't tell him I was a student," I say. "He didn't tell me he was a professor, I didn't mention that I was an undergrad, I just thought he was someone who lived in town and had probably graduated a year or two ago."

"You never asked what he did? He never asked you?"

Margaret sounds suspicious.

"No," I say, putting my laptop back on the desk and plugging it in.

"What did you talk about?"

Magic and sea monsters and pickup artists and stars, I think.

"Other stuff. You want a transcript?"

"Were you talking?" she asks, both eyebrows lifted. "I thought you said Excalibur didn't happen."

Excalibur is what the four of us have named the possibly-mythical dick that finally takes my virginity, after the time that I referred to myself as a 'reverse sword-in-the-stone situation' during one late-night chat. It's become both a running joke and a useful shorthand, and yes, I know that King Arthur took the sword *out* of the stone.

"Yes, we talked," I say, looking away so she doesn't see me blush. "Just not about that."

She's still watching me from my bed, concern all over her face.

"We already broke it off," I say. "You'll notice that I'm sitting here talking to you and not getting ready to go on another date."

"It's just that professors who date students —"

"He's not *a professor who dates students*."

"Q.E.D., he is," she points out. "I'm just wondering if we should tell someone about this —"

"No!" I practically shout.

" — In case it's a pattern," she finishes.

Suddenly, I'm a little uncertain.

Last night *seemed* special. It *seemed* like a bolt from the blue, totally genuine, but now I can't help but wonder. Am I the first? He doesn't routinely try to date undergrads, does he?

One accident is understandable, but a professor with a thing for undergrads is… worrisome.

"Look, it was one date," I say, trying to sound reasonable. "All we did was make out, agree on a second date, and then call it off when I showed up in his class today."

Margaret looks skeptical, and I can't quite blame her because 'professor who dates his undergraduate students' does sound very, very bad.

"It's over," I say. "No harm, no foul, it's already ended. Caput."

She takes a deep breath, then lets it out, nodding.

"I'm sorry," she says, then gives me a searching look. "You okay? You seemed really into him last night."

I'm not okay. Actually, I'm crushed. Maybe even heartbroken, which is a stupid way to feel after a single date, but oh well. I guess I feel stupid.

"I'll be fine," I say.

"C'mere," she says, holding out one hand.

I scrunch up my face at her.

"Come get physical affection, dammit," she goes on, still holding out her hand. "It'll lower your cortisol levels and give your brain a hit of dopamine, which you probably need."

It's impossible to argue with Margaret sometimes, so I go flop down on my bed, legs hanging off one side. She flops next to me.

"There's a dildo poking into my spine," I sigh.

"That's not where it's supposed to poke," she teases.

I squirm, then finally pull out a long, thick, red, knobby length of silicone that looks more like modern art than a penis. Next to me, Margaret wriggles, then whacks my dildo with the ridiculously-sized purple one.

"On guard!" she says, and finally, I laugh.

CHAPTER NINE
CALEB

I look at myself in the mirror and sigh, scrutinizing the point of my tie where it crosses my belt. I stand up straighter. I slouch. I loosen it ever so slightly, because this thing always feels like it's strangling me.

In all positions, the point of the tie stays firmly within the boundaries set by my belt. By Jove, after five different tries, I think I've got it.

" — is going to overflow if one of Mom's church friends brings another lasagna, I swear," Seth's voice says from the foot of my bed, where my phone is on speaker.

"Is it Mom's church friends or is it Eli?" I ask, still regarding myself in the mirror, hoping that I don't look as ridiculous as I feel.

"Eli would never freeze a lasagna," Seth says. "Are you kidding? 'Freezing cheese breaks down the cellular walls and affects the melting point of blah blah blah,' I can just hear him now."

I grab my glasses from my nightstand and put them on, but even when I'm no longer slightly blurry, I can't get over the notion that I look like some sort of corporate douchebag in a suit. It doesn't matter that it's dark gray and properly tailored, and it doesn't matter that after several thousand tries, I finally got the tie right.

I don't belong in a suit. I belong in t-shirts and jeans, maybe fleece and flannel in the wintertime, whatever lets me get outdoors and move around. Suits are too restrictive. By the end of the night I'm going to feel like jumping out of my own skin.

Because I don't like suits. That's the only possible reason that attending the Madison Scholars beginning-of-year banquet might make me feel like I want to jump out of my own skin.

The single reason.

"I've been getting twice-daily updates from Daniel," Seth is saying. "Usually he follows them up with a quick monologue about how they're totally prepared for a newborn and how he's feeling very calm, so..."

Seth and Daniel are two of my brothers who own a brewery together in our hometown, so of course Seth is well-informed about our future nephew.

"And Rusty?" I ask. "How are the nursery decorations going?"

Rusty is Daniel's nine-year-old daughter, and as a way to include her in the arrival of a new brother, Daniel and his wife Charlie asked her to be in charge of nursery decorations.

It's gone... interestingly.

"Well, they talked her out of the photorealistic Kraken for the wall over the crib," he says. "And I believe they're negotiating toward a friendly-looking octopus," Seth says.

"Progress."

"She tried to argue that since the baby's living underwater right now, the Kraken would be a soothing kindred spirit," Seth says.

"We're sure she's not somehow Eli's daughter, not Daniel's?" I ask, and he just snorts.

"How's the job?" he asks. "What's with the sighing and rustling? Hot date?"

"I have to go to a banquet for undergrads," I say. "Suit required."

Not just any undergrads, I think. *Madison Scholars.*
Like Thalia.

It's been two weeks now. Six class sessions. Six hours of her sitting in the back of my classroom, taking the world's most studious notes while I talk about calculating limits.

Two weeks of classes. Six hours of calculus instruction, and every time she walks into the classroom the world still tilts on its axis for a moment.

I hate it.

I hate lusting over a student. It makes me feel like I'm a dirty old pervert, like I'm one step away from hanging around cheerleader tryouts just to leer at undergrads in workout gear.

I hate that I can't stop thinking about her this way, as the girl who told me about magic and then kissed me in the starlight, and not as a student.

I'm starting to hate myself.

Virginia Southern University has an undergraduate enrollment of 17,289 students, and 17,288 of them look like children to me. I've never been attracted to one before. Not my first year teaching, when I was a graduate student who was barely older than some of them; not any of the years afterward.

The thought's never even occurred to me. They're *students*.

17,288 of them, anyway.

For two weeks, I've been waiting for Thalia to make

that switch. Every day I wake up and think, *maybe today's the day she finally looks like a student and nothing more.*

"Undergrads get banquets these days?" Seth asks. "I just got credits for soggy chicken tenders at the dining hall. No wonder tuition keeps going up."

"What do you know about college tuition?" I ask, giving up on looking at myself in the mirror and opening my sock drawer.

"Who do you think does Daniel's tuition forecasting?" Seth laughs. "He's only got nine more years before Rusty's in college. You know how he likes to be prepared."

"Is anyone ever really prepared for Rusty?" I ask, digging through a layer of hiking socks to find the ones that go with a suit.

"Well, no," Seth admits. "Has anyone told you her latest thing?"

Finally, I grab a pair of black socks, a sudden pang of guilt working its way between my ribs. Between moving and the start of the school year, I haven't visited home or seen any of my family in nearly a month.

"Computer hacking," I guess. "She wants Eli to buy a whole pig so they can have a proper luau. She's mastered alchemy and managed to turn lead into gold."

Seth just laughs.

"Close," he says. "Medieval siegecraft. Levi's helping her build a model trebuchet."

I'm not even a little bit surprised.

CHAPTER TEN

THALIA

"I should pull my hair back," I say, frowning at myself in the mirror.

"Stop it," says Victoria, leaning forward to check her teeth for lipstick.

"A bun wouldn't look more dignified?" I ask. "Maybe a bun with a pencil through it, like, oh, I was so busy studying I didn't see you there, that's how studious I am."

I've got on a black sheath dress that falls to the knee, black pumps, a royal blue cardigan, and right now I can't tell if my outfit says *smart, focused, and serious about scholarship* or *dowdy librarian*.

I suspect I'm overthinking it.

"Thalia, you look extremely studious," Victoria assures me again, adjusting the scarf in her hair. "As if you could quote me the whole DSM-IV."

"It's the DSM-V now," I correct her.

"See?" she says. "Earrings or necklace?"

We're in the bathroom of our apartment, both crowded in front of the only full-length mirror in the place. I study Victoria's reflection in the mirror for a moment: she's wearing a red dress with an asymmetrical neckline, her natural hair pulled back and wrapped with a patterned headscarf, along with her usual ten million bangles and bright red lipstick.

She's an art major, so making things visually appealing is kind of her thing, but she still looks effortlessly amazing.

"Earrings," I say. "The neckline is very dramatic all on its own, you don't need a necklace."

"I think you're right," she says. "God, I envy men. If they manage to show up wearing a suit jacket that's not utterly ludicrous they get a pass. And if they've put a tie on without strangling themselves?"

"Right?" I sigh. "Has any man ever thought *they'll take me more seriously if I wear lipstick?*"

"It's not my impression that men worry about being taken seriously," she says, half-turning, the backs of her thighs against the toilet tank as she checks out the back of her dress. "They just assume that they will be, and they're usually right."

There's a knock on the bathroom door, and a moment later, it opens and Harper's head pops through.

"Come on, we gotta go," she says, giving us a quick once-over. "You both look very smart and or artistic and or accomplished and or sexy. Also, Margaret is going to have kittens if we make her wait much longer."

"I'm not going to have kittens, I just don't want to be late," I hear Margaret say. "Is that so wrong, not wanting to be late?"

Harper gives us a look, then disappears. I give my hair one last finger-comb, then shake it out, open the door, and follow her, Victoria right behind me.

Tonight is the annual Madison Scholars banquet. Even though it's my fourth time going, since I'm a senior, I haven't been this anxious about it since I was an itty bitty freshman who was brand new to college and, quite frankly, thought I was in over my head.

Every year, VSU offers twenty-five Madison Scholarships to incoming freshmen. It's a long, intense application process on top of the already-exhausting process of applying to college, but a Madison Scholarship is worth it.

Not only do you get a full ride *plus* a very small stipend for school-related expenses, you get access to special Honors classes. There are networking events with professors in your field, special mentorship opportunities, work-study programs, and on and on.

The banquet is one of those events — and three hours ago, I found out that one Dr. Stephen Rossi is going to be not only in attendance, but sitting at my table.

He is, of course, the leading researcher on the use of virtual reality in treating post-traumatic stress disorder, and he heads up the Virtual Lab at the Virginia Institute of Technology.

Naturally, he'll be one of the people considering my graduate school application there in a few months. My advisor, Dr. Castellano, arranged for him to come to the banquet tonight almost entirely so I can meet and impress him.

For the first time in two weeks, I've stopped wondering whether Caleb will be at the banquet in favor of praying that I don't spill soup on myself or accidentally mix up the frontal and parietal lobes in conversation.

However, in that two weeks of thinking about whether Caleb will be there or not, I've come to some conclusions and made some guidelines for myself.

1. He probably won't be there. VSU has a billion faculty members. Most don't go to this banquet; why would he?

2. If he *is* there, it doesn't matter. Who cares? We're not

together. We're not anything. There's nothing between us and nothing to hide.

3. And if he's there — which he probably won't be — I'm not going to talk to him. I have no reason to talk to him. Why would I talk to him?

4. If I find myself in a social situation in which I must talk to him because to do otherwise would be impolite, I will talk casually about: the weather. The loveliness of the ballroom in which this event is held every year. The deliciousness of the cheese platter. What kind of salad dressing he likes.

But really, he won't be there, and leaves me free to not make an ass of myself in front of Dr. Rossi.

"Here," says Harper, holding out a small, slim packet as I grab my purse, ready to leave.

Despite myself, I blush.

"Caleb's not going to be there, for crying out loud," I say, ignoring the offered condom. "And I told you, we shut it down as soon as realized that he was —"

They're all looking at me like I've started speaking in tongues, and I stop speaking mid-sentence.

"If you don't want a Shout wipe, don't take the Shout wipe," Harper says, one eyebrow raised. "You don't have to get weird about it."

I look at the thing she's offering me. It's not even square. It looks nothing like a condom.

It's possible that I'm feeling a little high-strung right now.

I clear my throat, grab it, and shove it into my purse.

"Thanks," I tell my three grinning friends.

· · · · ★ ★ ★ ★ ★ · · ·

The banquet takes place in Randolph Hall, right in the center of campus. Even though it's the second-oldest building on campus, it's been beautifully maintained and renovated every so often, and it's got a certain old-Virginia charm that's hard to put into words.

When you stand in front of it, you feel like if you turned around, you'd see horse-drawn carriages on cobblestone streets, ladies in long dresses and men in suits, gas lamps lighting the dark.

It's brick, four stories high, a colonnade on each side, the copper roof now a dull pale green. Each window has a single candle in it, as if it's waiting to welcome us.

Just in case, I check behind myself. There are no cobblestones, just a few guys wearing shorts and playing frisbee.

Inside Randolph Hall looks just as old-world as the outside: wooden floors with wide planks, ceilings with intricate plaster molding around the light fixtures, lamps in walls sconces, the whole nine yards.

Aside from the ballroom, this floor is a series of small salons, each set up with arm chairs and tables, bookshelves, a fireplace. Originally this building was the center of student life at VSU, where undergraduates could come and discuss their intellectual ideas with one another, back when there were three hundred of them.

"Everyone has a cheese plate," Harper mutters to me as we make out way through the network of rooms. "How?"

"I imagine there are appetizers somewhere," I tell her.

"But where?" she asks as a skinny guy in a badly-fitting suit walks past holding a small plate filled with cheese, crackers, and grapes.

"In the foyer," I tell her, as we walk single-file through a doorway. "It's always in the foyer. Every year. Cool your tits."

"My tits are an excellent temperature," she says, reaching up like she's going to pat them.

At the last second, she touches the neckline of her dress instead.

"Good save," I say.

"I'm a demure, sophisticated lady who would never grab my boobs in public without thinking first," Harper says. "Oh! There it is."

With that last statement, she grabs my arm, and I can't blame her. The cheese table is a thing of wonder, just like it is every year: there are cubes and chunks and wheels surrounded by crackers and grapes, some artfully spilled and some neatly stacked.

The cheeses are stacked on multi-level plates, interspersed with other bite-size snacks. Some cheese plates also contain charcuterie, and I even grab a minuscule pickle from one, hoping it's not merely decorative.

I also get some grapes, but they're mostly for show because in front of all these professors and colleagues, I'd like to seem like the sort of person who looks at four metric tons of cheese and chooses fruit.

I snack. I even eat the grapes, though admittedly I eat them last. I chat with some other students about the best non-library study spot on campus (it's in the basement of the Economics building), and inform a few freshmen about the best sandwich place on Main Street (it's called Shorty's).

Just as I'm about to grab more cheese, I catch sight of a short, serious, gray-haired Latina who's practically barreling toward me.

I forget the cheese and stand up a little bit straighter.

"Thalia," Dr. Castellano says. "I was hoping I'd find you here. Could I have a word?"

· · · · ★ ★ ★ ★ · · · ·

As I follow her, I automatically catalog all the things that this could possibly be about. I just saw Dr. Castellano a few hours ago, and everything seemed fine then.

Did I screw up the bibliography that she asked me to put together for her paper?

Are the page numbers wrong? Did I spell a name wrong?

Maybe she doesn't like the sources I found.

My brain is still whirling as I follow her outside to the colonnade and she finally turns, her back to one stark white column, slowly going blue in the evening light.

She looks at me, her mouth a grim line.

"Is this about the bibliography?" I blurt out, but she just shakes her head.

"Nathaniel was expelled this afternoon," she says, her face grave.

I just stare at her, trying to process this news.

"Johnston?" I finally ask.

"Yes," she confirms.

"Nathaniel Johnston was expelled," I say, putting it all together in one sentence.

I have to be getting something wrong here. There must be some other Nathaniel that she's talking about besides the guy on my work-study project with me.

Nathaniel is... nice? Quiet? Responsible?

Whatever he is, he's not the kind of person who gets expelled from college.

"I'm afraid that's right," she says.

"What?" I sputter. "Why? How? He's got all the citations on the neurolinguistics paper, if I have to redo those it'll take me weeks —"

I stop talking, because I realize I'm missing the point.

"The committee made its decision this afternoon," she says. "Ethical misconduct."

"Ethical misconduct," I echo, still trying to wrap my

brain around it. "Plagiarism? Was he taking money to write papers?"

That, at least, makes a little bit of sense. Writing papers for money is big business and college students always need money, even the ones on full scholarship.

I've been offered money to write a paper. I know Harper and Victoria have been, too.

But Dr. Castellano shakes her head.

"I'm afraid it was behavioral," she says, lips still tight. "I'm not at liberty to discuss much more, but I wanted you to hear it from me, rather than the rumor mill, since the two of you worked together."

I have no idea what *behavioral misconduct* even means in the context of getting expelled from college, and I really can't imagine quiet, respectful, polite Nathaniel participating in any such thing.

He was a nice guy. Smiled at puns. Showed me a picture of his parents' dog once. Seemed to drink mostly tea.

"Thank you," I finally manage to say. "I appreciate the heads up."

She sighs, then nods.

"I'm sorry to tell you like this, right before you meet Dr. Rossi," she says. "Please understand that this sort of extreme punishment is quite rare in the Scholars program. In fact, to be honest I can't think of another case quite like this one where…"

As she's talking, there's a slow trickle of people walking past us and into the building. Most look like students. Some I recognize, some I don't, and I'm nodding absentmindedly and I'm trying to figure out what the hell Nathaniel *did*.

Behavioral. What does that even mean? Did he get into a bar fight? Threaten someone?

Doing drugs? Dealing drugs? Does that count as behavioral, or —

Someone walks around the corner, and instantly, my attention shifts. Before I can even see who it is, my attention shifts. It's like on some subconscious, cellular level, I already know.

It's Caleb, of course. Dr. Loveless. Whatever I'm supposed to call him.

In a dark gray suit with a skinny black tie. Glasses. Hair tamed, face clean-shaven, suit well-tailored. Even though I've had two weeks to get used to seeing him, I am unprepared.

My heart speeds up. I blush. I do my damnedest not to smile, but by the time he's walking past us, I've failed at that.

He smiles back, nods once. I nod back. That's all.

Then he's gone, into the building, and Dr. Castellano is reaching out and patting me on the shoulder.

"In short, you've got nothing to worry about," she says with an encouraging smile. "Now, let's go back inside so I can introduce you to Dr. Rossi."

CHAPTER ELEVEN
CALEB

I turn to the young man seated next to me at the banquet, because now that dinner's over, it's time to attempt a conversation again.

"What sort of creative writing will you be focusing on?" I ask.

"Fiction," he says.

I wait another moment, just in case he'd like to put some effort into the conversation.

He wouldn't.

"What authors do you particularly admire?" I ask.

This is making me feel like a nagging aunt at Thanksgiving — *what are you majoring in? What are you going to do with that? Can you get a job with a mathematics major? What about econ, there's always business.*

The young man — I think his name is Aidan, but I can't even remember any more — shrugs.

"Denis Johnson," he says. "Raymond Carver. Richard Ford."

"What have they written?" I ask, because they all sound

medium-familiar, like I've read them and forgotten the name.

"Short stories mostly," he says, and then goes quiet and blank again.

"Anything I might have read?"

He shrugs, which seems to be his only body language.

"Probably not," he says.

It's like talking to a rock, but an uninteresting rock. This is at least my third attempt tonight to lure him into conversation, and it's also my third failure.

Behind me, a table breaks into laughter. Without turning, I can't tell which one, but I focus in sharply on the fork in my hand, on the floral bouquet in front of me, and I banish the thought that I can hear Thalia's laughter.

Suddenly, that's all I can take.

"Excuse me," I say, and stand, pushing my chair away from the table. The undergrads on either side of me look up at me briefly, then nod, go back to what they were doing: on one side, talking about fancy airplane travel; on the other, an apparently deep contemplation of the basket of dinner rolls.

Then I look over at Thalia's table. I don't mean to do it. I don't even want to do it, I just *do*. She's facing toward me but intently listening to the man next to her, a middle-aged white guy with glasses and graying hair. She's hanging onto every word he says, nodding along, smiling.

Jealousy pins me like an arrow out of the blue. It's a surprise. It blows the breath from my lungs for a moment with unexpected tightness, and I look away before I can make it worse.

As soon as I exit the ballroom, I take a deep breath. The air out here, in the foyer, is already cooler, and I feel like I can breathe again. I make my way through the other rooms in the building, all small chambers that look like something out of the year 1750, until I find one that's empty, the lights off.

It's blessedly, blessedly quiet, and I sink into a chair in front of the window. This window is candle-free, and through it I can see the backyard of this building, walled in by five-foot-high brick walls, wrought iron benches stationed along brick paths. A strange thing to be in the middle of a college campus, but when a building is this old, no one wants to change it.

Outside, the moon is a sliver. I can't see the stars over the light of the street lamps, but I imagine them all the same, the constellations that my mom taught us all by heart.

I wonder, not for the first time, if I should be outside with them and not inside with antiques, oriental rugs, and sophomores who own yachts. I wonder if I'm cut out for wearing suits to events and hobnobbing when all I really want to do is go hiking and think about prime numbers.

I think, again, about Thalia looking at another man, smiling, nodding. I wonder if I should be teaching at all, if seeing a student taking an academic interest in another professor — I'd bet a thousand dollars that's who he is — is going to turn me green with jealousy.

I've walked away from everything before, literally, but I think it was easier when I was twenty years old. I have more to walk away from now.

Besides, you can't walk away from yourself.

I'm still looking outside, naming the invisible constellations to myself when I hear the slightest of creaks behind me.

Before I even turn, I know who it is. I know it in my bones.

"I don't think you're supposed to be in here," Thalia says.

I should say *I'm sorry* or *you're right* or even *we shouldn't be in here together*, but I don't.

"You gonna report me?" I ask.

She laughs.

CHAPTER TWELVE

THALIA

I didn't think he'd be alone. I didn't think he'd be in the dark, staring out a window, tie loosened and sleeves rolled up, looking slightly disheveled and somehow even more attractive than before.

"You look like you're about to howl," I say, because Caleb makes my mouth function without my brain, and I bite my lips together, close my eyes.

"The moon isn't full," he says, as I walk over to where he's sitting, take the chair next to his, half turned toward his, half-turned to the window. "It's waning. I've got at least two weeks before I transform, according to my math."

"I suppose your math is trustworthy," I say, leaning back.

The chair's upholstered in velvet, the frame wooden. It's not particularly comfortable, but it'll do.

"It had better be," he says. "If I can't even add up the days of a lunar month, what chance do I have of proving Glessmacher's theorem?"

"That one's wrong," I say. "There, I saved you all that work. You're welcome."

In the other chair, Caleb laughs and the sound works itself into my chest, unwinding the knot that had taken up residence there.

"Thank you," he says, his voice low, the lilt of his accent there even in those two words. "Doubtless, you've just saved me years."

"Glad I could help," I tease, and then we both go quiet again, looking out the window together.

I shouldn't have followed him. I know that. I know nothing can come of this, I know nothing *should* come of this, and I know that I'm just torturing myself by following after him like a lost puppy.

But I'm not sorry. Not yet. I might be, sooner rather than later, but not yet.

"Do you think werewolves ever get the urge to howl at the moon while they're human?" I ask. "Just a little yip, while they're driving home at night and the moon's a sliver, like this?"

"Werewolves don't exist," he points out, and I sigh.

"I'm not asking whether werewolves exist," I tell him. "I'm asking whether they want to howl at the moon even when they're human."

"So, to clarify, I'm supposed to know the innermost desires of a creature that doesn't exist?" he asks, his voice low, teasing.

"You don't have to know," I say. "You can guess."

He props one ankle on the opposite knee, his elbow resting on the arm of the chair, his hand in the air by his face as he regards me carefully, slowly, then glances back out the window, at the moon.

"Of course they do," he finally says.

"Of course?" I ask. "That's a lot of certainty for a creature that doesn't exist."

"Well, they're human, right?"

"Sort of."

"Then of course."

He pauses, and I feel rather than see his gaze slide from the window to me. In my lap I press my palms together, like that can fight off the heat I feel.

I shouldn't have come here. I shouldn't have.

But now we're here and we're talking about the moon, and I can already tell that in a few hours I'll be alone in my bed, remembering the way he looked at me.

"You've howled at the moon, haven't you?" he asks, and now he's looking over at me, a grin on his face.

"Never," I say.

"Come on, Thalia," he says, his voice even lower, a cajoling note there, like he already knows the answer and wants me to say it. "Not even once?"

I start to laugh.

"I swear I haven't," I tell him. "Why on earth would I howl at the moon?"

"Because it's the moon and it's right there," he says. "You've never looked up at night and been struck by that wild, primal urge to howl?"

I'm breathless, wordless for a moment, because I can't help but imagine him outdoors, shirtless, howling at the moon, and I can't help but want to hear more about his wild, primal urges.

"You have," I finally say.

"I can't believe you haven't," he says.

"My urges are civilized," I say, looking back through the window, at the sliver of moon hanging low in the sky.

There's a long, long pause, and I have the chance to really mull over what I just said and wish I'd said something else instead.

"Are they?" he says at last, and I don't have an answer, because he's right and they're not. They're wild and primal as anything and it's all I can do here, now, to take another deep breath and press my hand into the velvet of an antique chair and remind myself where I am, what I'm doing.

There isn't a night that's gone by without me lying in bed, thinking of him saying *I want to see what you sound like when you come*. It's been almost two weeks and that memory is as potent as ever, tinged with the frustration and allure of wanting what I know I can't have.

"Do you howl at the moon often?" I ask.

"Not any more."

"But you did."

"I'm not sure I should answer your questions," he says. "You're going to think I'm a werewolf."

"That often?" I tease.

"It was a long time ago," Caleb says, stretching out his arm, resting on it on his knee. "Don't worry, I'm civilized now."

My heart beats in my throat for one, two, three.

"Are you?" I ask, my voice low, soft.

Caleb gives me a long, slow, searching look.

"When it counts," he finally says. "But that doesn't mean I don't howl sometimes."

Before I can ask when he still howls, my phone buzzes in my dress pocket. Yes, this dress has pockets. All dresses have pockets.

"Sorry," I say, as my brother Bastien's name pops up on the screen, and I hit the red button, sending him to voicemail.

"Junk call?"

"Little brother," I say, sliding my phone back into my pocket.

"I hear those are annoying," he says, grinning, and I laugh.

"Sometimes he drunk dials me on the weekends," I say. "I don't even know why, it's not like I'm —"

My phone buzzes again, and I sigh.

"Dammit, kid," I mutter. "Chill."

"He's in school?"

"William and Mary," I say, shoving my phone into my pocket again, hoping that Bastien moves on to drunk dialing someone else. "It's not exactly a party hot spot, but he's having a pretty good time with all the football players who graduate high school and then start questioning their sexuality."

"Does he help them find answers?" Caleb asks dryly.

"He's very helpful in that regard," I say, then sigh, looking out the window again. "And I think he drunk dials me because I'm the only one in the family who knows he's gay."

"I see," Caleb says, just as my phone buzzes one more time.

Bastien. Again. He hasn't left a voicemail yet, just keeps calling. I flop my head against the back of this chair and sigh.

"Fine, you win," I say aloud. "Sorry, I'll be right back."

Caleb just nods as I walk for the door, pulling my phone from my pocket.

"Hey, what?" I ask, facing the far wall of the room we're in.

On the other end of the phone, there's a long, long intake of breath, and I frown.

"Did you drunk dial me *again*?" I ask.

As I do, his breathing hitches, just for a moment, almost like it's static on the line or something, but I know it's not.

Just like that, I know something's wrong, and a seed of fear takes root in my heart.

Bastien told Dad and now he's disowned, I think, mind racing. *He hit on some homophobe and got beat up.*

On the other end of the line, my brother clears his throat.

"What is it?" I ask, my voice tight, high-pitched. I walk for a door, open it, and instead of another cozy, antique-filled room it leads outside, to a brick walkway and a wrought-iron bench. I go through it anyway, too distracted to care.

"Bastien."

They found Javier.

No. They found Javier's body.

"*Bastien*," I say, ready to scream, shout, tear out my own hair. "Talk!"

"It's Mom," he finally says, his voice a ragged whisper. "She was in an accident."

It sucks the air from my lungs, feels like the floor is opening under me.

"What?" I ask, my voice high-pitched, shaky, the words spilling out of me like floodgates have opened. "Is she okay? What happened? Was it a car accident? Did someone hit her? Was she driving? Who was in the car? Was it —"

"She's in the hospital, Ollie," he says, and it sounds like he's dredging the words up from somewhere deep inside him, against their will. "They're taking her to surgery, there was a car crash, she was coming home, we don't know —"

He takes another long breath, and I don't move a muscle, staring blindly at the brick walkway and the bench and a wall and a few ornamental trees.

"We don't know," he finished.

"Is she gonna be okay?" I ask. I know he doesn't know, but I can't stop myself from asking. "Tell me she's gonna be okay."

"I don't know," he whispers.

CHAPTER THIRTEEN
CALEB

It's not your business, I tell myself, hands in my pockets as I pace in front of the window.

You're her professor and that's all.

I should go back to the banquet, talk to smart undergrads about the wonderful world of mathematics. I've already been in this dark room for too long, anyway. I don't need anyone reporting back to Gordon that I disappeared two-thirds of the way through the banquet.

But I can't erase her voice from my head, the way she said *what is it, Bastien?* then yanked the door to the outside open and practically fled the room.

I'm not psychic, but I know panic when I hear it.

And I know that she hasn't come back inside yet. Maybe she's still out there, talking to her brother. Maybe this door doesn't open from that side.

I give it one more minute, then two, and then I can't stand it any more and I pull the door open, the uneven old wood scraping over the threshold.

Thalia's head jerks up, her face still lit from below by the glow of her phone, her cheeks streaked and smeared with black. She's on her knees, on the grass next to an ugly bench, curled into herself, and I'm already down the uneven stone steps, already next to her, kneeling on the ground.

"What is it?"

She just shakes her head, gasping.

"Thalia," I say. My knees are an inch from hers and I curl my hand into a fist against the ground, lean on it so I don't reach out and touch her.

"I'm sorry," she whispers, swiping at one eye with the back of her hand, her knuckles coming away streaked with black. "I'm fine, I'm sorry —"

"Bullshit," I say, and the force of the word makes her look at me, deep brown eyes ringed with black, already puffy and swollen. "Tell me."

Now there's a hand cupping her cheek, a thumb wiping away tears and black streaks.

Mine? Mine.

"My mom was in a car accident," she says, voice shaking.

It's like my lungs are lined with lead, suddenly too heavy and stiff to let air in or out, the weight of them pulling down in my chest like it'll sink me to the ground. Then the bolt of horror, quick, brutal, fresh every single time.

And then I make myself breathe, and it's gone.

"Is she okay?" I ask, and I force myself to sound calm, to sound collected, like I'm capable of being in charge right now.

"No," Thalia whispers, and she looks away, pushes at one eye with the heel of her hand, swiping black everywhere.

My heart drops like a bullet through a glass of water.

"That was my little brother," she says, gasping for air,

swallowing convulsively. "He thinks they're taking her into surgery right now but he's not sure, he's in the car on the way there from school so he doesn't really know anything, he doesn't even know what she's having surgery on or what kind of surgery or what happened or —"

Thalia hangs her head and a sob explodes through her, fingers tightening on the bench next to her.

"Not my mom," she whispers. "Please."

I pull her into me. I do it automatically, unconsciously, like I'm driven by gravity. I push her head against my chest and loop my other arm around her quaking back, and I hold her there as hard as I can, both of us on our knees, and I let her cry.

And she does. She buries her head in my shirt and wraps her arms so tightly around me that I think she's trying to break me, her breathing ragged, gasping sobs breaking through when she can't stop them.

There's nothing I can say, so I don't. I close my eyes against her onslaught and I count my breaths, even and steady: in for one, out for two. In for three, out for four. I open my eyes and look up at the moon, and I don't think of anything.

Eventually, her arms loosen, her breathing get less ragged.

"I'm sorry," she whispers, pulling away, still wiping at her eyes. "I'm sorry, I'm sorry, I'm —"

"Where is she?" I ask gently, cutting her off.

"The hospital," Thalia says, looking down at herself. "Maybe she's in surgery now, I don't know —"

"Where's the hospital?" I ask, forcing myself to stay calm.

She shoves the back of her hand against her other eye, smearing black outward toward her temple as she fumbles for her phone, clicks it on again, opens a map with shaking fingers.

"They took her to Randolph General, Bastien said, I think that's the one at Lynnhaven and Broadway," she says, staring down at the little screen, swiping jerkily from side to side like she can't stop moving. "I don't know why, he said she was closer to St. Agatha's but they didn't take her there, they took her to Randolph instead and he didn't say why —"

"Thalia," I say, softly, to get her attention before she spirals. "In Virginia Beach?"

"Norfolk," she says, and then looks up at me, face blotchy with tears, eyes bloodshot and red. She takes a deep breath. "It's in Norfolk. She's all the way in Norfolk, fuck, *fuck.*"

I don't think, I just speak.

"I'll take you," I say.

For a moment, she's silent, no sound but her ragged breathing, her sniffles.

I rise, holding out one hand.

"Caleb, you can't," she says softly, looking at it.

"Yes, I can."

"It's a four-hour drive," she says, looking at my hand like it's some sort of ancient artifact, like if she touches it it'll crumble into dust. "It's clear across the state, I'll borrow a car, I'll find a bus, it's fine. I'll figure something out."

"Let me take you," I say, and I sound calm, even as my pulse is racing with remembered panic. "Please?"

"You could get in trouble," she says, suddenly whispering.

"I know."

She studies me for a long moment, still on her knees in the grass, her phone held limply in one hand, my arm outstretched toward her.

The knees of my suit are soaked through, grass stained, and my shirt has black smudges from where she cried against me, but it doesn't matter. It doesn't matter at all.

"Okay," she finally says, and puts her hand in mine, lets me pull her up. "Thank you."

For a moment, we don't let each other go. We just stand there, next to a building older than the country, sliver of a moon above, and look at each other.

I know I should say something to her, some platitude like *it's gonna be okay* or *your mom will be fine* or *I'm sure she's a fighter*, but I know better than to lie. I don't know shit about the future. I only know about the gaping hole that's opened underneath Thalia. I know that doing something, being in motion, will put it off for just a little longer.

Then we walk to my car, silent except for the click of her heels on pavement.

CHAPTER FOURTEEN

THALIA

I stare at the toothbrushes in the cup on the bathroom sink. I stare and I stare because I can't figure out which one is mine.

When did I call home? Was it Sunday, or Monday?

Is it the orange one? The pink one?

What does my toothbrush look like?

What did we talk about?

My brain feels like sludge, like my IQ has suddenly dropped so many points that something as simple as a toothbrush is utterly baffling. I take a deep breath and my eyes fill with tears again because I can't even figure out which toothbrush is mine and I can't do anything, not one single thing to help my mom besides hope that she's going to be okay and —

"Fuck it," I mutter to myself, savagely, as I bend down, wrench the bathroom cabinet open, and grab a new toothbrush, still in the package.

I go back into my room, shove it into my backpack with my laptop and my phone charger and a few shirts and pairs of underwear. I'm sure there's something else I should take but I've already been in my apartment, packing this bag, for a little over three minutes, and what if that three minutes makes the difference? What if I'm three minutes too late, what if she wakes up and asks for me and I'm not there, I'm three minutes away and then —

"No," I say out loud to my dark apartment, slinging my backpack over my shoulder, glancing back at the now-dirty dress that I tossed on my bed, the heels haphazardly kicked off next to it. "No. Come on."

I leave. I close the door, lock it, barrel down the stairs. Caleb's car is still there, waiting in front, and I practically throw myself into the passenger seat.

"All right?" he asks, putting it into gear.

"All right," I say, and we pull away from the curb.

Then I realize I left something behind. Without thinking I pull the door handle and the car door swings open, nearly hitting the parked sedan next to us.

"Whoa!" Caleb shouts, slamming on the brakes. "Thalia, what —"

"I forgot something," I say, already running back to the apartment, taking the stairs two at a time. I drop my keys twice as I'm unlocking the door, practically counting the seconds because this is two more minutes, and what if five minutes is the difference between seeing my mom one last time and —

The door swings open. I leave the keys in the lock and dart into my bedroom, open my closet, find the jewelry box on the floor. It's dark but I find what I'm looking for anyway, worn wooden beads that I know by touch.

I leave, lock, run. Caleb's back in the spot where he was waiting, and I get in again, buckle up.

"All right?" he asks for the second time, and I nod.

"You're sure?"

I turn in my seat, look at him. I search his face for clues that he's ribbing me, giving me a hard time for nearly jumping out of a moving car, but he's calm, serious, intense.

"Sorry," I say, squeezing the wooden beads in my hand, letting them dig into my fingers.

We drive in silence. In ten minutes Marysburg is in the rear view mirror, fading. The road we take out of town narrows from four lanes to two and then we're in the country that surrounds the college town, where farms give way to forests that give way to farms, over and over again.

Caleb doesn't say anything, just drives, the rear windows of the car cracked for air, the breeze shuffling my hair. I check my phone every thirty seconds, I think, but we're in and out of cell service and nothing comes through.

After twenty minutes, I unclench my hand and the wooden beads click against each other softly, rearranging themselves in the absence of pressure, and I look down, take it in, like I'm seeing it for the first time.

I forgot to call her on Sunday, I think. *I had so much homework and I had to meet with Nathaniel about the sources for Dr. Castellano's paper and I just completely forgot until it was almost ten.*

I pull the beads up, through my fingers, until I'm holding the crucifix between my thumb and fingers. I can't see it in the dark but I can feel the figure of Jesus there, on the cross like always, and I press it against the pad of my thumb until it hurts, trying to remember the last time I talked to my mom.

Was it the Sunday before that? I think, still pressing the metal into my thumb. *Had it been that long? What did I say? What did she say?*

I can't remember. I can't remember a sentence, a word,

a phrase. We end every conversation with *I love you* and *you too*, but did we end the last one that way?

We must have. Please, God, we must have.

I run my thumb over Jesus again, in the dark, and just like that the words are there in my brain, fully automatic.

I believe in God, the Father Almighty, creator of heaven and earth...

I look down again, and the words feel wrong. They feel like school assemblies, like going to Mass every Wednesday and Sunday, like the one time that I got detention for being late to class.

They don't feel like my mother. I open my palm, still looking down, and the light from the dashboard catches the centerpiece.

It's faded with the years, but there she is, La Virgen, resplendent and sad. Cloaked in stars. Crowned by faded red and gold.

Creo en Dios, Padre todopoderoso, creador del Cielo y de la Tierra...

I close my eyes and keep the prayer to myself, and I think not of myself and not of the last time I spoke to my mother and not of her on a gurney, being wheeled into surgery, but of her mother, my grandmother.

I think of her, near the end. Sitting in her chair in the living room of the house in South Texas, all the doors and windows open despite the heat. I think of coming and sitting by her feet, the way she'd put her hand on my head and keep praying, the Spanish words flowing over me like cool rain in the blistering heat.

It was the only Spanish she taught my mom and her siblings. She and my grandfather wanted their children to assimilate, to be comfortable in the country where they were born, so they never spoke to them in her own native tongue.

My fingers work up to the next bead and quickly, silently, I recite the *Padre Nuestro*, three *Ave Marias*, the *Gloria*, and even though I'm not sure I'm really still Catholic, saying the words makes me feel a little bit better, brings me some tiny measure of peace that I'm doing what I can.

CHAPTER FIFTEEN

CALEB

I glance at the speedometer. Seventy-five. I take a deep breath and ease my foot off the gas, forcing myself to slow the car down to sixty, even though these roads are empty on a Friday night.

I don't need a speeding ticket. I don't need to whip around a curve too fast and hit a deer. I don't need to fly off the road, into a tree.

The last thought sends a shudder down my spine, a chill through the air.

Thalia is sitting in the passenger seat, whispering to herself. I think it's Spanish. I think she's praying. She hasn't moved since she got into the car except to turn her head every so often and look out the window.

I don't interrupt her. There are a hundred thousand things I could say, but they're all useless. I know because I've heard them all, every last one of them, from well-meaning people who only wanted to make me feel better after my father died.

The truth is that there's nothing. Words are empty

vessels, only said so the speaker can feel as if they've helped somehow.

I look down, let the needle rise to sixty-five.

Then her phone rings and shakes in the cupholder, and we both jump.

"Sorry," Thalia says, grabbing it.

"We're almost to the interstate," I tell her. "Sounds like you've got service again, though it might cut in and out a little. There are some pretty empty parts between here and the tidewater."

She clicks her phone open, face glowing blue, flicking through her notification screen.

"Shit," she hisses, softly.

"News?" I ask, evenly, calmly, like my chest isn't constricting, but she shakes her head.

"Nothing since she went in," Thalia says, and holds her phone up to her ear. "But I forgot to tell my roommates what was going on and I think Margaret's about to call the — hey, it's me."

On the other end of the line, Margaret says *oh, thank fuck* loudly enough that I can hear it perfectly.

"I'm fine, I'm not kidnapped," she says. "I'm not — what? No, my kidnapper didn't make me say that."

She pauses, the voice on the other end quieter now.

"My mom's in the hospital," Thalia says quickly, a gasp for air at the end of the sentence. She inhales, exhales. "She was in a car accident. She's in surgery right now. Bastien called me, that's all I know, we're driving to Norfolk and we're about to get on eighty-one."

The narrow two-lane road I'm on widens, the trees suddenly further from the shoulder. Through the forest I can see bright fast food signs, a lone Hampton Inn.

Thalia clears her throat, and suddenly I can feel her looking over at me, eyes glassy, lips puffy.

"One of my professors was at the banquet and volunteered to give me a ride," she says.

There's a long spell of silence, then: "Does it matter?"

More silence. She leans back in the passenger seat, closes her eyes.

"I know," she says. "I know. Thank you. Thanks for checking on me. I'll let you guys know when I've got more info."

Another small pause, and then she says, "I love you too," a smile in her voice. "Later."

Thalia puts her phone back into the cupholder, pulls one foot onto the seat.

"They know I'm with you," she says.

"I told you, I don't care," I tell her as the road opens to four lanes.

We go around a wide curve in the road and suddenly a Wal-Mart looms in front of us, two gas stations, a Chick-fil-a, a brightly lit green sign announcing Interstate 81.

"They also know that we went on a date," she says, the lights passing over her face. "And why we didn't go on another one."

"Then they know we didn't do anything wrong," I tell her, and turn onto the on-ramp.

"Right," she says, and goes quiet again as I merge onto the interstate, speeding up until I'm doing eighty.

"Can I ask you something?" she says, after a spell.

"Shoot."

"How old are you?"

I steal a glance away from the road at her: watching me, her eyes glassy and puffy but dry for now. I understand. There's only so long at once that you can stay mired in the grief and misery of unknowing; every so often, you have to come out.

"You're trying to figure out how much of a creep I am," I say, smiling at the road.

"That's not quite how I'd phrase it," she says, and for the first time since she got the phone call, I hear the smile in her voice. "I'd say I'm just after some information."

"Twenty-eight," I tell her.

"Oh," she says, and she sounds relieved.

"Should I even ask how old you thought I was?" I tease. "It's the glasses, isn't it?"

"I like the glasses," she says, not answering my question. "They're your professor costume."

"It's not a costume."

"You weren't wearing them when we met," she points out. "You don't usually wear them to class, only the first two sessions. And you wore them tonight, to the banquet."

I touch the bridge of the glasses with one finger, like I'm checking that they're still there. I try not to read into the fact that she knows how many times I've worn my glasses to class.

"What else have you been taking notes on?" I ask, suddenly aware of the weight of my glasses on my face, the few tiny scratches on the lenses. "Have I worn any shirts twice?"

"I'm not the fashion police," she says, as her phone dings softly and she looks down at it. "I just notice whether you're Caleb or Professor Loveless on a given day."

Which do you prefer? is on the tip of my tongue, but I swallow it. I adjust my glasses again, the solid frames against my face reminding me that tonight I'm Professor Loveless and she's my student, that I'm giving her this ride because I'm a good Samaritan and nothing more.

"Any updates?" I ask, as she types something into her phone, then clicks it off again.

"She's still in surgery," she says, taking a deep breath.

"Bastien's been texting me, but there's no news. Apparently my father's been standing in front of a window and staring out of it without moving for twenty-six minutes. It's just the two of them for now, none of my aunts and uncles are local. And me."

"Your other brother's not local either?" I ask.

No answer. I look over, and she's flipping her phone around in her fingers, the rosary wound around one wrist.

"Didn't you say you had two?" I ask, suddenly feeling unsteady, like I've wandered into the wrong territory.

"And you're teasing me for remembering when you wear your glasses," she says, but there's something in her voice that makes me glance over at her. "Do you remember everything I said that night?"

She's trying to smile but it's not quite working, her lips not fully cooperating, the smile not reaching her eyes.

"I try," I tell her, honestly. Too honestly, but Thalia has that effect on me. "I'm sorry, that was the wrong question."

Thalia is silent for a long moment, thinking. I just drive and listen to the silence.

"I don't think Javier is local," she finally says. "But I don't know, because I don't know where he is."

I stay quiet, respect her silence.

"I don't think anyone knows," she goes on, her eyes forward, watching the interstate as we rush toward it, white lines disappearing under my car. "Not my family, at least. The last time we heard from him was last March. He was sleeping in a car with a friend of a friend of a friend in Richmond, and he managed to borrow a phone to call my mom."

She clears her throat.

"I don't even know how to tell him about Mom's accident," she says, and now she's whispering, her voice ragged again. "No one knows how to reach him, we don't even know if he's…"

I reach over and take her hand in mine. I do it without thinking, the movement automatic, the need to comfort her and protect her almost overwhelming even though I know I can't.

"It's a whole fucking mess," she says, and she laces her fingers through mine, squeezing.

I squeeze back, hold her in my grip, the wooden rosary beads pressing into my wrist.

"You don't have to tell me if you don't want to," I say.

There's a long, long silence, long enough that I think she's chosen not to say anything, to take me up on my offer.

"He was a Marine," she finally says.

CHAPTER SIXTEEN

THALIA

This is a story that I don't know how to tell because I never tell it. It's our ugly family secret, our shame, a gaping hole that we've slapped a band-aid over so we can pretend that we're all fine. We tell people that he's in North Carolina or Washington, D.C., working some job, and then we change the subject because the truth is too much.

I don't know what would happen if my father found out that I told a complete stranger. He'd be furious, for starters. Even my roommates don't know the ugly details of it, just the broad strokes, because they've watched it go down.

"He didn't really want to be," I go on, trying to start at the beginning, not exactly sure where that is. "When we were kids he wanted to be an artist. The two of us used to watch Bob Ross on PBS for hours. You know, happy little trees and all that?"

"Of course," Caleb says, his fingers still anchored between mine, warm and strong.

"He was pretty good at it," I go on, trying to remember how to get back to the main point of the story. "Took all the art classes in high school, did really well, and for a while he talked about applying to art school or something. But I guess he wanted Dad's approval more because one day he came home and he'd enlisted."

Caleb changes lanes, speeds up, passes a big rig. I look up at the driver for a moment, and he's staring straight ahead, dead-eyed.

"He did two tours of Afghanistan, and on the second one he tore his rotator cuff, blew out his knee, and compressed three vertebrae in his lumbar spine when they took fire and he dragged his best friend's body behind a wall while wearing fifty pounds of equipment," I go on. "He left active duty. Started drinking. They gave him fistfuls of pain meds at the VA and not much else."

I don't tell Caleb that last year, when I went home for Christmas break, Javier woke me up nearly every night, screaming. I don't tell him that he used to disappear for two or three days, then come back wearing the same clothes, rings around his eyes, smelling awful and looking worse.

"I see," Caleb says.

"He got addicted," I say, simply. "What he got prescribed wasn't enough any more, so he found it on the street until my parents put him into rehab. Which worked, until it didn't, and when they found out that he'd been using again my dad kicked him out and cut him off. And now we don't know where he is."

Caleb looks over at me, and I can see the disbelief written on his face, the disgust, the horror. I can't say I blame him.

"My father believes that the only real love is tough love," I say, and I try to keep my voice from shaking. "My mom had to fight with him over sending Javi to rehab in the first place. He's the kind of person who thinks that all help is weakness, that if Javi really wanted it he'd be able to magically *will* his way back to being better instead of needing sissy bullshit like therapy and rehab and psych meds."

I take a deep breath, even though I feel like someone is strangling me.

"And now I don't even know where he is so I can tell him that Mom is in the hospital," I finish. A tear splashes down my cheek and I wipe it away, exhale a long, shuddering breath, close my eyes and lean back against the headrest. "I guess Bossy and I will start calling all the shelters and halfway houses tomorrow, but they hadn't heard of him last month, so I'm not really expecting a miracle."

Inhale, exhale. I bite my lips together and try to keep myself from crying more, because Caleb's seen enough of my tears by this point in the night. He's already volunteered to be my driver. He doesn't need to be my therapist, too.

"I'm sorry, Thalia," he says, holding my hand even tighter, the pressure warm, steady, reassuring. *I'm sorry* isn't enough, but what is? What could someone possibly say that could fix this?

"Thanks," I say, and then I realize the car is slowing down. I open my eyes as we decelerate, coming to a stop sign at the end of an exit ramp off of I-81. Caleb looks both ways, then turns right and right again, into a gas station so brightly lit that I have to shield my eyes.

He doesn't say word, just parks across three parking spots, gets out of the car. Bewildered, still trying not to cry, I watch as he crosses in front of the car to the passenger side door.

He pulls it open and I look up at him, one hand stretched out, and I stare like I've never seen a hand before, utterly uncomprehending.

"C'mere," he finally says.

I unlatch the seatbelt. I unwind from the car, still blinking in the bright lights, stand, and then his arms are around me and my head is buried in his chest, and all I can think is *oh*.

Then I cry, and Caleb doesn't say a thing. He just stands there and holds me.

I don't know how long we stay like that. Too long, probably, but he never tries to back away, never tries to let me go. He just stands there and holds me while I cry because I'm scared for my mom and furious for my brother and afraid that I'll never see either of them again.

"I'm sorry," I finally gasp, coming up for air. "I'm sorry, I'm sorry —"

"Don't be," comes his calm, steady voice.

"I'll be sorry if I want," I say, petulant, and that gets a chuckle from deep in his chest.

"Fine," he says. "But I don't have to accept it."

I finally pull away, wiping my eyes, clearing my throat. Trying to act like I didn't just cry my eyes out in a Mobil station in the middle of nowhere, and failing.

"We should go," I say. "We're not even to sixty-four yet, are we?"

"We're close," he says, and reaches out, takes my face in his hand.

He swipes away my tears with his thumb, and then, for a long moment, he just looks at me.

I think he's going to kiss me.

I want him to kiss me.

I've wanted him to kiss me for two weeks. I've wanted him to kiss me every time I walk into calculus class.

But right now, I really, really want him to kiss me. I feel raw, like the inside of my skin has been scrubbed out, and I feel needy, and I want him to kiss me and fill the void and make me feel something good. I want to climb him like a tree and I want him to shove me against his car, trap me here, whisper more dirty things in my ear.

And then his hand leaves my face and he gives me a half-smile and nods toward the car.

"Come on," he says, and he walks back around the front of the car, the moment shattered. "We've still got a ways."

There's no kiss.

Of course there's no kiss.

There can't be a kiss.

CHAPTER SEVENTEEN
CALEB

We leave the lights of the gas station and slink back into the darkness of the interstate, illuminated only by headlights, the occasional billboard.

It's after eleven at night, and we're sharing the road with tired families and long-haul truckers. I can still feel the warmth of her face on my hand, the wetness of her tears on my shirt, and I try to knock the feel of her body against mine from my mind.

She's a student. An undergrad. I'm her professor.

Everything about this is inappropriate, yet here I am.

I drive north on I-81, get on I-64, drive east, out of the mountains. Thalia asks me to tell her about my perfect family — her words, slightly sarcastic, not mine — so I tell her about being the youngest of five brothers, about never being called the right name on the first try, about never wearing anything but hand-me-downs, about always being the worst at everything because I was the youngest.

But I also tell her about learning to drive at thirteen because my older brother Eli decided it was time, even after I ran the truck into a ditch. I tell her about the times that

Daniel let me sneak out with him, and I thought I was the world's coolest high school freshman.

I tell her that Levi's the one who took me hiking and camping when I was a teenager. That his house in the woods is still my refuge, though since his fiancée moved in I make sure to call first before I go over.

I tell her that I talk to Seth, who's a little less than two years older, almost every day, that he's my best friend, that I've been worried about him lately.

And I tell her about my niece Rusty and how much I love being an uncle. I tell her about my nephew who's supposed to show up in a few weeks and how excited I am for him.

I don't tell her about my father. Not now. It's not the time and it's not the place.

We drive through Charlottesville, over the Rivanna river, through the woods. Twenty minutes later, trees flashing past, she laughs for the first time since we got into the car. Her face is still tear-stained. Her eyes are still bloodshot and puffy. I know she'll probably be crying again before morning, because that's how these things go, but she laughs that one time and I feel like I've won a gold medal.

We drive through Richmond and I see her looking out the window at the still-lit city, and I know she's wondering if her brother is out there, beyond her reach. We stop for gas just outside the city, and she offers to pay. I don't let her.

The closer we get to Norfolk, all the way on the eastern end of the state where the Chesapeake Bay meets the ocean, the quieter she gets. She checks her phone, again and again, fidgets, looks out the window at the low-slung suburbs outside the car windows, bathed in orange light.

"Anything?" I ask, nodding at her phone, and she sighs.

"Bastien's just complaining about my dad," she says,

opening it, flicking through the screens, turning it back off. "Apparently he's alternating between standing perfectly still, staring at the wall, and freaking everyone out, and driving the nurses crazy."

"How's Bastien?" I ask. I've never met her younger brother, obviously, but since she's been reading me his texts all night I feel like we've become close friends.

"Scared," she says. "Freaked out. Climbing the walls. I think he's glad I'm almost there so he doesn't have to deal with my dad by himself any more."

We drive through city, then through a tunnel under the Chesapeake Bay. I swear it's ten miles long, and by the end of it, my palms are sweating on the steering wheel from the thought of being surrounded by that much water.

Finally, we pull into the parking lot of Randolph General. Thalia grabs her backpack, pulls it onto her lap.

"You can just let me out by the doors if you want," she says.

I almost don't dignify it with a response, but then she looks over at me as I keep driving.

"I didn't take this road trip to just push you out of the car and drive away," I tell her. "I'll walk you in."

That gets half a smile, even as her hands twist in the straps of her backpack.

I park. We get out. She puts her backpack on, looks toward the looming hospital. Then she looks at me, and I hold my hand out.

She takes it, and we walk toward the hospital doors.

"They're in the fourth floor family waiting area," she says, looking at her phone. "In the north wing."

The closer we get, the tighter she holds onto my hand until finally, we're standing in front of two big white double doors, a red-lit keypad on the wall next to them. Thalia looks down at her phone.

"Bossy's gonna come let me in," she says.

"I'll wait," I tell her.

Thalia turns to me.

"Did I say thank you yet?" she asks.

"I think you did," I say.

"Thank you," she says, and her eyes fill with tears again before she turns away, dashing them away with the back of her hand. "Thank you for the ride, and thank you for keeping me company, and thanks for taking my mind off this a little bit, and —"

She stops, takes a deep breath.

"Sorry," she says, shaking her head. "Thank you for everything, Caleb. No, wait."

Thalia lets my hand go, then reaches up and very, very gently, lifts my glasses from my face, pushes them until they're resting on top of my head.

"Now you're Caleb," she says, her hands still gently resting on the frame of my glasses. "Thank you."

"You're welcome," I say, and my whole body feels like a neon sign that's just been switched on because suddenly I'm aware of her nearness, of the way her lips are just barely parted, of the fact that my blood is pumping through my veins so hard they must be able to hear it in North Carolina.

I know what's going to happen a second before it does. I have a second to stop it, to back away, to leave and preserve myself.

I don't take it.

Thalia kisses me. She winds her fingers through my hair, stand on her toes, pulls me down to her. She kisses me and I kiss her back, one arm around her waist, one hand cupping her face, and it feels like something inside me unravels, something I didn't even know was knotted.

It's a fierce kiss. It's needy, tinged with desperation.

There's a manic energy to it that presses her teeth against my lip, makes her pull my hair a little too hard, but I don't mind. I savor it all the same, knowing I should pull away, trying to memorize every second of her lips on mine.

Finally, she ends it. She keeps her hands on my face, her eyes searching mine, and we stand there, locked in the moment.

Then door opens, and we both turn toward someone who looks like Thalia but taller and wider and male.

"Ollie!" he says, and then he's wrapped Thalia in a huge hug and she's crying again and he's squeezing her so tight that I get a little worried, but I step back, out of the scene.

"What's happening?" she gasps when he finally lets her go. "Is there anything new yet?"

"They just wheeled her out of surgery," another voice says from the doorway, older, deeper. "We can see her once she wakes up."

"Dad," Thalia breathes, and then she's in his arms, in another tight hug.

"I'm glad you made it," he says into her hair.

"Me too," she says, her voice muffled.

Quietly, I take a step back, not wanting to intrude. Still holding the door open, Thalia's dad releases her, then looks at me.

It's an appraising, not-particularly-kind look. Thalia clears her throat.

"Sorry, this is Caleb," she says, holding one hand out to me. "Caleb, this is Bastien, my brother, and Captain Lopez, my father."

Her father holds out his hand, and I shake it.

"Thank you for giving Thalia a ride all the way here," he says, looking me dead in the eye.

"My pleasure, sir," I say, and I think I see Thalia almost smile at *sir*.

I turn, shake Bastien's hand.

"Thanks," he says.

"No problem," I say.

Then her dad is opening the door wider, motioning Thalia and Bastien through.

"Thank you," she says, one last time, and I wave.

She leaves. The door shuts behind her.

It's almost two o'clock in the morning, and I'm almost three hundred miles from home.

But Thalia's mom made it through surgery. Thalia's here, with most of her family.

And I can still feel her on my lips. It's the last thing I should be feeling. I should be feeling relieved, that her mom is out of surgery and the worst is over. I should be feeling guilty that I kissed her back, that I wanted it so badly, that among the thousand things I considered doing, ending the kiss wasn't one of them.

I should be feeling concerned that her brother and father saw us, that now someone knows *something*.

But I'm not. I walk out of the hospital and back into the parking lot, toward my car under the orange lights, and all I feel is elated.

CHAPTER EIGHTEEN
THALIA

"How long until she wakes up?" I ask, and my voice echoes through the nearly-empty beige hallway.

"That depends," my dad says, walking along efficiently. "Her doctor said anywhere from thirty minutes to two hours."

As long as she wakes up, I think. I know people don't, always, especially when it's emergency surgery and there's a lot of bleeding and possible brain injuries —

He turns sharply, into a small waiting room lined with cushioned chairs and side tables covered in old issues of *People* magazine.

Instantly, I can tell that this is the special waiting room. The overhead lights are off, and the room is lit by floor lamps, making it slightly more welcoming than most waiting rooms.

I stop in the door, looking in, thinking *this is the nice waiting room where they put families before they tell them someone is dead*.

"Move your butt," Bastien says behind me.

"Don't tell me to move my butt," I say, stepping into the

room. "I'll move my butt when I want to. There, I just wanted to."

"You moved your butt as you were told," Bastien says, but neither of us really have our hearts in this dumb sibling argument, so I let it drop and take my backpack off, put it on one of the padded benches.

My dad and Bastien look at each other.

"Come sit by me," my dad says, easing into one of the chairs.

I sit next to him. The fabric is the same fabric as every doctor's waiting room: stiff, plasticky, clearly waterproof. A single wooden armrest separates the two seats, and Bastien sits on my other side, his elbows on his knees.

They look tired. I think Bastien's been crying. My father looks like he's aged twenty years, and he leans forward, rubs his hands together, his gold wedding band glinting in the low light.

"Your mother was t-boned making a left turn on a green arrow," he says. "The force of the initial impact on the passenger side spun her car around, and the car coming after her didn't stop in time and hit the driver's side rear."

I just nod. There are already tears pouring down my face, and Bastien puts one arm around me, pulls me into his shoulder.

"She had an open forearm fracture, broken ribs, and a collapsed lung," my dad goes on, his tone still clipped, formal, even though I can feel the blood drain from my face. "The surgery seems to have gone well, but we'll also need to see how the next day or so goes. It's possible that her oxygen levels could dip and that would require further intervention."

I take a deep, deep breath, and stare at the dark beige flecks in the light beige floor tiles.

"But she's out, right?" I whisper. "She made it through surgery? She's gonna wake up?"

"She made it through," he says, tone still grave, slightly formal. But then again, he's always sounded slightly formal. "And the doctors say they have every reason to believe that other than a possible concussion, she has no brain damage."

Bastien hugs me tighter as I breathe in, then breathe out, trying to control myself. I want to collapse into the floor and sob with a mixture of sadness and relief and anxiety, but I don't.

Suddenly, there's something on my hand. I look down to see my father, taking my hand in his, then holding it tightly.

I look at him. He nods once, his mouth a tight line, his jaw flexing.

"Thanks," I whisper.

* * * * * ★ * * * * *

A WHILE LATER — I don't know how long — the door to our waiting room opens, and a woman in scrubs leans in, nods at us.

"She's awake and wants to see you," she says.

Silently, we follow her through the brightly lit beige hallway, past nurses at stations, past closed door after closed door. Finally, she stops in front of an open door, the inside curtain drawn around it.

For a moment, I wonder why all hospital rooms have a curtain inside the door. Why not just a door or just a curtain?

"Paloma?" she calls, softly. "Your husband and children are here."

"Come in," responds my mother's voice. It's hoarse and froggy, but it's her.

My heart thumps. I have to remind myself to breathe, and before I pull the curtain back I hesitate for a second because I'm afraid of what I'm going to see.

Then I do it anyway, and there she is. She's propped up on pillows, and she looks terrible, but when I come into her room she smiles at me through cracked, swollen lips.

"Ollie, Bossy," she says, as Bastien and I come in, one on each side of her bed. "Hi. Did you get my voicemail?"

Bastien and I glance at each other, over her bed.

"The anesthesia is still wearing off," the nurse says, checking something off on a clipboard. "She might be a little loopy for a while yet."

"Of course, that's why we came," Bastien tells her, shrugging at me.

"Good," my mom says, and she sounds relieved. "You shouldn't get the tiramisu from D'Agostino's, they've started — "

She breaks off, looking past us, and we turn.

"Javi?" she whispers.

My father, standing at the foot of the bed, clears his throat, his face practically set in stone.

"It's me, Paloma," he says.

She blinks, like she's trying to see through a haze.

"Of course, Raul," she says. "I'm sorry."

He steps forward, next to me, and takes her hand in his.

"How are you feeling?" he asks, and my mom closes her eyes, settles back on the pillow.

"Like shit," she murmurs.

· · · · ★ ★ ★ ★ · · · ·

"You're getting the big one?" Bastien asks, looking over at the paper cup in my hand.

"Yup," I say, already pouring coffee into it.

"That's a lot of caffeine."

"Good. I'm also going to pour a shitload of cream and sugar into it, *and* I'm getting a donut. And Froot Loops. And chocolate milk. And a package of M&Ms! And you can't have any!"

I stop pouring coffee into my very large cup and grab a handful of creamers.

"I'll just steal some when you're not looking," Bastien says.

"I know," I grumble.

I grab all my sugar items, and then we head to the register, where I pay with the twenty dollar bill that my dad handed me for breakfast before he went back to the house to get some things for Mom.

Just because I'm an adult doesn't mean I'm grown, I guess. I didn't argue with him.

Bastien and I take our trays full of caffeine, sugar, and one banana to a booth by the wall and sink into it, exhausted. My eyes are so dry that they feel like they're made of sandpaper, and if I weren't still a mess of nerves and anxiety, I think I could fall asleep right here at this table.

After we'd been with my mom for a few minutes, a doctor came in and proceeded to practically drown us in medical information: what had happened, what could happen, what else could happen, what decisions would need to be made. The moment she left, another doctor came in and did the exact same thing, only with completely different information, somehow.

Then, finally, the nurse kicked us out so she could rest

and Bastien and I came downstairs, to the hospital cafeteria, because we didn't feel like going anywhere else.

But she's awake. She's not out of the woods yet — bleeding could restart, something could rupture, there could be an infection — but the worst is over and I can eat junk food with my brother.

"So," he says, peeling the banana.

"So," I agree, biting into the donut. It's not a good donut. It's stale, probably from yesterday, but it's sugary and it's *food* and I'm not really particular right now.

"Mom's not gonna forgive him, is she?" he asks.

"I don't think so," I say, wiping frosting from my bottom lip.

"Yeah," he sighs, then bites into his banana, looking off at the far wall of the cafeteria. There are only a few other people in here, and they look like they're having the same kind of day that we are.

"You haven't heard from him, have you?" I ask, already knowing the answer.

Bastien snaps his fingers and gasps.

"Oh, that's right," he says, in mock-surprise. "I found Javier and he moved into my dorm room with me and my roommate and I signed him up for crew team, he's doing really great. Totally forgot to tell you, sorry!"

"All right, then I won't make conversation," I say, grumpily.

"You don't think the *second* I knew something I'd tell you?" he huffs.

"You need a nap."

"You need to not ask dumb questions."

"You need to…" I trail off, because my brain is refusing to come up with an end to that sentence. "Shut your dumb face," I finally say, shoving the rest of the donut in my mouth.

Bastien just laughs, his mouth full of banana.

"How's school?" I ask, changing the subject. "Have you taken a single class for your engineering major yet?"

"Technically, yes," he says, lifting his coffee cup to his lips. "I've fulfilled most of the general education requirements."

"And zero of the engineering ones," I finish.

Then I rub my knuckles against my forehead, brutally aware of what an obnoxious older sister I sound like.

"Something like that," he says.

"Just tell them," I say. "They're going to figure it out when you graduate with a B.A. In Comparative Literature instead of the B.S. In Engineering they were expecting, just tell them now."

"I know," he says. "I just... I haven't yet."

I look across the table at my little brother, though *little* is the wrong word because he's been taller than me since the moment he hit puberty. Objectively, I'm pretty sure he's handsome, though subjectively, he's my brother so *ew*.

"New topic," he says, leaning back in the booth. "Tell me about Caleb."

I clear my throat and look down at my tray.

"What about Caleb?"

Bastien looks at me like I'm an idiot.

"What do you *think* I want to know about him, Ollie?" he says. "You show up at two in the morning with an honest-to-God *hunk* on your arm and you think there's not going to be questions?"

"He's a friend," I say.

"You have hot friends, then," he goes on. "Who apparently play full-contact rugby in suits, judging by the grass stains he had on him. He straight?"

"Yes," I say, a little too quickly. "I mean, I think so."

Bastien grins.

"He questioning? I'd be happy to provide some answers."

It is very, very weird to realize that you and your little brother have the same taste in men.

"I haven't asked whether he's settled in his sexuality," I say, primly taking a sip of coffee.

"And he hasn't given you any clues?"

I'm blushing, my face bright red, and I know it. I also can't look directly at Bastien right now or I might accidentally tell him everything.

"We're just friends and we're going to stay that way," I say. "It wouldn't work out, so we're just friends. For reasons."

Bastien gives me a long, thoughtful look.

"He's really into Insane Clown Posse," he guesses.

I roll my eyes.

"He legitimately thought that *Suicide Squad* was a good movie," he says.

"You think I'm that much of a snob? They're good reasons, okay?"

"He's married."

I nearly spit out my coffee, because *that* escalated quickly.

"No!" I say, coughing. "God, Bossy, no he's not married. Are you insane? Of course he's not married. I would never —"

I pause as words fail me for a moment. Bastien is just looking at me, uncertainty written all over his face.

" — *Take up with* a married man," I hiss, leaning across the table.

"*Is* he married?" he says, leaning forward, his voice hushed, horrified.

"*No!*" I whisper-shout.

He doesn't say anything for a long moment. Then he

swallows, frowning at me, giving me a look I've never really seen from him before.

"Ollie," he starts. "If —"

"He's my math professor," I hiss, leaning across the table. "There. You happy? Is that better?"

"Holy shit," he says, and now he looks surprised, but no longer horrified. "I didn't really think he was married but that's the problem? He's a *professor?*"

"Assistant professor," I say. "It's his first year, he just got his Ph.D. in May."

In the four hours we just spent together in the car, we did manage to talk about more than my stupid, tragic family. For example, Caleb now knows the entire plot of the anime *Neon Genesis Evangelion* and I know all the ways in which the Lord of the Rings movies differ from the books.

"I would be amazing at math if he were my professor," Bastien says, his face dead serious. "I'd declare a major."

"No, you wouldn't," I sigh.

"I might if he were driving me across the state and kissing me goodbye," he says, stealing a chunk of my donut and popping it into his mouth.

Then he looks up at me, and my thoughts must be written all over my face because he immediately looks horrified.

"I won't say anything," Bastien says quickly, a few donut crumbs flying from his mouth. "Sorry. I would never, Ollie, I can hardly go and tell everyone your secret."

He chews, swallows.

"Besides, you've got leverage on me," he points out.

"That's not leverage," I protest. "I'm not a monster."

"Sorry, bad joke," he says, and rubs his eyes with the heels of his hands.

Speaking without thinking first is probably genetic. I know better than to take it personally.

"You're at least getting an A in his class, right?" he asks, leaning back in the booth and crossing his arms.

"I think so, but not —"

"Wait, no," he says, pointing one finger at me and grinning. "You're not getting an A."

I shut my eyes and wait for the stupid joke.

"I bet you're getting a D," he says, still grinning like it's the funniest thing anyone has ever said.

"I'm not getting a D," I say calmly.

"You're getting *the* D," he says.

"He's my professor, Bossy, nothing like that is happening."

"You know, D for dick?" he says. "So if he's giving you the —"

"I get the joke, Bastien," I say, and toss back the rest of my coffee.

CHAPTER NINETEEN
CALEB

I only get about thirty miles from Norfolk before I realize that I'll never make it all the way back to Marysburg without either taking something illegal or falling asleep at the wheel, so I pull off the interstate somewhere on the Northern Neck and find a Motel 6.

It's fine. It's clean. It's a Motel 6. I toss my dirty clothes into a heap at the foot of the bed, splash some water on my face, and fall asleep within seconds.

I swear it's five minutes later when I wake up to the relentless buzzing of my phone, rattling away on the wood veneer side table.

"Fuck," I mutter to myself, reaching for it.

It's my brother Seth, and it's seven-thirty, not five minutes later. My mouth tastes like a swamp, but I answer it anyway.

"What?" I ask, still face-down on the scratchy pillow.

"He's here," Seth says.

"What?" I ask again, feeling like I've walked into the middle of a conversation. "Who's where?"

"Charlie had the baby," he says.

That gets me to sit up in the bed, even as I feel like my brain is water, slowly going down a whirlpool.

"I thought she wasn't due for another week," I say, blinking at blackout curtains, trying to gather my wits. "Is everything okay?"

"Everyone is fine, he's just huge," Seth says. "Nine pounds, thirteen ounces. Total chunker, he's got the chubby wrists and everything. He's actually really cute, Caleb, even though newborns are usually kind of funny looking."

Seth is smitten.

"What's his name?" I ask, standing.

Where are my clothes?

There are my clothes.

"Thomas William," Seth says, and I stop, one leg halfway into my pants.

Of course. The moment he says it, I can't believe that it hadn't occurred to me that that would be his name, that the first boy born to one of us would be named after our father.

"Did you know?" I ask, sitting back on the bed.

"Not officially," Seth says, slowly. "I had a feeling, though. Daniel wouldn't confirm or deny."

I wonder, fleetingly, whether I should tell them the truth, a thing I've wondered so many times that the thought is a worn pathway in my mind, smooth like a worry stone.

Then I put it away, back into the same drawer where it's been for years. Not every ugly truth needs to be brought out and aired, and that's something I decided a long time ago.

"Thomas," I say, trying out the name in my life. "I like it."

"Me too," says Seth. "You coming?"

"Of course," I tell him, pushing my foot the rest of the

way through my pant leg as I hold my phone between my chin and shoulder. "Are they still in the hospital?"

"Yup. Second floor, maternity ward. Text Mom or me first, though, in case they're napping. Charlie might go full mama bear if you wake him up," he says.

"Will do," I agree, grabbing my shirt from the floor. "I'll be there in… five hours."

There's a brief silence on the other end of the line.

"Five hours?" Seth asks.

* * * * * ★ * * * * * *

It's close to three in the afternoon when I finally walk into Sprucevale Memorial Hospital, almost six and a half hours after I talked to Seth. Sprucevale is further from the interstate than Marysburg, then there was an accident so I got off the interstate anyway, and by 1 p.m. I thought I might starve so I stopped and grabbed a sandwich.

I text my mom and Seth from the waiting room, then stand there for a moment. I'm the only person in there. Apparently late September isn't a popular time to be born in Sprucevale.

"You got here just in time, they're about to —"

Levi comes in, then stops short.

"What happened?" he asks, giving me a good, long, head-to-toe look.

Oh, shit. I put one hand over my chest, like it can hide the black eyeliner stains that Thalia left there last night.

"It's a long story," I tell my oldest brother.

"Is the long story also why it took you six hours to get here?" he asks, both eyebrows raised so high they're practically in his hairline.

"I'll tell you later."

"Is everything all right?" he asks, coming across the room, lowering his voice.

"Fine," I say, pushing my sleeves up, like that'll help. "I'll tell you later, promise."

Levi just nods.

Then he starts unbuttoning his plaid shirt, revealing a white undershirt beneath it.

"Uh… ?" I say.

"Take your shirt off and give it to me," he says, pulling his shirt over his shoulders. "Then put this on. You stand a zero percent chance of being allowed to hold Thomas if you come in wearing that, though we're going to have to risk the pants as I'm afraid those are personal."

He holds his shirt out to me, and I don't argue. I just take my shirt off, hand it to Levi, then put his shirt on. It's a tiny bit too wide in the shoulders and a tiny bit too short in the sleeves, but for all intents and purposes, we're the same size.

"I trust that this will be part of the explanation later," he says, holding up the shirt in one hand. I just nod.

"Room two-forty-one," he says.

Surreally, it's the second time today I've been in a hospital, and I follow Levi as he walks, nodding at nurses who inevitably smile back at him.

"Where's everyone?" I ask.

"Mom's here," he says. "Seth went home for a bit and Eli's making dinner for everyone. Elizabeth and her husband just left. June and Violet are with Rusty. It's me again."

The last part is directed into a room, a curtain separating us from the interior.

"Come in," Daniel's voice calls, and Levi pulls the curtain back.

"Got him," Levi says, and gestures me forward.

Daniel's sitting in a chair, shirtless and holding a tiny pink baby, both of them draped with a blanket, and Charlie's propped up in a hospital bed a few feet away, my mom folding an afghan onto an armchair across the room.

Charlie and Daniel don't look up, but my mom glances from Levi to me, looking slightly puzzled.

"Hi," I say, keeping my voice low. "How are you guys doing?"

"You know, normal weekend," Charlie says from the bed, her eyes never leaving Daniel and Thomas. "Pretty chill."

"You look good," I tell her. "How do you feel?"

That gets a tired, woozy half-smile from Charlie.

"Bless your heart, Caleb," she says. "All things considered, I think I feel pretty good. Better than I did this time yesterday."

Daniel stands from his chair, both his hands spread over Thomas's small back. He looks like he's carrying a sack of loose eggs or something, he's so careful.

"You want to hold him?" he asks.

I do. I really, really do, but I'm also never sure I've seen anything so terrifyingly small and fragile before. I'm the youngest, after all, and though Daniel does already have Rusty, he didn't know about her until she was almost a year old.

Rusty's biological mother isn't a nice person. It's a whole story.

"Can I?" I ask, pretty certain that Daniel's kidding and there's no way he's going to let me touch this tiny, hours-old human.

"Sure," he says. "Thomas, this is your Uncle Caleb. I promise he's the last one."

Thomas's head is turned toward me, his eyes barely

open a crack, his head covered in a pink-and-blue knit cap, his face puffy.

"Hi, Thomas," I say, bending forward and talking softly. "Pleasure to make your acquaintance."

Thomas doesn't move, but I swear he looks me dead in the eye and then holds my gaze like he's studying me, one tiny fist next to his face. I don't know how far newborns can see. I don't know if he can see my face or whether I'm a big peach blob, but I swear there's a connection.

Then Daniel is carefully wrapping him in his blanket and my mom is coming over, fluttering a little, supervising.

I wonder, briefly, how she feels about his name, but then Daniel is standing in front of me, Thomas in his arms, nothing but his tiny face visible, eyes now closed.

"You ready?" he asks.

"Do I have to take off my shirt?" I ask, since he's not wearing one, but he shakes his head.

"We're supposed to do skin-to-skin bonding with him," he says. "Apparently it helps to regulate his body temperature, and it releases hormones, and... I don't know, I'm just following instructions. Here."

Carefully — so, so carefully — he holds the bundle out, and I take it from him, cautious to put one hand under Thomas's head, my other arm under his body.

Thomas opens his eyes for a moment, then closes them again, and I just stare down at him. And stare. And stare.

And then, suddenly, I'm nine years old and in the forest, kneeling on the leaves. In front of me are sticks tented together on a patch of cleared ground, thicker on the outside, the interior of the cone filled with pine needles and a wad of newspaper.

Behind that is my father, on one knee, and he's got a box of matches in one hand.

This might take a few tries, he says.

Making a fire takes patience, he says, and I'm hanging onto every word he says because this is one of the rare times I don't have to share him with anyone. It's just him, and me, and his calm voice that Seth got and his dark hair that Eli got and his unflappable nature that Daniel got, his deep love of nature that Levi got.

The first match doesn't take, and he tosses the burnt stub into the pile of tinder, sits back, and looks at it for a moment. He's analyzing, thinking, considering the best way to go about improving this, and right there, in this twenty-one-year-old memory of his final summer, I see the parts of my father that I got.

I blink away tears. I swallow hard, take a deep breath, refocus on this tiny, tiny human in my arms.

"He's perfect," I say. Levi squeezes my shoulder. Daniel pulls a gray t-shirt over his head. Across the room, I can see Charlie smile.

"I know," Daniel says.

CHAPTER TWENTY

THALIA

The days while my mom's in the hospital blend together. Sunday is like Monday is like Tuesday with no real differentiation between them other than the date on my phone.

I visit my mom in the hospital. After a little while, I somehow get used to the tube in her chest and then learn to ignore it. The doctors say it'll be there for several more days, until her collapsed lung is getting enough oxygen.

Besides that, she's loopy on pain meds for her broken arm and ribs, and every time I so much as make her smile, the nurses admonish me lest I make her laugh. She spends most of her time fading in and out of sleep, and sometimes Bastien and I take turns napping with her, in the uncomfortable arm chair next to the bed.

My father's there, too, though he never naps next to her, but he attends to her dutifully. He charges her phone, brings her his iPad, makes sure she has good snacks and plenty of water. He brushes her hair and helps the nurses give her a sponge bath.

I know that they're on the rocks. They have been ever

since he cut Javier off and Javier disappeared, breaking my mom's heart. But he's still there, every day, because if there's one thing my father understands, it's duty.

· · · · ★ ★ ★ ★ ★ · · · ·

I DO, eventually, remember to email my professors and explain my absence, even though it's Tuesday before I suddenly realize that it needs to be done. I beg forgiveness and offer doctors' notes, copying and pasting the same email to all of them.

Though I hesitate over Caleb's. I wonder if I should tell him more, expand on the fact that my mom is okay but will still be in the hospital for a little while, if I should thank him for giving me a ride all the way across the state.

Then I remember the kiss. The frantic, anxious, frayed-nerves kiss that I practically forced on him at the end of the night. The kiss that I gave him in a moment of weakness and helplessness even though I knew that I shouldn't, because it's not me who will get in real trouble.

If a student and a professor get caught kissing, the student probably gets a stern lecture, maybe a warning.

The professor probably gets fired.

I decide not to say anything, at least not in this email from my university address to his. It was a mistake, an accident, something that I've solemnly sworn up and down to myself that I won't do again, and I'd rather just bury it.

· · · · ★ ★ ★ ★ ★ · · · ·

MY ROOMMATES, on the other hand, get blow-by-blow text updates. We have a group chat and I tell them every time that my mom seems a little extra woozy, every time there's some decision to be made, every time a doctor has new information.

They send my mom flowers and a balloon. They send me chocolate. One night, as I'm complaining to them about how there's no food in the house because my father is clueless and my brother is back at school and no one ever seems to think about the fact that we have to eat except me, the doorbell rings.

There's a delivery man standing there with a pizza.

From them.

Margaret, Harper, and Victoria are my lifesaving angels, and I owe them big time.

Finally, after a week, it's decided that I'm going back to school. My mom is still going to be in the hospital for another few days, just to monitor her, but there's no reason for me to stick around. She's doing well, her broken bones are beginning to mend, and the tube is finally out of her chest.

The night before I leave, I finally, *finally* decide it's time to relax. I pour myself a glass of wine from a bottle in my parents' pantry and load up a dumb movie on my laptop.

Just as I'm about to hit *play*, my phone rings.

It's Harper, and I frown. She's calling me? Harper never calls. I mean, no one ever calls, at least without texting me first and warning me, but Harper in particular never calls.

I cross my fingers before I answer.

"Hi," I say.

"Hi! Sorry for calling," she says.

"It's important," Victoria says, on speakerphone.

"Did something happen?" I say, twirling my wine glass between my fingers.

"Hell yes it did," Victoria says.

"Do you have your laptop nearby and is it on the internet?" Harper asks. "And are you at least medium-alone?"

"I'm fully alone," I say. "Why? What's going on?"

"Okay, okay, hold on," Harper says. "You tell her."

"You worked with Nathaniel Johnston, right?" Victoria asks.

"Yeah, he was Dr. Castellano's other research assistant," I say. "But he got kicked out last week —"

"See, I told you she'd know," Harper says to Victoria. "Well, do you want to know why?"

"Obviously."

"Check your email."

I take a gulp of wine, then lean forward, toward the laptop. I pull up my email, click the link that Harper just sent.

"If this gives me a virus I'll — uh, what?"

A video pops up of a woman, naked on all fours, on a bed. She looks over at the camera like she's checking on it, then tosses her hair back.

"Come on," she says in a weird, breathy voice. "I'm so horny for you."

"Did you send me porn?!" I ask, pushing the laptop away from me. "Why did you send me porn?"

"Just wait," Harper says grimly.

I drink the wine and watch. It's very clearly amateur and looks like it was made by propping a phone up on a dresser or something.

Not that I'm an expert. I've watched porn on occasion — hi, I'm human — but overall I find it so chemistry-less and mechanical that I may as well be watching a video of someone putting legos together.

A man climbs onto the bed behind the woman, both their faces blurry and in shadow, his dick fully visible. I take another sip of wine.

I hope Dad doesn't have some sort of tracker set up on the wifi here, I think.

The man inserts his penis into the woman. She makes a theatrical noise. I make a face.

No, if he had a tracker set up he'd know Bastien was gay. I'm good.

"Oh, daddy, I like that," the woman says. I am unconvinced by her performance.

"Yeah, you like that?" the man says, pumping harder.

"Wait," I say, bells going off in my head, leaning closer to the screen.

"Mhm," says Harper, in her *I told you so* voice.

"I like it, daddy," she moans again.

"You like that?" the man says, repetitively, and I gasp.

Not because of the bad dialogue, but because I know that voice.

"No," I tell Harper and Victoria, scandalized. If I had pearls, I'd clutch them. "No *fucking* way."

"Fucking way," Victoria says.

"The money shot is about thirty seconds in," Harper says.

"That fast?" I ask, trying not to wrinkle my nose.

"Not that money shot!" she says. "Ew."

"Harper, you are literally showing me porn!"

Victoria is laughing hysterically in the background.

"I mean the regular kind of non-porn money shot. Ew."

"You do know the term *money shot* originated in porn? That's what money shot *means*."

Now we're both giggling. I can hear Victoria snort-laugh.

"Just pay attention for like ten more seconds, okay? There's a non-literal money shot."

I take a long drink of the wine and watch my laptop

screen through the glass. Frankly, it improves the experience.

Then, suddenly, something shakes whatever the camera is on, and the camera tilts until nothing's visible but the ceiling.

"Shit," the man's voice says.

"Thalia!" Harper says. "Here. Right here."

Despite my better judgement and serious reservations, I lean in.

A few seconds later, Nathaniel's face fills the screen.

I yelp and slam my laptop shut, then just stare at the closed lid in horror. It takes me several seconds, first of slow, controlled breathing, and then of gulping the rest of my wine, to process what I just saw.

And what I just saw was my quiet, polite, and utterly nondescript co-research-assistant nailing some girl on the internet.

"What *was* that?" I ask, the only question I can get my mouth to say right now.

"Well, Thalia, when a man and a woman love each other very much, they set up a camera —"

"That's the reason that Nathaniel is no longer a Madison Scholar at the Virginia Southern University," Victoria interrupts. "He's got a whole RedTube channel. Username NastyNatty."

The wine sloshes in my stomach, and there's one second where I honest-to-God think it might come back up.

"NastyNatty?" I ask, weakly.

"It's all been pulled down, of course," Victoria goes on. "But the internet remembers everything."

"Who's the girl?"

"Her name is Allison or something, she's not a student," Harper chimes in. "I guess she's his girlfriend, she's in most of the videos."

I narrow my eyes at TV across the living room, staring into its blank space like it can provide me with an explanation.

"Most? How many have you guys watched?"

Victoria's laughing again, but Harper huffs.

"We fast-forwarded through several of them out of curiosity," she says. "I'm not sure he lives up to his moniker. It's all very straightforward."

"Not nearly nasty enough," adds Victoria, still laughing.

"Ew," Harper tells her, but then they both start giggling.

I stand and head into the kitchen, my phone still with me as I open the cabinet and pour myself the rest of the wine. I haven't drunk at all this week — as far as coping mechanisms go, I prefer long showers, sleeping too much, and binge-watching bad period dramas — but this is it. This is the straw that broke the camel's back and drove me to drink.

"This is why he got kicked out of school?" I ask, watching the red liquid glug into the glass. "For having the wrong side hustle?"

"He was kicked out for *sexual misconduct*," Harper says, very officially. "At least that's what I heard. You agree not to do it when you sign the papers accepting the Madison Scholarship."

I shake the last few drops of wine off the bottle, then place it carefully in the recycling bin next to the trash.

"I thought that meant actual misconduct, though," I say, leaning against the counter, glass held in front of me. "Like sexual assault or something? I never want to see that again, but it looked consensual."

"Well, we also agreed to comport ourselves with the highest degree of moral and ethical standing, and also to represent the Scholars program well, and I imagine that uploading your dick onto RedTube wasn't what the founders had in mind," she says.

"Though you can bet your ass they'd have loved internet porn," Victoria offers.

"Everyone loves internet porn," Harper says.

"Are we even sure that he uploaded it himself?" I ask, still trying to wrap my brain around this. "What if it was someone else trying to get him kicked out of school?"

I did not enjoy the video. I'm already dreading having to open my laptop again, because I know the video is still pulled up.

But it's two adults having consensual sex, for Pete's sake. It's not illegal or anything.

"Oh, he did it himself," Harper says. "They've been investigating for months. One of the other TAs for Roman History was on the ethics committee that got the job, and I finally got her to talk about it the other night. It's him. He did it. Apparently they were considering giving him a year-long suspension and just pulling the scholarship until he uploaded a video that's got a VSU sweatshirt visible."

There's a long, companionable silence over the line. I can just imagine the two of them, on our couch, feet up on the coffee table. I stare at the wall in my parents' kitchen and drink the wine I poured and try to remember anything besides vague feelings and blurry images from the past week.

It has been a *week*.

"Anyway, don't make porn and if you do, don't put your face in it and if you do, don't put it on the internet," Harper says.

"And if you do, don't put a VSU sweatshirt in it," Victoria adds. "The real crime is making the school look bad."

"The real crime was a total lack of screen presence," Harper objects.

"There were a lot of crimes," I say. "Including you two for showing this to me, because now I've seen Nathaniel's dick and I didn't want to see his dick. Not even a little. I barely even realized that he had one."

"Sorry," says Harper.

"I'm not," says Victoria. "You're still coming back tomorrow night, right?"

"As long as everything goes according to plan, yeah," I say. "Barring further emergencies."

"Good. I miss your face."

"I miss your butt," says Harper, and I snort.

"I miss you guys, too," I say. "I'll be back. Tell Margaret I said hi. She with some new conquest?"

"Something like that," Victoria says. "She called it a date but I watched her put a condom in each of her pockets and like five in her purse."

I wonder, briefly, whether it's my virginal status, or whether having a condom in each pocket really doesn't quite make sense. How hard is it to reach across your body, even in the throes of passion?

"Attagirl," I say. "See you dorks tomorrow."

CHAPTER TWENTY-ONE

From: tylopez4nb@vsu.edu
To: clloveless@mathematics.vsu.edu
Subject: Absence due to family emergency

Professor Loveless,

I hope this email finds you well. Unfortunately, I've had a family emergency come up, and I will be unable to attend class on Monday, September 20, and I may also be absent on Wednesday, September 22.

I would be happy to provide doctors' notes for my absence, and to discuss making up any missed classwork when I return.

Thank you for your understanding.

Best,
Thalia Lopez

From: clloveless@mathematics.vsu.edu
To: tylopez4nb@vsu.edu
Subject: Re: Absence due to family emergency

Dear Thalia,

Thank you for letting me know. We can discuss your coursework when you return to campus, and your absences will be excused.

Best wishes to you and your family.

Sincerely,
Caleb Loveless

From: tylopez4nb@vsu.edu
To: clloveless@mathematics.vsu.edu
Subject: Re: re: Absence due to family emergency

Professor Loveless,

Apologies, but I'll also be absent on Friday, September 24. I expect to return to school the following week, however.

Best,
Thalia Lopez

From: clloveless@mathematics.vsu.edu
To: tylopez4nb@vsu.edu
Subject: Re: re: re: Absence due to family emergency

Thalia,

Take all the time you need. How's your mom doing? How's the rest of your family?

Best,
Caleb

* * * * * ★ ★ ★ * * * * *

From: tylopez4nb@vsu.edu
To: clloveless@mathematics.vsu.edu
Subject: Re: re: re: re: Absence due to family emergency

She's much, much better, and expected to make a full recovery. We still haven't been able to take her home, but it should only be a few more days. There's nothing I can really do here, so I'm coming back to campus.

My dad and Bastien are as well as can be expected.

Love,
Thalia

* * * * * ★ ★ ★ * * * * *

From: clloveless@mathematics.vsu.edu
To: tylopez4nb@vsu.edu
Subject: Re: re: re: re: re: Absence due to family emergency

Glad to hear it. See you in class on Monday.

Caleb

CHAPTER TWENTY-TWO
THALIA

The tile floor is freezing. I didn't take that into consideration when I planned my outfit for the day. In my head, I just knocked on the office door, Caleb called out 'come in,' and I waltzed into office hours.

I should have known better. Office hours are never waltzed into. There's always a wait, and it's usually a long one, and more often than not I get tired of standing and wind up sitting on a cold tile floor, trying to get some reading done.

Currently, I'm trying to read an article in *Neuroplasticity Bulletin* about brain cancer survivors who forgot their first language but learned a second, and I'm not having much luck.

Instead, I've read the same paragraph at least five times, but the only thought I've managed to have is *Love, Thalia*.

I didn't mean to sign my most recent email to Caleb that way. I meant to sign it *Best, Thalia*, or *Sincerely, Thalia*, or *Professionally and Platonically, Thalia*, but I'd been at the hospital all day, then come home and watched *The Tudors* for four hours straight, and then finally, at two o'clock in the morning when my brain was fried and filled with nonsense, I'd emailed Professor Loveless.

And I signed it *Love, Thalia*, sent it off, and didn't even realize what I'd done until he responded.

With any other professor, I'd feel awkward for a few minutes and then shrug it off, because I'm sure people sign their emails without thinking all the time.

But given that the last time I saw this particular professor, he'd just dried my tears and driven me across the state and I'd repaid his kindness by kissing him, this feels more awkward. A lot more awkward.

His door opens. A girl I don't know comes out, clutching a textbook in front of herself and looking slightly worried about math.

"Next?" Caleb's voice calls from inside, and the guy sitting across the hall from me stands and goes in while I try to get back to my reading, butt freezing on the floor.

I've been back on campus for a week. It's currently almost five on Friday evening, which means I've spent three class periods trying to fight off thoughts of *Love, Thalia*. I feel like that student in *Indiana Jones* who wrote on her eyelids, and that thought doesn't make me feel good.

I sit there for ten more minutes, then fifteen. I finally make some headway with the *Neuroplasticity Bulletin* and when the guy comes out of Caleb's office, I've finally read three entire pages.

"Anyone else out there?" Caleb's voice calls.

I clear my throat, getting to my feet.

"Just me," I say, and push his door open, heart beating faster than I'd like.

"Thalia," he says, and he smiles a smile that makes my heart skip a beat.

I've imagined this moment several more times than

strictly necessary, and in those imaginings, Caleb didn't always smile. Given that the last thing I did was kiss him without permission, I couldn't blame him for any other reaction.

"Have a seat," he says, gesturing. "I've been wondering all week whether you'd come by."

"You have?" I ask, heart thrashing again as I sink into one of the chairs opposite him.

The building may be new, or at least newly revamped, but the chairs are clearly a holdover from its former life, old wooden things upholstered in avocado-colored leather.

"I have," he confirms, sitting himself, his chair creaking slightly as he looks down, grabs a pen from his desk, holds it between his fingers. "You've got a fair amount of homework and a quiz to make up, and you seem like you prefer to have your ducks in a row."

"I do," I say, and the knot in my stomach unwinds.

Apparently we're taking the simplest approach to what happened: we're pretending that it didn't. I can do that. Much better than talking about it.

He's wearing his glasses. He's worn his glasses every day since I've been back, at least that I've seen, and because I'm a chronic overthinker I wonder if it's about me.

I know it's probably because he's been running late in the mornings, or hasn't gotten his contact prescription renewed, or his eyes have been bothering him, or one of ten thousand reasons a person would wear glasses instead of contacts.

But I can't help but wonder whether it's got anything to do with the fact that I said *there, now you're Caleb* before I kissed him.

"And I apologize for not contacting you or coming to office hours earlier," I say, spine straight as I pull a notebook from my bag, along with my day planner. "To be honest, I've had a lot of work to make up and I've also gotten slightly behind with grad school applications, so my ducks aren't as in a row as I'd like."

"Understandable," he says, turning the pen in his hands end over end. "Do you want to start with any questions you've had about the lectures or the homework? I trust you got the notes from a classmate."

"I did," I say, and I look down at the problem sets I brought with me, and I make myself focus on them and only them.

Together, we go over the homework that I've managed to get done so far. He stands from his chair and walks to a whiteboard against one wall of his office, erases a set of symbols that I don't even pretend to understand, and answers my questions simply, thoroughly, and completely.

He's a very good teacher. He's probably the best math teacher I've ever had, and I'm not just saying that because he's hotter than an August heat wave. Unlike every other math teacher I've ever had, he can understand *why* something doesn't make sense to me. If I'm not getting one approach to a problem, he can approach it from another angle, explain it a different way.

Admittedly, I'm not bad at math. I'm perfectly fine at math; it's not my favorite subject, but I'm not terrified of it like so many people seem to be.

But Caleb is very good at math, and he's very good at teaching math, so good that in a purely professional, non-sexual way, it's a pleasure to watch him do it because it's so rare that you see someone doing exactly what they should be in their life.

I don't know how long we've been talking about integrals and limits when his phone goes off several times in a row.

"Right, so that will be the asymptote as the limit of

that particular function approaches zero," he says, pointing with one hand and pulling the phone from his pocket with the other. "Which, actually, is what we're covering Monday, so you're officially all caught up. Is it really seven-fifteen?"

"That's gotta be wrong," I tell him, reaching for my own phone, since he doesn't seem to have a clock in his office.

My phone says it's 7:16.

"I'm so sorry," I tell him. "I swear, I thought it was maybe six."

He's still got a dry-erase marker in one hand, both sleeves rolled up, and he runs that hand through his hair, ruffling it slightly.

"Well, everyone knows how easy it is to get lost in a discussion of calculus," he deadpans, his voice teasing as he looks at the whiteboard again. "If you're not careful, *poof*, there goes your whole weekend."

"It should come with a warning label," I agree.

"Do you have any questions? I'll leave this up here for a moment, but I actually need to leave," he says, capping the marker and putting it back into the tray.

"Where are you going?" I ask, casually, copying the last equation from the board into my notebook.

"Home," he says, moving behind his desk and grabbing a pile of papers. "Well, not home. My mom's house, for the weekend."

Then he pauses, the stack of papers held in one hand, and considers me for a beat.

"Charlie had the baby," he says, and a smile takes over his face slowly, from the inside out.

It's the first time either of us has alluded to the four hours we spent together in a car, and it's a relief, pure and simple. Pretending that the kiss didn't happen is hard enough; pretending that I don't know him as well as I do would be impossible.

"I thought she wasn't due for another week?" I say, keeping my voice down.

"She was about ten days early," he says, maneuvering the stack into a manila folder. "Though I've since learned that anything between thirty-eight and forty-two weeks is considered a perfectly normal length for a human pregnancy."

"Have you met him yet?" I ask, putting my notebook away, slinging my bag onto my shoulder. "You said it was a boy, right?"

It's oddly heavy, and after a moment, I remember why.

"I went up last weekend," he says, then glances at the door. There's silence in the hall, and after a moment, Caleb smiles. "I've got pictures. Want to see?"

I just laugh.

"Of course I want to see, I'm human," I tell him. "We're genetically programmed to be attracted to babies. Not like that! I just mean attracted in a regular way. Humans like looking at human babies. In studies people always look at pictures of babies for much longer than anything else, even sexual pictures of other adults."

I am not making this better. I am not making this better at *all*.

I think Caleb is laughing at me, scrolling through something on his phone.

"It activates the reward center in our brain," I go on, for some reason. "Some scientists actually think that it's the reason that we've selectively bred domestic animals to be cuter —"

He holds his phone out to me. On the screen is a picture of him, wearing a plaid shirt, holding a brand-new infant swaddled in a blanket.

I feel like my whole body turns to jello, right there and then. One second I'm a person and the next I'm a melting pile of goop, and I don't even entirely understand why.

I wasn't expecting it. I've seen babies before, even tiny ones, but this picture in particular has activated some deep, instinctual part of my brain that I didn't know was there.

"Oh my God, Caleb," I whisper. "He's adorable."

I tell myself it's just the baby. It's a very cute baby, and my over-the-top reaction has nothing at all to do with the person holding the baby.

"Yeah, he's pretty cool," he says, looking down at his phone indulgently. "We hung out for a little while. Here, you can take that."

He hands me the phone, then goes back to putting papers into a briefcase.

"Are there more?" I ask, suddenly awkward.

People don't hand other people their phones. Everyone's got something they don't want found — dating apps, naked pictures, a really embarrassing playlist.

I wonder if Caleb has those things. If he just handed me his phone, does he want me to see them? Does he not mind if I see them? Has he simply never taken a naked selfie?

Sometimes a phone is just a phone, I remind myself.

"I took about a hundred," he says, grabbing another stack. "You can just flip through."

I'm tentative at first, but I go ahead and look through the pictures, shot after shot of various people holding the baby, who seems to be mostly asleep.

However, one thing becomes clear very quickly: Caleb's brothers are all hot. There are four of them, they all held this baby, and all five of them are handsome beyond reason.

It's astonishing, really.

"That's Seth," he says, his voice rumbling over my shoulder. "and then that's Levi lurking over in the corner."

I wouldn't say that Levi is lurking. I'd say that he's standing normally, hands in his pockets, attractively looking toward something off-camera.

"What's his name?" I ask, still staring at the picture.

"The baby?"

I shoot Caleb a look over my shoulder.

"No, this year's Nobel Prize winner," I say. "*Yes*, the baby."

He's laughing at himself, the strap of his briefcase over his shoulder, a rakish smile on his face.

"Thomas," he says.

I look back at Thomas, this time in his dad's arms.

"That feels like a big name for a small baby," I say.

Caleb's quiet for a moment, and I wonder if I've said the wrong thing again.

"He's named after our dad," he says, his voice quiet as he looks at the picture of his brother and his nephew that I'm still holding.

It hits me like a bolt from the blue: his father is dead.

I look at the tiny, scrunchy face in the picture and it all falls into place. We talked for four hours straight, and he didn't mention his father once. He's not in any of these pictures. The way he reacted when I told him about my mom, holding me without saying a word, letting me cry into his shirt in a gas station parking lot. Suddenly, it all adds up.

"I'm so sorry," I say, the words out before I think to get confirmation.

"About the name?" he teases, voice still soft, his eyes still on the picture. "It's not so bad."

"No," I say, flustered, wondering if I just read this all wrong, if I'm being really weird for no reason. "It's a good name, I mean about... aren't babies usually named after..."

Don't say dead people. Do not say dead people.

He turns and looks at me, a sudden realization coming over his face when he sees the look on mine.

"The dead?" he asks, eyebrows raised.

"That's what I'm sorry about, not the name," I say, still floundering. "Unless he's alive and I've really messed up my social cues, which does definitely happen sometimes, so maybe your dad is alive and really excited and not in any of the pictures for some reason? It's a good name. I like it. Strong. Solid."

Stop. Talking.

"I thought I'd mentioned it," he says, and runs one hand through his hair, a hint of an embarrassed smile on his face. "Yeah, he's dead. Car crash. I was ten."

I gasp, one hand over my mouth. It's more dramatic than I mean to be but I can't help it.

"That's so young," I say. "I'm sorry."

"Thanks," he says, simply, then reaches for his phone, slides it back into his pocket. "I should get going, I think everyone else has gone home."

"Actually, wait," I say, reaching into my bag. "One more thing."

CHAPTER TWENTY-THREE
CALEB

I never know how to talk about my father. All these years and I've never quite understood how people think I should react about it. Do they expect me to gnash my teeth and weep? Open my heart to them about how much it sucked to lose my father as a kid?

Am I supposed to say *nah, it's fine, everything is perfect now?*

Because the truth is that it's complicated. It's thorny. It's been eighteen years and somehow, my father's death is still reaching through time and grabbing at my ankles with ugly, bony fingers, but it's also been eighteen years, and that's a long time.

"I wanted to say a proper thank you for giving me a ride to Norfolk," Thalia says, and she pulls a bottle from her bag, holding it by the neck. "It was really kind of you. And it really meant a lot. And I'm sorry that I probably ruined that shirt, and just... thank you."

I reach out and take the bottle of wine. There's a ribbon around the neck, a folded notecard hanging from it.

"You're welcome," I say, and it feels too formal. I shift the wine bottle to my other hand. It's a cabernet from

2015, a howling wolf on the label, and I remember our conversation that night, before she got the phone call.

"You didn't have to," I say, trying something else, but it also feels wrong in my mouth.

What I want to say is that I'm glad that, by some miracle, I was there when she got the call. I want to say that, despite the awful circumstances, the time we spent in the car might have been the best four hours of my year.

I want to tell her how desperately I wish she wasn't an undergraduate. I want to tell her that I'd drive her again in a heartbeat, that I didn't do it for thanks but because I like her and I wanted her to be okay.

"I know, but I wanted to," she says. "And also, politeness and manners are the glue that hold society together."

"I thought the glue that held society together was little white lies," I say.

"We went to different finishing schools, then," Thalia laughs. "What are they teaching you down here?"

"Mostly how to fix things with nothing but duct tape and fishing line while drunk on Bud Light," I say, putting an extra twang into my accent. "It's my understanding that the girls took a course in making flowerbeds out of tractor tires."

"Practical," she says, grinning. "Probably more practical than learning to curtsey or waltz."

"You know those things?" I ask, opening my briefcase and finding a spot for the wine.

"I had to learn before my *quince*," she says. "I'd need a refresher before I met the Queen, though. And I've got no clue how you make a tire into a flowerbed."

"Fill it with dirt, then plant flowers," I say.

"If you ever get tired of math, you could teach redneck finishing school," she laughs.

I nod at the door, then follow her as she walks for it.

"I'll consider it my backup plan," I say, as I close the door behind us.

The hall is still lit but completely quiet, every other door long-since closed. Most nights there's still someone here until late, but tonight's Friday, so they're all gone.

Yet again, I've found myself alone with Thalia. I don't know how it keeps happening. It shouldn't keep happening. I should be making sure that it doesn't, but here we are.

"Can I walk you home?" I ask, checking that my office door is locked.

The question comes out of my mouth without me meaning to ask. It's habit, borne of being mostly raised by my mother: I offer to walk women home, to see them to their cars, make sure they get where they're going.

"I'm just going next door, to the Crown," she says, pointing toward the library, though she doesn't meet my eyes.

"On a Friday night?"

"I've got calculus homework to do," she laughs, but she still doesn't look at me. We walk through the empty hallway, down the stairs, toward the side entrance nearest the library, talking about nothing.

"You don't have to walk me to the library, you know," she says once we're out of the math building, walking down the sidewalk between the two buildings.

"I'm going this way anyway," I lie.

"I don't think I'm going to meet a grisly end in the next five hundred feet," she says, glancing down the sidewalk, dotted with other students. "And if I do, there'll be witnesses."

"You object to my presence?" I ask, dryly, both hands in my pockets as we go up a short set of stairs.

"No, just afraid I'm making your route home inefficient," she says.

Another hundred feet, and then we're there at the steps of the Crowninshield Library — aka The Crown — named after some colonial-era bigwig who probably donated a lot of money.

"I guess I trust you from here," I tell her.

Thalia rolls her eyes, but she's smiling.

"If I require assistance getting into the elevator I'll call you," she teases.

"Is this where I curtsey?"

"Thanks for the homework help," she says. "And sorry I took your whole evening."

"It was nothing," I say, and I mean it. I'd teach her math all night if she wanted. "Come back if you've got more questions."

"Sure," she says.

We say goodbye. I turn away, something warm and fuzzy still glowing in the center of my body.

I haven't gotten two steps before Thalia calls my name, and I turn back.

She's still standing where she was, rooted to the spot, both hands on the strap of her bag. She's holding her breath, lips slightly parted, like there's something on the tip of her tongue.

"Thalia?" I say after a moment, stepping forward, but it breaks the spell. She blinks and breathes and her body relaxes and she looks away, then smiles.

"Nothing. See you Monday," she tells me, then turns and climbs the steps into the library.

· · · · ★ ★ ★ ★ ★ · · · ·

"How many onesies can an infant own?" Seth asks, holding up a tiny white garment.

"I suppose that depends on the wealth of the infant and

the number of available onesies for purchase in the world," I tell him. "But it's a finite number, albeit a large one."

Seth folds it in half, then carefully places it on one of the several piles next to him.

"The correct answer is *so fucking many*," he says, half to himself. "And there's another pile. How is there another pile?"

"We can switch if you want," I offer.

We're sitting on the floor of Daniel and Charlie's living room. Next to Seth are three separate laundry baskets along with a pile of clean laundry, and in front of me is a mess of plastic and metal pieces that claim to be an infant swing.

On one hand, the swing does have instructions.

On the other, they're a garbled mess that barely counts as English. I've been sitting here for fifteen minutes and I've put pieces together and then taken them apart about seventeen times.

"I'd rather fold laundry and complain about it," he says, grabbing another onesie.

"Delightful," I say, staring down at the instructions. They're telling me to fit together a piece that looks like a fire hydrant, sort of, with a piece that looks a little like the letter F, only none of the pieces I have look anything like the drawing in the booklet and also, I'm starting to hate everything.

"Just wing it," Seth says. "You've got a Ph.D., for crying out loud, it's just a baby swing."

"I can't wing this," I object.

"Of course you can," he says, folding. "What could go wrong?"

"The swing falls apart and Thomas gets hurt?" I say, looking over at him, a piece in each hand. "There's no speed control, so the swing launches him across the room and toward certain doom? I can't be responsible for a baby launch, Seth."

He grins.

"I'll tell Daniel that I suggested it. We'll share blame," he says.

"You say that like you think I've forgotten The Skateboard Incident."

"If you haven't, you should have."

"Never," I tell my older brother, leaning over the useless instruction booklet again. "Never."

I flip a page, carefully consider a few pieces, and then fit two of them together. It appears to be the right choice, though I honestly have no idea. I've never put a baby swing together before.

It's closing in on ten o'clock Friday night, and the four people who actually live here are all asleep for now, which is probably a small miracle. Seth and I did the dishes and cleaned, and now we're trying to accomplish a few more things before heading back to his place for the night.

"Are you really going to not tell me who you took to the hospital last weekend?" he asks, lifting a piece of fabric from the pile. "Also, what is this?"

I snap one more piece onto the first two and look over. He's holding up something that's blue with white clouds and looks like a wide T with a pocket at the bottom. I tilt my head, studying it.

"A baby hat?" I guess. "Maybe that part is a chin strap?"

"You mean the wings? These things?" he says, wiggling them. "They're huge."

"I don't know," I protest. "Thomas has a lot of hats."

"Tell me who," he says.

"Just a friend," I say, turning back to the instructions.

Seth just sighs.

"If it were a friend, you'd tell me who," he says. "Remember when you lost your virginity to Christine Schmidt your junior year and I drove you to buy more condoms and never told anyone? I've *still* never told anyone."

"I can buy my own condoms now," I say, dryly.

"And are you?" he asks, snapping a towel.

I decline to answer.

"If you won't tell me, it's someone I know," he goes on, talking mostly to himself. "An ex you don't want us to know you're back with?"

I stop what I'm doing and look over at him.

"What?" he asks after a moment.

"Are *you* seriously asking *me* that question?" I say.

"We're friends."

"Is that why you've been celibate since she moved back?"

He freezes for a moment, holding a crib sheet with sleeping bears on it up, like he's contemplating it. Then he puts it down, folds it, folds it again with the kind of exacting, studied movements that mean I just got to him.

"Who told you that?" he asks.

"It didn't take a genius to figure it out," I say, snapping another part onto the swing.

"I'm just dating women who don't live in town," he says, grabbing more laundry. "And taking time for myself, to do some personal and spiritual growth and shit."

"Well, which is it?" I ask.

He doesn't answer right away, like he's thinking.

"Or it's someone who we don't know but who you're not supposed to be with," he goes on, ignoring everything I just said. "A fellow professor? Your advisor?"

"Pretty sure Oliver's parents have been dead for a while now," I remind him.

"The Dean? A student? A research assist — Caleb."

I'm not moving, my eyes practically boring holes into the page of the manual that say *sliding the pole into shaft A, then rotated*.

"You didn't drive one of your students across the state," he says, sounding extremely reasonable.

"Not a student," I say, still staring down.

He doesn't believe me. I can tell from here, without looking, that he doesn't believe me.

"Shit," he whispers, and I can hear him swallow. "Caleb, be fucking careful, you can get fired for —"

"Thank you," I say stiffly.

"I'm serious," he says. "You just got this job, there's no way —"

"I'm not looking for advice from the guy who's following his ex around like a lost puppy dog, even after she broke his heart and rubbed his nose in it," I say, angrily snapping two more pieces together. "Thanks, Seth, I'm fully aware of the rules and regulations on this one."

"Are you? Also, fuck you," he says, yanking a towel out of a hamper.

I flip him off.

He flips me off.

I go back to the baby swing, heart pumping like mad even as I try to breathe through it and concentrate on what I'm supposed to be doing, which is helping Daniel and Charlie in their hour of need, not getting into a stupid fight with Seth over our respective woman problems.

That said, I might kill him if he gets back with his ex. I didn't go through that with him just for her trashy, lying ass to move back to town and instantly re-bewitch my brother.

Finally, I've got the frame put together. I stand it upright.

It stays. It even looks sturdy. Carefully, I attach the swing, then plug it in and turn it on.

It swings, gently, at nowhere near launch velocity, and I look over at my brother.

"Sorry," I say.

"No, I'm sorry," he says. "You're a grown-ass man, you can handle yourself."

The swing creaks slightly as it rocks, and I turn it off, cross the room, and grab a pair of pajama pants.

"Her mom was in a car accident," I say, folding them. "She was in surgery in a hospital in Norfolk when Thalia got the call and they weren't sure if she'd make it."

Seth understands. I know he understands.

"How is she now?" he asks.

"Much better. They're expecting a full recovery," I tell him, grabbing more laundry.

"Her name's Thalia?" he asks.

"Just a friend," I say.

Seth doesn't say anything, but he gives me a look. It's a big brother look, an *I've known you all your life and I know your bullshit* look.

"Careful," he says.

CHAPTER TWENTY-FOUR

THALIA

Victoria: Wonderbread Woman
Victoria: a One Night Stand
Harper: Chicken Strip! That one gives you an excuse to be sexy.
Margaret: It's Halloween, she doesn't need an excuse.
Victoria: Fifty Shades of Grey! We'll go to the hardware store and steal paint swatches.
Margaret: Or, hear me out, just wear something slutty, it'll do the trick.
Margaret: Trust me.
Harper: Don't peer pressure her.
Me: Yeah, Margaret, don't peer pressure me.
Margaret: What?
Margaret: You said last night that you just wanted to find some random guy and make out with his face!
Margaret: We're just helping.

I put my phone face-down on the scarred wooden desk of my carrel and rub my eyes. It's nearly one-thirty in the morning, and the library closes soon, which means I should leave.

It's entirely possible to get locked in here. No one checks all the floors, they just make the announcements and lock the doors. I know more than one person who's had to call the campus police to let them out.

My phone buzzes again, but I don't check it right away, because last night around this time — tired, overworked, and eating cereal around our kitchen table during a study break — I expressed this desire to make out with someone's face, and my roommates jumped on it.

Of course they did. I knew they would, because they've all been a little bit worried about my whole date-with-my-professor situation, and then they were *more* worried about the whole got-a-ride-to-Norfolk thing, and now that everything between Caleb and I has been perfectly, one hundred percent platonic and above-board for the last few weeks, they think I'm moping.

I'm not moping. I'm busy. And, fine, *yes*, still masturbating to the memory of our single make out session, but I have to think about something, right? A person can't just not masturbate, and I can't get off if I'm thinking about writing a paper.

I probably should just find a random guy and make out with him. Sure, my casual make outs have never been spectacular in the past, but it could help me get my mind off of *my calculus professor*, and I would welcome the respite.

Harper: You did say that.
Margaret: What about two guys?
Me: Three guys! Four guys!
Margaret: You're making fun of me, but it can be arranged.

I put my phone down again. I look at my laptop screen, where I'm trying to write a paper on the intertextuality of avian themes in García Marquez and Cervantes, and it is not going well.

I should probably just go home and go to bed so I can tackle this in the morning, but first I stand from the uncomfortable wooden chair. My knees pop like I'm seventy.

When's the last time I stood up? I think, and I have no idea.

I roll my shoulders, flex my hands, bend backwards, and then stroll along the wall, between the book stacks and the other carrels. There's no one in any of them, but the ones on this floor are reserved for seniors doing their theses.

I walk all the way to the corner and then stand there, looking out the window.

At the mathematics building.

Dammit.

It's been a little over three weeks since I showed up at his office hours and gave him a bottle of wine, which means it's been a little over four weeks since the time I kissed him in the hospital.

I still haven't apologized. I've been in class with him three times a week and back to his office hours twice, and I still haven't apologized. At this point I don't even know if I should apologize any more, or just pretend it never happened. Which is worse? Which makes me more of an asshole?

Meanwhile, I've been so busy that I've barely had time to breathe, between making up for the week of school I missed, graduate school applications, taking the bus home every weekend, and now midterms.

Just survive this week, I tell myself, looking out the tall, skinny window at the math building and the campus beyond, bathed in the orange light of street lamps.

Just get through this week, and then you can breathe for a minute before the last round of grad school applications and then —

There's an office light on in the math building. Just one, on the top floor, and the moment I see it I have a bad, sinking feeling.

I also have butterflies. It's a weird combination.

I should walk back to my carrel, pack my things, and leave before I get locked inside the library. That is what I, a reasonable and rational human woman, should do.

I don't. I cup my hands to the glass to block out the light, then look out the window.

It's the wrong office, I tell myself. *What are the odds —*

It's not, of course, and as I look closer I can see a man sitting in an office chair, at a desk, in front of a computer. Doing something or other.

And I can tell it's him. I don't know how but I can, even from here: it's shaped like him and it's wearing a shirt that looks like his and he's running one hand through his hair like Caleb does, pushing his glasses up like Caleb does, turning around like —

Caleb turns to face the window, and I freeze, hands still around my eyes, so obviously spying that I may as well be wearing binoculars.

He looks straight at me. Of course he does.

Slowly, I stand up straight, take my hands away from my eyes.

After a moment, he waves. I wave back.

Then, not knowing what else to do, I flash him a double thumbs-up and walk back to my carrel, where I sit, the paper still open on my laptop screen, and stare at it for a long moment.

The Crown, in its current incarnation, was built in the 1960s, a time that was pretty bad for VSU, architecturally speaking. It's square and made of concrete, with tall, narrow slit windows that let almost no light in.

One of those windows is next to my carrel, and slowly, cautiously, I look through it.

Yup. There he is, though at least now his back is to me again and he's on his computer, acting like I didn't just spy on him and then act extremely weird about it.

Okay, I tell myself. *Two more paragraphs and then —*

An email notification pops up at the bottom of my screen with a *ding*, and even though I should be writing, I open it.

From: glassesoff@secretemail.com
To: tylopez4nb@vsu.edu
Subject: Chivalry

You're not walking home alone at this hour, are you?

I LOOK through the window and there he is, facing the window, one ankle crossed over the opposite knee.

True to his new email address, his glasses are off.

From: tylopez4nb@vsu.edu
To: glassesoff@secretemail.com
Subject: Re: Chivalry

I usually take the campus shuttle.

HIS REPLY TAKES all of two seconds.

From: glassesoff@secretemail.com
To: tylopez4nb@vsu.edu

Subject: Re: re: Chivalry

I'll meet you on the steps.

I close my laptop as the PA system crackles, and a bored-sounding woman announces that the library will be closing in fifteen minutes. Suddenly, my heart is pounding, my stomach fluttering, and I am very, *very* awake.

· · · ★ ★ ★ ★ ★ ★ ★ · · ·

"Are you usually here this late?" he asks as I walk down the concrete steps, zipping my jacket up to my chin, the chilly autumn breeze bracing at this time of night.

"Usually I manage to leave around midnight," I say. "But it's midterms, plus I missed that week of classes, so I'm behind."

Caleb's standing off to one side of the stairs, wearing a black peacoat and a red plaid scarf, a bicycle leaning against his hip, a helmet hanging from the handlebars.

"Are *you* usually in your office this late?" I ask.

"Midterms," he says. "I've got a lot of students trying to get caught up before the test, plus I've been going home weekends."

Together, we start walking down the brick path across the quad, buildings looming around us, stars and moon above. It's a clear night, which is probably why it's so cold. I shove my hands into my pockets and scrunch into myself, trying to get warmer.

Tomorrow's a scarf and gloves day, I think.

"Cold?" Caleb asks.

"I'm fine," I say.

He's already pulling at his scarf, unlooping it from his neck.

"No," I say.

"I can't watch you shiver all the way back to your apartment," he says, pulling it off.

"I'll warm up in a minute, now that we're walking."

Silently, he holds it out to me. I don't take it, just keep walking.

"Are you going to freeze just to prove a point?" he teases. "I'm not even sure what point you're proving."

"That I'm independent and self-sufficient and don't get cold easily?" I say. My fists are clenched in my pockets, but my fingers are going numb anyway. "That I didn't forget to check the weather report this morning, I *chose* not to?"

"It's just a scarf, not a moral judgement," he says. "C'mon. It's wool. From my mom's friend's sheep."

It does look really, really nice, and I'm still cold.

"Don't make me carry it like this all the way back," Caleb says. "My shoulder's gonna cramp up."

I sigh, then reach out and take the scarf, then pull it tight around my neck.

It's still warm from his body heat, still smells like him, like pine and pencil shavings. The tiniest shiver makes its way down my spine despite my best efforts in that arena.

"Thanks," I say, tucking the ends under my jacket. "You usually get your way, huh?"

He looks at me, one hand in his pocket, the other on the seat of his bicycle, guiding it alongside us.

"It doesn't feel like I do," he says.

"Then it's just with me?"

There's a long pause, and I mentally smack myself on the forehead. He just gave me a scarf. Why am I being a jerk? Why didn't I just say *thank you for lending me this scarf made from some sheep of your acquaintance* and leave it at that?

"I'm fairly sure I've never had my way with you," he

finally says, his voice so low it feels like it's bumping along the path below my feet. "I think I'd remember."

Suddenly, this scarf is way too hot and I think again, for the thousandth time at least, of being pushed against the wall at the botanic gardens, his lips on mine, his body pressed against me, the way I felt like my skin was electrified.

I stop in my tracks.

We're right where the brick walkway meets the sidewalk, though the street is empty this time of night, a single stoplight changing endlessly from green to yellow to red even though there are no cars to obey it.

"Gotten, not had," I say after he also stops, two paces ahead of me. "Don't get it twisted. There's an important semantic difference."

"Then tell me how I've been getting my way with you, Thalia," he says.

"I'm wearing your scarf even though I said I didn't want it," I say, pointing at my neck. "You emailed me and *informed* me that you were taking me home and I didn't even get to argue."

"I'm walking you home," he points out. "There's an important semantic difference."

Just like that, my temper flares.

"Right, because walking me home is the sort of completely above-board thing that any nice professor would do but the minute *walking* becomes *taking* it's wildly inappropriate for you to be doing with a student," I say. "And you would absolutely never be inappropriate."

Even in the dark, his eyes flash.

"Have I been?" he asks, taking a step closer.

I swallow hard, stand my ground.

"Because if I recall correctly, you're the one who came and found me at the Madison Scholars banquet while I was sitting alone and minding my own business," he says, his voice low, nearly a growl. "You kissed me in the hospital. You wrote *Love, Thalia* on that email and you gave me a bottle of wine."

"The email was an accident," I snap.

"Was the kiss?"

"That was just a mistake," I say, and I'm frustrated and tired and hurt and stressed and hungry, and on one hand I feel like crying and on the other I feel like shouting at Caleb and on the third, non-existent hand, I want to make another mistake and kiss him again.

"My mom had just been in a car accident and we'd been driving all night, it was late, I was tired and stressed and emotional and there's study after study that shows people in heightened emotional states have poor judgement," I say, my eyes closed.

I will not cry. *I will not cry*.

"It seemed like a great idea at the time, but obviously, it wasn't, and I'm sorry. If I could take it back I would, but to the best of my knowledge no one has figured out how to interrupt the time stream yet and if they had I'm sure it wouldn't be available to private citizens who did something dumb."

"Apology accepted," Caleb says, his face stone.

"Great," I say, way, *way* more sarcastically than he deserves. "I'm walking home. Don't come with me, I think I'll make it two blocks without getting mugged or abducted."

I turn on my heel and stomp away, down the street. Full-on *stomp* because if I'm behaving like a child, why not go all the way and really sell the performance?

"Good night," he calls after me.

I feel like shit. More than anything, I suddenly feel like too much, all at once: I feel like I want to march back there and kiss him hard and tell him to take me home and have his way with me. I'm witheringly, incineratingly angry that the one person I've felt that way about in my life is a man I absolutely, positively cannot have.

I'm mad that he keeps flirting with me when he knows the same. I'm mad that he's so genuinely kind, that he's sharp and smart and looks hot holding a baby, that he's not like anyone else I've ever met.

I stomp to my apartment and unlock the building's front door without looking back at him. Somehow, I know that he stood there and watched me until I got inside, making sure I was safe. Yes, that also makes me mad.

I'm a wreck, I think, slogging my way up the stairs into my building, an old house that now has an apartment on each floor. *Just a damn useless wreck.*

Then I take a deep breath, keep slogging.

You're not a wreck, I tell myself. *You're tired and stressed and overworked. Your family circumstances have you emotionally stretched thin.*

And, okay, you're frustrated because you want someone you can't have.

Also, hungry. Don't forget hungry. When was dinner?

When I get upstairs, Margaret and Victoria are in the living room, Margaret on her laptop on the couch, Victoria eating cereal at the table.

"Halloween," I announce.

They both look over at me, eyebrows raised, as if they can see the storm cloud over my head.

"Two guys," I say, holding up two fingers. "That's how many guys I'm gonna make out with. *Two*. I'm gonna dress sexy and have sexy fun and make out with people."

Who are not my calculus professor.

"Okay," says Victoria.

"Attagirl," says Margaret. "Are we talking successive or simultaneous makeouts?"

"Don't care," I say, heading through the living room for my bedroom. "Either one, as long as there's two, because I am getting on the express train to Makeout City. Good night!"

"Night!" they both call, and I shut my bedroom door behind myself, sling my laptop bag onto the floor.

Then I take off my jacket, and when I do, I realize I'm still wearing Caleb's scarf.

In one final fit of pique, I take it off and fling it into my closet.

CHAPTER TWENTY-FIVE

THALIA

"Okay, wait, give me a few more guesses," Josh shouts over the thump of the bass from the next room, leaning in toward me. "You're a sexy CEO."

"No," I shout.

He takes another sip from his red solo cup. I'm not sure what's in there, but I'm pretty sure it's blue, so it's not beer. I assume the frat brothers here have some special booze stash in the back that's only for them.

I, on the other hand, have some pretty strict guidelines about what I'm willing to drink at a frat party. If I don't see it come out of a bottle, or preferably a keg, it doesn't go in my mouth.

"Sexy lawyer," he shouts.

I take a tiny sip of my drink — a now-warm beer that I got from the keg my very own self — and shake my head.

"Give me a hint," he says.

"I'm a specific person," I say, and point at the cigar in my pocket.

He gives me one more up-and-down look, and I glance away from him, back at the doorway to the dance floor.

"Sexy Bill Clinton!" he says, grinning, like he's certain he got it. "The cigar is a total —"

"No," I shout.

I knew I should have gotten a beard, because no one has any idea who I am, but I really didn't want to wear a beard. It seems like a huge pain in the ass.

"Well, whatever you are, you're totally sexy," he shouts. "It's a good costume."

"Thank you," I shout back.

I'm supposed to be making out with Josh. Well, not with Josh specifically, but the idea of tonight was that I would make out with *someone* and it would scratch my itch and I would stop thinking about Caleb and thus be freed to find a more suitable match.

It's not working. This is the same story as always: some guy talks to me. I get intensely uncomfortable. He flirts. I try to imagine making out with him, and it weirds me out so much that I make some excuse and leave.

I don't know what my problem is. It seems like everyone else I know has no problem doing this kind of thing, why do I?

"Guess what I am," he shouts.

I take another step back and regard his outfit: basketball shorts, flip flops, and a tank top. It's not really seasonally appropriate, but other than that, he looks like one of the several thousand guys on campus who wear that every day.

"An off-duty lifeguard," I guess.

Josh looks mildly puzzled and drinks some more.

"Nah, man," he says.

"A surfer on the weekend," I try again, and now he laughs.

"I'm a Rho Gamma Delta!" he shouts, holding his drink way up, like it's a torch. "Haha! Get it! They're always wearing shorts and flip flops and shit, it's like they don't even own real shoes."

"That's really good," I lie. "Super funny."

I try smiling at him. Is this how you flirt? You tell a guy he's funny and smile at him?

"Thanks," he says. "Me and a couple of my buddies are gonna go over there in a little while, they're having their own party and man, are they gonna be…"

He keeps talking, but I stop listening to stare at his mouth as his lips move.

Can I make out with him? I just have to put my face right there and then get my lips against his…

To be clear, there's nothing wrong with Josh. He's nice looking. Good face. Athletic body. My own age. Not my professor.

And yet, the idea of putting my face on his and making out makes me feel like there are worms crawling over my skin.

I don't want to. Even though, in the abstract, I really do want to accomplish my stated goals for tonight, I just don't want to make out with this guy.

"That'll be great," I say when he's finished with his plans for pranking another frat, or… something. "Super funny. Hey, I gotta go get a refill, cool talking to you!"

I don't even wait for a response before I flee.

Like all the frats on campus, Kappa Chi Kappa is in an old house, and I duck around a staircase decorated with fake cobwebs and giant (fake) spiders, then through a hallway hung with skeletons and then past the party room, music pumping out.

I scan it quickly, but I don't see anyone I know in the writhing mass of bodies, so I skip it.

The kitchen. Another hallway. A room that's just filled

with Christmas lights and people making out on beanbag chairs.

Then, finally, in a room that I think is some kind of closed-in porch, I find Harper and Victoria.

"Heyyyyy!" they chorus when they see me.

"Heyyy," I say, flopping on the couch next to them.

I choose not to think about the things a frat house couch has probably seen.

"How's the mission going?" Victoria asks.

"The mission is stupid," I say.

"So, bad?" Harper asks, taking a sip of her beer. I think they're both slightly drunker than me, but it's Halloween. Everyone should be drunk. That's the point of Halloween in college.

"I tried," I say, leaning my head against the back of the couch. My extremely-short-cutoff-shorts are giving me an intense wedgie right now, but I don't care quite enough to fix it. "I just... don't wanna."

"Then don't," Victoria says. "If you make out with someone just to make out with someone, you'll only wind up feeling bad about that."

"It's okay to only make out with people you actually want to make out with," Harper joins in.

"I know," I say. "I just wish I wanted to make out with more people."

"Do you?" Victoria asks.

"More beer would fix that," Harper offers.

"I don't want more beer either," I say.

"Then I don't know how to help you," she says, finishing her own off.

"Where's Margaret?" I ask, even though I probably know the answer.

"One of her harem boys is in this frat," Victoria says. "They're probably upstairs."

Margaret is — in her own words — a slut, which she defines as "a woman who likes sex and isn't shy about it." At any given time, she has several friends-with-benefits relationships going on, all of which seem pleasurable and safe and consensual and am I jealous?

Yes. Kinda. It's complicated. I'm jealous of some aspects, at least. Such as the ability to make out with someone without making it weird first.

"How come she can bang like twenty guys at once and I can't even make out with one?" I complain.

"Because you're different people," Victoria says, her tone of voice suggesting *duh*. "People are different, it's not a big deal."

"You want to fuck your professor, she wants the whole frat to run a train on her," Harper says. "Different strokes for different folks."

I don't think that's quite what Margaret is looking for, but I take Harper's point.

"I need more beer," Harper announces, then points at Victoria. "You need more beer. And you need more beer!" she finishes, the last statement directed at me.

"Accurate," Victoria says, and shoves herself off the couch. "Then we should go dance before the organ concert. Shake that booty, you'll feel better."

I let her help me off the couch.

"Okay," I agree. "We'll dance."

· · · * ★ ★ ★ ★ * · · ·

I'M NOT A VERY good dancer. I know that, as a Latina chick, I'm supposed to have rhythm in my soul and salsa through life or whatever, but apparently I missed that memo.

I dance anyway, with Victoria and Harper. After a

while, Margaret comes down, looking pleased with herself, and she dances too.

We dance with some guys. We dance without some guys. I have another beer and loosen up a little and don't care that I'm not a great dancer.

We've been dancing for a while when Harper shimmies over to me, grabs my wrist, and shouts in my ear.

"It's eleven thirty!" she says. "We gotta go."

We collect Margaret and Victoria, say goodbye to some other friends, and then grab our coats before we leave the booming frat house. The cold night air feels good against my sweaty, flushed skin, and I pull my hair back into a knot as we walk.

"You make out?" Margaret asks.

"Nah," I tell her. "Not my night."

She flings one arm around me and squeezes me close, nearly sending both of us stumbling off the path, and we giggle.

"I still love you," she says, overly effusive and definitely somewhat drunk, but I appreciate it and slide my arm around her waist, and we stumble to Scarborough Hall.

Scarborough Hall has one of the largest pipe organs in the United States, so every Halloween, the school organist puts on an organ concert.

Yes, we have a school organist. I think he's a music professor in his spare time, though I like to imagine that his main job is playing organ concerts, which also happen at Christmas, Easter, and graduation.

The concert is at midnight, so every Halloween, a huge chunk of the student body stops partying, grabs some blankets, and goes and sits on the floor of a huge, Baroque hall that's got a pipe organ at one end and portraits of old white men adorning the walls.

We get there in plenty of time and find a space near the

front, at the end of the hall opposite the organ, which is situated in a loft above the front door. The lights are off, except for a few spooky-looking sconces, and we sit on the blankets that Harper remembered to bring, bless her.

"Did anyone guess your costumes?" Margaret asks.

"Everyone," says Harper.

"A couple people, but they really liked it," says Victoria.

I just sigh.

"I told you that you needed the beard," Victoria says. "You just look like *A Clockwork Orange* meets *Rocky Horror Picture Show* without it."

Even though I'm lying on the floor, I look down at myself: ankle boots, thigh-high fishnets, thrift store gray trousers cut off to make booty shorts, a half-unbuttoned vest over a pushup bra, and a blazer with a cigar in the pocket.

I've been slightly self-conscious all night, but I also saw a girl wearing nothing but a thong under a fishnet dress with stickers over her nipples, so by college standards I'm practically a nun.

"Yeah," I agree.

Harper took the *Fifty Shades of Grey* idea and stapled paint swatches to a black outfit. Victoria spent all week creating a complicated getup that's half poofy prom dress, half football uniform, and has fairy wings attached.

She's fantasy football.

Margaret's just wearing a miniskirt and a crop top. It's not even a costume, though I did overhear her tell someone that her costume was "college girl."

We wait for the concert to start and talk about nothing at all: which of the white men's portraits on the wall looks grumpiest, whether hot dogs count as tacos or sandwiches, how many times per week you can eat cereal for dinner and still claim to be an adult.

Finally, at five 'til midnight, the lights flicker once, warning us that organ music is imminent. Harper squeals and claps her hands, and Margaret laughs and tell her to simmer down. I sit up, leaning back on my hands, looking up at the huge golden pipes gleaming above the entrance to the hall.

Then I look down, at the back of the huge hall.

Caleb's standing there, leaning against the wall, his hands in his pockets.

I take a deep breath, close my eyes, and lie back on the floor.

CHAPTER TWENTY-SIX
CALEB

I get there just as the lights go dim. Perfect timing.

I almost didn't come, even though I've come every year for the past seven, since I started graduate school here. The organ concert is awesome in the biblical sense of the word, unlike anything else I've ever experienced.

But it's also filled with undergraduates, and even though I always taught undergrads as a grad student, being their professor is somehow... different. Seeing them drunk and dressed as sexy butterflies didn't feel creepy when I was just a graduate student.

It does now. On my bike ride to Scarborough Hall I passed a girl who was — I think — dressed as a sexy mummy and seeming to be wearing nothing but haphazardly placed crepe paper, and I nearly stopped her just so I could offer her my coat, praying the whole time that I didn't recognize her.

It's bad enough that every time Thalia walks into my class, I have to remember pushing her against that wall, hard as hell, the way she gasped and dug her fingers into me. I can't imagine having to teach calculus to someone whose nipple I've accidentally seen.

The floor in Scarborough is completely covered in students, most lying down, Halloween costumes dimly visible. I take off my coat and stand near the back, under the organ loft.

The lights go down. The crowd hushes. I close my eyes, and it feels like church.

"Good eeeevening," a voice booms from above, affecting a cheesy Transylvania accent. "And velllcome to the annual All Hallow's Eve midnight organ concert!"

I can't see Mike from where I'm standing, since I'm half-below the loft that holds the pipe organ, but I grin anyway. I appreciate a guy who knows how to play to his audience.

The students on the floor cheer and stomp. It's more raucous than you'd expect for a pipe organ concert.

"Tonight, ve vill begin vith an arrangement of Handel's Organ Concerto, Opus Seven, Number Vun, in B flat major," he booms. "Please enjoy."

The entire hall is dead quiet. It feels like the building itself is holding its breath, waiting.

I wait, eyes closed.

The first note floods the room like dark sunshine, low and vibrant, the sound so thick I feel like I could reach out and touch it. The hairs on the back of my neck stand up. The wall behind me hums.

I've never heard anything like this before. I've been to plenty of other concerts, but there's something particular about this one: the way it feels like the air itself is the music, like the building and the organ and the people listening are all part of the same song, the same power.

And I needed it. I needed to go somewhere and feel

something new and get away from myself, just for a little while.

It's been a bad week. It's been a long week, a rough week, because on top of everything else I've had to see Thalia sitting in the back of my classroom, taking notes and turning in homework and generally pretending that I'm invisible.

Of course she was angry. I'd been pretending that, as long as I didn't touch her, the nature of our relationship didn't matter. That it was appropriate to contact and walk her home and give her my scarf and flirt with her, as if all that wasn't also wildly inappropriate.

I shouldn't have. My entire life is laced through with *shouldn't* and *don't* and it's laced through with an intense longing that knocks the breath from me sometimes, and underneath all that it's laced through with the queasiness at the knowledge that this is over a twenty-two-year-old student.

In that way, Halloween has brought a small measure of relief, that after seeing countless girls in various states of undress, my only thought has been *she must be cold*.

The organ booms and I feel the music on my skin, in my lungs when I breathe, and I make myself stop thinking about anything else.

I don't know how long that lasts. The first song ends and another begins, then another and I stand there, against the wall, and float away on a wall of sound.

At last, the music stops. The last note echoes through the hall, a ghost floating away until it dissipates in a hall so silent I swear I can hear the building settle.

Then a thump, a creak from above, and I hear Mike's voice.

"Sank you for your kind attentions," he says, still with the same accent. "Ve vill now have ze briefest of intermissions and ven ve return, I vill be playing Louis Vierne's Organ Symphony Number One in D minor, Opus Fourteen, and of course, Bach's Toccata and Fugue in D Minor."

Mike drops the accent when he names the songs, and right when I open my eyes there's a swish and I see the brief flick of a red cape disappear over the railing of the balcony.

And then, before I can move from the spot where I'm leaning against the wall, I see Thalia.

Walking in my direction, though she's not looking at me. Wearing short shorts and fishnet stockings with garters, the thin black strap snaking up her thigh, under her cutoffs.

She's got on a vest that's half-unbuttoned over cleavage and a gray sport coat over that, something poking out of the pocket.

My whole body floods hot, then cold. I swallow hard and shove my hands in my pockets and try to look away, I swear I do. I can't. I feel like a cartoon dog going AAAOOGA, eyeballs popping out of their sockets, tongue lolling practically to the ground.

Stop staring. Stop staring.

I can't. I hate this, but I can't, and for long seconds I'm standing against the wall, just watching her, like some sort of pervert. She closes the distance between us, still not looking at me, and I dream of cold showers. I imagine standing naked in a snowbank. I think of hiking ten miles in the rain over rocky ground.

I promise that when I get home I'll immediately put a profile on every dating site in existence just so I can meet someone else and forget about this inappropriate girl, and then she looks at me and tilts her head slightly and smiles.

"Oh hi," Thalia says, folding her arms in front of herself, like she's self-conscious. "I didn't know you were coming. And I didn't see you there, I was just walking to… that way."

She nods vaguely behind me, so I turn and look, and it's just as well because her folded arms only give her more cleavage, her breasts straining at the already-unbuttoned vest like they're planning a jailbreak.

There's a hallway. It looks mostly dark. I don't know where it goes. I don't think she does, either.

"Walking to that way, of course," I tease. "Don't let me stop your walk. To that way."

"You're not going to offer to come with me to keep me safe?"

My skin prickles, my defenses slightly up, because I don't want a replay of the last time we talked. I didn't even do anything besides attend a concert this time.

"Are there many unknown threats back in the mystery hallway?"

"If I knew, they wouldn't be unknown, would they?"

"Touché."

She's got black eyeliner with dramatic wings and red lipstick, and she reminds me of the night we met, the only other time I've seen her look anything like this though there was no fishnet or cleavage then.

"What's your costume?" she asks, arms still folded in front of her.

I look down at myself: boots, jeans, and a t-shirt that's got a drawing of a bear and some trees on it.

"A professor who doesn't stick out like a sore thumb at an undergrad event," I say, pushing a hand through my hair. "How am I doing?"

"If you were about fifty percent drunker I think you'd blend right in," she says, laughing. "At least you didn't wear spectacles and bring a briefcase."

"They're not spectacles, they're glasses," I correct her,

smiling. "Dr. Schwartz assured me they were *very* cool."

"Dr. Schwartz wasn't wrong," she says.

"Was he right?"

She pauses for a moment, glance flicking away, her lips twitching like she's about to either laugh or say something, and I don't know which.

"He wasn't wrong," she says again, and now she's laughing.

"Are you wearing a costume, or is this just Saturday night?" I ask, risking a look at her again.

"Oh, God no," she says quickly, taking a step back, looking down at herself. "It's a costume, and it's a little more than I thought it would be because I told my roommates —"

She pauses for half a breath.

"— they kind of took control of things since I've been so busy," she finishes.

"Who are you?"

That gets a smile, a sparkle in her eye.

"Guess," she tells me, and the lights go low again.

I try to take her in as cooly and clinically as possible: shorts that look like they were once slacks, fishnets, the vest, the sport coat.

No idea, and then my eye catches on whatever it is in her pocket, and I point.

"May I?" I ask, and she nods.

It's a long cylinder, paper covered, and as soon as I take it from her pocket I know it by its scent.

Thalia lifts one eyebrow.

"It's just a cigar," she says, and there's a tease in the curve of her lips and in the way she's looking at me, and instantly, I know who she is.

"Sigmund Freud," I say, flipping the cigar through my

fingers. "If Freud was in a production of *The Rocky Horror Picture Show.*"

"Congrats on being the first," she says, and I slide the cigar back into her pocket.

"I wouldn't have gotten it without the clue."

"No one else got it *with* the clue," she says.

I try not to imagine who else has been looking at Thalia, touching the cigar, trying to guess who she is. It's absolutely none of my business but the thought of some drunk frat boy ogling her and asking if she's the sexy Monopoly Man makes my stomach curdle.

"Do I win something?" I ask. "Free psychoanalysis?"

Thalia laughs, then steps forward, and now she's even closer. Too close, close enough that it sends my pulse skipping and racing, and she puts both hands on my temples.

And stares deeply into my eyes.

All my alarms go off at her touch. All of them. She shouldn't be doing this and I should be stopping her, but she is and I don't.

"I was expecting to lie on a couch," is what I say.

"Shh, I'm analyzing," she says. "And it turns out —"

"Vellllcome back to ze second portion of our eeevening!" announces Mike, and we both look up, to the balcony, where his voice is booming from though we still can't see him. "Next, I vill be playing anozer delightful piece by Johann Sebastian Bach..."

She's still looking at me, dark eyes made wicked by black wings, by the shadows of the organ loft, by the low lights and the moonbeams just barely coming in through high windows.

I don't hear what Mike announces. It's another organ piece, the opus and movement or whatever lost on me anyway.

"It's your mother's fault," she says quickly, the moment he stops talking. "Also, I'm sorry for last week."

"What's my mother's fault?" I ask, my voice hushed in the quiet, and Thalia just shakes her head.

"Forget it, it was a dumb psychotherapy joke," she says, taking her hands off my face. "Freud had a penchant for blaming everyone's problems on their mothers —"

Then the organ notes hit, filling the room, and the rest of her sentence is lost, her red lips still moving but her voice drowned as she scrunches her face quickly, shoots a glare over our heads at the organ loft.

"I'm sorry!" she shouts. Someone to our right turns, looks at us. A run of organ notes ripples through the air between, and I bend down, my lips an inch from her ear.

"What for?" I ask.

CHAPTER TWENTY-SEVEN
THALIA

I close my eyes. I pull my jacket tighter around myself, as if it can erase the fact that I walked over to Caleb and struck up this conversation with my tits and ass basically out.

Until he looked at me, I didn't feel almost naked. Slightly underdressed, yes; not wearing as many clothes as I normally would, yes. But the second he looked at me I suddenly felt like I'd gone on a romp through a Victoria's Secret catalog and was now wearing the barest minimum of clothing that could be considered clothing.

I stand on my toes, put one hand on his shoulder to steady myself.

"I'm sorry I was such a bitch last week when you walked me home," I say, as succinctly as possible.

I meant to do this in a reasonable tone of voice, while the intermission was going on, but it's like I hate making things not-awkward.

"You weren't," he says, his voice deep and rumbly, cutting through the organ music, both of them raising goosebumps on my skin, making me feel like I could float away.

I tighten my grip on his shoulder — his hard, muscled shoulder — and try not to think about it.

"I kind of was though," I say, still half-shouting to be heard, even into his ear like this. "I didn't have to say it that way, I was just tired and stressed and hungry and —"

I wobble slightly on my toes, and then his hand is on my waist, steadying me. I catch another glare from the same girl as before.

"And felt like I was taking advantage?" he asks, removing the hand.

"What? No," I say, now to his face, now shouting, and now this girl is full-on glaring me down, lasers practically shooting from her eyes.

I am fucking this up. I'm not good at apologizing, I'm not good at talking about my emotions, and I'm really not good at talking to men I'm interested in, so this is some sort of horrible hat trick of Thalia Makes Things Weird.

Caleb just raises his eyebrows. I glance around, organ music humming and soaring around me, and spot a door in the wood paneling of the entryway.

Without thinking twice, I make for it, stepping over a few people and dodging around a few more. I look over my shoulder just enough to make sure that Caleb's following me, and sure enough, he is.

The door's unlocked. I'm pretty sure it shouldn't be. I'm altogether sure that I shouldn't be opening it and going through it, but I do it anyway and find myself in a short, narrow hallway that leads to a tall, narrow staircase, a bannister running the length of one side.

Caleb steps in behind me. He closes the door, and suddenly the organ music is dimmed, louder coming down the stairs than through the door.

I take a deep breath.

"I'm sorry I was a jerk on Friday night," I start over, moving closer. "I still think that what I said was valid, but I didn't have to —"

He steps closer, leans in.

"—I didn't have to be an asshole about it," I say into his ear.

"I think I deserved it," he says. His lips brush my ear, and my eyes flutter closed.

Don't, I tell myself. *Don't do a single thing that isn't apologizing for your behavior.*

As if I didn't seek him out. As if I didn't drag him into this tiny, cramped back staircase.

"No, you were right," I tell him, automatically reaching out, steadying myself against his shoulder. "I found you at the banquet. I kissed you later. I gave you a bottle of wine."

"But I'm the one who should know better," he says, and then his hand is on mine, holding it against his warm chest. My heart beats harder, faster.

"You think I don't?"

"I shouldn't be giving you rides and walking you home," he goes on. "Pretending that those things are perfectly fine and innocent, because they're not."

We shift in the tiny space and suddenly our bodies are touching from shoulder to hip, the jolt of his heat like an electric current.

"We shouldn't be seeing each other at all," I tell him, even as I close my eyes, press myself into him so softly I can tell myself I'm not doing anything, my lips millimeters from his ear.

"No," he says. "The more I see you the harder it is to pretend I don't like you."

A hand on my hip, his fingers touching bare skin above my too-small shorts.

"And the harder it is to pretend I don't want you," he whispers.

My heart's beating so hard and fast that it feels like my ribcage is rattling in my body. Outside and from above, the organ hums thickly, surrounding us.

"What if it were my fault?" I ask.

"What do you mean?"

I know I should walk away. I know that. I know Nathaniel got expelled for *sexual misconduct* and while I have no intention of making porn, I'm fairly certain that sleeping with my professor also falls into that category.

I know he could get fired and his career could be over.

I know a million things wrong with this scenario, and not one of them stops me.

"I mean," I say, and plant a kiss on his neck, right below his jaw. His fingers curl into my spine.

"What if —" another kiss, higher up, "— it were my fault?"

The last kiss lands on his jawline, right below his ear, my fingers now woven through his hair, his slight stubble sharp on my lips.

He moves his hand until his palm is flat on my back, in the space between the shorts and my vest, underneath the jacket I'm still wearing. He swallows hard, his breath on my neck.

Then his hand is on my face, his thumb stroking my jaw, and he pulls me back, his green eyes nearly black in the dark, his lips parted, his gaze roaming my face. I don't breathe. I don't think my heart beats.

And he kisses me.

He kisses me so softly and gently that, for a moment, I think I'm imagining it. The kiss is over almost as soon as it starts, the lightest touch, but he nuzzles his nose against mine and he's still holding my face, his thumb on my cheekbone now, and he kisses me again.

Still gentle, but firmer, harder. He pulls away, both hands in my hair, leans his forehead against mine. We're both breathing like we've been underwater for minutes on end, our eyes closed as our mouths find each other again and again.

With each coupling there's less gentleness, more need. I wind my hands through his hair and pull his face to mine. He pushes me backward, walking with me until I'm up against the bannister that runs the length of this short hallway.

He grabs my hips, running his hand up my waist, under my jacket, until his fingers hit my ribcage, his mouth rough on mine, his erection pressing against my hips, pinning me against the bannister.

This time I don't panic when I realize what it is. This time a delicate, secret warmth blossoms inside me and I curl my fingers into a fist around his shirt, bite his bottom lip between my teeth.

"Your fault," he whispers, teasing. "What else are you going to make me do, Thalia?"

"Kiss me again," I say, the only thing that comes to mind as words.

I want more. I want so much more but the words stick in my brain, refuse to come out in sentences.

"Done," he says, his mouth already on mine, seeking, plundering.

Then, his lips still on mine: "What else?"

I want you to take my clothes off right here and ravish me and make me come and shout and scream like you said you could two months ago and I want you naked and on top of me and oh, God, I want everything.

"Take my jacket off," I whisper, and as the words leave

my mouth he's already pushing it over my shoulders, lips on my jaw, on my neck, on my now-bare shoulders as it falls to the floor, his arms around my waist, pulling me into him.

"What else?" he murmurs, and I can hear the smile playing across his lips.

I reach behind myself, grab the bannister, hop up, my knees now on either side of his hips as I balance, precarious.

"Come closer," I say.

Caleb moves an inch, one hand flattened on the wall next to my head, a teasing eyebrow raised.

"Closer," I tell him. "Closer. *Closer.*"

I pull him in until my legs are wrapped around his hips and his hardness is against my heat, making me grip the bannister in both hands as he kisses me and his body moves against mine, hungry and needy and wild.

"What else?" he growls.

"Touch me," I say.

He lights two fingers on one shoulder, draws a slow circle.

"Here?" he murmurs.

I grab his wrist, drag his hand to my chest where a pushup bra and a pair of socks are giving me much more cleavage than I actually have. For the record, the socks are clean.

"Here," I say, and he groans, both hands closing around me, cock throbbing. "And here," I murmur into his mouth as we kiss again, unbuttoning the last few buttons on the vest.

His mouth leaves mine as he opens it, traveling to my neck, my shoulder, my collarbone. He slides his hand under one bra strap, twists it around his finger, tugs lightly.

"Like this?" he asks.

"Yes," I whisper, and he pulls the shiny black strap over

my shoulder, onto my arm, and then my nipple is out and he slides his thumb over it, the rough pad skipping along as I arch my back and gasp.

"Jesus," he says, the word half a whisper and half a moan, the fingers of his other hand already under my other bra strap. "And like this?"

I can only nod, and then he has both my breasts in his hands and he's pressing himself into me, groaning, and he's pinching my nipples between his fingers and his very hard cock is rubbing against me, finding my clit even through layers of fabric.

He kisses me again and this time I moan into his mouth, wrapping my legs around him, sliding my hands under his shirt and along the warm, rigid muscles of his torso.

"And you want me to touch you like this?" he rasps, the organ music still soaring, his fingers pinching my nipples, rolling them as he bucks against me.

"Please," is all I can say.

"What else, Thalia?" he asks.

"Can I touch you?" I ask, already touching him, my hands under his shirt, fingers skimming along the waistband of his jeans, and Caleb grins.

"Always," he says, thumbs sliding over my nipples, sending a spasm through my body. "Thalia, you can touch me whenever and wherever you want. My body is yours to plunder."

"Plunder?" I ask. "Are you sure?"

"Do your worst," he says, and slowly, carefully, I slide the flat of my hand along the length of his clothed erection as he groans.

His head finds my shoulder and his hands find my thighs, clamped around them and he pushes himself into me and groans again like he's lost.

So I do it again, and then again, and I'm definitely not a dick expert but I think we might be working with a lot here.

I expect the thought to make me anxious, given my virginal status.

It does not, so I pull on the button of his jeans until it pops open.

Before I can grab his zipper, his hand catches my wrist.

"I thought you were mine to plunder," I say.

"I am," he says, and slides his hands up my thighs, palms skipping and catching on the fishnet. "But I also believe in chivalry, and most particularly in ladies coming first."

With that he grabs the waistband of my shorts, pulls me off the bannister, lowers his mouth to mine.

"Can I make you come?" he asks, fingers already dipping below my waistband, teasing at the elastic of my thong. "Please?"

"Yes," I whisper, and almost instantly I'm undone and he slides his hand past the garter belt that Margaret got me a discount on, under my thong and then his fingers are exploring me, his mouth on mine, his other hand thumbing my nipple.

"You're wet as hell," he whispers, catching my lip between his teeth. "Thalia, you're so —"

His fingers glide over my clit, and my whole body jolts.

"Turned on?" I whisper, an arm around his shoulders like he's a life raft.

"Fuckable," he says.

Suddenly, it occurs to me that he's missing an important piece of relevant information, even as he strums my clit again and my back arches, my arm tightening around his shoulder, the bannister behind me.

"Caleb," I murmur, and I'm met with a growl from somewhere deep in his chest, his fingers speeding up.

It takes all my presence of mind to grab his wrist, but I do.

"Wait," I say.

"You all right?" he asks, going perfectly still.

"I have to tell you something. I'm a virgin," I say, getting it all out in one breath.

Caleb just looks at me for a long moment. He studies my face like I'm a math problem, the solution slowly falling into place.

"By philosophy or happenstance?" he asks.

I'm still holding his wrist, his fingers still in my shorts, between my slick folds.

"Happenstance," I say.

"Do you want to stop?"

"No!" I say, then clear my throat, release his hand. "No. It just seemed like…"

His fingers start moving again, and I bite my lip mid-sentence, eyes sliding shut.

"Relevant information," I force myself to say.

"It doesn't change my plans, if that's what you mean," he says, and pulls me away from the bannister, pushes me toward the ascending staircase. "I've thought about this at least once a day for two months, and it was usually with one hand on my cock."

With that he lowers me to the stairs and then he's on top of me, my legs around him, and he strokes my clit and kisses me hard and just as I'm getting close to the edge, breath coming in gasps, he stops stroking me and slides his hand down further until his fingers are between my lips, teasing my entrance.

"Yes," I gasp, not waiting to be asked.

He plunges his fingers into me, all the way to the

knuckle, and he crooks them forward and tugs my shorts down with his other hand and then massages my clit with his thumb, in perfect time with his fingers, and every stroke brings me closer and closer and closer to the edge until finally, I lose control.

His forehead is against mine, our faces together, and I've got one elbow under me the other in his hair and I'm pretty sure I'm whimpering *oh fuck yes* over and over again, because other words escape me.

I've never come like this before. I've had plenty of orgasms — my best friend works for a sex shop, where she teaches a class called *The Art of Self-Pleasure*, so I'm more than aware of how to get myself off — but never one like this.

No one else has ever made me come. I've never *needed* it like this, to the exclusion of anything else. I've never come and still wanted more, still wanted to tear another person's clothes off and beg them to fuck me, right here on this staircase.

"Holy shit," Caleb whispers, his thumb skipping past my clit one last time, my whole body jolting. "That was beautiful."

I'm still lying back on the stairs, trying to catch my breath and Caleb pulls his fingers out of me, pushes my legs apart, climbs on top of me. I reach down and find the undone button on his jeans, acutely aware that he's still hard as a rock and that despite what just happened, I *want* him.

And then, just as I find his cock, the organ music stops. I wrap my fingers around him and he groans softly, his hips driving forward, pushing his long, thick shaft through my hand.

"Sank you all very much!" the organist suddenly

declares, his words floating down from the top of the stairs. "And may the rest of your All Hallow's Eve be... *delightful.*"

With that, steps cross the ceiling above us, creaking along the old wood and instantly, Caleb and I realize the exact same thing.

This is the staircase to the organ.

We're about to get caught.

Caleb leaps up, grabs my hand, pulls me to standing as I'm already putting my shorts back into place, zipping them, and stuffing my boobs back into my bra. I grab my jacket from the floor just as the top step creaks, and then Caleb's opening the door and we're out in the foyer in the middle of a flood of undergrads, all leaving Scarborough Hall at the same time.

We just got caught, I think, my heart nearly exploding in my chest.

Oh God, we fooled around once and instantly got caught.

But I look around. I glance over at Caleb who's standing there, rigid, affecting a casual pose that doesn't convince me at all, and I realize: I don't see anyone I know.

Seconds later, the door behind us swings open and the organist comes out, read cape swishing behind him. Caleb nods at him, and he nods back, and I start to relax because even though we did the dumbest possible thing, we didn't get caught.

I take a deep breath. We didn't get caught. I look over at Caleb, who's looking at me, and I button my vest and pull my jacket on and sidle over to him, his face still flushed, his eyes still bright.

"Take me home?" I murmur.

Before he can answer, I hear my name.

"Thalia!" Margaret shouts and I glance toward the crowd of people, my heart sinking. I step away from Caleb, anxiety swirling in my chest, and then the three of them come through the crowd one at a time.

"There you are!" Harper is saying, dodging a guy wearing a cardboard robot suit. "I was afraid you were..."

Margaret and Victoria are already standing there, silently looking at me, then at Caleb, then back at me.

"*Oh*," Harper says, and that's all. The hum of people talking and shouting and laughing rises around us, but none of the five of us say anything for a long, long moment.

I'm positive that what I just did is written all over my face. I'm positive that my three best friends can guess, probably almost verbatim, what just happened and with whom.

"You ready to go home?" Margaret asks pointedly, shooting a glance at Caleb.

"Yep!" I say, about ten times too excitedly. "Sounds great! Let's do it!"

Victoria says nothing, but I know the press of her lips, even the disapproving cock of her hips in her half-football-half-fairy outfit.

I don't want to go with them. I want to go home with Caleb and I'm pretty sure I want to ride him like a race horse, but what choice do I have?

I can't tell them *sorry, I gotta go bang my professor*.

I glance over at Caleb, catch his eye. He nods, ever so slightly. There's a half smile and then Margaret clears her throat *very* obnoxiously and I turn away and follow them out of Scarborough Hall.

The entire way home they talk about how bummed they are to graduate and how *still*, no one has guessed my Halloween costume, and how they have so much homework to do tomorrow because they got nothing done today.

And I walk and chat and I'm half afterglowy and half

cold because I love my friends but I'd rather be elsewhere, with someone else.

Someone who I didn't even manage to give a handjob to.

It's something I've never felt guilty about before, but I guess it's a fun new experience.

CHAPTER TWENTY-EIGHT
CALEB

I jerk off twice when I get home. I don't think I've done that since I was sixteen, but I lay on my bed with the lights off and I can't stop thinking about Thalia, about the noises she made when I rolled her nipples between my fingers, or about the way her hips bucked when I found her clit, or about the way her eyes rolled shut and she moaned when I sunk my fingers knuckle-deep inside her.

I come hard, just thinking about it. Then I think about it ten minutes later and take care of that, too, because apparently she's made me a teenager again.

But even after that, I can't sleep. I can only lie awake, looking at the popcorn ceiling that I'd like to redo, thoughts of Thalia and transgressions swirling in my head.

I think, black-hearted, *oh God, what have I done?*

I think, *I'd do it again in a heartbeat. Half a heartbeat.*

I wonder if her friends are going to turn us in and I wonder if anyone else saw us and I wonder if we can possibly keep this up without getting caught.

I wonder if it matters that she's a virgin. I wonder if it matters that I'm not. I wonder what she's done and I wonder with whom and I think about what I've done and with whom, and I wonder if I should tell her that our encounter on the stairs might be the peak sexual experience of my life.

Finally, hours after getting in bed, I go to sleep.

· · · * * ★ * * · · · ·

"Okay, but — hear me out, dammit June don't even open your mouth, you don't know what I'm going to say — a drone is the ring-bearer."

My soon-to-be-sister-in-law stares at her brother with an expression so stone-faced I start to worry.

Finally, she lifts her drink to her mouth, still regarding her older brother with a mix of wariness, contempt, and plain bafflement.

"Who's piloting the drone in this scenario?" she asks.

Silas just shrugs.

"Nope, wrong answer," June says. "You can't just come up with these half-baked ideas and then not have thought them through. You want a drone ring-bearer? You tell me who's piloting that shit. You tell me their skill level and you tell me who's catching it and you tell me who's troubleshooting this mess and you tell me *who is bandaging up Grandma Enid when the drone inevitably hits her* and then, maybe then, I will consider your moronic idea."

"Are you still trying to weasel your way into the wedding party?" I ask Silas, taking a sip of my iced tea.

Silas puts one hand on his chest and tries to look hurt and offended.

"I would never," he says solemnly.

June just rolls her eyes.

"I was trying to weasel a drone into their wedding party," he says. "It's completely different."

"You want to know a secret?" I ask, sidling closer to Silas.

He lifts both his eyebrows.

"Levi told me Hedwig is his best man," I say, keeping my voice low. "Saves him the agony of having to choose a human, you know?"

I probably shouldn't be baiting poor Silas, but I'll do anything to get my mind off the fact that I had sex with a student last night.

Even though it's not working at all. Even though the knowledge of what I did feels like a boulder on my chest.

It's unconscionable. Even if it wasn't technically intercourse, there's no mistaking that what we did last night was anything but sex.

If I were someone else, I'd be appalled, no matter what. It's an abuse of trust and it's an abuse of power and even though it doesn't feel at all like any of those things, it feels like I've met someone who lights up every room she walks into and makes me want to believe in magic, that's the cold hard truth.

It's wrong, and I know it's wrong, and now I feel awful about myself, and I don't know how to walk into class tomorrow and look at Thalia, so I'm hassling Silas and June instead.

"I don't believe you," Silas informs me. "Though I almost do, because Levi would do that. But I don't."

"It's kind of a good idea," June says, thoughtfully. "All you assholes can just sit in the front row and chill. Hedwig's a very good dog, and you've still got two more weddings to fight over, probably."

"No, *he* has two more to fight over," Silas says, pointing at me. "Well, he's got one because the other is his wedding —"

"I'm getting married?" I ask, and even though I'm

kidding and I know what it means, the thought sends an odd ripple through me.

They both ignore me.

" — But for me? This is my one shot," Silas finishes.

June, his little sister, is marrying my oldest brother Levi. Levi is also Silas's best friend, and he's also the entire reason they still haven't picked wedding parties for a wedding that's just months away.

Does he stand on Levi's side, as his lifelong closest friend?

Does he stand on June's side, as her brother?

He can't do both, and not being in either wedding party seems so wrong that it's unconscionable. In the meantime, the rest of us have quietly decided that the suits we wore to Daniel and Eli's weddings will do nicely for groomsmen suits when we're inevitably asked two weeks before the wedding.

"Besides, I would make *such* a good toast," he goes on.

"We already asked you to make a toast," June says. "Don't make me regret giving you a microphone in front of everyone we know."

Silas just grins.

"Remember that time when you were thirteen, and you wanted to impress that guy you had a crush on, so —"

"Dinner!" Eli shouts, pushing open the back door.

"Thanks!" shouts back June.

Then she turns to Silas.

"You think I won't kill you at my own wedding," she says. "I will."

· · · · · ★ ★ ★ · · · · ·

AFTER DINNER AND DESSERT, I help Seth and Violet clear the dining room and do the dishes, and then I tell them that I'm going to check the back porch for more glasses and plates, just in case, and I head back outside.

There aren't any glasses or plates out here. I knew there weren't, but I have the world's nosiest family. I love them, but I'm not sure they've ever once respected someone's desire to be alone with his thoughts.

Somehow, astonishingly, I get a full seven minutes before the door opens and footsteps cross the deck toward me. Seven minutes of staring out at my mom's backyard, half thinking about how next time I'm here I should rake the yard and clean out the gutters for her, half thinking about last night and Thalia and how I haven't even texted her today even though I've thought about her every three-point-four seconds.

I don't know if I can text her, or at least, I don't know if I should. Can the school administration find that? I know they can track the emails we send from school accounts, but my phone has nothing to do with the school, right?

I'm hyper-aware, hyper-alert, more on edge than I've ever been.

Breaking the rules and keeping a secret is so, so much harder than I thought it would be. I don't even know whether to text a girl.

"What's wrong?" my mom's voice says, and I look over in surprise because I assumed it was Seth, coming out here to badger me.

I sigh.

"Nothing," I tell her.

"Caleb," she says, in the same tone she always uses when she knows I'm lying to her.

"Mom," I mimic back.

"Don't get sassy with me," she teases. "Come on. Seth mentioned Delilah *twice* during dinner and you didn't even react."

"That's because he's none of my business," I say, raising the dregs of my iced tea to my lips. "If he thinks befriending Satan is a good idea, that's on him."

She laughs, resting her forearms on the deck railing, looking out at the backyard with me.

"I did something I really shouldn't have and now I feel shitty," I finally say.

"What did you do?"

"I don't want to say."

My mom gives a long-suffering sigh, still looking out at the forest.

"How bad?" she asks. "Am I gonna want to call the cops?"

I roll my glass slowly between my hands and consider the question.

On the one hand, Thalia's a consenting adult, so I've done nothing illegal.

On the other, it's ethically murky at best, and my mom is both a college professor herself and an ardent feminist, so there's no way she'd take this well.

"Maybe not the cops, but you'd want to call someone," I tell her.

"Lord," she says, mostly to herself. "You know, once upon a time I thought that if I kept the five of you alive until you hit eighteen I'd be done with parenting? I was an idiot."

I just laugh, and she does too.

"Some people believe sharing your secrets cleanses the heart and mends the soul," she offers, and now I frown at her.

"You don't," I say. "Clearly."

"No," she agrees. "I think that white lies are the only thing standing between polite society and utter barbarism."

"And also regular lies," I point out, without venom.

We've had some version of this conversation a thousand times in the past ten years. She knows where I stand and I know where she stands, and it's been a long time since either of us got angry about it.

"I still wish you'd never found out," she says.

"Me too."

"Doing a bad thing doesn't make you a bad person," she says, after a moment. "Neither does choosing the wrong thing. It just makes you human."

I swallow, staring forward into the late-autumn night.

"But what are we, if we're not the sum of our actions?" I ask, not expecting an answer. "What else even matters?"

"Intentions," my mom says, thoughtfully. "Hopes. Feelings. Thoughts. Desires. All those things matter. If they didn't, we'd never forgive people who made mistakes."

"Have you forgiven Dad?"

The question hangs in the air for a moment. For all we've talked about this, I've never asked about forgiveness before.

"No," she says, simply. "I haven't and I'm probably going to be angry with him until the day I die, which doesn't mean I don't feel other ways, but I'm pretty sure that one's here to stay."

"Oh," I say, a little surprised at her honesty.

"Just because it's a virtue doesn't mean I can bring myself to do it," she says, shrugging. "He robbed me of a husband, and a partner, and he robbed you of a father, and I *really* could have used some help around here. God, if someone else could have picked Daniel up from the police station once in a while it would've been huge."

I snort, because the man currently holding a sleeping baby inside raised some serious hell as a teenager.

"I think I'm close to it," I say, surprising myself. "Forgiveness, not picking Daniel up from the police station."

"If he got hauled down there now, he'd have Charlie to reckon with," my mom says.

"I don't know which is worse."

"What about your brothers?" she asks, back to the topic at hand.

"I never told them," I remind her. "You know that. They don't know there's anything to forgive."

She taps her fingertips together, still leaning over the railing, then cocks her head at me.

"And you're really not going to tell me what this bad thing you did was?"

I consider it. For half a second, I consider it, but there's no way.

"I'm really not," I confirm. "You'd hate it, and I'm pretty sure I'm going to do it again."

"That's not like you."

"I know."

"Still," she says slowly, thinking, watching the dark back yard and the forest beyond. "It's better to do a bad thing with intention than slide into it half-assed. Own your actions and then, when the shit hits the fan, own up to them."

I almost ask her if that's what she wishes Dad had done, but it's a moot point because he never got the chance. Maybe if he'd owned his actions he'd still be here, but that's a long road with too many *what if's*.

"Language," I tease her instead, and she just sighs.

"It's the one downside of having grandchildren," she says, straightening, both her hands going to her lower back. "Are you spending the night or heading back?"

"Heading back," I say, holding up my glass. "It's iced tea."

"I know," she says, then nods her head for the back door. "Come on, I made pie."

When I get home that night, I go straight for the pile of graded quizzes in a neat stack on my kitchen table. I flip through them.

I find Thalia's and pull it from the stack.

I spent dessert holding Thomas with one hand and eating pie with the other, since I offered to hold him while Charlie ate, and he promptly fell asleep on me.

Then I spent the entire drive back thinking about what my mom said, about owning your actions. About choosing the wrong course of action with open eyes.

And I think about what I said to her, something that I hadn't even thought about yet: *I'm pretty sure I'm going to do it again.*

Open eyes.

I grab a red pen and, before I can change my mind, write on Thalia's quiz in neat block letters.

Then I put it back into the stack and go to bed.

CHAPTER TWENTY-NINE
THALIA

Sunday morning, I wake up at seven a.m. and I'm at the library by eight, leaving my apartment before any of my roommates get up and make eye contact with me.

It's the coward's way out, but I'm fine with it. I'll be a coward all day long if it means I get to skip confronting what happened last night, or, more accurately, confronting the fact that my roommates know what happened last night.

If I hide out in the library, I'm free to pretend they don't know. I can pretend that they're never going to confront me, never going to ask me what the *fuck* I think I'm doing and whether I know it's wrong and whether I shouldn't report Caleb for being a dirty old pervert and whether he's a terrible, terrible person for wanting me.

I don't think he is. Maybe I'm naïve. Maybe I'm stupid for thinking that I'm special. Maybe he's got a revolving door of young, easily duped students who he seduces for a semester and then discards.

But I doubt it.

I'm at the library all day. Every time my phone buzzes,

I scramble to look at it, thinking that it's either my friends or Caleb, but none of them texts me at all. The only person who does is Bastien, asking me if I have any idea where my high school copy of *Moby Dick* might have wound up.

I do not.

Meanwhile, I work on graduate school applications with the fire of a thousand suns. I ruthlessly edit my personal statement. I format my resume. I email psych departments up and down the east coast to double-check that VSU has, in fact, sent them my official transcript.

To hear my applications tell it, I was born with a passion for neuroscience. I was reading psych journals while I was still in diapers and asking my kindergarten teacher about the latest in experimental PTSD therapy.

It's not all that far from the truth. I'm a Navy brat, and while I think my own father is one of the lucky ones who escaped that kind of psychological damage, I was surrounded by it.

And then, of course, there was Javier. I write and delete and re-write and re-delete a paragraph about him over and over again, because I don't know what I should say and I don't know whether I should say it in a graduate school application.

I grapple with that. I look at my planner and wonder when I'm supposed to do everything that I'm supposed to be doing. I stare at the wall in the Absolute Quiet room and my mind floats back to last night, and before I know it I'm having dirty fantasies in the library.

When I finally go home that night, Margaret and Harper are both there, and they each give me a *look* but thankfully, they don't say anything.

· · · · ★ ★ ★ ★ ★ · · · ·

THE HOOKUP EQUATION

PLEASE SEE ME AFTER CLASS.

I don't like those words. I've never once read them and thought, yay! I get to talk to a teacher after class! I'm sure they have some positive news for me!

Admittedly, I don't see them a lot. Teachers rarely ask to see straight-A students after class.

I glance over at Caleb, his back to me as he hands back the last few quizzes, and I think for at least the thousandth time about his mouth on mine in the dark, the way he groaned when I touched him.

I'm yours to plunder.

I uncross and re-cross my legs under my desk, desperately trying to quell the heat there and focus on the matter at hand.

It makes for a very, very long fifty minutes, but finally, it's over. I took four pages of notes but to be honest, I have no idea what today's lecture was about. For all I know he told us about his favorite Disney Princesses for an hour, though I seem to have written down lots of numbers, so it was probably math.

The other students leave. I hang back, putting my stuff into my bag as slowly as I can, trying to ensure that I'm casually the last one in line to speak with Professor Loveless as he goes over a particularly thorny problem from last week's quiz. I half-listen, because it was the problem I lost points on, but I'm too distracted.

Then, finally, they leave and it's my turn. I walk up to the lectern, heart kicking in my chest because I don't know what he's going to say and I don't know what I'm going to say, but I'm pretty sure it's not going to be about calculus.

Please don't say we can't see each other again, I think. *We tried that and it didn't work.*

"Hi," I say.

"Hi," he says, and he smiles.

Then he takes his glasses off, looks at them, folds them in one hand.

"Can you see without those?" I blurt out.

"Pretty well," he answers, shrugging. "My eyesight actually isn't too bad, I just think they make me look smart."

"Right, your Dr. Loveless costume," I say, and he laughs.

"Not a costume," he says, putting them down on the lectern.

Then he looks at me, and I feel like his emerald eyes can see all the way to the bottom of my soul.

"I fucked up," he says, his voice low and soft. "What happened Saturday night never should have, and I broke basically every ethical guideline pertaining to student-teacher relationships."

I feel like a balloon, slowly deflating.

"It was wrong," he goes on. "No two ways about it, Thalia, what we did was wrong as hell and if I had a lick of sense I'd never so much look in your direction again and pray you didn't feel like going to the ethics committee."

I'm not deflating any more.

"Is that why you asked to talk to me?" I ask, my voice matching his, soft and low. "To tell me how badly we fucked up and swear you'll never look at me again?"

"It's not," he says. "It's to ask what you're doing Friday and whether you'd like to come over for dinner."

He leans forward, his elbows on the lectern, his folded glasses in one hand.

"Just the two of us," he says. "With locked doors and a couch in the living room and a bedroom upstairs and tiramisu for dessert."

"Yes," I say, then swallow hard and take a deep breath. "Yes. I'd like that."

"Good," he says, and then studies my face, a smile

tugging at his lips. "I'd kiss you now if I thought I could get away with it."

As if on cue, a student for the next class walks into the classroom and sits at a desk.

"I'll pretend," I say, and then we walk out of the classroom and somehow, we manage to make normal conversation and then we part ways.

Friday can't come fast enough.

CHAPTER THIRTY
CALEB

I love research. I have a Ph.D. and work in academia; of course I love research. I love discovering information. I love digging deep into a topic I know nothing about. I love the way learning is its own reward. I love feeling prepared for every situation.

That said, I don't recommend Googling *first-time intercourse with a well-endowed man* without Safe Search turned on. Most of what comes up isn't educational in the least.

The last time I had sex with a virgin, I was sixteen. She was also sixteen. We were in her childhood bedroom while her parents were away for the weekend and inexplicably trusted her to stay home alone, and we did *not* know what we were doing. It's probably a minor miracle that we managed to fit Tab A into Slot B at all, and an even bigger miracle that we enjoyed it.

In terms of logistics, I don't know whether it matters that Thalia's a virgin, but it seems like I should prepare for a range of possibilities. I go a little insane and buy seven different kinds of personal lubricant, then pay for fast shipping. I take notes from one of the few helpful articles I find — go slow, make sure she's turned on, let her be on top so she can control speed and depth — and put them in my bedside drawer, just in case I need a handy, bullet-pointed reference sheet.

But beyond logistics, I don't care that she's a virgin. I see her face practically every time I close my eyes. Every time my mind wanders, it wanders to the sound she made when I slid two fingers into her, the way she arched her back. I want her beyond all reason and sanity.

Whether I'm her first lover or her fiftieth doesn't really matter to me.

· · · ★ ★ ★ ★ ★ · · · ·

THERE HAS NEVER BEEN A LONGER week in the history of time. Pointless meetings have never dragged on more. My office hours have never gone slower, and since it's shortly after midterms, every student who still hasn't grasped basic integration is there, panicking right into my face.

Then, at last, it's Thursday, and I walk home from campus while the sun is still up, for once, and then I drive to the fancy grocery store across town. That night I'm up past midnight layering tiramisu and texting an annoyed Eli for tips.

He doesn't ask why I'm making tiramisu, and I don't volunteer that information. It probably means that Seth has accidentally spilled his suspicions, and while that's annoying, I can't blame him. Keeping secrets from brothers who know you have them is basically impossible.

Friday comes. She's in class just like always, sitting in the seat in the last row that's become 'her' seat, listening attentively and taking notes, tapping her pen between her fingers the same way she always does. Leaning forward on her elbows, focusing on the blackboard, like she always does.

I, on the other hand, call an asymptote an arachnid and write the quadratic equation wrong on the board. I don't even notice that I write it wrong. A student has to point it out. It's not my finest classroom moment, but I survive it, even if I can barely think about calculus.

She doesn't say anything when she leaves. I consider asking to talk to her after class, just because I want to see her up close and hear her voice, but I don't. I don't want to raise suspicions.

When she leaves, she catches my eye, and she nods. Almost imperceptibly, but she does and my heart growls and sputters like a twenty-year-old car, and then she's gone and I realize that a sophomore is asking me a detailed question about the homework and I missed the first half of it.

· · · * * ★ * * · · ·

When I get the email, I'm standing in my kitchen, a notebook in my hand, a recipe pulled up on my phone, trying to take stock of my situation. It's six o'clock, so Thalia is due in two hours, and I admit I'm feeling a little lost.

I'm also feeling like an idiot for taking Eli's advice about what to make, because the more I read this recipe, the more I realize that each steps has sub-steps and timing that needs to work out properly. Of course he recommended this as an easy recipe, he's a goddamn chef. He could probably do this with his eyes closed.

I, however, cannot. I'm a perfectly adequate cook but I don't think I've ever impressed anyone.

I'm reading the recipe yet again when my phone

vibrates in my hand and an email slides in from the top of the screen.

The pit of my stomach goes cold before I even read the subject line. All it takes is the email address it's from.

From: secretknower@gmail.com
To: clloveless@mathematics.vsu.edu
Subject: I know

You're morally bankrupt.

That's all. Those three words. I stare at them until my phone screen dims and then goes black of its own accord, and I slowly put it back into my pocket.

Morally bankrupt?

Seriously?

Sex traffickers are morally bankrupt. People who take money meant for charity and buy themselves private jets are morally bankrupt.

I might argue that anyone who knowingly gets in the "15 items or less" line at the grocery store and *knows* they have twice that many is morally bankrupt, but I'd be willing to hear alternate takes on that one.

Even though it's silly and over-the-top, the email rattles me. It's not the charge of being morally bankrupt that does it — is dating Thalia against the rules? Yes. *Morally bankrupt?* No — it's the fact that someone knows, and that someone is clearly not happy about this.

But on the other hand, that someone hasn't reported us to VSU administration. They haven't even told Gerald, my department chair about it. They're just sending me emails about my qualities as a person. They're not even making threats.

And it's not like I thought I was making an ethically

defensible choice. I'm doing the wrong thing with my eyes wide open.

Fuck it.

I pull my phone out, ignore the email, and get back to the recipe that I should have started at least thirty minutes ago.

CHAPTER THIRTY-ONE
THALIA

I triple-check the address before I walk up the short path to the front door, even though I'm pretty sure I recognize the car in the driveway as Caleb's. I mean, I didn't memorize his license plate number or anything, but it's a silver hatchback at the address he gave me, so I'm probably in the right place.

As I walk I take the bottle of wine out of the black plastic bag it came in and shove the bag into my purse, alongside my toothbrush, a change of clothes, and a handful of condoms. My boots click on the flagstones, the porch light on, revealing a welcome mat at the top of a few brick stairs.

I take a deep breath before I ascend, because I'm nervous. I'm nervous that someone's seen me walking here. I'm nervous that I'll knock on the door and Caleb will tell me he was just kidding about this.

I'm nervous that I'll say something dumb and make him not like me any more, that he'll realize I'm not actually that interesting, that I'll be bad at sex.

I've spent twenty-two years being the good girl, who got

the good grades, who joined the right sports teams, who did the after school activities and had the right friends and won the accolades and made her parents proud.

They would not be proud of me right now. My father would be furious and my mother would *strongly* not approve of me losing my virginity to my math professor who I'm not even technically dating, I guess, let alone engaged or married to.

I love my mom. I think she's an amazing woman. But she's a hundred percent positive that all men have a *why buy the cow* philosophy, while I prefer to imagine that my worth as a person and potential partner doesn't reside entirely in my hymen.

Anyway, I knock on the door, gripping the wine bottle by the neck.

There's no response. I wait, patiently. I check the time on my phone. It's five 'til eight, so maybe he's in the shower, or maybe he's still getting dressed, or doing something else that prevents his answering the door.

Or it's not his house because you somehow got the address wrong, and this is about to get awkward.

I wait a full minute before I knock again, and this time the door opens practically under my fist and then Caleb is standing there, in gray sweatpants and a black shirt with flour all over it and a smear of something on his cheek.

"Sorry," he says, and he smiles that smile he has, the one that's charming and sheepish and rakish all at once, and my heart goes *thadunk* and I can't help but smile back.

"It's my fault, I'm early," I say, and hold out the bottle of wine. "Thanks for having me."

"I haven't yet," he says, lifting an eyebrow, and I laugh, my anxiety dissolving because this isn't some high-stakes drama about a scholarship student having a torrid affair with her professor, it's just Caleb and I being us, together.

"Take the wine and don't be saucy," I tell him.

"You look nice," he says, taking the bottle from my hand. His eyes drift from my face, down my body, and he doesn't even bother to try and hide it.

"Thanks," I say, casually, as if I didn't spend a full forty-five minutes shoving through my closet over and over again, as if somehow the perfect outfit would magically appear among the jeans, t-shirts, two going-out outfits, and a recent deluge of business-appropriate clothing.

What says *I really want to have sex with you but also have a twenty-minute walk from my place to yours, during which I might well see someone I know?*

What says *I quite enjoyed being fingerbanged on a staircase last weekend and would like a repeat performance, but not in a trashy way?*

Apparently, a deep red knee-length long-sleeved wrap dress and the same high-heeled ankle boots I was wearing the night we met.

"You look covered in flour," I say, and he looks down at himself.

I also look down at him. He's covered in flour but the black shirt is tight across his shoulders and hugs his biceps in a way that makes me feel... things.

That's not even mentioning the sweatpants. If you'd asked me before this moment whether I like men in sweatpants I'd have give you a resounding *ew, no*.

But now, I've seen Caleb in sweatpants. They hug his hips enticingly. They skim his thighs attractively.

And there's a bulge.

A notable one. My thoughts turn NC-17.

"It turns out I have terrible kitchen time management skills," he says. "I meant to put on real clothes half an hour ago. Here, come in."

"Don't worry, it's just me," I say, stepping in as he closes the door behind me.

"Just?" he says, then leans in and kisses me.

His fingertips just barely brush my face, and after a long moment, he pulls back.

"I don't want to get flour on you," he says, apologetically.

"This dress is washable," I tease, running one hand over his shoulder.

"Are you asking me to get you dirty, Thalia?" he asks, pressing his lips to mine without waiting for an answer, and this time his body follows suit, his heat melding to my skin from chest to knee.

And the bulge. Sweet Jesus, the bulge. I never want Caleb to wear anything but sweatpants again, because I can feel practically every ridge and curve, every hardening inch—

"I did promise myself one thing about tonight," he says, his free hand skimming my hip, his lips brushing mine as he talks.

"Only one?" I ask.

He puts the pad of his index finger in the hollow of my throat, then drags it slowly downward, over my chest, until it hits the V of my dress.

"I swore up and down that I'd have dinner before dessert," he says.

"What's for dessert?" I ask, as innocently as I can. "Pie? Ice cream?"

"It's a euphemism, Thalia," he says, laughing softly. "You're dessert. Obviously."

"How subtle," I tease.

"I was trying to be classy."

"In a flour-covered shirt and *those* sweatpants?"

"I told you, I meant to change before you got here," he

says, and kisses me again.

Then, after a beat, he pulls away.

"What's wrong with these sweatpants?" he asks, suddenly suspicious.

I can feel myself color instantly.

"They're sweatpants," I say. "That's all."

"No, you said *these* sweatpants," Caleb says, eyes narrowing. "Spill it, Thalia. Do you not like gray? Is there an enormous mustard stain on the back?"

"Have you looked at yourself in a mirror?" I ask.

"No," he says, still suspicious.

"They're obscene," I tell him.

Just then, there's a loud, repeated beep from further inside the house, and Caleb grins his most rakish grin down at me.

"I've gotta go get dinner from the oven," he says, dropping a quick kiss on my lips. "You're welcome to come along if you can handle the obscenity."

"I'll try," I answer, and he leads me into the kitchen.

I also note that the sweatpants highlight his ass in a way I never would have predicted.

Sweatpants. Who knew?

We walk down a short hallway, over creaking wood floors, and take a left into the kitchen.

It smells *incredible*. It's also a mess, which does explain Caleb's current state.

Every burner on the stove has a dirty pan on it, the scent of browned meat hanging in the air. There are two separate chopping boards on different parts of the counter top, one covered in flour and one strewn with discarded vegetable parts. There's also a food processor, a colander, mixing bowls, a roll of aluminum foil, a couple of empty plastic clamshells, and a spilled bag of pistachios.

All the way at the end of the kitchen, alone on the

table, is a square brownie pan with something in it.

Caleb grabs two hot mitts, then flips his oven light on and peers in.

"*Golden brown* is so subjective," he says, staring intently.

"Baking's an art, not a science," I say, walking behind him, toward the brownie pan.

"Baking is essentially chemistry, which absolutely makes it a science," he counters. "At the very least, each recipe should give you a color chart with their definition of golden brown."

I walk back, crouch next to him. In the oven are two things that look a little like pizza, but clearly aren't.

"That's golden brown," I say, with somewhat more authority than I feel.

"All right," he says, and we both stand as he opens the oven, pulls the baking sheet out. He balances it on top of a pot on his stove, and since I don't want to watch something tragic happen to something that smells so delicious, I investigate whatever's in the brownie pan.

It's not brownies. I looks like some sort of pudding or maybe a cake, with a thick layer of cocoa powder dusted on top.

Experimentally, I reach one finger out and very, very gently touch the powder.

Caleb's hand wraps around my wrist, pushing my fingertip into something white and gooey.

"No stealing," he says, his voice surprisingly close. I look over my shoulder and he's standing over me, his right hand over my right wrist, the length of our arms touching to the shoulder.

"I wasn't stealing until you interfered," I protest. "I was just gathering information."

"Well, now you've put a dent in my perfect tiramisu," he says.

"Call it a sample if it'll make you feel better," I suggest.

"Samples are offered. That was purloined."

His hand is still around my wrist and there's a wicked, teasing smile tugging at the corners of his mouth. He doesn't let go, fingers gritty with flour and crumbs.

"So I'm doing something I shouldn't?" I ask. "Here? Alone with you, at your house?"

He laughs, his voice low and raspy and melodic, and lets my wrist go.

"Touché," he says, leaning one hip against the counter, arms folded over his chest.

I look down at my fingertip, then back up at him.

Slowly, I put it into my mouth and suck it off. It's sweet and tangy, followed by the bitterness of the cocoa powder, and I keep my finger in my mouth longer than I need to.

Caleb's just watching me. As I pull my finger out of my mouth, he swallows, his Adam's apple bobbing up and down.

"Thalia," he says. "You are trouble with a capital T."

"Good trouble or bad trouble?" I ask.

"I thought there was only the one kind."

"I'm bad trouble, then."

"You disagree?"

Caleb steps toward me, anchors his hands on the counter on either side of me, leans in. I'm wearing heels and he's barefoot, and he's still got a good six inches on me.

"I think I'm at least neutral trouble," I say, anticipation prickling down my spine.

There's a swipe of flour on his cheek, so I reach up and brush it off.

"You're the most dangerous kind," he says, in a voice so low I can practically feel it in the soles of my feet. "Bad trouble that feels good."

The bulge makes contact just before his mouth does,

and I summon all my willpower and grab his shirt in my fist instead. He presses me backward, into the counter, and he kisses me harder and I open my mouth under his and he's got one hand in my hair, fingers sifting through it, the other around my ribcage, his thumb stroking the spot just below my bra's underwire.

Tentatively, I put one hand on his chest, over his shirt, and I slide it down, feeling the warm muscles under the fabric as he pushes into me a little harder, the countertop digging into my back.

I think of what he said last time we were like this. *My body is yours.* My breathing's gone erratic as his thumb slides up and over the curve of my lower breast until it finds my nipple, and even through two layers of fabric I inhale sharply, heat twisting through me.

My hands dip under his shirt, wandering, exploring. He runs his thumb over my nipple again, now a stiff nub, and he circles it slowly, his other hand skimming down my body, landing on my thigh.

I kiss him harder, deeper, and he grinds against me, very hard and very big against my lower belly, and I don't mind or panic or wonder what I should do.

I just like it. I like the effect I have on him. I like that he so unabashedly wants me, and he twists my skirt between his fingers, drawing it up and I hook my fingers into the waistband of his sweatpants and I pull at them, ever so slightly.

He groans, softly. He flicks his thumbnail over my stiff nipple and now his palm is against my thigh, moving up, and then he pulls his mouth away from mine as his thumb slides under the elastic of my panties, over my hip.

"How serious were you about dinner before dessert?" I ask, pulling his sweatpants another millimeter lower over the hard muscles of his hips as he rocks against me.

Caleb hooks one finger through my underwear, twisting it, playing.

"I'm willing to reconsider," he teases, his voice raspy.

"And?"

"And my bedroom's upstairs, first door on the left."

He doesn't wait for me to respond, just gives me one more kiss and then releases me, takes my hand in his, and pulls me through the kitchen and into the dark upstairs, then through a door and into a bedroom.

The bed is made. The only light is from a small lamp on one of the two bedside tables, books stacked next to it. The room also has a bookshelf crammed with books, more books stacked on the floor, two dressers, and a shelf with a few plants on it.

It's simple, clean, cozy, a far cry from the dorm rooms and student apartments that my few other experiences have been in. Everything feels at home, like it's exactly where it should be, including me.

The door clicks shut, and I turn just in time to se Caleb pulling his shirt over his head.

At exactly that moment, I realize I've never seen him with his shirt off before. Even in the stairwell he was still dressed — we both were — half-blind and in the dark, exploring each other by touch.

No professor should look like this. It should be illegal to have a Ph.D. *and* a six pack, shoulders that broad, arms that muscled, and an Adonis belt.

That's the pelvic V that points right to the dick. I learned the name in an Art History class I took, but this is the first time it's ever come in useful.

Oh, and the bulge is still there, only now it's less of a bulge and more of a sideways Mt. Everest.

"Ta da," he says, walking toward me. "I forgot to offer you the tour. This is my bedroom. Office is over there."

He jerks one thumb over his shoulder as he closes the distance, my fingers find the tie on my dress.

I pull, slowly.

"Is that going to be on the quiz?" I ask.

He watches my fingers as I pull the bow undone, then release the square knot at its base.

"Quiz?" he echoes after a long pause, stopping midway to where I'm standing, by the bed.

"Dumb joke," I say, and let my dress fall open, pulling the tie loose from around my waist. My heart is pounding and I feel like I can barely breathe, but it's not from nerves or anxiety. I'm not afraid of what's about to happen, not even a little.

I'm just excited, breathless with anticipation. Caleb's staring at me, stopped in his tracks, all his attention utterly focused on me.

It's a powerful feeling, the sensation that right now I could tell him to walk to me on his knees and he'd do it. I push my dress over my shoulders, pull the sleeves off, let it drop to the floor.

"Jesus, you're beautiful," he whispers, still motionless.

He takes one tentative step forward, then another.

"Can I touch you?" he asks, reaching out, curling his fingers around the back of my neck, his thumb across my jaw.

"Please," I whisper back, a shiver snaking through my body, carrying pure heat with it.

"Here?" he asks, sliding a finger under my bra strap, a slight smile tugging at his mouth.

"Yes," I answer.

His hand continues down, over my stiff nipple, sliding down my belly.

"Here?" he rumbles.

"Caleb," I say, stepping forward into him, my hands on

the warm hard flesh of his torso. "Touch me anywhere you want."

With that, his lips crash into mine, needy and powerful, and I'm in his arms so hard I can barely breathe. He touches me and groans, the noise low and deep in his chest, and I slide my hand down and find his erection as it throbs against me and I squeeze him through his pants from tip to root and he pulls away from the kiss, panting, his lips to my ear.

Then my bra is off. I'm still stroking his cock as he pushes me backward, and then I'm against the bed and then I'm on the bed and he's on top of me, between my legs, his erection right against my clit so that every pulse of his hips sends a jolt of pleasure through me. He holds himself up on one elbow and kisses me feverishly and rolls my nipple between his fingers, palming it, pinching.

He shifts, kneels. I lock my legs around his hips and squeeze, and I reach down into his pants and when I grab his cock he presses his face into my neck, biting me softly as he groans. We rock together, our hips bucking in time, my hand stroking him.

Finally, he shifts again, and this time he's upright on his knees, still between my legs as I lie back on the bed, and he hooks one of my knees over his shoulder, turns his head, kisses the inside of my knee.

With his other hand, he skims his thumb over the thin fabric of my panties, his light heat on my lips and clit, the fabric probably soaked through.

"Anywhere?" he says.

"Anywhere," I say, and before the word is out of my mouth he's sliding my panties off, both legs in the air, and then he's pushing me further onto the bed and grinning like he just won the lottery.

Fingers brush my lips, teasing them, pushing them

apart, exploring the length of my slit as Caleb drops a single kiss on my belly, next to my belly button, then another on the curve of my hipbone.

I inhale and just as I do, his tongue finds my clit at the exact same time that his fingers slide inside me.

I make a noise. It's half moan and half grunt and half shout and it's *loud*, and Caleb digs his fingers into the soft flesh of my inner thigh and doesn't slow down.

His tongue circles, flicks, laps, and I don't know what exactly he's doing but it feels incredible, his fingers inside me stroking my sensitive inner wall in the exact same rhythm.

It doesn't take long. With every stroke, soon my whole body is trembling, both hands fisted in his comforter, my back arched, my head to one side as I whimper and moan and say things like *oh my God that feels so good*.

I come hard and fast, my body an unstoppable rush as I shout *oh! oh! oh!* again and again until I regain my senses, panting for breath, in a haze of satiety. Caleb pulls his fingers out and kisses the inside of my thigh again, my hip, my belly. He briefly sucks one nipple into his mouth and swirls his tongue around it, moving my legs around his hips.

"Turns out the answer is *sexy as all hell*," he says, leaning over me, taking my mouth again in a kiss. He tastes like me, but it's not off-putting.

It's actually kind of hot, like I've claimed him.

"What answer?"

"To what you sound like when you come," he says, as if it's obvious. "I told you I wanted to find out the night we first met."

I kiss him harder, my tongue in his mouth. I snake my hand downward, realize he's still wearing pants.

"Get these off," I order.

"I'll need a proper data set of your orgasms, of course,"

he says, standing on his knees, pushing his pants and boxers over his hips, releasing his cock.

Hypothesis confirmed: it's very big.

"And we'll need to control for variables, obviously," he goes on, that rakish smile back on his lips. "It's not as if I can compare the second or third orgasm in a session to the first."

I push myself up on my hands, look up at him as he pulls his pants the rest of the way off, tosses them on the floor behind the bed.

"Caleb," I say, my voice still raspy, sultry. "If you try to get data from a control group I'll kill you."

He leans forward, kisses me. I grab his cock in one hand and stroke it and bite his lip, and just like that the fire inside me reignites.

"Never," he says. "Why, when I've got you?"

We kiss again, and we move together and I pull him against me as hard as I can, and then we're going over and suddenly I'm on top, straddling him, both my hands on his chest and my clit pressed against his cock, already slippery with my wetness as I'm pressed against him.

In the back of my mind, a warning light flashes. I ignore it but for the first time since I got to Caleb's house I hesitate for a split second before flexing my hips again and pressing myself into him.

"You like that?" he asks, a quiet growl.

"Yes," I say, the word escaping me in a breathy whisper as I roll my hips over him again, savoring the pressure and the friction.

I keep ignoring my sudden hesitation. Stupid nerves.

"You're sexy as hell," he says, one hand wandering over my thigh, fingers closing around my hip. "Especially when you're using my cock to get off."

I fold forward, give him a deep, long kiss, keep rocking

and grinding, try my best to ignore the alarm that's slowly getting louder.

I tell myself that Caleb's not taking advantage of me. I tell myself that virginity is a cultural construct at best and a tool of the patriarchy, used to control women, at worst.

I tell myself it doesn't matter and I'm not actually losing anything. Practically speaking, this changes nothing.

"You okay?" Caleb asks, his hand still on my hip.

"Yeah," I say, and take a deep breath. "Do you have any condoms?"

He stretches one arm out, opens the drawer on a bedside table, and grabs a small foil packet and a bottle of lube.

My heart hammers, slamming into my ribcage, and there's a knot in my stomach. Caleb rips the packet open, takes out the condom, tosses the wrapper back onto the bedside table.

Then he looks at my face and stops.

"I'm sorry," I say. "I can't, just — not yet. I'm sorry, I know I just —"

"Don't apologize," he says, pushing himself up on his hands, the condom disappearing somewhere.

"Sorry," I say again, then shake my head. "I mean, I don't — I don't know. It's just…"

It's just *I have no idea what my problem is*, other than at the very last moment I suddenly just couldn't. In the most perfect moment ever, I just couldn't.

I'm gonna die a virgin.

"It's okay," he says, cups my head in his hand, brings my lips to his. "Thalia. It's fine."

I kiss him, and the knot in my stomach unwinds slowly.

"It's not you," I whisper. "I swear."

"I didn't think it was."

"Virginity's not even real," I go on, eyes closed, my

forehead against his. "It's a made up thing, and I doubt I even have a hymen any more, I've ridden bikes and horses, I don't know why…"

"Made up things can still be important," he says, his voice soft. "I get it."

He kisses me deeply, his lips still tasting faintly of me, and I kiss back and after a moment my hips move again, like they've got a mind of their own, gently bucking against him, still pleasure-seeking.

After a moment he pulls back and I can tell he's half-smiling again, even though he's too close to see.

"Can I eat you out again, though?" he asks.

My insides swirl at the thought.

"Please?" he says, and finally, I just nod.

Then he's lying down again and he grabs me, pulls me forward. I yelp and grab the headboard of his bed, surprised at his strength, though I probably shouldn't be. He loops his hands over my thighs, pulls me down to his face.

This time there's no fingers, only tongue. Before he was controlled, steady, but this is fast and hard and furious. In moments I've got my forehead against the wooden headboard of his bed, leaning against it, arching my back as he pulls me in harder and licks me.

I'm moaning. I'm gasping, whimpering, and I put my arms over my head so I don't grab Caleb's hair like I want to.

The only phrase I manage to gasp out is *don't stop*, and I say it over and over again: *don't stop, don't stop, don't stop don't stop don'tstopdon'tstop* and then I'm coming again and it's nothing but a single long moan, shouted into the headboard.

CHAPTER THIRTY-TWO
CALEB

I love watching her. Even from this angle I love seeing the way her chest heaves, the way her back arches. I love the way she sounds, all breathy moaning and gasping, telling me not to stop like there's some possibility I was considering it.

When I'm sure she's done, I stop. She relaxes, slumping against the headboard, drawing a long breath, and I slide out from underneath her, kneel behind her, wrap an arm around her and plant a kiss on the back of her neck.

I'm disappointed, but barely. As much as I admit I've been thinking about watching her while she rides my cock, it's not as if licking her until she comes twice is a step down.

Thalia looks over her shoulder, still kneeling, resting against my headboard, and she smiles.

"You're delicious," I tell her, my chin resting on her shoulder. "I could get addicted to making you come over and over again, you know."

"Oh, no," she deadpans, turning around, still on her knees. "Sounds terrible."

"I wouldn't want to interfere with your studies," I offer as she puts one arm over my shoulder, tilts her face up to mine.

"I can make time for that," she says innocently, and bring her lips to mine.

As she does, her other hand wraps around my cock, and I groan. It's involuntary but it only makes her squeeze harder, stroking me from root to tip.

"You're not the problem," she murmurs, still stroking. "I don't know what it is, but it's not you."

Thalia pushes me backwards until I'm sitting and she's on all fours, kisses me again, and then she's spinning me around and I'm on the edge of the bed and she's standing, her lips on mine and her hand on my cock and then she's kissing my neck, my shoulder, my chest, and then she's on her knees in front of me.

I groan as she takes me in her mouth, one hand still wrapped around the base of my cock, and then she slides her lips down until I hit the back of her mouth and I whisper *oh, fuck* and there's a second when I think I might come on this, the very first stroke.

But I don't and she pulls back, her lips moving down my shaft, and when she reaches the head she flicks her tongue over it and looks up at me, wicked and innocent all at once.

I want to burn the image of Thalia with my cock between her lips into my brain forever. She's beautiful and sweet and seductive all at once, and somehow she's here and she's mine and even if this is dangerous, I don't care.

Then she does it again, and again, and in no time I'm seeing stars and I'm grabbing the bedspread so hard with both hands I'm afraid I might tear it.

"I'm gonna come," I tell her, my voice rough.

She just looks up at me again, and her tongue swirls

around my cock and then she pushes her lips down my shaft one more time and I hit the back of her mouth, warm and wet and tight.

"Thalia —" I manage to growl, but then I'm already coming. She pulls halfway back but then she swallows, her mouth working around me, and she swallows again and I'm coming for her harder than I've ever come before.

When I finish I feel wrung out, half-melted, like I'm floating in space. I lean forward and kiss Thalia, my musky taste still on her lips as she stands.

I pull her to me, still naked, press my face into her belly, lips against her soft skin. She gives a short laugh of surprise, and then I put my arms around her, hold her close.

"You okay?" she asks softly, sounding puzzled.

I can't help but laugh.

"I've never been better, and I mean that literally," I tell her.

"Never?"

"Never," I say, and I mean it. "You're staying the night, aren't you?"

"I brought a toothbrush," she says, running a hand through my hair. "Just in case."

"Just in case?" I tease.

"You weren't a sure thing," she says, laughing. "I didn't know if you'd want me gone right away or what."

I sigh, tighten my grip, and then lean backward. Thalia yelps as she falls on top of me, then rolls off, laughing.

"What, exactly, about me says *wham, bam, thank you, ma'am*?" I ask.

"People have uncharted depths," she points out.

"Those aren't mine."

"All right, fine, I didn't think that," she admits. "I was

pretty sure I'd be staying over but didn't want to jinx it. Happy?"

"Yes," I say, and I kiss her, and I've never meant it more because for the first time since we met, she's not my student and I'm not her professor. She's not the forbidden object of all my most fervent desires, and I'm not the dirty old man who should know better.

She's just Thalia and I'm just me, and the outside world can go fuck itself right now. She's lying here completely naked with her head on my shoulder, black hair fanned around her, the fingers of her left hand unconsciously tapping against my hip.

Even the email from earlier doesn't bother me, not right now. I know I should have told her. If someone knows and thinks I'm morally bankrupt, she should know, but not right now. Right now I'm selfish and I want her to myself, fully here, fully present, not thinking about some anonymous email.

Just then, my stomach rumbles, and Thalia laughs.

"I didn't even ask what's for dinner," she says.

"Too distracted by my obscene sweatpants?" I tease.

She turns her head and looks at me, her cheeks still flushed, a strand of hair stuck to her. I reach over and brush it from her face.

"I'm just saying, maybe don't leave the house in those," she laughs.

"They were less obscene before you showed up."

"Less obscene is still obscene, Caleb."

"Leek, goat cheese, and steak galettes with sesame-dressed snap peas and tiramisu for dessert," I say.

"That's so fancy I don't know what it is," Thalia says, both her eyebrows rising. "Of course you're also some sort of amazing cook. You do triathlons too, don't you? And spend your weekend rescuing puppies from burning buildings?"

"I'm an adequate cook with a brother who's a chef, triathlons sound exhausting, and I've never in my life rescued a puppy," I correct her. "C'mon."

We both sit up, slowly. I gather my discarded clothing, toss it into my hamper, then pull a fresh shirt and jeans from my dresser.

When I turn back to the bed, she's still sitting there, one foot tucked under her, reading a piece of notebook paper. Next to her, the bedside drawer is still open.

It takes me all of two seconds to realize what she's reading.

"I'm not a serial killer," I say.

She looks up at me, brow slightly furrowed.

"Should I have been worried?" she asks, and I just nod at the paper she's holding.

"I did some research," I admit. "And I've always found that the best way for me to truly learn information is to rephrase and summarize it myself, and then I left that there in case I needed a quick refresher."

I'm not making myself sound good, because what kind of weird dork keeps his notes on first-time intercourse in his bedside table, even though they've also memorized it? Me, that's who.

I can't see it from here, but I know that the piece of paper says:

- Lots of lube
- Go slow
- Be sure she's aroused
- Make her come first, it'll help her relax
- Let her be on top so she can control speed, depth, &c.

Thalia flips it over, checks the back to see if there's more writing, then puts it back in the drawer on top of the condoms and lube, then closes it carefully.

"Sorry," she says. "It was still open and… I really like lists?"

"Did you like that one?"

She laughs, stands, grabs her bra and underwear from the floor.

"I did," she says, still laughing, face still flushed. "It's sweet."

I walk over and give her a quick, soft kiss on the mouth.

"Come back in a few days," I tell her. "I'll make a flow chart. Maybe a PowerPoint, too, if you're lucky."

She's still laughing, still naked, head cocked to one side.

"I can't wait to see the clip art," she says.

· · · * * * ★ * * * · · ·

WE HAVE dinner at the kitchen table, then dessert on the living room couch. We each have a glass from the bottle of wine she brought, and while we drink we talk, and talk, and talk.

We talk about nothing: about which Marvel movies are good and which ones are dumb, about which dining hall on campus has the best chicken fingers, about what the weird smell in Hayes Hall could possibly be.

Together, we decide that some enterprising biology student is farming magic mushrooms in the basement, then selling them to other students. It's much more exciting than my real answer, which is *mold, probably*.

We talk about everything: about her brother who's gay and her brother who's missing, about how every time she gets a phone call from her family, she imagines that he's dead. About moving constantly when she was a kid, about her grandparents who immigrated from Mexico to south Texas, about how sometimes people tell her she could pass for a "really tan white girl" and then expect her to think it's a compliment.

We talk about my brothers. I tell her the whole story about Rusty coming to live with Daniel, the story of Eli and Violet almost-eloping, the saga of Seth and Delilah and how much I wish she would just leave town again.

And then, somehow, it's two o'clock in the morning and we've been sitting on the couch with empty wine glasses for three hours, so we leave the dishes for the morning and go upstairs to bed.

* * * * * ★ * * * * * *

Just like that, I'm having an affair with a student.

I hate thinking of it that way. I much prefer to just think of Thalia as my girlfriend who happens to be in a class I'm teaching, but I know that's glossing over the murky truth of the situation.

The truth that it's wrong, even if nothing's ever felt more right. The truth that this is unethical, immoral, reprehensible; the truth that I shouldn't be getting blowjobs from the girl whose papers I grade.

Three days a week, she sits quietly in the back of my class and takes notes. Sometimes, she asks questions. She got an A on the midterm and she gets mostly A's on her weekly quizzes, and it's got nothing to do with the fact that she's naked in my bed several times a week and everything to do with the fact that she's smart and studious.

A week passes, then two. She comes over a few times a week, sometimes for dinner, sometimes not. I learn her body as well as I possibly can: what makes her gasp, moan, what makes her eyes roll closed, what makes her bite her lip and curl her toes.

Technically, she's still a virgin, a fact which throws the entire concept of virginity into question. And technically, I don't care. She knows where the condoms are, and she knows I'll do anything she asks of me.

I also keep getting the emails. Every other day, like clockwork. Always vague. Always one line.

Taking advantage of her like this is wrong.
This is against university guidelines, isn't it?
If you had a shred of decency you'd stop.

Et cetera, et cetera. I still don't tell Thalia. They're squarely aimed at me and my wrongdoings, as if the writer thinks I'm a supervillain with a maiden chained to the tracks.

CHAPTER THIRTY-THREE

THALIA

I lean back in the creaky old wooden chair, stretch my legs in front of me, my arms over my head. It's one of those chairs that doesn't feel so bad when I first sit down, but after a few hours I always feel about seventy. I swear every joint in my body pops when I stand up.

The worst part is that it's the best chair on this floor of the library. I know this because, at one point or another over the past two years, I've sneakily tested out every chair on this floor and taken the best one.

On the desk, my phone buzzes.

Caleb: What are you up to?

I lean further back in the chair, let my head hang down, and smile to myself. Even though I just saw him last night for a date — sex, pizza, and a movie, because it's not like we can go out — for the past hour I've been debating sending this very text.

Me: Finishing up a response paper for my comp lit class.

Me: I swear this class is more work than my actual thesis.
Me: But I'll be done in twenty minutes, if you're asking what I think you are.
Caleb: You're at the library?
Me: Yup.

Well, there's my incentive to type this as fast as humanly possible. I get out of my chair, joints popping, do ten jumping jacks, sit down again, and type like the wind. I'm not completely sure that my opinions on bird imagery in Urrea's work make much sense right now, but this isn't even due for another week, so I can edit later. I just wanted to get it out of the way before I leave tomorrow morning for Thanksgiving break, because I know better than to think I'm going to get much work done while I'm home, particularly since my mom's still in a cast and God knows my father can barely make a peanut butter sandwich.

I'm four and a half pages into a five-page paper when I hear soft footsteps moving through the stacks, so I instinctually hit *save* and then turn.

Moments later, Caleb emerges from between two bookshelves, twenty feet away.

"Are you the only one up here?" he asks, looking around, keeping his voice low in case I'm not.

"If you were anyone else that question would be terrifying," I point out, and he glances over his shoulder, then walks toward me, smiling.

"Good thing it's just me, your dirty old professor," he says.

"You're not old," I tell him as he stands behind my chair, puts his hands on my shoulders.

"Just dirty, then?"

A ripple of excitement splashes through my chest, and I

tilt my head back, look up at him as his thumbs dig into the knots in my shoulders.

It feels *really* good.

It feels even better when he leans down and kisses me, the angle new and a little strange, slow and sensuous.

And public. Even if no one else is here, and I'm pretty sure they're not, this is the most public we've ever been and it sends a thrill spiraling through my whole body.

I reach up, hook one hand over his shoulder, catch his lower lip between my teeth. He responds by taking a hand off my shoulder, skimming it along my throat, then under the sweater and shirt and tank top I'm wearing, under my bra, sliding two fingers around my nipple.

I make a soft, uncontrolled noise into his mouth. My back arches and my hips push back, against the chair, because my body knows what to expect next and it's ready.

"You finish your paper?" he asks, still fondling me softly.

I take a deep breath and try to focus.

"Yes," I lie.

Surely I can write one single conclusion while I'm at home, right?

"Good," he says, growly, gravelly, his voice traveling straight to my core. "Because I just realized how long it's going to be until I see you again."

"It's four days," I tease.

"I know," he says, mock-seriously. "Ninety-six whole hours."

"You did that math fast."

"How unexpected."

He kisses me again, then releases me. I shove all my stuff into my bag, put on my jacket, sling the bag over my shoulder. Caleb takes my hand as we walk through the dark stacks toward the elevators and my heart skips a beat even though there's no one around.

On the elevator he leans against the wall, grabs my hands, pulls me in and we make out slowly, teasingly, one of my hands underneath his jacket and shirt. When the elevator dings I pull away, but he keeps my hand in his, and we walk to his car like that: sweetly, dangerously, even though campus is practically a ghost town.

Then, when we're in the car he says, "I should tell you something."

"If you're married, I'll kill you," I say, the first thing that pops into my head, and I instantly shut my eyes and make a face. "I'm sorry. That was nonsense. I'd kill you, though."

He releases the parking brake, pulls away from the curb.

"I'm not married," he says. "I mean, I think."

"Not funny."

"That was kinda funny," he says, glancing over at me.

"Caleb."

"Hand to God, I'm not married," he says, raising his right hand from the steering wheel as he stops at a stop sign. "I've been getting emails, though."

I sit up a little straighter, look over at him.

"What kind of emails?"

He doesn't answer right away, looks through the windshield like he's thinking of the best way to answer.

"Short ones that say they know my secret and tell me I'm a bad person," he says.

My heart leaps into my throat, and I try to swallow it back down.

"Who are they from?"

"Secret Knower at gmail dot com," he says.

"How creative," I say, leaning my elbow against the

window ledge, looking out at the dark university buildings going by.

"So far, nothing's come of it," he says, and sounds calm, calmer than I am right now. "Whoever it is just… seems to want to make sure that I know what I'm doing with you is shitty."

"It's not."

He's silent, one thumb tapping on the steering wheel.

"It's complicated," I amend myself, tapping the knuckle of my pointer finger against my lips.

After the organ concert incident, we've been careful. I've barely made eye contact with him in class, only texted, never sent emails. Maybe someone's seen me walking into his house or coming out in the morning, but he lives in a neighborhood that's mostly student-free.

It could be another professor. Caleb's told you how vicious academia is.

"You think they'll do anything else?" I ask, softly.

"I think if they were going to, they'd have done it already."

Already?

"How long has this been happening?"

Caleb turns down a residential street, slows, then turns into his driveway.

"A little over two weeks," he finally admits.

I pause. It's not the answer I was expecting. I thought he'd say two days, maybe.

"That long?"

"I'm sorry."

"Why didn't you say anything?"

He turns the keys, pulls up on the parking brake, turns and looks at me.

"They seemed mostly interested in me, and I didn't want you to worry," he says.

I take a deep breath, then get out of the car and walk around the front. By the time I get there, Caleb is standing in his driveway, hands in the pockets of his peacoat, waiting for me.

"I need something from you," I say, stopping in front of him, looking up.

"Anything," he says.

"Don't shelter me," I tell him, my voice soft in the cold, dark night, but it's quiet except for the wind rustling the nearly-barren trees, so the sound carries. "I know that on paper, this relationship looks pretty off-balance, and there's nothing I can do about that. But I need the truth of the matter to be that you're my partner, not my protector."

His eyes search my face. Then, slowly, he smiles.

"Of course, Thalia," he says. "I wouldn't want it any other way."

"Thank you," I whisper.

He reaches out, takes my hand, lifts it to his lips.

"As long as I can protect you sometimes," he says, lifting his eyebrows.

"As long as I can reciprocate."

He kisses my hand again, shifts his, laces our fingers together as we're standing there, facing each other, and I feel an echo of that first warm night we met, standing by the sea monster on the pond.

"We can stop the affair if you want, now that someone knows," he says, quiet, low, serious.

"I don't."

He opens his mouth like he's about to say something, pauses, smiles.

"Good," he says. "I don't either. Ladies first."

· · · · ★ ★ ★ ★ ★ · · · ·

INSIDE, coats off, bags on the floor next to shoes. He kisses me before the door is shut, after it's shut, while I'm unlacing my shoes and trying not to fall over. I leave my sweater on the railing of the stairs, my shirt on the floor, and by the time we're in his bedroom I'm in a tank top and jeans, Caleb shirtless.

We don't bother shutting the door. The room is lit by bedside lamps and Caleb walks me in, backward, one hand on my back and one twisting in the front of my skin-tight tank top.

"You know what the hardest part of Thanksgiving is going to be?" he asks, hands on my ribcage, his thumbs already brushing my stiff nipples through my bra.

"You?" I ask, and he laughs.

"I'm afraid watching my brothers argue isn't terribly erotic," he says, as I take my hands off him, reach for my bra clasp.

"What, then?" I ask, pulling it off through the arm holes of my shirt.

Caleb doesn't answer, just runs the length of his hands over both nipples, from fingertip to palm, and my eyes slide closed at the friction.

"I like this shirt," he says, his voice rough as he's tracing the outline of my nipples with his thumbs. "You should wear it all the time, and you should never wear anything under it."

I drape an arm over his shoulders, dip my fingers into the waistband of his jeans.

"To class, maybe?" I tease, and he looks at me in slight alarm.

"No," he says, pinching my nipples between his fingers. "Jesus, never to class. You want me to forget what three times three is?"

"You've got a calculator," I murmur, and slide my palm down the long, hard, thick ridge of his cock.

"Don't you dare," he growls, playful, pushing me back again toward the bed. "You're supposed to be my partner, not my temptress."

The backs of my knees hit the bed and instead of falling over, I climb on, kneeling, facing him, one hand on his cock and the other pulling at a belt loop.

"I'm not your temptress?"

"I'd prefer if you weren't in class," he says. "Just give me two more weeks, and then you can have your nipples out in class all day long. Wait. No."

I laugh, tugging at the button on his jeans, practically tearing the zipper down.

"Shut up and take your pants off," he teases, already shoving them over my hips.

I fall backward, wriggle out of my jeans, and Caleb leans over the bed and pulls my panties down too. I shove at his pants as he crawls on top of me and a few moments of maneuvering later, he's naked and I'm wearing nothing but this shirt, my legs wrapped around him, his thick cock bumping against my clit, my hands on the hard muscles in his back.

I am *aching* with need and every touch, every thrust makes it worse, like he's taunting me. I reach between us and grab his cock, the underside already slippery with my juices, and he thrusts into my hand and groans into my shoulder. I stroke him hard once, twice, and then I've made up my mind.

"Roll over," I murmur, and he does, catching my wrist, dragging me on top of him. He pulls my shirt off as I straddle his hips, hands on his chest, automatically grinding against him, my body pleasure-seeking.

In the back of my mind, something ugly and old whispers *good girls don't*, and I squash it.

Instead I kiss him again and I push myself against him and think of his list: *make sure she's aroused*.

Yeah, check.

I lean over, stretching away from him, open the drawer, and grab a condom.

Then I remember the first bullet point and go back for a bottle of lube. I straddle him again, lower, tear the condom wrapper with my teeth because my hands are too slippery, then pull it from the wrapper.

I've never done this part before. I know the theory, and it's not rocket science, but when you're putting a condom on a banana as practice you're never so turned on you think you might explode. You're never tempted — so, *so* tempted — to toss the condom away and bareback a banana because you're just that impatient.

I make sure the condom is right side out, center it on the head of his cock, and it slips a little but then Caleb pushes himself up on one hand and his fingers are on mine as we unroll it onto him.

He grabs the bottle of lube, drizzles it on himself, pours some into his hand and strokes himself a few times, lies back on the bed, his hand on my thigh.

"C'mere," he says in a voice that turns my insides even gooier.

I lean forward, kiss my lover, push away that tiny voice telling me I shouldn't because I know, completely and unequivocally, that it's wrong.

He moves his hand from my thigh, grasps himself, guides himself to my opening.

At last, I take him. I take him a millimeter at a time I ease myself down, my hands spread on his chest as the tip of his cock slides into me and I open, stretching, filling.

It almost hurts, but not quite. It's a sensation right on the edge of pain, right at my limit.

If he moved it would hurt. If I went too fast it would hurt but he's gentle, patient, lets me go at my own pace. After a moment he lets his cock go, touches my clit with his thumb lightly.

"Is this okay?" he asks, and I nod. He strokes me and I keep moving, up and down, slowly working him inside me, and then he hits the spot.

I groan and Caleb moves the tiniest bit, his hips flexing and his cock throbbing. I gasp at the quick pinch of pain but then it's gone and he's deeper, pressing against a spot I've found before on my own but holy shit, never like this. Never *anything* like this.

"Did I hurt you?" he murmurs, and I just shake my head, dig my fingers into his shoulders.

"I'm fine," I murmur.

I'm fighting with myself, caught between the almost-pain, the knowledge that I'm on the edge of it, and the instinctual, primal urge to ride Caleb as hard as I possibly can.

I know I need to be careful, take it slow, this first time at least, but I don't want to. I don't want to at all.

"Fine?" he asks, thumb still drawing slow circles over my clit, his hand slippery with lube and my own wetness.

"Good," I say, voice low and rough, and as I say it I flex my hips and move back and for one second there's another pinch but then it moves his cock against that spot again, harder and longer.

This time I moan out loud, and this time I don't care that it might hurt and I take him deeper, harder.

Caleb groans, and even though it was too deep and too hard and I should stop, I don't because it also feels so good that I don't think I can. I don't think I can do anything but ignore the sensation that I'm at my limit and take all of him, every last millimeter, my fingers and toes curling and his thumb moving faster on my clit.

I'm whimpering, my eyes half-closed, my lips parted. My hips are barely moving against his but it's all I can take, stretched and filled, my whole body a live wire.

"Still good?" he rasps.

"So good," I half whisper, half whimper. I swallow, gulp air, lean in, rock back on his cock.

I find that perfect angle again and I groan, my eyes going closed and slowly, carefully, I ease into a rhythm of small, shallow strokes as he strums my clit.

"Fuck, it's so good," I breathe, barely aware of what I'm saying. "God, you feel so good."

"Tell me how much you like it," he growls, and his other hand wanders up my body, caressing me. His cock twitches and I inhale sharply then moan, every single movement magnified times a hundred.

"Do that again," I say, taking his hand, sliding his palm over one breast, his callouses skipping over my nipple. "Please?"

He moves, barely, and my body trills a quick warning but it's lost among the feeling that I'm a symphony in crescendo.

"You like that?" he says, doing it again, his voice raspy and heavy, his breathing hard and fast. "Just like that?"

"Yes," I breathe. "Don't stop. Please don't stop. God, more, don't stop. Don't stop, don't stop…"

Now I've got his hand in both of mine, his knuckles pressed to my lips, eyes closed, and I can barely move but I'm rocking back and forth on his cock and he's thrusting barely, just barely, and it almost *almost* hurts and I can barely breathe but I manage to whisper *I'm gonna come oh God Caleb I'm gonna come so hard*, and then I do.

I come so hard it hurts, so hard I nearly fall over, Caleb's hand clutched in mine. I shout into his knuckles and whimper and say *oh God oh God*. I'm wracked. I feel like I'm melting, like I'm a bell being rung for the first time.

It fades slowly, into an afterglow that makes me dizzy, lightheaded. I kiss Caleb's knuckles again and he stops stroking my clit, moves both hands to my hips, pulls me down another millimeter.

"I love the way you feel when you come," he whispers, and then he explodes inside me, throbbing and pulsing. He grabs my hips even harder, the muscles in his arms flexing and I rock back, wanting more of him. I need more. In this moment, fuzzy-headed and sated, I feel powerful and wildly possessive, like I've been blessed that he's mine and *this* is mine, and also like I want to go exact blood revenge for anyone else who's ever seen him this way.

He slows, stops. He pushes himself up on his hands, still breathing hard, looking wild and untamed and sexy as hell.

"Kiss me," he says, and I do.

CHAPTER THIRTY-FOUR
CALEB

When I come back from tossing the condom Thalia's still lying on my bed, one knee up, her arms overhead. She's naked and beautiful and on display, and I pause for a moment, just trying to memorize this moment.

I wonder if she has any idea how she looks right now, whether she knows that she's temptation come to life, desire personified. I wonder if she knows my bed looks like there's a goddess in it.

"You're sure you can't stay?" I ask, glancing at my bedside clock. One-thirty in the morning.

"I shouldn't," she says, glancing at the clock herself, then making a face. "I still have to pack for break, and my ride's gonna pick me up at nine so we hopefully don't hit too much traffic in Richmond or the Tidewater."

I get into my bed next to her, ignoring the large, sticky spot where I used *way* too much lube. Thalia looks at it, then rolls over, onto her stomach.

"Also, I should shower," she says.

"The instructions said lots," I point out, perching two

fingers on her shoulder, then running them softly down her back, to her tailbone.

Just barely, her back arches, hips rising to meet my touch. I flatten my palm against her.

"Well, the instructions worked," she says, laughing. Her cheeks are faintly pink and I can't tell whether she's still flushed from sex or whether she's blushing anew.

"Once more proving the power of research," I say.

"Is that what we just did?" she teases. "Prove the power of research?"

"I don't hear you complaining."

"I've got nothing to complain about," she says.

Then she catches my eyes, pauses for a beat.

"That was really good," she says, and now she's definitely blushing. "Thanks."

"You don't have to thank me."

"What if I want to?"

"Trust me, I got all the thanks I need," I say, sliding a finger back up her spine, watching the way she rolls her shoulders as I do.

She's addictive, this girl. The more I get of her the more I want.

"Can I shower here?" she asks, glancing at the clock again.

"No," I say.

She gives me a look, and I laugh.

"What, you can sleep in my bed and hop on my dick but not shower? Of course you can shower here."

"I think I'm gonna need to work up to hopping," she says, then leans in, gives me a long kiss on the mouth.

"I'm available for practice," I tell her.

"Good," she says, her lips still against mine. "I've brainstormed some ideas for next steps."

"Already?"

"I'm a planner. I like to think ahead," she says, then pushes herself off the bed, stands, and walks for the bathroom, still utterly naked. A few minutes later, still on my bed, I hear the hiss of the shower and even though I'm tempted to go in there and offer to get started on those next steps, I don't.

Instead I change the sheets and set an alarm for six, so she doesn't miss her ride. When she gets out of the shower I take one as well, then crawl into bed next to her already-sleeping form.

In her sleep, she snuggles back against me. I stay awake a little longer just to savor it.

* * * * * ★ * * * * *

Seth: Caleb, who are you staying with?
Levi: I thought it was me.
Daniel: If you like being awake at three in the morning, you can stay here.
Daniel: Charlie approved of your laundry folding skills last time you were over.
Eli: You say that like she's the one in the relationship with opinions on how laundry gets folded.
Daniel: Fine. Caleb, you folded the laundry nicely.
Seth: I folded laundry, he put together the swing.
Seth: But thank you.
Levi: Caleb, the spare bedroom is yours if you want it.
Seth: I've also got a spare bedroom. And also, wifi.
Levi: We have wifi. We've had wifi for two years.
Seth: You mean June has wifi?
Levi: We live together. It's our house and therefore it's also our wifi.
Eli: We know whose wifi it is, Levi. Do you even know the password?

Levi: Yes.

Eli: Caleb, you're welcome to our couch, but sounds like you've got better offers.

Eli: Maybe he's staying at Mom's house?

Seth: Earth to Caleb.

Daniel: Caleb, please bring one of those huge chocolate chip cookies from that place near the park when you come. They're very good and I would like to eat one. This is Daniel.

Eli: Daniel left his phone unguarded again, didn't he?

Levi: Looks like it.

Daniel: I did not leave my phone unguarded and I would like the big cookie please insert this patch itch extra extra wish bag etc

Eli: Definitely seems like Daniel over there.

Seth: For sure. Better get ten cookies.

Daniel: Sorry. I went to grab Thomas and Rusty got my phone.

Eli: Wow, that wasn't you? She even said "this is Daniel."

Daniel: Don't laugh. I live in terror of the day she learns to lie well.

·· * * ★ ★ ★ ★ * * ··

I'M a quarter mile from the trailhead when my phone starts beeping, ringing, and buzzing like it's possessed, though it turns out to just be the group text I've got with my brothers, not a demon.

The group text is probably better. Probably. A demon might be less nosy, though.

Caleb: Anywhere is fine. I actually hadn't thought about it yet.

Seth: Your mind elsewhere?

I decide to ignore him, turn my phone to silent, and keep hiking. I should probably be figuring out what I'm bringing to Thanksgiving tomorrow — Eli sent an email about what he's assigned each of us — but more than anything, I needed to escape, clear my mind, and get some exercise.

Admittedly, I'm mostly thinking about Thalia. I'm thinking that we should go hiking out here instead of only ever having dates in my house. We'll go somewhere far from campus, and no one else is ever out here. We won't get recognized.

I'm wondering when I can bring her to Sprucevale to meet my family. I'm wondering if I can get Seth to keep his mouth shut about the fact that she's my student.

And about last night.

I think about last night a lot, actually. Hard not to. The way she said *fuck, it's so good*. The sounds she made. The way she fit me like a glove, the way I could feel every tiny move she made, the way she looked as she slid down my cock —

I sigh out loud and glare at a squirrel, forcing myself not to think about it any more. The squirrel glares back.

"What's your problem?" I mutter, and it runs away.

· · · · * ★ * * · · ·

Me: I hate Monopoly.
Thalia: Did you lose to Rusty again?
Me: When you play Monopoly, doesn't everyone lose?
Thalia: That's not very sporting of you.
Me: Monopoly's not sporting, it's stupid.
Me: How was the drive to Norfolk?
Thalia: Uneventful. How's Sprucevale?

Me: Well, I've lost twice at Monopoly and Seth gives me a knowing look every thirty seconds or so.
Me: But otherwise, it's good. I hadn't seen Thomas for a couple of weeks and I swear he's twice the size he used to be.
Thalia: You can't just say that and not send a picture.

I OBLIGE and send her one that Daniel took of me and my nephew. He's yawning in my arms, and I'm making that same face back at him.

Thalia: Ugh, what a cutie.
Me: Thanks. I really think this shirt brings out my eyes.

I can practically hear her sigh and try not to laugh.

Thalia: The baby is also cute.
Me: How's Norfolk?
Thalia: It's been better.
Thalia: Oh, Bastien wants to know if any of your brothers are single and gay.
Me: Seth's technically single but not gay, unless he's REALLY closeted.
Thalia: What about that guy who's not your brother?

I'm standing in the upstairs hall of my mom's house, briefly escaping the madness of Thanksgiving Day, and at that question I look up at the wall in puzzlement.

There are a great many guys in the world, and the vast majority aren't my brother.

Thalia: The one whose sister is marrying Levi.
Thalia: I mean, they look alike.
Thalia: June? Is that her name?

Me: Oh, you mean Silas?
Me: Also, what, did you make flash cards of everyone?
Thalia: If I'd made flash cards I'd have known his name.
Thalia: And yeah, Silas. Hetero?
Me: Hetero and too old for Bastien.
Thalia: Bastien says he'll be the judge of that.
Me: Nope, I'm doing the judging.
Thalia: Suddenly critical of age differences?
Me: Fifteen is a lot more than six.
Thalia: You're so good with numbers, have you ever thought of doing something with that?
Me: Nah, I don't think I've got much of a future in math.

· · · · ★ ★ ★ ★ ★ · · · ·

"How's THALIA?" Seth asks, holding a huge tray of leftover turkey and staring into the refrigerator.

"Who?" I ask, standing beside him. "We should probably turn the fridge off for a minute. This looks like a whole project."

"I meant to come over here and clean it out before today," he admits. "And don't play dumb, idiot."

I reach up and turn down the temperature dial on the fridge, because finding spots for all the leftovers is going to take a while, and there's no sense in wasting all that electricity.

There were over twenty people at Thanksgiving, and even though we sent everyone home with food, there's still an astonishing amount of leftovers, and it's fallen to Seth and I to figure out how to fit it all into my mom's fridge.

"Can we move these shelves? That one's a weird height," I say, pointing.

"Ignoring my question won't make it go away," he

points out, taking more stuff out of the fridge, putting it on the chair currently propping the fridge door open.

"Yes, it will," I say.

"No, it'll make me ask it louder," he says. "Eventually, I'll have no choice but to ask how Thalia's doing so loudly that everyone in the house will hear me, and I bet they'll also want to know how Thalia's doing. They might also have follow-up questions."

"Come on," I say, as we both reach into the fridge and begin rearranging.

Seth pulls out a small plastic container of something and regards it suspiciously, then tosses it into the sink.

"Not bluffing," he says.

I say nothing.

"How's Thalia doing?" he asks, ten percent louder than before.

"Don't."

"How's Thalia doing?"

Twenty percent. I close my eyes and tell myself that he'll knock it off before someone else actually gets interested.

"HOW'S —"

I punch him in the arm, and he breaks off, grinning.

"Ow," he says.

"She's fine," I mutter. "Doing well."

"How are her grades?"

"Seth."

"She still getting a D?"

I don't answer, even though I already know that it won't work. For all my cleverness and book smarts, I've never figured out how to make any of my brothers knock it off when they're being obnoxious.

"That stands for dick, specifically yours," he explains.

I keep rearranging the fridge and do not, repeat, do *not* make eye contact.

"And asking if someone is *getting the D* is a colloquialism for —"

"We're not talking about this," I say.

"Q.E.D., we are, actually."

I take a deep breath, stand up straight, push one hand through my hair and gather my thoughts. Generally, I'm a fairly calm, unflappable person.

Siblings, though.

"Things are really good, and they're not supposed to be," I say, keeping my voice low. "Because she's my student, and there aren't supposed to be things at all, which means that no matter how good they are, I don't want to talk about them because every person who knows is one more who might let something slip, and that could be disastrous."

Seth's quiet a moment, his eyes searching my face, his dark hair slightly mussed like always. I think, for a flash, of how much he looks like our dad, even though his hair was always neat and never out of place. A far as I recall, at least.

"But things are really good?" he says, softly. "Despite the fucked-up nature of your relationship?"

I don't take that last part personally, because I know exactly what he means.

"They are," I tell him. "I've never met anyone like Thalia before. I really like her, and I really want it to work, I just wish…"

"Right," Seth says, nodding as he pushes a container into the fridge, then frowns. "Is this gonna keep the door from closing?"

"Dunno, try it," I say, and move the chair holding the fridge door open.

It swings shut, and then Seth and I both jump.

Levi's standing right there.

"Who's Thalia?" he asks.

"How long have you been behind that door?" I hiss.

"Ten seconds. Maybe fifteen, I came to see if you needed help. You all right?"

I don't know why I've ever tried to keep a secret in my entire life.

"I'm fine," I say.

"A relationship with a fucked-up nature sounds less than fine," my eldest brother points out, folding his arms over his chest.

"Caleb's dating someone he shouldn't be," Seth explains.

Levi shrugs, looking skeptical.

"No, *really* shouldn't be," Seth says, keeping his voice low. "This isn't *my friend is gonna be mad* —"

"He punched me," Levi points out.

" — This is *Caleb's life is gonna be ruined if people find out*," he finishes.

Levi just turns and looks at me, silently. And looks. And waits.

I lean my head against the cool metal door of the fridge, close my eyes.

"She's my student," I finally admit.

CHAPTER THIRTY-FIVE
THALIA

Bastien looks down at his mocha, then up at me.

"It would be frowned upon to put vodka in this, right?" he asks.

"Did you bring vodka with you?"

"It's more of a theoretical question," he says. "In theory, let's say you're at your parents' house for Thanksgiving break, and they've barely spoken two words to each other since your dad kicked your ex-junkie brother out of the house while your mom was at work, and also your mom has a cast on her good arm but would literally rather drop a full knife rack on her foot than ask your father for help with something in the kitchen. Vodka in your coffee: yes or no? Also, you're gay and they don't know."

"Thanks, now I want vodka," I say.

"There's a liquor store down the street," Bastien volunteers. "I'll wait here."

"This was all a ploy to get me to buy you vodka, wasn't it?" I ask, taking a sip of my non-alcoholic coffee.

"I don't need a ploy," he laughs. "I'd just ask you to buy

me liquor. Actually, speaking of which, will you buy me liquor?"

"It's illegal," I tease, and Bastien rolls his eyes.

"You're fucking your math professor, you can —"

I nearly spit out my coffee and kick him under the table.

"Ow," he says while I cough.

"Don't," I hiss, still coughing.

"I'm just saying, on the spectrum of *no bigs* to *big deal*, buying your pretty-close-to-legal little brother some booze ranks way below some of your other activities."

Bastien is utterly and completely delighted that I'm having an affair with my professor. He might be even more delighted than I am, and I'm pretty delighted. He claims it's because he likes seeing me happy, but I'm not buying it.

Well, I'm sort of buying it. I think he likes seeing me happy, but I think he's even more relieved that at last, I'm doing something wrong and he gets to know about it.

He's also enjoyed the (perfectly innocent) pictures that Caleb's been texting me, and I can't blame him. Caleb's hot and he has hot brothers.

"Fine, I'll buy you booze," I say.

"You're my favorite sister," he says, grinning.

We both take a long sip of our respective coffees, then look out the plate glass window we're sitting by. This coffee shop is across the street from a big shopping center, which makes for pretty good people watching.

Particularly today. There's definitely a certain level of schadenfreude involved in watching people shop on Black Friday while peacefully sipping a drink across the street.

"You weren't actually going to try and buy something, were you?" I ask him, my chin in my hand as I watch two people shout at each other in their cars, both in the wrong lane.

Bastien's just staring out the window, his coffee in one hand, resting on the table, and he doesn't say anything.

"I figured you just said that to Mom and Dad as a reason to leave the house because if you said 'we just really want to not be here right now,' they'd get all weird about it," I go on.

He still doesn't answer. I follow his gaze, but I can't tell what he's looking at, other than a general shopping madness.

"Bossy," I say, and he finally turns to me.

The look on his face stops me cold.

"I think I found Javi," he says, voice low, eyes locked on mine.

Then he swallows.

"That's the real reason I wanted to get out of the house — I mean, Mom and Dad are also unbearable, but —"

"Is he dead?"

The question comes out flat and emotionless, my lips and fingers already going cold, my heart a knot getting pulled tighter with every second.

Bastien just shakes his head. He looks away. He looks at me again, and suddenly he doesn't look like my college student brother who plays soccer and volleyball and rock climbs and is constantly apologizing to girls for being gay.

He looks like my kid brother, young and scared and lost.

"No," he says. "I mean, I don't know. That was misleading. I didn't find him, I found where he was a month ago."

"A month?" I echo, the knot still tightening.

I don't want Javier dead. I want to say that first, that I want my big brother back. I want back the guy who taught me to write in cursive long before I learned in school, the guy who drilled me endlessly at kicking soccer goals, the guy who beat up the boy who pulled my hair in fourth grade.

But I saw Javier after he came back, and before he went to rehab, and he may as well have been a ghost. He barely talked, couldn't joke, couldn't laugh. The only time he ever seemed alive was when he'd wake up screaming.

In other words, I think Javier might already be gone.

And the truth is that I don't know which is worse. He's on the streets and he's addicted to opiates and winter is coming, and I'm one hundred percent positive that when he sleeps, he still wakes up screaming.

"I've been calling around to shelters and churches and groups that work with the homeless," he says, softly. "A volunteer with the Richmond needle exchange program said she helped someone matching his description at the end of October, right after Halloween. She gave him a bunch of syringes, some medical supplies, and a couple doses of Narcan. Said he turned down an HIV test."

I nod. I swallow hard, and I keep nodding and I stare out the window at the zillions of cars fighting to get their cheap TVs and underpriced pants, and I have a thousand thoughts all at once.

I think, *he's still using* and *at least he's using a needle exchange* and *at least he has Narcan in case he overdoses* and I hate the first, hate that he needs the last two.

I think *he was exchanging needles while I was having fun with Caleb.*

I think *I can't believe I've been so happy while Javi's been out there, still using, still on the streets...*

"When did you find out?" I finally ask, still staring blankly out the window.

"A week ago," he says.

"I should have been calling too."

"Ollie."

"I've done *nothing*."

"Ollie, knock it off," Bastien says gently. "Don't start guilt-tripping yourself."

"But I should have been —"

"I mean it. I finally talked to someone who'd seen him and what does it help? Jack shit."

"We know he's still alive and still in Richmond," I point out.

"We know he was three weeks ago."

I look at my hand on the table, my nails shiny and dark blue because I painted them yesterday, listening to my parents ignore each other. It's good, if minor, stress relief.

"Do Mom and Dad know?"

"No," he says simply.

"Are you going to tell them?"

He sighs and looks down.

"I don't know," he says. "I'm not sure what it helps. I'm not sure *if* it helps. I mostly told you because I needed to share it with someone and talk about what we should do or if there's anything we *can* do."

"I wish you'd told me earlier," I say.

Bastien just shrugs.

"You're really busy," he says. "And you and Caleb seem like you're really happy and I didn't want to harsh your buzz, you know?"

"Telling me Javi's still alive isn't *harshing my buzz*," I say, more forcefully than I mean to. "He's my brother. I want to know."

Now he looks young again, lost.

"I'm sorry," he whispers. "You're right."

I shake my head, trying to clear my brain out.

"It's okay," I say. "I'm sorry, I didn't mean to…"

I trail off, my words not quite operating at the moment.

"We should tell Mom and Dad."

"Yeah, you're right. I was just being a pussy about it because —"

I clear my throat, and Bastien rolls his eyes a little.

"— being a *coward* about it —"

"Thank you."

"— because I didn't want to make things worse between them, but that's not really my problem, is it?"

"Nope," I agree.

We're quiet for another moment, drinking our coffees. People come in and out of the coffee shop, get drinks, sit down. The baristas call names and kids run back and forth and two people hug, laugh, sit down together.

"You find out anything else?"

"That's all she knew," he says. "I think a lot of people go through there."

"They didn't chat? He didn't casually tell her that he's been living in a car in Foggy Bottom or visiting a shelter near VCU or on the streets Downtown or something?"

Bastien just shakes his head again.

"Sorry, Ollie. That's all I got."

"It's good. Thank you."

· · · · ★ ★ ★ ★ ★ · · · ·

Me: Buy anything good today?
Caleb: God, no. I went hiking with Levi, June, and Silas, and then when we got back Thomas fell asleep on me for nearly three hours.
Caleb: Daniel said he must find my funk soothing.
Me: You should bottle it as a baby sleep aid.
Caleb: If this teaching thing ever falls through, maybe.

I MAKE a face and laugh quietly. I'm sitting on the couch in my parents' den, feet on the coffee table. The TV is showing some action movie and Bastien is sitting at the other end of the couch, both of us looking at our phones.

When I laugh, he glances over at me, then back.

"Are you talking to your *lovahhhh*?" he asks, and I snort.

"You can't call him that."

"Call him what? Your *lovahhhh*?"

This time he uses a funny voice, and I start laughing.

"Lov-ahhhh. Looo-vahhhhh."

I throw a pillow at him, giggling almost too hard to talk.

"Thalia," he says, still looking at his phone. "Has taken a…"

He looks at me, grinning.

"Don't," I say.

"LOVAHHHH," he stage-whispers, raising his eyebrows and doing jazz hands.

I grab the pillow I threw by a corner and start beating him with it.

"Don't. Wake. Up. Mom. And. Dad!" I hiss, giggling, punctuating each word with a pillow smack.

"You don't want them to know about your —"

I shove the pillow over his face.

"Uhhhhwuhhhhh," he says.

· · · · ★ ★ ★ ★ ★ · · · ·

TELLING my parents that Javier was alive and at a needle exchange in Richmond doesn't do much for the atmosphere in the house. My mom asks Bastien a million questions that he doesn't know the answer to — *Was he okay? How did he look? Did he have a coat, did he have shoes?* — and my father pretty much turns to stone while she cries.

I think he regrets turning Javi out. It can be hard to tell, and to be honest, I've never been particularly close with my father. He's not exactly the warm, fuzzy type.

I've suspected more than once that my grandfather, the son of Mexican immigrants and also a military man, was abusive. I'm pretty sure that my grandmother was an alcoholic, possibly as a result of having an abusive spouse and trying to raise six children essentially on her own. They both died before I was born, so I don't really know. I just know that my father, the eldest, didn't grow up in a happy household and joined the Navy the second he turned eighteen so he could get out of there.

Not that it excuses anything, but thinking about it helps me to be a little more compassionate.

The rest of the weekend is very, very rough. I try to stick around and be there for my mom, but I don't know how much I'm helping.

And I can't stop feeling guilty about my own secret. I can't stop thinking about how much she'd disapprove, how disappointed she'd be, and she wouldn't be completely wrong.

Needless to say, I'm pretty relieved when my ride Natalie picks me up, and we head back to Marysburg.

CHAPTER THIRTY-SIX
CALEB

"Why would you assign a paper to be due *one week* before the final?" Thalia asks. "Who does that? What educational purpose can it possibly serve? No one is doing their best work at that point. No one is really absorbing information, it'll all just be incoherent nonsense brought on by too little sleep and too much caffeine."

"Sadists?" I ask, leaning back on the couch, lacing my fingers over my head. "Or maybe masochists, because then they'll have to grade the final and also read all those papers?"

I've never once assigned a paper. I had to write them occasionally in undergrad, and every single time, it made me regret taking a humanities course for 'fun.'

Turns out that I like reading books, but writing papers and analyzing them feels like someone pounding nails into my brain. What's the whale symbolize in *Moby Dick*? I don't know, a whale?

"It's monstrous," Thalia says, also leaning back, looking up at me. "And stupid. And dumb."

"So you're not staying over?" I ask, even though I already know the answer from her brief tirade.

"I can't," she sighs. "I gotta go back and finish this dumb thing, it's due by eight a.m. And I still have to write four more pages and a conclusion, and then put together my bibliography because Callahan is a *maniac* about bibliographies."

Then she curls into me, one knee over my thigh, her head on my shoulder, and I wrap an arm around her smooth, bare skin.

"Sorry," she says.

We're both naked on my couch because we didn't make it upstairs this time. Forty-five minutes ago she texted me and asked me what I was doing, and fifteen minutes after that she was on my doorstep.

Then, in short order, she was naked and I was naked, on the couch, her knees on my shoulders and I was wearing a condom that she'd magically produced from somewhere, and she was breathing hard, both hands on my thighs, and then I carefully, slowly slid inside her and she moaned.

She didn't last long. I didn't last long.

I'm starting to think that Thalia might be a sex fiend, and I'm okay with it.

"Better you than me," I tease, and she laughs.

· · · * * ★ * * · · ·

When she comes over the next night, the first thing she does after she comes in the door is hand me a neatly written, numbered list.

"These your demands?" I tease, before I actually read it.

Thalia just laughs.

"Sort of," she says, and then my eyebrows go up as I actually read the list.

1. Cowgirl
2. Missionary
3. Doggy
4. Froggy
5. Plow
6. Wheelbarrow
7. Reverse Cowgirl
8. Pretzel
9. Piledriver
10. Side-lying

"Tell me more about how you're a shy, innocent virgin," I say.

"I never claimed the first two, and I got over the third," she laughs. "I did some research during a study break and you know how I like lists. And goals. And achievements. And achieving goals."

"And fucking me silly," I say, still scanning the list, and she laughs. "Is there a Powerpoint? I don't know what all of these even are, and if I try to Google them you know I'll just get porn."

"You *have* to start using Safe Search," she says.

"That only works sometimes," I tell her. "If you're searching, I don't know, *best corkscrew* it'll work but there's no such thing as a Safe Search when you're trying to look up *doggy style*."

"I thought you'd know that one," she teases.

We're still standing in my front hallway as she takes off her coat, puts her bag down, then runs her fingers through her hair, shaking it out.

"Want to help me figure it out?" I ask, grinning, and I pull her to me.

"Duh," she says, laughing. "That's the point of the list."

* * * * * * * * * * * *

FOR THE NEXT TWO WEEKS, I essentially become Thalia's late-night booty call. It's the end of the semester and then finals, not to mention the last few grad school applications are due, and she's completely swamped with work.

I'm not mad. There are far worse things in life than Thalia coming over for sex and then either leaving or falling asleep in my bed.

Far worse.

We do talk. She tells me about how Bastien found Javier, sort of. I admit that Levi and Seth both know about us. We talk about our families and Thanksgiving and the upcoming Christmas break, about whether we should wait until she graduates to tell our families, or whether we can do it once she's no longer my student.

Though I could still get fired once that happens. The Virginia Southern University guidelines are very clear, but once I'm no longer grading her homework it just becomes wrong and ethically questionable, not Wrong and Unethical.

Speaking of Wrong and Unethical (and *an affront to professors everywhere*, and *a perverse man who gets off on having power over her*, and *unambiguously corrupt*), I'm still getting the emails. Every other day, like clockwork. In a twisted way I'm starting to look forward to them. They're at least creative.

I keep Thalia's list on the bedside table, along with a pencil, so we can cross things off and also make programming notes as appropriate.

For example, on the line next to *#9, Piledriver* is the single word **no**. Next to *#8, Pretzel*, it says **actually impossible**; *#7, Reverse Cowgirl*, **not nearly as good as regular cowgirl,** and the line next to *#6, Wheelbarrow*, just reads **who comes up with these?**

But she likes when I put her legs over my shoulders and take her slow and hard and deep, which turns out to be *#5, Plow*. When we try *#3, Doggy*, she fucks me back so hard that I'm afraid she's going to hurt herself, but she doesn't. She just whimpers my name and then comes, clenching around me so tight it almost hurts.

She likes the variation on *#1, Cowgirl* in my office chair when she takes me all in one stroke and then rocks back and forth while I'm buried inside her. She likes *#4, Froggy*, which we try by accident when she collapses onto her elbows during Doggy and then buries her face in the mattress, moaning. She likes *#10, Side-lying*, in the morning when we're both half-awake and don't want to get up yet.

······ ★ ★ ★ ······

THE DAY before the calculus final, she comes over in the afternoon and brings sandwiches. She texts first, but she's got a key, so she just comes in to find me grading papers at the kitchen table.

"Any of those mine?" she asks.

"Why, are you offering a bribe?" I ask.

"I brought sandwiches."

I tap my pen on the table, like I'm considering.

"What kind?"

"Turkey, brie, and arugula on baguette," she says. "And I brought two cookies from Mason's. Regular size, not face-size."

She puts them on the counter, then leans against it, watching me while I sit there, thinking.

"Do you hate brie or something?" she finally asks, puzzled.

"No," I admit. "I'm trying to think of a good way to offer you my meaty baguette but I don't think there is one."

Thalia laughs, her eyes crinkling.

"I brought lunch because I'm starting to feel like I'm using you for sex," she says. "Shouldn't we be having deep conversations about life and meaning and the universe or at least what movies we've seen?"

"What movies have you seen?"

"I haven't seen any movies, I've been studying," she admits.

"How about books?" I tease, leaning back, crossing my ankle over my knee, still tapping the pen on the table.

"I've been plowing through this really great read called *Principles and Theories of Cognitive Neuroscience*," she says. "It's a real page turner. Ask me anything about the amygdala."

"What is it?"

"Part of your brain."

"Thanks," I deadpan.

"It has to do with emotional response. Mostly fear and aggression. We think it's very involved in PTSD emotional responses, though also maybe not, because the brain is very complex and sometimes it feels like no one knows anything about it and we may as well be diagnosing mental disorders based on what lumps people have on their skulls," she says.

"You need a study break," I say.

"Are you turning down my offer of scintillating conversation over lunch?" she says.

"Never," I say, still tapping my pen. "I'm just offering a stress-relieving appetizer."

"Of a meat baguette?"

"I already regret saying that out loud."

Thalia walks over to me and I sit up straighter, uncross my legs and she straddles me, resting her arms on my shoulders.

"You should, because it was pretty bad," she teases, then gently takes my glasses by the arms, carefully places them on the table. "There. One more day."

"Probably two," I admit, my hands already cupping her ass as she rolls her hips toward me, my cock stiffening. "The class officially ends when final grades are in."

"I'm not leaving for Norfolk until Monday," she says. "We get a whole weekend when you're not my professor."

I grasp her hips harder, rock her against me, my thumbs on the soft skin of her belly, and even though yesterday we tried some variations on #2, Missionary, I already want her again with a fervor that surprises me.

Can you get addicted to a person? I think I might be.

"Want to go on a real date?" I ask. "Somewhere outside town. Saturday night. Somewhere no one knows us."

"Do we still know how to act in public?" she asks, her fingertips already on my chest, rocking forward along the length of my cock.

"Did we ever?" I ask, and she laughs.

· · · * * ★ ★ * * · · ·

I DON'T SEE her the day of the calculus final except at the test itself. It's not in our usual classroom, but rather, in an auditorium with the two other sections of honors calculus, the students spaced far enough apart that there's no way they can cheat off of each other.

Well, that's the idea, at least, but they're honors students. Most would never cheat, but the few who would are probably smart enough to come up with ways around being seated far from someone else.

When Thalia comes in, she glances at me briefly, sitting in the front with the other two Honors Calculus instructors. She nods and I nod back, the exact same way I've nodded to my other students today, then go back to grading the finals from my Differential Equations class.

The final starts at eight in the morning, and they've got until eleven to finish it, but Thalia's gone by ten, presumably to the library to finish her Research Methods final paper, which is due at 11:59:59pm tomorrow, the last day of finals.

CHAPTER THIRTY-SEVEN
CALEB

I haven't checked grades this often since I was a college senior myself and wondering what I got on my Introduction to Knot Theory final. I submitted them by noon Friday, and at 6:30, they still haven't gone up.

I'd say it usually doesn't take this long for grades to be posted after I submit them, but I have no idea. Even though I've taught for years as a grad student, I've never really cared when the students got their grades before. I never had much of a reason to.

Briefly, I turn in my office chair and look through my window, lean a little to the right until I can see Thalia, still at her carrel. I can't quite see what she's doing from here, but she looks studious.

I turn back to my desk, where a stack of end-of-semester paperwork is waiting for me. I grab my headphones, put on a podcast, and get to it.

· · · · ★ ★ ★ ★ ★ · · · ·

An hour later, my phone dings and I grab it instantly, grateful for the distraction from Building Form 59B, which is for requesting special permission to use a seminar room in the Mathematics Department for next semester's graduate student seminar, rather than a classroom with shaky desks and a window that doesn't quite close all the way.

I don't know why the permission is special. Aren't seminar rooms for seminars?

Thalia: Only an A, not an A+?
Me: You didn't earn an A+.
Me: You got two C's on quizzes and I don't even want to talk about the question on the final about asymptotic limits.
Thalia: Thank God, I don't either.

I turn around and look at her, still at her carrel, through my window and hers. She waves, and I wave back.

Thalia: Do you feel better now?
Me: About?
Thalia: Me.
Thalia: Now that I'm not your student any more.
Me: I've always felt good about you, that's the problem.
Thalia: Don't be willfully obtuse.
Me: Yeah, I do.

I stand from my chair, crack my knuckles on the desk, and stretch. I take a deep breath.

We made it. We didn't get caught.

Even though we're still a semester away from being able to admit we're dating, I feel better already because even though I know that I never treated her any differently than my other students when it came to class, it still felt awful to know I was doing something that *wrong*.

I spent most of yesterday and today figuring out what to do tomorrow, to celebrate the end of finals and the fact that she's no longer my student. I've considered art shows in Richmond, hikes in the mountains, and several different alleged haunted houses and abandoned sanitariums. There's something called Foamhenge. There's an amusement park called DinosaurLand, which has lots of statues of dinosaurs.

I finally settled on taking her to Luray Caverns, because it's cool, interesting, and no one there is going to have any idea who we are. We can hold hands and display affection publicly, and we'll just be some couple who wanted to come look at stalagmites, not a dirty old professor taking advantage of an innocent student.

That's what I hate the most about this situation, why I'm relieved that she's not my student any more. I *know* that what we have is real and true and deep, but the simple facts of it feel so shameful: professor, student; older, younger.

I hate that I'm supposed to be ashamed of falling for the most fascinating person I've ever met. I hate that I can't even brag to my brothers about how great she is.

I take my glasses off and rub my eyes with the heels of my hands, then will myself to get back to the last of the paperwork. I don't usually stay late in my office, but I'm hoping to have this all done so I can go to Sprucevale on Monday and spend Christmas week with my family.

I got Rusty a skateboard. Daniel's gonna pass out, but she'll love it.

One last time, I glance through the window, but Thalia's gone. All the more reason to finish this dumb request form and go home.

I've just signed it and am double-checking all the boxes one last time when there's a knock on my slightly-open door.

"Yeah?" I call, hoping it's not someone with more paperwork.

"Do you have a minute?" Thalia's voice says, and my head jolts up. "I know your office hours are over."

"Miss Lopez, come in," I say, taking a stack of papers and straightening them against my desk. "Did you have a question about the final?"

She enters, bag slung over one shoulder, her winter coat open, my scarf around her neck. She's been wearing it lately. I like that she wears it.

"No questions," she says, then glances out the door and raises one eyebrow at me. "I'm just glad it's over."

I nod, and she closes the door. I stand and twist the vertical blinds shut over the window behind my desk, because even though campus is pretty empty no one needs to see us together in my office, after hours, when the semester's finished.

"Me too," I say, walking around the desk and leaning against the other side.

Thalia puts her bag on one chair and shrugs her coat off. Underneath it she's wearing an above-the-knee skirt over tights, and despite everything, the slight glimpse of her thighs pings something in my reptilian brain.

Maybe it's my amygdala. My hippopotamus? Thalia knows, I don't.

"I'm officially done with my semester several hours early," she says, grinning, her hands on her hips. "I saw you were still here and figured I'd come say hi before I meet Margaret and Victoria for beers at the Rail."

"Congrats," I say, also grinning. "And no using the men's bathroom while you're there."

"Why?" she asks, laughing. "You're afraid that I'll meet another handsome, charming math professor?"

"That could be your move," I tease. "Lock yourself into

a bathroom, play the damsel in distress, next thing you know some poor hapless sucker is so besotted with you that he takes to the botanic garden that very night."

Thalia glances around quickly, like she's double-checking that we haven't overlooked a brand-new window in my office, then steps forward and puts her feet between mine, her arms resting on my chest.

"Okay, one, I'm not a damsel," she says. "Two, you're not exactly a poor hapless sucker —"

I grab her ass and give it a quick squeeze. Thalia yelps, then giggles.

"Shh," I admonish. "People are going to think I'm hurting you. With *math*."

"Sometimes math hurts," she says.

"You mean hurts so good."

"Do I?"

"You do," I say, grinning at her. "When dispatched correctly, mathematics can be *very* erotic."

"And I assume that you know how to dispatch math erotically?"

"Of course."

"Go on."

I give her ass another good squeeze, pressing her a little harder against me, and she laughs again. We're both in goofy moods, feeling a little punch-drunk from the semester, and she wriggles slightly against me.

"You can't get out of a discussion by grabbing my ass," she says.

"I bet I can," I say, and do it again.

"It's not working."

I've still got her ass firmly in both hands, and I give it a little jiggle.

"Yes, it is," I counter. "We're not discussing erotic math

any more, and I've got my hands full of the best ass on campus."

I'm also starting to get hard. I should never have grabbed her ass. I knew what would happen, and we're in my office, on campus, not to mention she's about to go get drinks with her friends.

"Well, the best ass just came by to say hi, give you a quick kiss, and ask what you're doing later tonight," she teases, looking up at me.

I release her ass and cup it gently, instead. It's a nice ass. I like touching it.

"You, I presume," I say. "When you show up at my door drunkenly demanding a good time."

"Is that a request?" she says, and now she's got her hands on the desk on either side of me and she cocks her hips and she grinds against me a little as she does, and it doesn't help my erection situation.

"That you drunkenly demand a good time? You don't have to be drunk," I tease back. "I'm happy to give you a good time whenever you demand one."

"I'd noticed," she says, a half-smirk on her upturned face.

"Sorry," I say, grinning. "Should I be saving that for your demands later tonight?"

"Thank you," she says, sweetly, and tilts her face up to mine for a kiss.

I kiss her quickly, not quite chastely but close enough, and a thrill goes through me. I shouldn't be kissing this girl at all and I definitely shouldn't be kissing her here, in my office, where a colleague could theoretically knock on my door at any moment.

Thalia pulls away for a second, still leaning against me, perched on her toes, my hands still cupping her ass, and her eyes search mine like she's thinking of something.

Then she kisses me again, and this time I lean into it. I know I shouldn't but I open my mouth, dart my tongue along her lower lip, feel her open to me as she pushes against me a little harder, her ass still in my hands.

By the time we part I'm hard as a rock, and we both know it. Thalia's slightly flushed, her eyelids slightly heavy, and I know for a fact that she's wet as all hell right now.

Half of me wishes she hadn't come by to say hello.

The other half wants to push her skirt up, her tights down, and make her come *before* she meets her friends for drinks.

"I should go before I land you in hot water," she says. "Just because I'm not technically your student any more doesn't mean it's a good idea to start getting it on in your office."

"It's a very bad idea," I agree, and I finally take my hands off her ass, take hers, give them each a quick kiss.

"Tonight?" she says, with that half-smile and head-cock I've come to dream about.

I intend to say *of course, tonight, I can't wait*.

What I actually hear myself say is, "The door *does* lock."

She turns her head, looks at the door, like she's confirming this information, then looks back at me.

"And if someone hears suspicious noises and knocks on it?" she asks.

"We'll pretend no one's here," I say, still leaning against the desk, letting myself cup her ass in my hands again. "What are they gonna do, knock down the door?"

Her lips quirk and move in that way that I know means she's thinking about it. I force myself to remain calm as the blood pounds through my veins, mildly worried that my cock is going to burst through my pants at any moment at the thought of Thalia bent over the desk where I graded her homework.

"I'm trying to keep you out of trouble, you know," she murmurs, teasing.

"And I'm trying desperately to get into it," I say, one eyebrow raised.

Then I lean in, kiss her slowly, deeply.

When I pull away, my lips still brushing hers, I murmur, "Tell me you're not wet thinking about getting bent over my desk and fucked."

Thalia smiles and leans into me, her belly against my hard cock, her fingers gently hooked under the waistband of my pants.

"All the way from *erotic mathematics* to this?" she teases.

"You're right, it wasn't math," I concede, and Thalia stands on her toes again, pushing herself up until her lips are against my ear.

"I was such a good girl until I met you, Professor Loveless," she murmurs, and pulls away.

She crosses the room. Locks the door. Double-checks that it's actually locked, surveys the blinds, then flips off the overhead lights leaving nothing but my desk lamp on.

"Someone outside might be able to see shapes through the blinds," she explains, coming back.

"Smart," I say, and gather her in my arms again. "I knew there was a reason I liked you."

She presses herself against me, rolling her hips along my hard cock, fingers through my belt loops.

"I thought it was my great ass," she teases.

I grab it again, obviously.

"The ass doesn't hurt," I say, and we kiss. I slide my hands down her hips, grab the fabric of her skirt, and pull it up until I can reach underneath, along the smooth surface of her tights, and between her legs from behind.

Thalia makes a noise that I've learned by heart and she presses forward, into me, asking for more as her fingers find the button on my pants, quickly pull it apart, grab the zipper and pull.

If there's a greater anticipation in life than the feeling of Thalia's hand pressing against my cock as she undoes my zipper, tooth by tooth, I've never found it. I growl and grab her ass again, hiking her skirt up higher, this time pushing my hand between her legs from the front, though she may as well be a Barbie doll with these tights on. I can't feel a damn thing.

Then she sighs and a tiny *oh* escapes her mouth while it's still on mine, and I know I've found her clit so I circle that spot slowly, gently, as my zipper reaches the bottom and Thalia grabs my cock through my boxers.

This time we groan together, and then she laughs and I bite her lower lip and she squeezes me a little harder, lightens her grip and strokes me gently with the fabric still between us, the friction thrilling.

I grab her hips again, her ass, slide my hands up her body. I slide them down. As I do she moves her hand inside my boxers and grasps me hard, stroking me from tip to root and back. I groan into her mouth, grab her ass one more time, and she smiles.

Finally, I give up searching for a way into her tights.

"Get these off," I growl. "Now."

She pulls back, cocks a smile, looks up at me in a way that's half sultry and half teasing.

"Yes, Professor," she says, and reaches way up under her skirt, past her waist, and pulls her tights down, shimmying her hips from side to side as she does.

I make a note of this, for later use, and the moment her tights are past her thighs I grab her again, pull her in, hook my thumbs under her panties and pull them off until they're tangled with her tights.

She strokes my cock again and I kiss her hard, fast. I slide my fingers between her legs and find her soaking wet.

"I love being right," I murmur. "I'd ask if you're ready but I've already got my answer."

"I just really like desks," she teases, and I give her one more kiss then step around her, pushing her against my desk, one hand on her hips and the other already between her legs again, strumming her clit, fingertips nudging between her slick folds at her tight entrance.

She braces herself, arches her back. I can hear her inhale sharply, hips moving back as my fingers tease at her, asking me to enter.

Then, finally, a thought occurs to me.

"Shit," I hiss, just as Thalia flexes backward again, taking me to the first knuckle.

"Inside pocket of my bag, all the way to the left," she says without missing a beat.

I pull away for a moment, open her bag. Find the pocket on the inside, rummage through one side. Just pens. I rummage through the other, hoping, praying.

After a long moment where I find nothing but more pens and a few stray tampons in their wrappers, my fingers search out that square, shiny foil packet that I've come to know and love.

Thalia's watching me, still bent over and arched, grinning like her plan's come together and in two steps I'm behind her again, the condom held tightly in one hand, my cock nestled between the perfect globes of her ass as I kiss the back of her neck.

"You planned this," I say, my voice low, raspy.

"I swear I didn't," she says, looking at me over her shoulder.

"I should have known better than to think you wanted to come say hi," I tease her, my lips still on her neck.

"That's been there since the night we made out in the library," she says, laughing and arching against me at the same time and *fuck* she feels good. "I figured that sooner or later we were going to do this somewhere stupid, so we should at least be safe about it."

It's no wonder that I'm so desperately in love with this girl. She's perfect.

I tear the condom open with my teeth, roll it down my cock while she watches me over her shoulder. When I'm done I slide my hand into her hair, move it from the back of her neck, and give her a long, slow kiss.

While I kiss her I tease her with my cock, sliding it between her lips, rubbing the tip against her clit, letting her push fruitlessly back against me while her breathing goes ragged.

Then, when I can't take it any more, I find her tight entrance with the tip of my cock, look down, and take her with one long, slow thrust.

Thalia groans softly as I enter her, clenches around me as I watch my cock disappear inside her, holding my breath as I sink into her tightness until she's taken every millimeter and I'm hilted, feeling her squeeze me like a fist.

Then I wait a moment, listening to her breathe, letting her adjust while I hold onto her hips, and after a few seconds she pushes back against me, asking for more.

I give her more. I do it slowly at first, pulling myself nearly all the way out before sinking in again, making sure I hit every single nerve center inside her. I do it carefully, adjusting the angle with every stroke until her moans are nonstop. I give myself to her and I look down and I watch myself fuck her because in the most pure, primal way I love watching my cock disappear inside her.

But I can't be careful for long, and Thalia doesn't need me to be. She moans and she whimpers and she whispers my name, bent over my desk.

She whispers *oh that feels good* and I fuck her a little harder, slide my hands under her shirt, and she glances over her shoulder, eyes heavy-lidded, lips parted.

"Does it?" I growl, driving hard, deep, listening to the noise she makes. "Does it feel good to get bent over my desk and fucked?"

"Yes," she says, half moan and half whisper.

"Does it feel good to make me lose my damn mind?" I ask, bending closer to her ear.

"Yes," she whimpers, her breathing sharp, erratic. "Don't stop, Caleb."

She's about to come.

"Please don't stop," she gasps. "Don't stop."

She doesn't always beg me not to stop but when she does it's her tell, a surefire sign that she's close, ready to explode.

I drive deep, hard, and she tells me again, again and I wrap an arm around her, hook it over her shoulder, pull her back against me as hard as I can.

"Does it feel good to be my bad girl, Thalia?" I whisper.

"Yes," she gasps, and then she comes.

There's nothing like it in the whole world: the way she clenches around my length, the way she moans and whispers and says *oh fuck, Caleb* and pushes back against me. The way she loses control and lets go. The way she grabs my hand and presses my knuckles to her mouth, she way she practically collapses onto my desk.

I don't stand a chance and I come hard, too, right after she finishes. I bury my face in her shoulder and my cock deep inside her, holding her tight against me and I growl her name into her ear while the aftershocks are still moving through her body and she's still rocking back and forth against me.

Finally, we stop. I've got my arms wrapped around her and we stand here, braced against my desk, towering over the paperwork that I didn't quite get finished earlier, my office spooky in the low light of the single desk lamp.

"We should probably never do that again," she murmurs.

I grin, then kiss her on the cheek.

"Probably not, but you liked it."

"True," she admits, leaning back against me, laughing softly. "True."

CHAPTER THIRTY-EIGHT

THALIA

I'm ten minutes late to the Rail, and they're already suspicious the moment I walk in the door. I can tell. I get a beer at the bar and slide into the round booth next to Victoria, and even though she, Margaret, and Harper all try to act like they don't notice I'm late, they do.

"Okay," says Harper, who seems determined to get this back on track. "Here's to the end of another semester, and to one more ahead of us."

"Hear, hear," says Victoria.

"Aye, aye," says Margaret.

"You're a pirate now?" Harper asks, and we all drink.

"I've always been a pirate," Margaret says when she comes up for air. "Not my fault you haven't noticed."

"I did think all those times you told me to walk the plank were odd," Harper admits.

"And that hook hand is pretty notable, but I didn't want to be rude," I add.

Victoria's got her beer in one hand, then points at Margaret with the other, her nails a deep, shimmering purple. That's how you can tell Victoria's stressed: she's painted her nails, something she always does when she needs to assert control over a situation, even if the situation is what color her nails are.

"Wait," she says. "Wait, no, this is a joke about booty and how much of it she finds."

"Yarr?" says Margaret, and with that whatever nervousness I had about this dissolves, and I start giggling like a schoolgirl. I start giggling and I can't stop, and after a moment Margaret and Victoria and Harper are giggling too, and then there are tears running down my face and I can't look at any of them and I also can't stop laughing.

"Stop," Harper gasps, hiding her eyes.

"I can't," squeaks Victoria.

"It's okay," says Margaret. "It's okay, it's under —"

Then she snorts and starts laughing all over again.

"Do you bury it?" Victoria asks, wiping tears out of her eyes.

"Booty?" snorts Margaret.

"Those poor boys," I say. "They must have sand in the worst places if she buries her booty."

"Oh no," giggles Harper. "Oh no. No, now I'm picturing it."

"Margaret's buried booty?" I ask. "I'm sure she gives them straws to breathe through."

"Those aren't straws," says Victoria.

"This is too weird, stop it," says Margaret, laughing almost too hard to talk.

"Is there a treasure map?" I wonder aloud. "Is this an 'X marks the spot' thing, or…?"

"Here be dragons?" says Victoria.

"Here be booty," corrects Harper, and Margaret just covers her face.

"I'm dying," Margaret says from behind her hands.

"We have to talk about something else. Med school placements. Anything. How's Todd?"

"Well, and back in Boston," answers Victoria. Todd's her boyfriend of a little over a year. "I guess that's where the X on my booty map would be."

I snort.

"Don't laugh or we'll talk about where *your* booty map X is," she says. "What's Josh the frat boy up to right now?"

I look from her to Margaret to Harper, then drain the rest of my beer.

I may have told them that I'm dating someone named Josh, a frat guy. None of them believed me for a single second.

"He went home," I say. "To… California. Does anyone else want another drink?"

· · · · ★ ★ ★ ★ ★ · · · ·

AN HOUR AND A HALF LATER, we're all on our fourth beers. Should I be having four beers? No. I should never be having four beers, because four beers is *so many beers*, but The Rail is having a 'last day of finals' special and most of campus has already gone home, and why not have four beers for once in my life?

That said, my fourth beer is still practically untouched, sitting in front of me, because three beers was already a lot.

"No," Margaret is saying, leaning forward over the table. "I hate it. I refuse to accept it. It's *wrong*."

"There's scientific evidence," Harper points out.

"My argument is a moral one," Margaret insists. "I reject this assertion on moral grounds."

Victoria just sighs.

"Margaret, that's stupid," she says, sounding very, very patient.

"No," Margaret says.

"Dinosaurs having feathers isn't immoral, it's just… a thing," I say, eloquently. "Like how you have skin. And hair. And a nose. Do you guys ever think about if aliens find human skulls a million years from now? They're going to reconstruct us *so ugly*."

I take a quick sip of my fourth beer.

"Dinosaurs must be pissed," I muse.

Harper reaches out and puts a hand on my arm.

"They're dead," she says gently. "Hence the reconstructions."

"Which are wrong, because fuck feathers on dinosaurs," Margaret chimes in.

"I think they're spectacular," says Victoria. "And fun."

"Dinosaurs are not *fun*," insists Margaret. "They're impressive. And awe-inspiring. And scary. And not feathered."

"You forgot *fabulous*," teases Victoria.

"And *funky*," I add.

"And…" Harper says, then blinks. Then narrows her eyes. "…flippant. Nope. Sorry, guys, my brain's out of words, I'm just gonna sit over here for a few minutes and be quiet. Few? Is that anything? No."

"She turned in her Taciturn paper ten minutes before we came over," Victoria says.

"It was Tacitus, and I hate him," Harper says through her hands. "I hope he's in hell."

"He probably is," I say comfortingly.

"Thank you."

"Speaking of things we were doing ten minutes before we got here, Thalia, what the fuck," says Margaret, who's the furthest through her fourth beer.

The table suddenly gets very quiet.

"What?" I ask, a bad feeling already worming its way through my stomach.

"You were *not* in the library. I went there to see if you wanted to walk over together," she says.

"I ran some errands after I finished my last paper," I say, drunk and defensive. Then I point at her. "And I don't have to tell you were I was. Fuck off. I wasn't running errands, I was in a secret location that I'm not telling you!"

"Not a secret," Harper says, looking down at the table.

"One last time to say *thanks for the A*?" Margaret asks.

Victoria puts one hand over her eyes.

"What the fuck?" I ask.

"We know Josh the frat boy is really Caleb the professor because we're not morons," she says, taking another drink of her beer and rolling her eyes.

"And you think I got an A because we're dating," I say. Anger flares in my chest, but I force myself to hold it back.

"Oh, come on, I was kidding," she says, smirking at me.

She wasn't kidding. We've been best friends for nearly four years, I know when she's kidding.

"What a funny joke," I say. "Thalia's not smart enough to get an A so she has to date the professor! Ha ha!"

"Sure, *dating*," she says. "That's what you're doing."

"Margaret, shut up," Harper says softly.

"Sorry, are you the only one who gets to call it that?" I ask. "When the rest of us go sleep with someone we're supposed to say 'hey I'm gonna go bang this dude' but you, Margaret, get to call it *dating*?"

"You don't get to call it dating when it's your professor," Margaret says, and drains her drink. "Calling it *dating* implies there's some level of —"

"Enough," declares Victoria, putting her half-full drink down loudly in the center of the table. "You two can talk about this when we're not all shit-faced because we're damn well not doing it now. Margaret, don't be a bitch. Thalia, stop lying to us about Josh the frat boy, we've all seen Caleb drop you off at one in the morning at our apartment and walk you to the front door. Maggie's at least right that we're not morons."

I drink.

"Don't call me —"

"Quiet, *Maggie*, or we'll do it for real," Harper says. "Thalia, I think it's weird that a professor is into a student but honestly he seems very sweet and you seem happy to be getting nailed by this dude, so power to you."

"This dude who you think gave me an A because I'm letting him nail me?" I hiss, leaning forward over the table.

"No one thinks that," Victoria says quickly, shooting a glare at Margaret. Margaret won't look at me. "You're obviously capable of getting your own A."

"And your own D!" Harper says, brightly.

No one laughs.

"Sorry," she says.

I close my eyes and lean my back against the booth behind me, but that just makes everything spin unpleasantly, so I hold my head upright, keep my eyes closed.

"Fine," I say, without opening them. "Fine. Yes, there is no Josh the frat boy and yes okay *fine* it's actually Caleb but it's not in exchange for grades, it just sort of happened, and yes I know it's bad, but…"

I don't know but *what*. All I know is that I shouldn't have had this fourth beer, end of the semester or not. I know that admitting that we're together even to my closest friends feels like I'm betraying Caleb, but lying to them about it felt like I was betraying them.

"…but I like him?" I finally say. "I don't know, you guys, I just like him. That's all. I like a guy and he sort of happened to also be my calculus professor, and now he's not any more and if you could please just keep this quiet until June, that would be really cool, okay?"

"Okay," agrees Harper, instantly.

"Okay," shrugs Victoria.

I open my eyes, and we all look at Margaret.

"Okay," she finally says, her eyes on her empty glass and not on us.

"Thanks," I sigh.

· · · * * ★ * * · · ·

I SLEEP over at Caleb's that night. We don't even have sex again, he just comes and gets me from the bar, then lets me drunkenly raid his fridge while I sober up a little and recount the should-dinosaurs-have-feathers argument that I had with my roommates.

For the record, he is very definitely laughing at me, even as he coerces me into drinking water and eating some bread. I tell him several times that dino feathers are no laughing matter, but I can't keep a straight face either.

I don't mention the other argument.

I wake up to Caleb's hand on my shoulder, shaking me softly.

"Thalia," he says. "Hey. Thalia."

I feel like someone's dragging me up from underwater. When I finally open my eyes and look at him, I'm not sure what's happening.

"Huh?"

"Your phone," he says.

"What?"

"Your phone is ringing," he says, groggy but patient, and I lift my head a little higher.

Then, finally, I hear the muffled, tinny sound.

"What time is it?" I ask, then glance at the bedside click myself.

Four-thirty in the morning.

"Shit," I mutter, then roll out of bed. At least I'm not drunk any more, but I'm not exactly at my best, either. I manage to find my way to my purse, tossed in a corner last night, and then rummage through it until I finally get to my phone.

The moment I find it, the thing stops ringing, and the missed calls pop up.

It's from Bastien.

Actually, I've got four missed calls from Bastien, and that's when the fear grips my heart. I let myself slide to the floor, the wood cold against my bare thigh, my head pounding, my whole body feeling heavy.

"What is it?" Caleb asks from the bed, just as my phone starts ringing again. This time, I answer immediately.

"What happened?" I ask, not bothering with a greeting.

On the other end, Bastien clears his throat.

"They found Javi," he says.

I can't breathe. I need to know, need to ask, but I can't find the air to do it with.

"Alive," Bastien says.

CHAPTER THIRTY-NINE
CALEB

Thalia bursts into tears.

I've never gotten out of bed so fast. I drag half the sheets and the blankets after me, spilling onto the floor, as I kneel next to her and put one arm around her, my other hand on her leg.

"Where?" she whispers into the phone as she turns to me, eyes wide, tears spilling out.

Then she shakes her head, looks away from me at the wall again, puts her hand over mine on her leg and I have no idea what any of that means.

"In Richmond?" she asks, pauses. "Is that — is he still? Can they keep him, or —"

Another pause, and even though I can only hear her half of the conversation, I've got a feeling that I know who this is about.

Thalia closes her eyes and tears drop from beneath her lashes. I plant my lips on her bare shoulder and keep them there.

"Okay," she says. "Right. But —"

Another long pause, and she looks over at me.

"He'll be okay, right?" she asks, into the phone. "From this, I mean? The worst is over from this?"

She waits a second for a response.

"Thanks," she says. "I'll let you know. Love you. Tell Mom and Dad that too. Thanks, Bossy. Bye."

She pulls her phone away from her face and hangs up, turns it off, plunging my bedroom back into darkness with nothing but the faint light of a street lamp around the edges of my curtains.

Thalia takes a long, unsteady breath, then lets it out, and I pull her toward me until her head is on my shoulder.

"Javier?" I ask.

"Yeah," she whispers, her voice rough. She clears her throat, takes another breath, wipes at her face. "He overdosed, but —" she takes another deep, rough breath, " — he got the Narcan in time and someone called 911, so now he's in the hospital in Richmond. Bastien and my parents are heading there now."

"But he'll be okay?" I ask, letting my fingers drift through her hair.

"He survived the overdose," she says. "*Okay* is... a big ask."

"That's all I meant," I tell her, already wishing I'd said something else, like *alive*.

"I know," she sighs, and I wrap my arms around her, let her lean against my chest.

"I'm ready to go whenever you are," I tell her, looking at the street light filtering through the window. It's close to the winter solstice, so the sun won't be up for nearly two and a half more hours. We might be there before the sun.

Thalia's quiet for a long, long moment.

"I can't ask you for this," she says.

"You're not asking."

"I've never given you anything back," she says, her

voice a scratchy whisper in the near-dark. "I came home way too drunk last night and ate all your snacks while I was complaining about dinosaurs, and you put up with me and got me to bed properly, and now it's not even five in the morning and my stupid family has more awful bullshit and I can't — you can't be this nice to me, Caleb. You can't."

All I hear is her saying *I came home*. She just called my house *home*, and something deep inside me grows wings and takes flight.

"I'm not being nice if it's what I want to do," I tell her. "I want you to see your brother. I'd want to see mine. It's really that simple."

"I'm sorry we're such a trash fire," she goes on. "I've got a junkie brother and a closeted brother and my parents don't talk and my dad's just a straight up asshole. Jesus. Meanwhile you've got this perfect beautiful family with an awesome niece and a cute nephew and four older brothers who are all functional adults and your cool mom is a fucking *astronomer*, I mean, come on."

"Those assholes are *not* perfect," I say, quietly, and Thalia lets out a single laugh.

"You know what I mean," she says. "You're so wholesome and here I come with all... this. I'm sorry."

I start laughing softly at *wholesome*. I try not to, but I can't help it.

"Okay, what?" she says.

"Levi's a weirdo who talks to trees and has personal relationships with every squirrel in his yard," I say. "Eli failed out of college and then disappeared for a while to backpack the world before he decided to become a chef. Daniel spent his teens and early twenties raising hell until he impregnated a monster of a woman who didn't even tell him he had a kid, Seth'll fuck anything with two legs and tits, and my cool mom's been lying to everyone for years."

Thalia's quiet a moment.

"Oh," she finally says.

I decide, right then, that I'm going to tell her the thing that I've never told anyone.

"And my father, the heroic policeman who has a road and a building named after him, was drunk when he died," I say.

Thalia goes very, very still.

"In the car accident?" she asks, her voice small.

"He hit a tree doing seventy down a mountain road," I say, heart still beating fast.

I can't believe I told someone. It feels surreal, like maybe I could still reverse time and undo it.

"Oh, my God," she whispers.

"The county coroner knew him," I say, suddenly unsure how to proceed. "And she knew my mom, and she knew us, so when she found out that he had a blood alcohol level of point twelve she covered it up. My mom was the only person she told. I guess she thought she deserved to know the truth."

I stare into the dark, remembering two things at once: the late-night knock on our door, watching from the stairs as my mom opened it, Levi's hand on my shoulder, and then also years later, when I was the only one still living at home, overhearing my mom on the phone.

I remember the fight we got into, the fight we had for weeks afterward: me, a know-it-all, righteous teenager; my mom, steely and pragmatic. I wanted to tell my brothers, to tell the town newspaper, to tell everyone. I wanted to share my disgust and horror with the world, but she talked me out of it.

She said he'd already paid for what he did. That at least he hadn't hurt anyone else, that we didn't need to pay for it too. That he wasn't a bad person — he wasn't even much of a drinker — he was someone who made a bad decision and paid for it.

So I never told anyone, not even my brothers. Thalia was the first.

"Did he hurt anyone else?" she asks, softly, looking at me like she's afraid of the answer, but I just shake my head.

"Even the tree lived," I say. "It's still there with a marker in front of it, though I never go that way unless I have to. It happened in January. Everyone blamed black ice, and no one but my mom and I know the truth, and we've both been lying about it for years."

"I'm sorry," she says.

I raise her hand to my lips, flip it over, kiss her on the palm.

"Everyone is fucked up somehow," I say. "Don't apologize."

"You forgot to tell me how you're fucked up," she says. "Other than lying to your brothers, I guess."

I start laughing again, despite everything. She pulls away and gives me a puzzled, amused look.

"Come on, Thalia," I say, leaning forward and planting a kiss on her shoulder. "I slept with my student."

"Right," she says, and she's laughing and wiping tears away all at once.

"Come on," I tell her, holding out my hand. "Let's go to Richmond."

CHAPTER FORTY

THALIA

When we get to the hospital, Bastien and my father are both outside, standing next to a bench in front of a dilapidated flower bed. They're not speaking, but when they see Caleb's car pull into the parking lot, they both nod once in exactly the same way.

Chapman Memorial isn't as nice as the last hospital Caleb drove me to. The outside is ugly, the gray concrete weathered and stained, the windows faded and ugly, a patchwork of slightly different colors. The first M is missing from the sign over the door that says Chapman Memorial. The garbage cans and ashtrays outside the door are overflowing.

It's also clearly in a bad neighborhood. I don't know Richmond very well — hardly at all — but the houses here are all in disrepair and all the stores have bars over the windows, even during the day. Tents dot the sidewalk, and I'm pretty sure I saw a drug deal go down on the way here.

Not that I should be surprised, given why I'm here in the first place.

Caleb parks his hatchback, jerks up the parking brake, turns to me.

"We're all fucked up," he says, softly. Despite myself, I smile.

"Thanks," I say, and give him a quick, chaste kiss.

We talked the whole car ride over. Or rather, I think I talked for most of it and he listened: the Javier I remember as a kid, the big brother who taught me to roller skate, who helped with my homework, who used to drive me to my friends' houses sometimes.

I talked about the brother Bastien and I both adored, who was sweet and gentle and kind. The brother who loved to draw, who had notebooks filled with sketches, who used to win every art show he entered in middle and high school.

And I tell him how he used to fight with my father. How he joined the football team just to get my father's approval. How, suddenly, my father was his biggest supporter who went to every game, learned every cheer.

He didn't apply to college. He didn't apply to art school. He joined the Marines straight out of high school, the only other thing he ever did that my father approved of.

Caleb and I walk up to the entrance holding hands, because there's no point pretending we're just friends. The whole walk from the parking lot, I can practically feel my father's eyes burning a hole through the back of my hand, he's looking at us so hard.

"Hi," I say, when I get up to them. "You remember Caleb, right? How's Javi?"

"Alive," says my father, stepping forward, offering Caleb a handshake while Bastien gives me a hug.

"Sir," Caleb says behind me, and I fight back a smile.

"He's already sucking up," Bastien whispers. "Dad's gonna hate him anyway."

"Stop it," I whisper back.

"Thanks for bringing her," Bastien tells Caleb when he releases me, shaking his hand as well.

"Of course," Caleb says, and takes my hand again. My father looks at it, looks at me, and then leads us through the doors of the hospital.

The inside isn't nicer than the outside. We walk past a gift shop that's got a crack running the length of the plate-glass window, masking tape over it. The tile floor is mismatched. Here and there, a fluorescent light flickers.

Bastien drops back to walk beside us, lets our dad lead the way down hallway after hallway, always walking as if a drill sergeant is watching.

I turn to my brother.

"How is he?" I ask, voice low, dread and anxiety knotted in my stomach. "And don't just tell me he's alive."

I shoot a quick glance at my father's back. I've spent a lot of the last nine or so months trying to, if not forgive him, reach a place of some understanding, some acceptance that he did what he thought was best.

It's quickly going out the window, now that I'm here. Now that I'm going to have to look my older brother in the eye.

"Please," Bastien mutters, then takes a deep breath.

I squeeze Caleb's hand, without really meaning to, and he squeezes back.

"He's bad, Ollie," Bastien says, simply. "He's not Javi any more. He doesn't look like Javi. He doesn't talk like Javi, he doesn't..."

We've come to a stop, my father standing outside the door to a hospital room, arms folded, facing us. Bastien, Caleb, and I are ten feet away, and it's obvious that we're trying to talk without him hearing us, but I don't care.

"He wasn't Javi when he left," I say.

"He was more than he is now," Bastien says. "Someone

found him on the sidewalk in front of a 7-11, sitting on the curb, doubled over. The only reason he's not dead is because he was holding the dose of Narcan he couldn't use in time, and whoever called 911 gave it to him first, then ran off."

I look at the door to the hospital room, my father standing in front of it, and suddenly I'm afraid of what I'll find. I'm afraid to look at him like this, afraid to confirm what Bastien just said, that Javier is really gone.

Next to me, Caleb is silent and I squeeze his hand again, grateful, because there's nothing he could say right now and he knows that.

"I need to ask you a favor," I say, looking up at him.

"Anything."

"Would you mind waiting while we go in?" I ask, softly.

"I can do that," he says.

"I don't want you to meet him like this," I say, the words rushing out, a little faster than I mean them to. "I don't — it's not fair to him, or to you, for you to meet him now. You should meet him once he's in recovery, once he's —"

I almost say *better* but I've already learned that addicts never are, not fully. They're forever in recovery, but I can't let this be Caleb's first impression of my big brother. I can't.

"—improved," I finish.

"Of course," Caleb says softly. "Just shout if you need me."

Then he bends and gives me a quick, sweet kiss on the cheek, and I squeeze his hand, and then I steel myself and let Bastien and my father lead me into Javier's hospital room.

It's not a nice hospital room, just like it's not a nice hospital, just like it's not a nice neighborhood. I can't help but compare everything to the last time I was in a hospital, three months ago, in Norfolk for my mom. I wasn't really paying attention at the time, but in comparison, it was the Ritz of hospitals.

There are three beds in Javier's room, separated by curtains. He's in the middle, and while I can't see either of the people in the other beds, I can hear the man in the first one breathing heavily and coughing occasionally the whole time I'm in there, and the man in the third bed keeps up a low, painful moan the entire time.

When I enter, my father's already pulled back the curtain around Javier, just enough for Bastien and I to enter, so I don't have time to prepare myself.

Not that I think I could have.

He's thin, cheeks hollow, once-golden skin nearly gray. The circles around his eyes look like black holes. His hair is combed but dirty. Someone's cleaned his face, but it's obvious from the smell behind the curtain that it's the only clean part.

There are bruises down his arms, most old. There are scabs and rashes, his fingernails dirty and broken. He'll be twenty-seven in May, and right now he looks a rough forty-five.

But none of that is the worst part. I stand there, just inside the curtain, taking it all in. I tried to prepare myself but it didn't help because I'm shocked, horrified, standing here gawking at him like he's a freak show and I've paid fifty cents to ogle.

The worst part is when he finally looks at me, his eyes flat and lifeless. They linger a moment, then look away again as he turns his head.

"Not her, too," he says, his voice rough. "Come on."

"Javi?" I say, his words finally breaking the spell. I step forward, into the space between curtain and bed, stand at his side next to my mom. She's still got one arm in a cast, the other holding Javier's hand.

"Did you have to get everyone?" he asks, his eyes still closed. "You just had to make sure that Ollie and Bossy saw me like this, too, didn't you?"

"Javi," my mom starts, squeezing his hand.

"They wanted to come," my dad says, standing at the foot of the bed, curtain still open behind him, arms folded over his chest. He's standing ramrod straight, as always.

"Raul," my mom says, without looking at him.

Silence takes over for a long moment, and then she turns and looks at my father.

He leaves without another word.

"He's right, I wanted to come," I say. "We've been looking for you."

"I've been looking harder than she has," Bastien says, standing across the bed from me, on the other side of Javier. "She's kind of been slacking."

"I'm not slacking," I say, making a face at Bastien. "I get through my list of phone calls once a week, I just don't fart around finding out which shelters are in buildings once used as hideouts on the Underground Railroad."

"So you admit I'm more thorough than you," Bastien says, and now he's grinning.

"That doesn't mean better."

"Bastien! Thalia," my mom says, in a tone of voice I know very, very well. "Knock it off and show a little respect, your brother's in the hospital."

Bastien gives me a smirk that clearly means *yeah, Thalia, knock it off*, but then we both look down at Javier.

His eyes are open again, he's looking at us, and I could swear there's the hint of a smile on his face. My heart doesn't exactly leap, but it sits up.

"You two need to help me convince him to go back into

rehab," she says, sternly. "That's why you're here. Javier, look at your brother and sister. Don't you want to see Thalia graduate this spring? She's even got a boyfriend!"

Anything that was on his face a moment ago is gone now, replaced by the same blankness that was there when I walked in.

"Bastien doesn't have a girlfriend yet but I'm certain the right girl is out there, just waiting for him," she goes on. "And for you, Javi. You just have to go to rehab and get clean before you can meet her."

I reach out and gently touch my mom's shoulder, and she looks over at me: red-faced and puffy-eyed, her white-streaked hair pulled away from her face in in a low bun, her reading glasses perched on her head.

"Could Bastien and I have a minute with Javier?" I ask, softly. "Just a minute. Please?"

She looks from me to Bastien to Javier and then back up to me. She squeezes Javi's hand again, then nods and stands.

"Of course," she says. "I'll be back, Javi. Promise."

"Thanks, Mom," he says, and she takes me by the shoulder, then kisses me on the cheek before she leaves. Bastien watches her go, then closes the curtain, walks back to Javier's bedside.

"Sorry, I needed to do something before she started naming your grandchildren," I tell them.

I love my mom dearly, but the way that she deals with hard emotions is often by imagining a happy-but-far-away future, and I don't think Javier needs that kind of pressure right now.

"Well, Raul and Paloma, obviously," Bastien jokes.

"Are those the names you and your future girlfriend will be using?" I ask, sweetly, teasing him right back.

Bastien just grimaces.

"Right," he says. "The sweet, innocent girl who's out there just waiting for me, and who is very definitely female and not a six-foot-one lacrosse player named Liam from Colorado."

My eyes go wide.

"*Is* there a Liam?" I ask.

Ever-so-slightly, Javier's eyebrows go up, and there's a flicker of interest in his dark eyes, but Bastien just snorts.

"I wish," he says. "Sorry, that was more of a request from the universe than a statement of fact."

"Colorado?" Javier asks, rough and scratchy, and Bastien shrugs.

"People seem like they're always outdoors in Colorado," he says. "It's *rugged*, you know?"

It's still weird that Bastien and I have the same taste in men. It makes sense, but it's weird. I like to think that it would also be weird if he were my straight sister, but who knows. Maybe I'm homophobic in this very specific way. Something to contemplate later.

"He still hasn't told Mom and Dad," I tell Javier.

"Can't blame him," Javier says.

"I'm not saying he should," I amend myself. "Just that he hasn't."

"They also don't know that Ollie's boyfriend is her calculus professor," Bastien says. "He's outside, she wouldn't let him meet you like this."

"He's not my professor any more," I point out. "Semester's over."

Javier swallows hard, and a bead of sweat rolls down his temple. His pupils are enormous, and it's impossible to tell where they end and his irises begin.

"You did that?" he asks. "Really?"

"Yeah," I admit, shifting my weight to my other foot, rubbing the back of my neck. "Yeah."

Javier shakes his head, almost like he's admonishing me, and for a moment there's a glimpse of the older brother I used to have.

"They're gonna freak the fuck out," he says, still raspy, unnatural sounding, still shaking his head. Now he's shaking it like he's in a trance and can't stop, his hands twisting in the bedsheets. "Dad's gonna flip his shit. He really is."

He's right, and several minutes too late, I realize that Caleb and my parents are now all together, somewhere outside this room, and I say a quick silent prayer that my dad hasn't made any veiled-or-not threats to him yet.

"That's my problem," I say, quickly. "We're not here about my problems."

Javier pushes his head back against the pillow, his hands still twisting, clenching, like he can't stop moving.

"Rehab didn't work," he says. "I tried it."

"If you look at the statistics, it almost always takes a couple of rounds," I say.

"Jesus," he mutters.

"Many people find Him helpful during the process, yes," Bastien adds in.

"It's not going to work," Javier says, and now he sits up a little, his face going even grayer, pushing at the sheets he's got over himself. "Last time I lasted a week after I got home. One whole week. Woo-fucking-hoo."

"That's got nothing —"

"Then stay clean for more than a week," Bastien interrupts me, suddenly grabbing the rails of Javier's bed and leaning over it. "Try two weeks this time, Javi. Maybe go for a whole three."

Javier swallows again, twice, convulsively.

"And if you relapse we'll put you back in rehab and

when you come out you'll go for four," Bastien says. "You're not escaping us."

We both know that we're not what Javi wants to escape, but neither of us say that out loud. I don't know how to deal with that. Bastien doesn't know how to deal with that, so we just stay quiet and hope that someone, somewhere will.

"If you go, I'll give you all the dirt on Bastien," I offer. "Here's a preview: his college major isn't what he told Mom and Dad it is."

Bastien grins awkwardly and gives Javier a thumbs-up.

"I want the dirt on her, too," Javier tells him.

"Done," Bastien agrees.

"And I want to meet this," he says, then swallows again, takes a breath, "shady-ass professor who thinks he can date my little sister while she's in his class."

"He's older than you, too," I volunteer. "I went full-on bad girl, and I'll tell you about it if you go to rehab."

"This is bribery," he rasps.

"Yes," Bastien and I both say at the exact same time.

I swear, Javier nearly smiles.

"All right," he finally says.

CHAPTER FORTY-ONE
CALEB

I take a seat in the waiting room. At least I think it's the waiting room; the sign has come off the door, just leaving a few lines of glue where it was once attached. There are blue vinyl chairs arranged in rows, fake plants, and old People magazines scattered around, so it seems like a waiting room.

I take a seat. I pick up a magazine. The cover has a badly-photoshopped picture of two celebrities on it, and a huge headline screams THIS TIME IT'S FOR REAL - BRAD AND ANGIE SPLIT!

I open it to a random page and hope that Thalia's okay. I understand why she didn't want me meeting Javier right now. I think I'd have chosen something similar if it were me and one of my brothers, but I wish I could be there for her.

Even if I don't know how, not really. The big tragedy of my life was a single gut-punch when I was a child, followed by an ugly, uneasy truth learned years later, and I only know how that feels. I only know how to slowly heal from something that's happened, not how to stay sane when the wound gets re-opened again and again.

I'm staring down at some women in evening gowns and thinking about Thalia when the door opens and her father walks into the room. He stops immediately inside the door, then scans the room like he's taking note of everything that's wrong with it.

Finally, he seems to notice me sitting there, and he walks over. He sits in a chair opposite me, his hands on his thighs, back ramrod straight. I put the magazine back down on the coffee table, sit up a little straighter myself.

"Captain Lopez," I say, and nod.

"Caleb," he says, and nods curtly back. The minor inequality of our names grates on me — we're both adults, I'm not his subordinate — but I have every reason under the sun to let it go, so I do.

"How is Javier?" I ask, the natural next question.

"Alive," he says again, then seems to catch himself. "My wife is in with him right now, trying to talk him into letting us put him through rehab again."

His jaw flexes, like he doesn't approve of this plan but has no alternative.

"I see," I say.

"How long have you been dating my daughter?" he asks, changing direction on a dime. "As I recall, you also drove her to see her mother in September. Quite a drive."

"A few months," I say, ignoring the second part of his statement.

"She hasn't said anything to us about having a boyfriend," he says, his tone perfectly neutral but somehow aggressive at the same time, like he'd like to start an argument with me in this hospital waiting room.

I am perversely tempted to say *well, sir, that's because she's one of the many women who I'm casually fucking right now*, even though it's completely untrue. There's just a part of me that wants to see this man's reaction to that statement.

"No?" I ask, perfectly neutral.

"No," he says. "Not a word."

"I guess that's her choice, isn't it?"

That doesn't get a response. Instead, he crosses one ankle over the opposite knee and puts an elbow on the armrest.

"And what is it you do?"

Shit. It did occur to me that this would come up, but then Thalia's phone rang again and it was Bastien with another update, and I forgot to tell her we should figure out a lie.

"I'm a graduate student," I say, since the lie that's closest to true is usually the best. "Mathematics."

"What do you plan on doing with that?" he asks.

"I'll be going on the academic job market soon," I say.

"Not too many opportunities there," he says. "You'd make a much better living going into cyber security or working with the dee-oh-dee. That's the Department of Defense."

"I'll see what I can find and consider my options," I tell him, just as the door to the waiting room opens again, and Thalia's mother steps through.

I've never actually met her before, but this woman looks so much like Thalia that it can't be anyone else. Raul turns and looks at her, and as she walks over we both stand.

"This is Caleb, Thalia's new boyfriend," her father says, and I hold out my hand.

"It's a pleasure to finally meet you, Mrs. Lopez," I say. "I'm sorry it had to be like this."

"It's Paloma, and thank you," she says, her grip surprisingly strong. "Thank you for bringing her. She and Bastien are in there right now, trying to talk some sense into him."

Her eyes are bloodshot, puffy, her cheeks splotchy, but she half-smiles at me.

"He's a graduate student who'll be going on the academic job market soon," Captain Lopez says to his wife.

Her face changes the instant she turns to look at him, her mouth going into a thin line.

"We're paying for rehab," she tells her husband. "We'll pay for it this time, and we'll pay for it the next time, and with God as my witness we'll pay for it until he's clean if it takes our entire life savings and both our retirement accounts."

"You're going to bankrupt us coddling him into getting clean?" Thalia's father says.

"It's better than turning him out onto the streets to —"

"Excuse me," I say, step around them, and leave the room.

· · · · ★ ★ ★ ★ ★ ★ · · · ·

THE DAY IS complete pandemonium before it's ten in the morning. I'm sitting on a bench, outside the hospital's back door, watching a man in a hospital gown chain smoke when Thalia texts me that she's done talking to Javier, where'd I go?

The hospital wants him discharged. They wanted him discharged hours ago, because his life is no longer in danger and they need the bed back, but Paloma had begged them and they relented.

I get Thalia's laptop out of my car, then head back upstairs with her and Bastien. Paloma is with Javier, somewhere. Captain Lopez has gone to the cafeteria to drink endless cups of coffee and presumably stare at a wall.

Our mission is simple: find a place that can take Javier today, now, before he has a chance to change his mind, and before he has a chance to start detoxing in earnest. Thalia finds locations and phone numbers; Bastien and I do the calling.

Thus begins my crash course in drug rehabilitation centers. Some are simple, affordable, relatively bare-bones. Some sound like resort spas. One offers something called crystal alignment therapy. One offers horseback riding therapy; neither has any openings for weeks.

Together, we work through the listen. Bastien finds a place with an opening, up in Northern Virginia, close to D.C., then I find a place in Maryland, near Ocean City. The list of options grows slowly. There are city rehabs and country rehabs, even a fishing rehab. One's on a working dairy farm. One is also a daschund rescue. Several are very religious.

But in the end, we choose the place that specializes in addicts who also have PTSD. Thalia is adamant, and neither of us argue. It's in the middle of nowhere, a few miles outside Lynchburg, and the only reason it has an opening at all is because someone didn't show up yesterday.

Bastien calls to make the arrangements, and as he paces back and forth, trying to answer questions that I don't think he knows the answers to, Thalia leans over and puts her head on my shoulder.

"Thank you," she whispers, and I put my arm around her, then kiss the top of her head.

· · * * ★ ★ ★ ★ * * · ·

WE SAY goodbye standing next to her parents' minivan after we put her stuff into it. She's going with them to take Javier to rehab, then back to Norfolk for winter break.

After we put her suitcase into the back, she looks at it, then rubs her eyes with her hands, and turns to sit on the tailgate and I follow suit.

"Did I apologize yet?" she asks, leaning her head on my shoulder.

"You did, and I told you to cut it out," I remind her.

"Did I say thank you?" she asks.

"Yes," I confirm, resting my cheek against the top of her head, my arm around her, looking out at the other cars in the parking lot, the gray sky, the spindly, leafless trees.

"I wish we were on a date right now," she says, kicking her feet out in front of her. "Whatever you had planned, I have a feeling it wasn't a questionable hospital in a bad part of Richmond."

"Should it not have been?" I ask, and she laughs. "Oops."

"My parents didn't get weird, did they?" she asks. "I didn't realize until it was too late that I'd accidentally left you alone with them, which probably wasn't a great move."

"I *am* a capable adult who can hold his own among other adults," I remind her. "I know how to act."

"Calling my dad *sir* was a very nice touch," she admits.

"But I also panicked a little and told them I'm a grad student," I say.

"I'll take it," Thalia says, and puts her hand on my thigh. I've got my right arm around her shoulders, so I put my left hand over hers.

Then she rotates her temple against my shoulder and looks up at me.

"I also didn't get to give you my Christmas present," she says, and then wiggles her eyebrows.

God help me, it works. I barely slept last night and then spent the morning driving and calling rehab centers, but that eyebrow wiggle still works on me.

"Is it the return of Sexy Freud?" I tease. "Tell me you didn't get rid of it."

"I mostly didn't," she says. "Though the bra was never

mine to begin with, and I should probably go ahead and confess that it was mostly socks anyway."

I stare at a young, leafless tree, quietly replaying select elements of that night in my head. I don't remember a single sock.

"Your bra was socks?" I finally ask, forcing myself to think of something else.

"Yeah, I stuffed it," she says, sounding surprised. "The socks were clean, but that was definitely not all boob."

"Oh," I say, and Thalia starts laughing.

"You never noticed that my boobs are, like, half the size that they looked in that bra?" she asks. "I couldn't even get the vest buttoned over the socks."

"I noticed *that*," I say. "But I can't say I do a lot of critical thinking when I look at your breasts."

She just laughs.

"Mainly, I'm thinking about how great it is to see them again," I admit. "How much I like looking at them. How fun it is to touch them. There's very little analysis."

"I should have kept my secret," she says.

"I would literally never have known."

"That wasn't your Christmas present, though," she says. "Can I give it to you when I get back?"

"What is it?"

"You'll find out when I give it to you, won't you?"

"Difficult," I tease.

"Nosy," she teases back, and I give her a long-but-chaste kiss.

When it ends, she takes a deep breath, then hops off the tailgate of the minivan and faces me.

"I should go," she says, softly. "See you in three weeks."

I've never lamented a long winter break before.

"Three weeks," I agree. "It's not that long."

"I think it might feel that way," she says, steps forward,

and kisses me. She kisses me sweetly, gently. It's a long, lingering kiss, and when it's over, I can still feel it in my bones.

When it ends I give her one brief, final kiss on the forehead, and then it's over.

"I'll miss you," she says, giving my land one last squeeze.

I nearly say *I love you*, but instead I say, "I'll miss you too," and she turns and walks back toward the hospital and I drive back to Marysburg, alone.

CHAPTER FORTY-TWO
CALEB

I pick up another cookie from the plate and pop it into my mouth as I walk through the kitchen.

"The usual," Thalia's saying. "Which over here is a big Christmas Eve dinner and then midnight mass. Per tradition, I nearly fell asleep in the pew and Bastien had to keep elbowing me to keep me awake."

"Midnight's not that late," I say, crumbly bits of cookie shooting out of my mouth. I try to catch some in my hand, but I don't. Oops.

"It was dark and warm and mass is very soothing sometimes," she says. "What are you eating?"

I swallow quickly.

"A cookie," I say. "My mom baked. You'll still be interested if I weigh an extra fifty pounds when I get back to campus, right?"

"We'll see," she says, laughing. "Did Daniel actually faint?"

"No, but he might still kill me," I say, finding a quiet corner of the kitchen and leaning against the wall. "It remains a distinct possibility."

Seth and I teamed up and got Rusty a skateboard for Christmas. It's electric blue and bright purple, and has a picture of a badass unicorn on the bottom. She loves it. Daniel, her father, hates it, even though we *also* got her knee pads, elbow pads, and a helmet.

We're very responsible uncles. Really.

"She'll be fine," Thalia says, as if she knows anything about skateboarding. "By the way, my family says hi."

"Hi," I say, and she snorts.

"They also want to know when you're graduating, what your prospects are, what your dissertation is on, what religion you are, whether you'd convert to Catholicism, when the last time you went to church was, whether you're *also* waiting for marriage, where your family is from originally, how long they've been in Sprucevale, whether anyone in your direct male line has served in the military, and if it's not too much trouble, they'd appreciate blood, saliva, and hair samples."

I glance over at the cookies and contemplate taking one more. On one hand, I've already eaten too many, but on the other hand, my mom's lemon-iced spice cookies are amazing.

"Can you repeat the first one?" I ask.

"The good news is that this means my mom likes you," Thalia says. "The bad news is that she has a couple of misconceptions about our relationship."

"Oh?"

"You know, one or two," Thalia says. "Probably starting with the idea that most of our time together consists of going on dates to the movies and leaving an empty seat between us for the Holy Spirit —"

"Ooh!" a voice says at the kitchen door. "Is that Thalia?"

Charlie's standing there, Thomas in a carrier on her

chest, utterly asleep and oblivious to the world in a way that only small babies can be.

"I've been discovered," I say *sotto voce* to Thalia.

"Hi!" calls Charlie, cheerfully coming over and grabbing a cookie on the way.

"Which one is that?" Thalia asks.

"Put it on speaker," Charlie says, grinning practically from ear to ear. "Come on. He won't quit talking about you!" she calls, standing on her tiptoes next to me and leaning in.

"Do you mind if I put it on speaker?" I ask Thalia, giving Charlie a dirty look.

She and Daniel, her now-husband, have been best friends since I was about eight years old, so she's the closest thing I've got to an older sister. Right now, that means she's been hassling me about my new girlfriend nonstop, along with the rest of my family.

Everyone knows that she exists and her name is Thalia.

Only a select few — Levi and Seth, and probably June since she's engaged to Levi — know she was my student, or even that she's an undergrad.

"Go for it," Thalia says, and I pull my phone away from my face.

"Behave yourself," I mutter to Charlie, before I hit the button.

"Hiiiiiii!" she says, grinning like a maniac. "He seriously won't shut up about you. Oh, now he's giving me a look like I wasn't supposed to say that so he could play it cool?"

On the other end, Thalia is just laughing.

"Anyway, how was your Christmas? If you celebrate. If not, how was your Friday?"

"It was nice," Thalia starts. "It was just my family —"

"Is that the new girlfriend?" Eli asks, suddenly darkening the kitchen door. "How come Charlie gets to talk to her first?"

"Because I found her first," Charlie says with a mouthful of cookie, spraying a few crumbs on Thomas's head, then brushing them off. He doesn't move.

"Hi! Who's that?" asks Thalia, who sounds like she's struggling to keep up.

"Pick a name, it doesn't matter," I say. "Now that there's two people here it's gonna be like —"

"I heard we were taking to the girlfriend?" Seth asks from the doorway.

"I'm sorry," I tell Thalia, one second before Eli grabs the phone from my hand, then spins and makes off with it.

"Hey!" I shout, but he's gone.

I've tried to get things back from my brothers before. It's never worked.

"Okay, I'm just gonna introduce you around to everyone," he says. "I'm Eli, Caleb's probably said a lot of really good stuff about me..."

I sigh, and Charlie pats my arm.

"Have another cookie," she says, grabbing one for herself. "And look at the bright side: if she's still answering your calls tomorrow, it *must* be true love."

· · · · ★ ★ ★ ★ ★ · · · ·

Winter break is three weeks long.

I last one and a half.

The first I'm in Sprucevale, with my family, before Christmas and after Christmas. I talk to Thalia every day and we text constantly, plus hanging out with my brothers and Rusty and Thomas more than keeps me occupied.

The next week, I'm back in Marysburg. I keep myself busy: working on papers for submission, making lesson plans, going out with friends, but it's not quite the same. There's nothing like the madness of Christmas and there's particularly nothing like the madness of my family at Christmas, and that's when it settles in that I miss Thalia.

It also settles in that there's no earthly reason for me not to see her. I've got a car. My job becomes *very* freeform during winter break.

And Virginia Beach, which is right next to Norfolk, has lots of very nice hotels with great off-season rates, so I book two nights at one of them and Thalia tells her parents she's visiting a friend.

It's glorious. It's glorious to be with her again, naked and gasping on the white hotel sheets while I've got my face buried between her legs, but it's glorious that no one here knows who we are.

We go out for every meal, just because we like being together in public. She takes me to the Back Bay Wildlife Refuge for the day, even though it's cold and windy because it's the beach in January, and we hike around holding hands because we're not going to get caught.

Then we go back to the hotel, and we have more sex. Afterwards, still tangled in the sheets, I show her the latest emails I've gotten from secretknower@gmail.com that call me a *predatory husk of a man* and a *shameless power-loving degenerate* and an *unscrupulous dirtbag*, and Thalia tells me that the sender is a shallow-brained moron who doesn't know their genitals from a bowl of cereal. Then she calls me an unscrupulous dirtbag, laughing.

Everything feels better when she's around. We talk about who the sender is but don't get anywhere — I'm nearly certain it's not Seth or Levi, she's pretty positive it's not Bastien. She mentions that her roommates have also figured it out, but she's adamant that they'd take their problems up with her, not send me weird emails.

That night we walk the boardwalk hand-in-hand and look out at the moon over the ocean and lights of the faraway ships, and for a moment I imagine that they're all sea monsters, raising their heads above the water for a few moments to get a taste of the salty air before diving back for the deep.

Thalia leans against me, looking out at the inky waves, and she tells me that when she was a kid they lived in San Diego for a few years, and Javier told her that if she looked out over the ocean hard enough, she could see Australia.

I ask her if she ever did, and she laughs and says only when she squinted really hard.

When I drive back to Marysburg the next morning, I'm certain of one thing: I have fallen desperately, utterly, and completely head over heels for this girl.

CHAPTER FORTY-THREE
THALIA

I lean my head back against the wall, the tile floor cold against my butt. I think the same thing I always think when I'm waiting to meet with a professor: *how come there's no waiting room?*

It's an academic department at a major university. There must be students waiting for someone in this hallway literally night and day. Why not have a waiting room? Some chairs, at least?

I yawn, stretch, arch my back, and change position ever so slightly. Even though I was supposed to meet with Dr. Castellano at three, and it's now three-thirty, I'm not particularly surprised that she's running late, and luckily my classes are over for the day.

School's been back in session for a week now, and it's... normal. Despite everything that happened last semester, a semester which started with me accidentally hooking up with my professor and ended with my professor-turned-boyfriend helping me get my brother back in rehab, so far this semester is just a semester.

My brother's still in rehab, and he'll be there until the end of March. I go over to my boyfriend's house several nights a week, and last Saturday he took me on a date to Luray Caverns. My roommates are insane, but the lovable, good kind of insane.

Yes, I've got too much homework, and yes, I'm working furiously on my thesis, and I'm still a part-time research assistant and I'm mentoring a high school student who wants to go into psychology, but that's all pretty regular, just busy. I'm always busy.

Finally — *finally* — Dr. Castellano's door opens, and another student comes out, followed by Dr. Castelllano standing in the doorway behind him, one hand on the door, and even though he's nearly a foot taller than her and looks like he plays sports, it's clear who's in charge.

"Thanks, Doctor C!" he says as he walks away, and she beckons me to get off the floor.

"Castellano," she says, half to herself. "I swear, they can all toss around *Gronkowski* no problem but they can't manage *Castellano*? Hi, Thalia. Thanks for waiting."

"No problem," I say, sitting in one of the chairs opposite her desk. "How was your winter break?"

She doesn't answer, just goes around her desk. Something tightens in her face, around her mouth, and she doesn't look at me as she sits, then opens a drawer, every movement exacting and precise in a way that makes me instantly nervous.

A shiver works its way down my spine, and suddenly, I notice how cold my fingertips are. *It's from sitting on the floor, that's all...*

Dr. Castellano pulls something from the drawer, shuts it again. It's an envelope, and for a moment, she holds it in front of herself, looking at it.

I feel like I might throw up, because I can tell that this isn't good, and there's almost nothing I hate more than bad surprises.

"Thalia, I'm afraid you're being accused of an ethics violation," she says, finally looking at me.

My heart drops to my feet. I can practically feel the blood draining from my face, and I can't move.

All I can think is, *I thought we'd dodged this.*

"A report has been made to the ethics oversight committee that you've been participating in a romantic relationship with one of your professors," she goes on, and now she's not looking at me, she's looking at the envelope again. "And I'm afraid it's been determined that that falls under the category of *behavioral misconduct.*"

I can't move. I feel like I've been encased in a layer of ice, like a tree after a storm, and all I can do is stare at Dr. Castellano and listen to my heart beat and think *this isn't really happening, I'm having a nightmare.*

"I specifically asked the committee if they would let me give you the notification in person, rather than send it through the mail system," she says. "And I have to say, this seems unlike you, Thalia. Is there anything you'd like to tell me?"

I don't say anything. I can't even breathe, and I feel like the walls are quickly closing in, white on every side of my vision.

"Thalia?" she asks, her voice sounding distant, far away.

Then, suddenly, I gasp and my lungs fill with air and the walls go back to where they're supposed to be and Dr. Castellano is just looking at me, concern written all over her stern face.

"Who reported it?" I ask, my voice thick. I clear my throat. "You said there was a report —"

"You know I can't say," she admonishes, gently. "There are policies in place to protect ethics reporters."

"Was it a student?" I ask, barely hearing her. "Another professor? An outsider?"

She just shakes her head.

"Thalia, is there anything you'd like to tell me about this?" she asks again.

I'm silent. I can't think of anything that won't incriminate me, and if I've learned one thing about any legal process, it's best to keep your mouth shut.

"The report alleges that this affair was mutual," she says, slowly, giving me a look I don't fully understand. "But, as I'm sure you know, the greater responsibility in these ethical entanglements would fall on the professor in question."

I want to say *you don't understand*. I want to say *I kissed him first, this was all my fault*, but I don't.

"Were you coerced into this relationship?" she asks, softly. "If you were, that might significantly change the outcome of the investigation."

"No," I say, so forcefully that I sit forward in my chair.

Dr. Castellano just nods, business-like, then pushes the envelope across the desk.

"Your hearing is Thursday," she says. "In the meantime, I'd encourage you to really think through the nature of this relationship and the power dynamics therein. I'd also encourage you not to have any contact before the hearing."

I nod, numbly. I stand. I take the envelope from her desk, grab my bag, walk for her door.

"Thalia," she calls, and I turn, still silent.

She's sitting there, fingers laced together, an expression on her face I can't quite place.

"If you need anything, don't hesitate to reach out," she says. "And please, think about what I said."

I turn back to her door, open it, and leave.

CHAPTER FORTY-FOUR
CALEB

My chickens have come home to roost.

I'm standing in the hallway of the mathematics department, halfway between the mail room and my office. People are swirling around me, putting on coats and taking them off, wrapping and unwrapping scarves, and I'm standing in the middle of all that, stock still, thinking *my chickens have come home to roost.*

It's something my father said sometimes, one of his little pieces of farm wisdom that I thought I'd nearly forgotten. He'd say it whenever the sins of our past caught up with us, like when I knocked over Daniel's block tower four times in a row and he finally stomped into my room and broke the Lego submarine I'd spent hours putting together.

I read the letter again: an ethics report, alleging improper conduct with a student, a serious violation. A hearing Thursday. A weight settling onto my shoulders, my chest. Consequences unmentioned in the letter but I know what they are.

I've always known. Not the first time I kissed her, true.

But I knew the second time and all subsequent times, and every single one of them I weighed the consequences of my actions against the feeling of her lips on mine. Every single time I found the consequences wanting.

And here they are, roosting. I can't help but imagine them as chickens — enormous, heavy chickens — perching on my shoulders and arms and the top of my head until I'm virtually covered with chickens, nothing but hands holding a letter sticking out between the feathers.

"Caleb," a voice calls, and I look up. The hallway's empty, and I wonder how long I've been standing there, holding this letter, thinking a lot about chickens and not at all about how I'm going to deal with this.

"I just heard," Oliver says, striding up to me. "Is that the letter? Can I see it?"

I hand it over, silently. His face is grim as he reads it once, twice, then hands it back.

"Come on," he says, and walks for his office.

I follow, chickens all aflutter, folding the letter and putting it neatly back into its envelope, then closing the door behind myself.

"I can't believe they're taking this seriously," he says, the instant we're inside, folding his arms over his chest and gazing through his window. "It's unconscionable how cutthroat this department has gotten. Do you have any idea who came up with this?"

I'm only half-listening to Oliver, the other half of my brain spinning wildly out of control, wondering if I should tell Thalia, wondering if I should tell anyone. Wondering if I can possibly convince the committee that she earned her A, that I don't make a habit of dating students, that it's only her. Only ever her.

"Came up with what?" I ask, not quite following.

"Who invented this improper conduct charge," Oliver

says, patiently. "It must be someone with friends on the committee, because otherwise I can't imagine this sort of thing sticking with no evidence whatsoever —"

"It's true," I say.

Oliver freezes, mid-sentence, his mouth still open. He blinks twice. Shuts his mouth. Opens it.

"What?" he says.

I push my glasses off my eyes and rub them, my brain still swirling. I feel like I'm stuck in one of those mirror houses they always have at the county fair, where most things are just reflections but one is real, and it's nearly impossible to tell which one.

"It's true," I say again.

Oliver walks to one of his chairs and sinks into it, his hands over his face. He doesn't say anything for a long, long time.

"You slept with a student?" he finally says, his voice echoing oddly through his fingers. "Jesus, Caleb, when?"

"I still am," I say.

He goes quiet again.

And then: "You did it more than once?"

I did it yesterday, I think.

"While she was your student?" he goes on. "She was in your class and you slept with her? While she was in your class? While you were grading her papers and her tests and —"

"Yes," I say, just to get it over with.

"Why?" he asks, looking up at me. "You? You've never done anything like that. Have you?"

"Not until now," I tell him. "Does it help if she's a senior?"

"I'm personally relieved that at least the student you're sleeping with isn't a teenager, but no, it won't help with your hearing," he says. "It wouldn't matter if she were fifty,

THE HOOKUP EQUATION

she'd still be your student. She, right? Or is there more I don't know?"

"She. Her name's Thalia," I say, as if that helps. As if anything helps. "Any advice?" I ask, though I've got a bad feeling about advice.

Namely, I've got a feeling that there's not much advice to be given: I did this, and someone found out.

"Say as little as you can in the initial hearing," Oliver tells me, instantly. "Don't lie, but don't give them anything, either. Figure out what they've got, if they've got anything beyond allegations, and pray that none of this has become public. If there's one single news story anywhere — even the school paper — about this, you're screwed, but if you can deny everything and keep it secret you just might survive it."

I just nod, wondering if I should take notes.

"More than anything, the University wants to come out of this looking good," he goes on. "They've got aspirations of being in the top ten public schools in the US, and perception has everything to do with that."

"Don't go on the six o'clock news," I say. "Got it."

"Find out who reported you and discredit them," he goes on.

I raise my eyebrows, and Oliver puts up one hand.

"It's dirty, I know," he says. "But I've seen people go through the wringer before, justified and not, and it's how the game is played. Your best-case scenario is that they decide the charges were baseless and dismiss them."

"They're not," I say.

Now Oliver's just looking at me, his elbow on the arm of the chair, one finger resting on his lips.

"I know I fucked up," I say, shoving my hands into my pockets. I shut my eyes, lean my head back against the bookshelf behind me. "I knew all along. It was wrong, and it was unethical, and it was immoral, and I did it anyway."

There's a long, long silence between us.

"I'd do it again," I say.

"Even knowing the outcome?" he asks, his voice quiet, serious.

I take a deep breath and think: that this week might be my last week spent teaching. That after this, if I'm lucky, I'll be teaching calculus to high school students. That my days in this office, on this campus, getting paid to think deep math thoughts, are nearly done.

And I balance that against Thalia, two days ago, lacing her fingers through mine as we walked to dinner in a town two hours away.

"Yes," I finally say. "Even then."

Oliver sighs, and even though I've got my eyes closed, I know exactly what face he's making.

"I know a few people on the ethics committee," he tells me. "I'll see if I can find out what they've got. It might be nothing, and you could do a lot worse than your word against theirs."

"Thanks," I say, just as my phone rings. Thalia's name pops up.

"I have to go," I say, already worrying. Thalia never calls without texting first. She told me once that she considers it incredibly rude to just interrupt someone's entire day by calling them out of the blue.

"That the student?" Oliver asks, looking like he already knows the answer. "This is probably obvious, but you shouldn't talk to her until this is over, and probably not even then if you want it to stick."

"I see," I say, looking down at my phone.

"Godspeed," Oliver calls, and I leave his office, walk toward my own, hit the green button despite his advice.

"Hey," I say, keeping my voice down.

On the other end, Thalia takes a deep breath.

"Someone reported us," she says, her voice shaky. "Dr. Castellano said I shouldn't be seen with you, but can you meet me somewhere? We have to talk, Caleb, I really need to see you —"

I stop in front of my office door, a slow realization dawning on me like an iron fist around my stomach.

"Thalia," I say.

"I'm sorry," she whispers.

"No," I say, turning the knob on my office door and entering. "No, Thalia, no, that's not what I'm — did you get a letter, too?"

"My advisor gave it to me," she says. "My hearing's Thursday, I guess that'll happen and then afterward they decide how much more they need to investigate and from there they'll hand down a judgement —"

"Why?" I ask, an utterly useless question.

"Because I was in your calculus class," she says, like she's confused about why I'm asking.

"Why are they going after you?" I ask, the fist around my stomach tightening. I'm nauseous, desperate, shaking. I want to grab books and throw them across the room, upend the whole bookshelf, throw it out the window.

This was my wrongdoing. I was the teacher, she was the student. I had the responsibility. I'm the one who fucked it up, who threw caution to the wind, and it should be me paying for it, not her.

"Because I agreed to uphold the university's standards of morality when I took their scholarship money," she says. "Can I see you? Please?"

I didn't know. There a tightness in my chest like someone's wrapped a chain around it, put an anchor on the other end, and thrown it overboard, because I didn't know.

This whole time, I thought it was just me. Maybe that was shortsighted, or naïve, or just stupid, but it's what I thought.

"What will happen to you?" I ask, staring down at my desk.

"I don't know," she sighs. "Can I come over?"

"You have no idea?"

There's a long, long silence on the other end of the line.

"Someone got expelled last semester for immoral behavior," she finally admits. "But it was for something completely different."

I close my eyes, the feeling in my chest nearly choking me.

This is my fault and my fault alone, I think.

"I don't think we should see each other until our hearings are over," I say.

"Caleb —"

"I'll talk to you later," I say, and hang up my phone as gently as I can.

I don't know what, exactly, I'm going to do, but I've got an inkling. The germ of an idea, if it comes to that.

What I don't know is whether Thalia will forgive me for it.

CHAPTER FORTY-FIVE
THALIA

When I get home, none of my roommates are there. I'm not surprised, because they're all at least as busy as me if not more so, but I wish they were because I ugly-cried all the way home and at least want someone to sit on the couch with me and pet my hair and tell me it'll all be okay.

But they're not, so I lock myself in my room and cry. It's pathetic. I know that I should be researching how to beat an ethics violation charge, or at least learning about the Byzantine process that I'll be navigating, but I can't. I'm useless.

I know I shouldn't be so shocked and upset that I'm reaping the consequences of my actions, but that thought only makes me feel worse, not better. I did something and I got caught and I'm just upset that I got caught, how stupid is that?

Really stupid.

I cry harder. I cry for myself, because I'm definitely at least getting put on probation for a year, which means I won't graduate in May and probably pushes graduate school right out of the picture. I cry because I might get expelled with one semester left to go.

I cry because I can only imagine my parents' reactions when they find out why I'm getting kicked out of college, because despite everything they were so excited about me graduating.

And I cry because I'm certain I've fucked Caleb over, too, and he won't even talk to me. I know he's probably just being smart, and I can't blame him, but right now everything hurts and especially that.

Finally, I cry myself to sleep.

· · · · ★ ★ ★ ★ ★ · · · ·

A FEW HOURS LATER, I wake up because I have to pee. The lights in my room are still on, and I'm still in my clothes, half under the covers and half on top of them. My bedside clock says it's two in the morning, and I feel like shit.

I drag myself out of my bed, pull my now-incredibly-uncomfortable jeans off, and head for the bathroom in my shirt and underwear. If they're not asleep, my roommates have seen me in my underwear before, and also, I'm about to get kicked out of school so who cares about anything?

I hit the lights in my room before I open the door, but our living room is dark, the only light the glow of a single open laptop on the kitchen table.

"Hey," I say, keeping my voice down, but Margaret's got her headphones on and doesn't move as I cross behind her, on the way to the bathroom.

I don't mean to, but I look over at her screen, glance at what's on it.

Then I stop in my tracks, because she's got an email inbox open in her browser, and it's for an email address I've seen before.

"What the *fuck*?" I say, and she jumps and whirls around, practically ripping her headphones off.

"Jesus!" she hisses. "Don't do that, it's two in the morning and I thought you were —"

"What the *fuck* is that?" I repeat, pointing at her screen.

She looks back, comprehension dawning instantly.

"I—"

"It was you," I say, disgust winding into my chest, taking hold. "Holy shit. Why the *fuck* would you do that, Margaret? You went right over my head like that and never even bothered talking to me? Not once?"

She slams her laptop screen shut, plunging us both into near-darkness, but it's way too late.

"I talked to you," she says, defensive. "You weren't interested in listening to me about how fucked up you were being, so I decided to try a different tactic so that maybe *someone* would listen and at least have second thoughts."

"*Second thoughts?*" I ask, and now I'm loud, nearly yelling, and I couldn't care less. "You think that getting me expelled and Caleb fired is the best way to make us have *second fucking thoughts*? You went that far over my head — you reported me to goddamn University Ethics — you're getting my scholarship taken away so I'll rethink my life choices?"

Now she's standing.

"Wait —"

"I'm sorry your dad fucked his secretary and left your mom!" I shout, my voice pitching higher and higher. "Okay? I'm sorry that you think every relationship is a transaction of power —"

"Shut up!" she shouts, and for a second, I do. "What the fuck are you talking about, *expelled?*"

"I'm talking about you reporting Caleb and me to the administration," I shout. "Because apparently it's not enough to send fucked up emails to him, you also had to make sure that we got punished for doing something wrong according to whatever moral code it is you follow so religiously —"

"I didn't report you."

"Right, you just called my boyfriend *morally bankrupt* and a *stupid dinglebat* and what was that last one he showed me? *Unscrupulous pervert* or something, but no, it was some other asshole who tattled on us?"

"I wouldn't get you expelled!" she says. "Thalia, I swear to God, I think he's a total fucking creep for dating you but —"

"Thanks," I say, practically spitting the word at her. "Thanks, sure, who could be interested in me but a total creep who just wants to pop my cherry for his trophy wall?"

"You can't act like it's not fucked up!" she says, pointing dramatically at the ground, like it's going to help her make her point. "There's no such thing as informed consent in a relationship where you are *his subordinate* —"

"You think I'm incapable of meaningful consent?" I shout, my voice wobbling. I'm half a second from crying tears of rage and trying desperately to hold them in, but it's not going to work for long. "Because I'm younger than him? Because I'm a student? You think I can't say *yes* and know what I mean? Fuck you."

"I think it's murky as fuck and he's a creep for going after undergrads!"

"He's not going after undergrads, he's going after me," I say.

Now I'm crying, my voice all over the place.

"You don't know that," Margaret says. "Maybe there's some girl every year who thinks *oh, my professor is really into me, I'm so cool and lucky*."

I feel like I'm going to throw up, or scream, or throw up while screaming and also strangling Margaret.

"Fine," I say, angry tears pouring down my face. "Sure. Every semester, he picks some girl from one of his classes and uses his immense powers of assistant professorship to coerce her into great sex —"

"How do you know it's great sex?" she fires.

"So you also think I'm a moron who's happy to lie back and take whatever dicking she gets because she doesn't know any better?" I say, sounding borderline hysterical because I can't stop crying. "Do you seriously think I can't tell when sex is great?"

I suddenly realize that Harper and Victoria are standing in the doors to their rooms, looking on, horrified expressions on their faces.

"How are you supposed to know?" Margaret snaps.

"Have I ever once given you shit for banging the entire men's diving team?" I shout. "No. Because I don't care who you sleep with, so how about you don't be an asshole and virgin-shame me."

"I'm not shaming you!" she shouts. "Fucking your professor is *inherently coercive* —"

"What a fancy phrase for *I think you're too dumb to make your own decisions.*"

"Are you really this dense?" she shouts.

"Guys!" Harper says, trying to yell over us.

"No, I'm not dense," I yell. "What I am is perfectly capable of making decisions about who I have sex with!"

"Stop it!" calls Victoria.

"Not if he's grading your papers," Margaret says.

"HEY!" Victoria shouts.

We both look over at her, wearing pajamas and a silk wrap around her hair. I'm crying and doing my damnedest to stop, and Margaret is breathing hard, like she just sprinted a couple blocks.

Victoria furiously points at the ceiling.

"If the bitch upstairs calls the cops on you two my Black ass is *not* answering the door," she says, then looks at me. "And your Mexican ass probably shouldn't either. Let the white girl do it."

"I'll talk to the cops," Harper says behind us, and we both turn. "What *happened*?"

Margaret and I look at each other, and she holds her hands up.

"Thalia, I swear I didn't report you," she says. "I fucking *swear*."

"You just sent fucked-up emails in the hopes that, what? He'd dump me?"

"Report what to *who*?" asks Harper, waving her hands, trying to get us back on track. "You and Caleb?"

"To the administration," I say, tilting my head back and taking a deep breath. "I have an ethics hearing Thursday."

The three of them gasp in unison.

"Oh, fuck," breathes Margaret.

"Oh no," says Harper.

"Shit," agrees Victoria.

"I didn't even know," Margaret says. "Thalia, I wouldn't, I would never ever do *that*, I just think it's fucked up —"

"Don't really care what you think," I tell her, and for once she has the good sense to shut her mouth.

I believe her, though. I'd kind of like to strangle her, but I believe her when she says she didn't report us.

Victoria covers her face with her hands, then takes a deep breath.

"Okay," she says, then uncovers her face. "Okay. Thalia, you sit on the couch. Harper, can you make some tea or something? Margaret, you should probably go to bed."

I sit. Harper goes into the kitchen. Margaret says nothing, but grabs her laptop and leaves, shutting her bedroom door behind herself. Victoria sits next to me on the couch, and a few minutes later, Harper comes in with three mismatched mugs full of chamomile.

"Okay," Victoria says. "Tell us."

CHAPTER FORTY-SIX
CALEB

I glance at the clock again and wonder, for at least the thirtieth time in as many minutes, why I've agreed to this. True, it seemed like a good idea at the time, but the closer I get to it actually happening, the more I'm dreading it.

I don't think I can plan any more. I can't visualize any more contingencies, come up with any more if-this-then-thats. I've spent hours on the phone with Seth, my most pragmatic, most forgiving, and least judgmental brother, going over all the options. I'm pretty sure he ran some statistical models.

I still don't know what to do.

Here's what I want: I want to go into the committee and explain what happened. I'll swear on a bible that I graded all her quizzes and homework and tests fairly. It's math, for fuck's sake; there's a right answer and a wrong answer, with not much open to interpretation. They'll nod their heads and fondly remember the first time they fell in love like this, tell me not to do it again, and send me on my way.

That won't happen.

Second most, I want to deny that it ever happened. If they have no evidence, only the allegation, it could work. Sure, lying is wrong and immoral, but it's not like I cared about those things when I got myself into this.

And if neither of those things happen — if they decide that someone needs punishing for this — I want to be the one punished, not her.

The university can have my head, but they can't have hers.

At exactly seven o'clock, there's a knock on the door. It opens before I can even stop pacing in the living room, and my brother's voice calls out.

"Hey!" he shouts. "We're here."

I take a deep breath, steel myself, and step into the hallway.

"Hey," I say, and Seth waves, hanging up his coat in my coat closet.

Behind him, my mom just sighs and gives me a very disappointed look.

God, it's worse than a knife to the heart.

Seth comes over, puts both his hands on my shoulders, and looks me dead in the eyes.

"It's gonna be okay," he says. "I promise."

"The depends on your definition of *okay*," I tell him.

"You'll see," he says, and gives me a few firm pats, then walks past me, down the hall, toward the kitchen. "Do either of you want anything to drink? I'm going to make tea."

Seth is *extremely* at home in my house.

"Earl Grey would be lovely," my mom calls, shutting the door to the coat closet

Then she walks down the hall to where I'm standing, and just looks up at me.

"This was the bad thing you didn't want to tell me," she says, matter-of-fact. "I guess I understand why."

My mom is an astronomy professor who mainly works at the Steinberg telescope that's about thirty minutes from our house and is owned by the Virginia Institute of Technology. She mostly does research and only teaches a class a semester, but still.

"I know," I say quietly, unable to look her in the eye. "I know."

"You worked so hard," she says.

"I know."

Before she can say anything else, there's a knock on my front door. I open it and Oliver's there, wearing a black coat with a green scarf, and he nods at me once.

"Thanks for inviting me to your strategy meeting," he says, as I usher him inside. "Hope I can be of some —"

He stops, just for a second, looking down the hall at where my mom is leaning against the doorframe of the kitchen, saying something to Seth inside.

" —use," he finishes, then shrugs his coat off. Underneath he's got on a fairly tame shirt, compared to some of the things I've seen him wear, though his shoes are a startling shade of blue.

"That's the idea," I say, taking his coat and scarf, but he's already walking down the hall.

"You must be Caleb's mom," he says, holding out a hand. "It's nice to finally meet you."

"You must be his advisor," I hear her say. "Clara Loveless."

"Oliver Nguyen."

"Be honest," my mom says as I close the closet door. "How bad has he fucked up?"

Oliver just sighs.

"Bad," he says.

"So they never get better?" my mom asks, sitting next to me on the couch.

"NSF grant applications? No, I think they get worse," Oliver says, sitting on a chair across from my mom. "I swear they add three pages of nonsense for you to fill out every year. Why do they need to know what the highest-paid employee at my institution is? Not my fault the football coach makes a pile of money."

"I was hoping that maybe if I did this for long enough everything would just click into place," my mom says, gesturing into the air. "Ten years, maybe fifteen."

"I wish," Oliver says, and my mom laughs.

Just then, Seth comes into the living room, carrying a tray with four cups of Earl Grey, a few cookies, and some grapes. I didn't know I had any of those things in my house, but leave it to Seth to find them and present them nicely to the rest of us.

"Thanks," I say, as he takes a seat, and we all lean forward for our tea, silence hanging heavy in the air between us.

Finally, Oliver clears his throat.

"I spoke with my colleague on the ethics committee," he says.

I can already tell it's bad news. Good news comes out immediately. Bad news waits.

"And?" I ask.

"They were sent a short video," he says.

My stomach drops. I put my tea back on the coffee table and lean my elbows on my knees, rubbing my hands together.

The organ concert, I think, a sharp prickle working its way down my spine. *The library. That time in my office. God, how thorough was I about closing the curtains when we were here?*

If someone has footage of Thalia naked without her consent I'm going to fucking kill them.

"What's on the video?" I ask, my voice surprisingly steady.

"It's you and — sorry..."

"Thalia," I supply, my voice tight.

"You and Thalia kissing next to a minivan," he says. "Apparently you're in some parking lot, but it's quite clearly you and pretty unmistakable what you're doing."

I close my eyes and sigh with relief. I'm pretty sure everyone sighs with relief, though when I open my eyes, Seth is smirking at me.

I wait for Oliver to look away, and I flip him off as subtly as I can.

Then, suddenly, I realize what Oliver just said.

Parking lot.

Minivan.

That really, really narrows down who the reporter could have been.

"Can he say it's Photoshopped?" Seth asks. "Academia's cutthroat, maybe someone wants him fired."

"It's a video," Oliver says.

"You can edit videos," Seth says. "Right now, the technology exists to make very convincing deep fakes. Just last week I saw a video that someone had made of the President saying —"

"It's not fake," I point out.

"Yes, I know," Seth says, in his most patient *you are a moron* voice. "But can you convince people that it's fake?"

"Seth," my mom says sharply.

"We're talking about a whole committee of people who

know what Occam's Razor is," I say. "And the simplest explanation is clearly —"

"That's actually not what Occam's Razor says," Seth interrupts. "Occam's Razor states that the solution that makes the fewest assumptions is likely to be correct, not the simplest."

"That's accurate," confirms Oliver.

I shift position, flopping backward onto my couch and covering my face with my hands.

"But I take your point," Seth concedes, sipping his tea.

I sit there, quietly, trying to think, but my brain feels like a disused path through the dense forest, like I'm hacking through kudzu and tripping over fallen trees every three feet just to get a single thought together.

"So it's unlikely that he'll be able to deny that the affair happened," my mom chimes in, ever pragmatic. Clearly, Seth got it from somewhere.

"Yes," says Oliver.

"What are his options?" she goes on. "Is this the sort of thing where he could swear that it's over and will never happen again, and he's very sorry? Or have institutions of higher learning moved on in the past thirty years?"

"It isn't over," I point out.

Even though I haven't spoken to Thalia in forty-eight hours and she hasn't called since I hung up on her, and not talking to her feels like slowly pulling my veins through my skin.

"Not the point," my mom says.

"That's very unlikely to work," Oliver says. "The University takes this sort of thing pretty seriously these days."

"I'm done," I say.

The proclamation is greeted by a long, weighted silence.

Then, finally, Oliver speaks.

"Yes," he says. "It does seem that way."

I have the sudden sensation that the ground I was standing on has crumbled, and now I'm on a precipice, staring into a black hole with no earthly idea what's down there.

"Okay," I say, and sit up straight, try to pretend like the world isn't tilting around me. "All right."

"I wish I had better advice," Oliver says, gently, but I just shake my head.

"I did it," I tell them, something I've said to all of them individually already. "I knew it was wrong and I did it."

There's another silence.

"Well then," says Seth.

"What about Thalia?" I ask, turning to Oliver.

"What about her?"

"She's a Madison Scholar," I explain, quietly, and his face changes.

Seth and my mom just look at each other.

"You really stepped in it, didn't you?" Oliver asks.

"She could lose her scholarship and maybe get expelled," I explain.

"An academic suspension at least," Oliver adds. "And this is her last semester?"

I nod, and he just lets out a low whistle.

"This was my fuck up," I say, my voice low. "It was on me. I was the teacher, I was the one who should have known better, I was the one with the responsibility…"

"You know, I've only talked to her on the phone, but I've got a strong feeling that Thalia's also capable of making decisions and exercising judgement," Seth says.

"Not my point," I tell him, and he just shrugs.

I turn to Oliver.

"Is there anything?" I ask, dreading the answer.

He doesn't say anything right away. Instead he leans forward slowly. He grabs a cookie. He sits back. He considers it for several long, long seconds, and then he takes a bite and swallows.

"There might be something you can do to help her," he finally says. "But it'll be ugly."

· · · · · ★ ★ ★ ★ ★ · · · ·

THE THREE OF them stick around to help me with the first draft, everyone crowding around me on my couch.

I hate writing, and I hate writing this more than I've hated writing anything in my whole life. I hate twisting the truth, making something beautiful sound so ugly and salacious.

We take a break. I'm sweating, even though it's a cold night. Seth goes into the kitchen, finds a beer, opens it, and hands it to me.

"I don't want it," I tell him, trying to hand it back.

"It'll help you feel better about lying," he says.

It's cold and smooth in my hand, the Loveless Brewing logo on the label, and for one wild second I consider telling him what I know about that dark January night all those years ago, that one bad judgement call can last forever, that alcohol has proven fatal to at least one Loveless man.

But I'm not driving. I'm not even getting drunk. I'm here, and I'm safe, with friends and family. A letter isn't a twisting mountain road.

And, for better or for worse, I forgave my father long ago, so I take a long drink from the beer that Seth offers me.

"Thanks," I say.

· · · · · ★ ★ ★ ★ ★ · · · ·

Oliver leaves after the second draft. After the third, Seth reveals that he's brought his work laptop and a few days' worth of clothing, so my mom goes back to Sprucevale and it's just the two of us and an awful, no good, very bad letter.

Finally, around three in the morning, we decide it's finished.

"We could ask June to proofread it," Seth says, his eyes on the screen as he reads it for the thirty thousandth time.

"I'm not showing her this," I say, also reading. "She'd stab me in the throat."

"Because it's poorly written, or…"

"Because of what it says," I say, and take another gulp of tea. One beer was more than enough, and I've switched back.

"Maybe," he admits.

Finally, he hits save, and we close the window, then close the laptop.

"You're sure?" he asks, just that one simple phrase.

I think of the first night I met Thalia, watching her face as she watched the light-up flowers. I think of her telling me she believed in magical, not magic.

And I think of the two of us alone on the boardwalk in Virginia Beach, two weeks ago, of how the lights of faraway ships looked like sea monsters coming up for air. Something I never would have thought before I met her, but something about Thalia bends reality in a way that only I can feel.

"I'm sure," I say, and Seth nods once.

"Good," he says. "I'll be on the pull-out bed in your office."

CHAPTER FORTY-SEVEN
THALIA

I lean toward the mirror, checking my teeth for lipstick. It's a dusky rose color, not the bright red I tend to favor, but this isn't a girls' night out, or a frat party, or even the psych major mixer.

This is my ethics hearing, and the last thing I need to look like is some trashy slut who wears red lipstick and has affairs with her calculus professor.

Yesterday, Victoria drove me to the mall on the other side of town and I blew nearly my entire paycheck at Sephora. I bought primer, concealer, foundation. I bought eyeliner and mascara and blush and eyebrow gel and lipstick and I nearly bought false eyelashes, though I changed my mind at the last minute.

I already own most of those things, but I bought new ones because I needed something, anything, to hide behind. If I put on new eyeliner and new mascara, if I paint my nails I'm-so-innocent light pink, if I have on the suit I bought for graduate school interviews, maybe I can get through this.

It's armor, and I know it. If I thought chain mail would

help, I'd wear that, too, but the best armor I've got is looking like the kind of girl who'd never, ever do what they're accusing me of.

Even though I did, and I think they know it.

I don't know what I'm going to do. The only advice I've gotten has been to say Caleb coerced me, and frankly, fuck that.

I'm not above tears, mostly because I'm pretty positive I won't be able to help it. I'm not above begging for forgiveness and swearing not to do it again. But I'm above throwing Caleb under the bus to save myself.

I take a deep breath. I fix a tiny smudge on my lipstick. I straighten the jacket of my suit, run my fingers through my hair, hope I look good enough to be believed.

Then I turn and leave the bathroom.

* * * * * ★ ★ ★ * * * * *

SMYTHE HALL FEELS LIKE A LABYRINTH. It was one of the first buildings on campus, so it's from before things like fire codes really existed. The corridors are smaller than other buildings, the ceilings lower, the floor oddly discontinuous because it was added onto and added onto again, which means you can only access parts of the second floor from the third floor, not the rest of the second floor.

When I find Room 233A, I'm three minutes late and I'm so nervous I'm shaking. I couldn't eat this morning, and already I'm making a bad impression.

It's a big, old, wooden door, the doorknob cold. I hold my breath and pray once and then push it open.

The room's empty. It's a meeting room, unexpected light pouring in from two big windows, with a big wooden oval table in the middle of the room surrounded by office chairs. Nice office chairs, the kind that cost hundreds of dollars each, maybe thousands.

I'm starting to feel like I'm in a Kafka book, but then something moves in the corner and I realize that Dr. Castellano has been there all along, a laptop open in front of her.

"Thalia," she says, taking off her reading glasses and holding them in one hand.

"I thought I had a hearing," I say. "Am I early? Did I get the time wrong? I know it's four past three already —"

"The honor case against you is pending dismissal," she says, matter-of-factly.

I stand there, in the doorway, and stare at her. And stare.

"What?" I finally ask. "What does that even mean?"

She leans forward slightly, her elbows on the table, twirling her reading glasses by one stem.

"It means that, as of a few hours ago, the university is no longer interested in pursuing a case against you," she says. "I apologize for not letting you know sooner, but I still wanted to speak with you."

"So they dropped it," I say, stepping into the room, letting the door slam shut behind me. "All that and they just dropped it?"

There's a dangerous, bubbly feeling deep inside me, like I'm about to burst into laughter at any moment, like my insides are shaking and I'm so rattled and sleep-deprived that I might just start cackling with relief.

"They dropped *your* case," she says. "Professor Loveless resigned this morning in a letter to the administration, effective immediately."

I close my eyes, replay her words quickly in my head, just to make sure she said what I think she said.

When I open them, I'm smiling. I'm still trying not to

laugh because that completely insane urge is still there, in the face of the unexpected, to just laugh like a maniac and maybe all this will go away.

"He did?" I ask.

He didn't tell me. We haven't even spoken since Monday, when he hung up on me. Even though I called. Even though I texted.

I just cost him everything.

She picks up a piece of paper and stands, walking toward me. I meet her in the middle of the room, and she hands it to me. It's a copy, the fold lines clearly visible, and it's on Caleb's letterhead.

I can hear the blood rushing through my veins, the sound of my own heart so loud it could drown anything else out, and my eyes skip down the letter, taking in phrases piecemeal because I need to get to the end, I need to understand what he did and why he did it, but I can't process anything.

To President Levenbaum

Resignation, effective immediately

With Miss Lopez, an undergraduate in my Honors Calculus section

Pursued relentlessly

Insinuated that she might receive a poor grade

"No, he didn't," I say out loud, jerking my head up, looking at Dr. Castellano. "That's not true, he never insinuated anything —"

"Are you sure?" she asks, and I look back at the letter.

I feel like I'm going to throw up.

Well aware of our relative positions

Improper abuse of authority

"That's not what happened," I tell her, and now my voice is shaking too. "This isn't true. None of this is true, he never threatened to fail me, or give me a worse grade, or give me a better grade if I slept with him, or…"

I am, somehow, sitting in one of the expensive chairs, the copy of the letter still in my hand, Dr. Castellano sitting opposite me. I don't remember sitting down but here I am, feeling like I'm in the center of a whirlpool.

I take a deep breath. I put the letter on the table, because I don't think I can hold it any more. And then I make myself read it, from start to finish, both my hands over my mouth.

It's simple. It's a straightforward, brief, no-frills account of how Caleb took advantage of his relative power over me to convince me to start a relationship with him.

It's also a complete lie, from top to bottom.

"This isn't true at all," I say, when I finally finish. My voice is a hoarse whisper, and I only realize I'm crying when a drop lands on the paper.

I swallow. I clear my throat, but before I can say anything else, Dr. Castellano speaks.

"Professor Loveless has already terminated his employment with the university, and anything you might say to me now won't change that," she says, slowly, looking me dead in the eye.

I clench my jaw, grit my teeth, will myself to stop crying.

"If you were particularly determined, you could request that your case be re-opened," she goes on. "But I want to be absolutely clear that this —" she puts her finger on the letter, "—is already done and cannot be undone, no matter what you might say or do."

I bite the inside of my lips together so hard I draw blood, then look down at the letter.

I hate every single word on that page. I hate every sentence, every paragraph, every punctuation mark. I hate it for being nothing but lies, and I hate it for being what the University administration wanted to hear.

"The only real question is whether you'd like to press charges," she goes on.

"No," I say, the word coming out half-sob. "No. Jesus, no."

She just nods, and I don't say anything else. I understand, with crystal clarity, what she's telling me.

"Then I think we're done here," she says, softly, and takes the letter back. She walks, ramrod straight, back to her laptop, picks up her briefcase, puts the letter back into it.

Then she stands again, turns, looks out one window.

"The administration isn't particularly concerned with true justice," she says, after a long pause. "But they're very concerned with the appearance of justice. If this ever comes to light, they want to be able to parade someone's head on a stick, and now that they've got that, they're happy. And forgive me, Thalia, but I don't see a reason for you to suffer needlessly."

I say nothing, but only because I have nothing to say. I'm cold, numb, and feel like any moment now I'm going to wake up from this stupid anxiety-induced nightmare.

"Is there anything I can do?" she asks, finally looking back at me.

I take a deep breath and close my eyes. I'm still crying and still trying not to, but it's not working.

"He's not a bad person," I say, quietly. "He's not the monster he makes himself sound like, I swear."

"I suspected as much," she says, slowly. "You're a smart woman who chooses your associates well."

"Who reported it?" I ask, the only other question I have. "It's over. Tell me that."

"I don't know," she says, but she walks toward me

again, puts her briefcase down on a chair. "I sincerely don't. We weren't told that information."

She pulls her laptop from her bag, and I can tell a *but* is coming.

"But this is the evidence they sent," she says, opening it, tapping at her keys, pulling up her email, clicking a link.

A video opens. It's shaky and slightly blurry, like it's zoomed in too far and shot through a window, but it's good enough.

On it, Caleb and I are sitting on the tailgate of my parents' minivan. We chat for a few moments, his arm around me. Then we stand. Embrace. Kiss. The video ends, the window going black.

"Thank you," I say, my voice strangely robotic.

"I hope it helps," she says, already packing up the computer.

"It does," I say, and my voice sounds faraway, like it belongs to another person.

Without another word, Dr. Castellano nods once, then leaves the bright, sunny room, leaving me alone.

I feel more wretched than I ever have in my life.

CHAPTER FORTY-EIGHT
THALIA

In the end, I make a list. It takes me an hour, maybe two, though most of the work isn't in writing the list. Most of the work is in pacing up and down the room, shoes off, angrily crying to myself while I try to sort through everything that just happened.

I'm a mess. I'm on overload, ten emotions at once, all of them ugly. I'm furious with the school for having this rule in the first place, but that's pointless and I know it, the rage just feels good.

I'm angry with myself, for not having one whit of self-control. I'm angry with stupid Margaret, just because she was such a bitch. I'm angry with Javier for overdosing, with my mom for putting up with my father, and with Bastien for no other reason than he's irritating sometimes.

I'm angry as hell with Caleb for not answering my calls. For not consulting me in my own fate, for letting people think that he's a monster and I'm some naïve, innocent victim.

And I'm furious with my father.

That what's the list ends up saying: School, *Me*, **Caleb, DAD.** That's all, but it's enough.

I pull out my phone, find a number, and hit the call button before I can lose my nerve. It rings six times and then goes to voicemail: *Thank you for calling Captain Lopez, United States…*

I hang up and call again. And again. And again.

I call seven times before, finally, he answers.

"What happened?" he demands, short and curt and no-nonsense as always.

Suddenly, words escape me and I wonder what he said when he reported us. Did he call? Email?

I wonder what he said, exactly, to Javier the day he kicked him out, whether it was the same staccato rhythms I'm hearing now or something else.

"Thalia," he says, the word a statement, not a question. "What is it?"

I look down at my list, and finally, I find my voice.

"Did you report me?" I ask, my voice oddly calm in my own ears.

He's silent.

"To the university?" I go on, and though my heart is beating so hard I can feel it in my fingertips, I sound completely zen, like nothing could ever bother me. "Did you report Caleb and I?"

More silence. The sound of a door closing.

"I reported Professor Loveless for a clear violation of his contract," he says, stiff and unyielding. "He should be ashamed of himself for taking advantage of you like that."

Deep breath in. Deep breath out. Ten thousand words fight to be the next ones out of my mouth.

"You didn't even ask me," are the words I finally choose. "Did it ever occur to you to talk to me about it? To ask me what was really going on? Whether I needed your help?"

I can hear the tears behind my voice, feel them heavy in my throat and in my skull behind my eyes, but they don't come out. I'm shaking with the force of keeping them in, but for once, I do.

My father answers with a silence so flat that for a moment I think the line has gone dead.

"You're my daughter," he finally says. "And I'm not going to let your professor sully you like —"

"Stop," I say, and to my surprise, he does. "Did you even consider talking to me about it?"

He doesn't answer me, but he doesn't need to because we both already know that the answer is *no*.

"Or did you just decide that someone needed to be taught a lesson and you were the perfect person to make it happen?" I ask, and now my voice is shaking. "How many times are you going to confuse cruelty for love before you don't have anyone left?"

There's a minuscule part of me that knows exactly why he thinks the only real form of love is tough love, that at least understands the theory behind what he was trying to do, how he was trying to protect me, but I'm not really interested in understanding right now.

After all, it's not like he was either.

"I'm withdrawing from our relationship," I tell him, slowly, each word coming to me as I say it. My voice quavers, dips, comes dangerously close to tears, but I don't give in.

He's not going to hear me cry. I'm not going to give him that.

"I don't want to speak to you for a while," I say, whispering, unsteady. "When I call home, I don't want to speak to you. I don't want you at my graduation. If you'd like to know how I'm doing, please ask Mom."

"You're choosing some perverted older man over your own family?" he snaps, finally angry. "Hasn't anyone ever told you that blood is thicker —"

"You turned your own son out onto the streets when he needed your help!" I shout suddenly, violently, the sound of my own voice bouncing from the walls of the conference room a shock.

I take a hard, deep breath but I'm not in time and the tears finally break through. I bite my lips together as I feel my self crumple inward, determined not to let him know.

Keep it together, just for one more minute, please keep it together keep it together...

"Don't you dare tell me anything about blood," I go on quiet, strangled. "I'm not choosing him over you, I'm choosing to no longer speak to someone who nearly got me expelled from college and doesn't seem to consider me a full person with thoughts worth seeking out."

"What do you mean expelled —"

"Bye, Dad," I say, softly, and then hang up.

Two seconds later, he calls. I send it to voicemail, then do it again and again, until finally, he stops calling.

Then I sit in a fancy office chair, put my head on the table, and cry.

CHAPTER FORTY-NINE
CALEB

"Put this on, you're making me cold," Seth says as I glance at my phone again. Nothing.

I open my texts. She hasn't read any of the five I've sent her in the last couple of hours, hasn't answered any of my calls.

Is she still in the hearing? I wonder, even though she can't possibly be because it's been hours, the sun now almost down.

"Earth to Caleb?" he says, and this time I turn. He's holding out a thick fleece blanket very patiently, his hair still wet from the shower, his feet bare beneath his pants.

"Thanks," I say, and take it, suddenly realizing that I'm standing on my back porch wearing nothing but a long-sleeved shirt, pants, and slippers, and it can't be more than forty degrees out here.

It must be over by now. It has to be. The letter must have worked or not, because although I know what's happened to me — I packed up my office while a security guard watched; my VSU email has already stopped working — no one would say a single word about what's going to happen to her.

"You're supposed to put it on," Seth says, his patience clearly running thin. "That's the thing about blankets, they reflect back warmth from whatever part you put them on. So if they're just wadded up in your hands, all they'll do is warm your hands, while your face falls off from frostbite."

"Sorry," I say, and unfurl the blanket, then slowly put it over my shoulders, wrapping it around myself.

He sighs, goes inside, comes back a moment later with a similar blanket wrapped around himself and his shoes on.

"Does your back yard know what the fuck you're going to do?" he asks, leaning against the wooden railing next to me.

It's midwinter, and the back yard looks shitty. The grass is dead. There's a small garden, left by the previous tenant, and that's dead. The two small trees and the oak on my property line are all leafless, spindly branches reaching into the darkening sky.

"No," I say.

"Has your back yard spent even a second thinking about it?" he asks.

"No," I admit, and Seth sighs.

I'll never teach again. Not at the university level, not community college, not high school. I confessed, in writing, that I used my position to coerce a student into a sexual relationship, and every job I apply to for the rest of my life will find that out with a single phone call.

I lean forward, crack the knuckles on one hand, my fingers freezing.

"I just want it to work," I say, softly.

"Moron," Seth says, matching my tone, looking out at my ugly back yard.

"I was getting fired no matter what," I remind him.

"And if you hadn't been?" he asks, gravelly, not making eye contact. "If they'd said *one of you has to go*, you'd have done the same thing, which is ridiculous and you're ridiculous."

He's right, and we both know it.

"You'd have done the same if—"

"Don't," he warns me.

I sneak a sideways glance at him.

"Still?"

"Just don't," he says, sounding weary, so I don't.

I already dragged the poor man on a five-mile hike through forty-degree weather today, after I turned in the letter, because I didn't think I could deal with people any more. At least not regular people, which Seth isn't.

After my dad died, it was twelve-year-old Seth who took care of us. Seth made sure that we all took showers, ate meals, did laundry. Seth made tea and built fires in the fireplace. He woke up in the middle of the night when I had nightmares about a car crash, talked me down.

We all reacted differently. Levi got quiet, Eli got spiky, Daniel got angry. I think I was just sad, but Seth somehow became nurturing. Out of everyone, he's the one who reached down deep and found something good within himself in those dark days, and I'm still grateful.

"Sorry," I say. "I should know —"

There's a knock on my front door, and I fall silent for a moment.

Then I drop the blanket to the floor, pull open the back door so hard it slams against the wall, and practically run through my house.

She's standing outside the front door, bag slung over her shoulder, wearing heels and a skirt, hands curled into fists and jammed into her coat pockets.

Thalia looks at me for a moment without saying

anything, and my heart drops through the floor. She looks like hell: eyes glassy and red, ringed with black; face splotched bright pink.

Without a word, she walks past me, into my house. I close the door behind her and she steps out of her shoes, then stands next to them.

"What happened?" I ask, almost afraid to know the answer.

"Nothing," she says, quietly. "I get to keep my scholarship and stay in school. But you knew that."

I start grinning, the relief flooding over my head like a cold rain, releasing tension I didn't know I was holding.

"Thank God," I say, and I step forward to take her in my arms.

Thalia steps back, and I just kick her shoes.

"Don't," she says, and now she's got her hands on her face, in her hair, on her hips, and she looks away and she sounds edgy and I stop in my tracks.

"I'm sorry I didn't answer your calls," I say, fighting to keep a smile off my face. "I thought it was best —"

"Did you?" she suddenly says, cutting me off, her voice wobbly and tired. "You thought it was best, just like you thought it was best to tell the story of how you *blackmailed* me into having sex with you?"

I feel like the moon must feel when it begins waning: the slow, unexpected march of darkness.

"You were going to get expelled," I point out, my mouth suddenly dry.

"You don't know that."

"There was a good chance," I go on. "And if you hadn't been expelled, you'd have at least lost your scholarship —"

"So you felt it was a good idea to make sure that you're remembered forever at the university as a professor who sexually assaults his students?" she says, her voice rising, eyes wide, face flushing. "You decided to just tell everyone that I was just your victim? Nothing but some innocent girl who wanted an A *so* badly that she was willing to fuck for it?"

The anger spreads through me with a chill, like frost in my veins.

"I just gave up everything for you," I say, my voice an ugly snarl. "Tomorrow morning you'll still be in class, still on scholarship, and I have no idea what I'm going to do."

"You didn't even ask me," she says, hard and flat.

"I spent seven years in grad school and now I can never teach again," I say, stepping forward again. This time Thalia doesn't budge, just looks up at me, jaw clenched, lips pressed together.

"You wouldn't even answer my calls," she says, her eyes shining, brighter red than before. "You wouldn't talk to me. You took everything into your own hands — you took *us* into your own hands — and you didn't ask me and you didn't tell me and at no point did you ask about my thoughts or my wishes and Jesus, Caleb, I'm so fucking sick of men thinking that they know what's best for me."

"What would you have said?" I say, and now I'm shouting too, taking a step back, pacing away in frustration and then back to her. "Would you have said oh, no, I'd prefer to be expelled from school?"

"I don't know what I would have said!" she shouts. "I'll never know because you didn't bother consulting me!"

"Well, you're welcome!" I shout, and now I'm pacing back and forth the width of the hallway, unable to keep still. I want to punch the wall and I want to open the door and rip it off its hinges, but I don't do either because I'm a damn adult.

"Did you think I was kidding?" she asks.

"What are you talking about?"

Thalia points furiously at the front door.

"There," she says. "When I stood right there after you told me about the emails and you promised to be my partner and not my protector, were you kidding? Were you just waiting for the next moment that you could be some kind of knight in shining armor and come and sweep this little lady off her feet?"

Now she's crying, tears running down her face, voice strangled and high-pitched and I keep pacing because if I don't keep moving I don't know what will happen.

"I'm sorry that you hate *not being expelled*," I snap. "I'm sorry that taking all the blame for the affair you're just as responsible for as I am wasn't enough, you also wanted pre-approval."

She stands perfectly still for a long moment, nothing moving but her eyes, glassy and bloodshot, as she watches me pace back and forth.

"What I want," she finally says, her voice quiet, shaky. "Is to be treated like I'm a person who gets to have input on her own damn life and not some sort of fancy pet."

"I promise I wouldn't blow up my entire life for a chinchilla," I snap. "Though maybe —"

"Jesus," Thalia hisses. She steps forward and jams one foot into her shoe and then the other, swaying as she does. "I'm sorry. I'm sorry I came here."

She jerks the door open, the cold hitting us both in the face.

"Sorry about your life," she says, then steps through and slams the door behind her, the click of her steps fading quickly.

I stare at the inside of the door, clenching and unclenching my fists. I think of a thousand angry comebacks and they crowd into my brain, elbowing each other out of the way.

"Fuck you," I finally say, the least clever of all, as I turn away from the door. "And fuck me for helping you and fuck — *WHAT?*"

"Sorry," Seth says, and instantly disappears back into the kitchen.

I stand there. I seethe. I resist the urge to destroy all my own things.

Then, finally, I grab my coat and my shoes and my keys and I jerk the door open myself, then go for a long, angry walk in the opposite direction of Thalia's house.

CHAPTER FIFTY
THALIA

Fuck it, I mope.

I spend that night in my bed, wearing pajamas, my suit crumpled in the corner, watching a pirated version of *The Borgias*. I've never pirated something before, but it turns out it's actually pretty easy.

Will the police come knocking on my door to arrest me? Maybe. After all, I'm a bad, *bad* girl who watches TV shows that she hasn't paid for, sleeps with her professor, gets away with it, and then gets mad at him for helping her.

Around midnight, Victoria knocks. She's got a mug of tea and a giant cookie from the Market Street Cafe, and she asks if I'm okay. I lie and say yes, but I let her come in and watch an episode with me in my bed while we eat the cookie, which is the size of my face and delicious.

She doesn't press me for answers. I think she knows better. I don't volunteer any, because I feel like a pile of garbage that someone should light on fire.

I skip all my classes the next day. Why? After that asshole *quit his job and torched his career* so I could keep my scholarship? Because fuck class, that's why. Once my roommates are gone, I come out of my room, still in my pajamas, and eat some of Margaret's ramen because she deserves to have her ramen eaten.

Around three, Harper knocks, then enters. She's got a burrito with her, and she makes up a long story about how she accidentally got an extra burrito from Jose's when they screwed up her order, but I don't really believe her.

She gives me the burrito — it's my favorite, a breakfast burrito, which probably makes me a bad Mexican but who cares — and when she does, I cry, and she comes over and hugs me, and then I eat the burrito in my bed and we watch another episode.

Harper maintains that no one in the fifteen hundreds was that clean or that sexy, and I maintain that I don't care, I just want to watch sexy historical figures have stupid escapades because I'm afraid that if I think too much about my situation, I'll come to some conclusions I don't like, and I'm still mad.

Saturday, I finish *The Borgias* mid-morning. I was already halfway through the first season when I started this binge, and it turns out there are less episodes that I thought there were.

After about ten minutes staring at my empty laptop screen, I decide I'm going to be a person, so I grab some clean pajamas and come out of my room, don't look at Margaret as I walk through the living room, and I take a shower.

As I shower, I wonder what I'm going to tell my mom. Does she already know? Is she going to be angry? Hurt? Will she understand?

Do I deserve understanding? Do I deserve anything?

I cry in the shower.

When I come out in my clean pajamas, at least feeling

slightly less gross, Victoria and Harper are in the living room, plugging a laptop into the television.

There are fuzzy blankets on the couch. There's a bowl of ramen on the coffee table, next to another giant Market Street Cafe cookie and an open bag of potato chips.

"Oh, hi," says Harper, as though she wasn't expecting to see me in my own apartment. "We were just about to eat this junk food and watch a historical drama called *Reign* about Mary, Queen of Scots that's supposed to be ridiculously over-the-top. There's also this extra bowl of Margaret's ramen, do you want it? And to join us?"

Bending over the laptop, Victoria's trying not to laugh at Harper.

"Yes," I say, and sink into the couch, then put my head on Harper's shoulder. "Thank you."

* * * * * ★ ★ ★ * * * * *

WE DO that for nearly four hours. I'm sure they have ten thousand things to do besides watch dumb sexy teenagers in period costumes make bedroom eyes at each other, but they don't act like it. Instead, we sit there and eat junk food and watch, entranced.

Around episode three, I start talking. I watch overly attractive people whirl around a ballroom in big ball gowns and half-face masks, and little by little, I spill the whole story.

The bar bathroom. The date. The classroom. The Madison Scholars banquet and the hospital; the office hours where we talked half about calculus and half about life; the walks home from the library.

I admit to the organ concert, and if they're even one percent surprised, they don't show it. I admit to the affair, to finally losing my virginity, to sleeping with my professor again and again and again and not even being slightly sorry about it.

And then, finally, I get to this week while Mary is sitting on the throne and the show cuts between shots of her face, looking toward a window, and her handsome lover riding a horse away from the castle.

When I tell them about the letter, they both gasp in unison. By the time I've finished with the phone call to my father and the fight, I'm crying again but it's a normal crying, not the ugly, breathless, snot-filled sobs of the last forty-eight hours.

"I think I might just be an asshole," I conclude, shoving a crumpled dining hall napkin against my eyes, trying to get them to stop leaking. "He's right, right? He did a nice thing and I should be grateful but I just feel so *bad* about it."

The front door opens, and there are footsteps on the stairs. Margaret comes in, looks at us on the couch, looks like she's about to say something but then just nods and takes herself into the kitchen without saying anything.

"Sure, fine," I mutter, mostly to myself.

"I don't think you're wrong to be mad that he didn't tell you," Victoria says, slowly. "That's a lot to spring on a person."

"It could also be a control thing," Harper says, reaching for the bowl of chips and settling it on her blanket-covered lap.

"Go on," I say, munching one.

"Well," she says, and then stops. She thinks. "Is he gonna be a martyr about it if you go back to him? Is this part of a pattern, where he decides things for you and performs some sort of self-sacrifice, and then expects you to be happy and grateful afterward?"

Victoria's just nodding.

"Exactly," she says. "He could have done this out of love, or as a mechanism for control."

I blink at the screen. Someone is dragging a feather over someone else's nude back. It looks... tickly.

"That's a lot to do for control," I say.

"It's a lot to do for love," points out Victoria.

"That's the big question," Harper says, and we both turn to her.

We wait.

"What's the big question?" I finally ask.

"Is he pure of heart?" Harper says, as if that's the obvious answer. "If he found a unicorn in the forest, would the unicorn befriend him or stab him?"

She crunches another chip, as if this is a totally normal thing to say. Which, for Harper, it kinda is.

"I thought that was virgins," Victoria says.

"He's not that," I point out.

"It's open to interpretation," Harper says.

"How do I find this out?" I ask, suddenly pragmatic. "Where do I find a unicorn? Is there witchcraft I can do?"

"Too bad you don't have ready access to virgin blood any more," Victoria says.

"Actually, that's a misconception," Harper pipes up. "Virgin blood in most rites doesn't refer to blood from a virgin, it just means blood that hasn't already been used. Like olive oil."

Victoria and I look at each other.

"Actually, that makes sense," Victoria says.

"I think you just have to use judgement about Caleb, though," Harper adds.

"Can't I at least ask a magic eight ball?" I say.

· · · · ★ ★ ★ ★ ★ · · ·

I shower again Sunday morning, and this time, I don't cry during it.

I still feel crappy, like my skin is lined with lead, making all my movements heavier and slower than they should be. I stand in front of the fridge for a full five minutes, trying to figure out what to eat for breakfast. I wear pajamas for the third day in a row, though I do change into fresh ones again.

That afternoon, I'm sitting at my desk, doing actual homework, when there's a knock on my partly-open door, and I glance over.

Margaret's standing there.

"Hey," I say, sitting up straighter.

"Hey," she says. "Can I come in?"

I just nod, and she walks into the tiny room, then sits cross-legged on my unmade twin bed and holds a green box out to me.

"There were girl scouts by the library, I guess it's cookie season," she says as I take the Thin Mints. "Also, I'm sorry I was such a bitch."

I look at the box in my hands, then back at her.

"But I swear to God I didn't report you," she says quickly, sitting up straighter. "I…"

She trails off, looks out my window.

"I know," I tell her. "It was my dad."

Margaret looks back at me, eyes wide, mouth open.

"We're not speaking any more," I say, carefully tearing the cardboard strip from the end of the box.

"Your *dad* tried to get your scholarship pulled?" she says, still goggling. "Holy shit."

Since talking to my dad, I've gone back and forth on whether I think he knew I could be punished.

"Yup," I say, matter-of-factly.

"Sending those emails was really fucked up of me," she

says, quickly, like she's nervous and in a rush. "I don't know what I was thinking. I mean, I do, I was thinking that it was pretty weird and creepy of some professor to sleep with you when you were literally *in his class.*"

I pull apart the plastic sleeve and shoot her a look.

"But I obviously should have just talked to you instead of… doing that shit," she says. "I'm sorry. I'm really sorry. Really."

I crunch into a Thin Mint and look at the cookie for a long moment, thinking.

"I should have trusted you. I don't know why I didn't," she finishes.

"Probably because you're an obnoxious know-it-all who thinks she's God's gift to men," I say, a small shower of crumbs escaping my mouth.

There's a long, long pause before she speaks.

"Are you trying to say I'm not God's gift to men, or…"

"You asshole," I laugh, and she grins at me. "Also, *morally bankrupt?* What the fuck, Margaret."

She hides her face in her hands. I almost tell her that she also has to apologize to Caleb, since he's the one she told was morally bankrupt in the first place, but I still haven't worked up the nerve to go talk to him yet because I think he's probably still pretty mad at me, and I'm still a little bit mad at him, and it's all still a mess.

"I'm sorry," she says again, through her hands.

"I haven't forgiven you yet," I tell her, eating another cookie.

"I deserve it," she says, and then looks up at me. "Oh, I have another apology. Wait here."

I wait, still eating cookies, and in fifteen seconds she's in my room again, holding something behind her back.

"I hope it's another box," I say.

She just grins wider, then pulls the thing out from behind her back.

It's a dildo.

I think. Actually, I'm only about sixty percent sure it's a dildo, because while it's definitely phallic, it's also tapered and green, the design on it pink and swirling in a series of dots to a somewhat fanciful tip.

I stare for a long moment.

Then I finally ask, "Is that a tentacle dildo?"

"Yep!" she says, holding it up proudly. "It's brand new from the store's new *hentai* collection. It's got a suction cup on the bottom so you can attach it to the shower wall or your chair or whatever and go to town. Also, it's still shrink-wrapped."

I take it from her. It's surprisingly heavy.

"Thanks, I hate it," I deadpan, and Margaret laughs.

· · · · ★ ★ ★ ★ ★ · · · ·

MONDAY NIGHT, I finally work up the courage and go to Caleb's house. I pulled up his name in my phone a hundred times that day and nearly called, but every single time I chickened out, and I can't bring myself to text a 'let's talk about forgiving each other and also maybe whether we can move on from this' message.

So I'm here. I'm walking up his sidewalk, onto his front porch. I've still got the key to his house, but this is not a *let myself in* scenario so I knock.

And I wait.

And I knock again, and wait again, and repeat that at least four more times.

Then I wait. I wait for a really, really long time, and I listen for signs that he's in there and knows it's me and is avoiding the door, but I don't hear a single thing.

Finally, I sit down on his porch steps, the concrete cold beneath my butt.

Me: He's not there.
Margaret: Where is he? It's not like he has a job.
Margaret: Sorry.
Victoria: The man still needs to run errands. Maybe he's at Target.
Harper: Maybe he's hiking the AT again.
Me: It's January.
Harper: He probably has a lot of psychic pain to work through.
Margaret: Dude, come on.

I really hope he's not hiking the Appalachian Trail again. I don't want to go months without talking to him, and I can't see myself hiking out there in search of him. For one, there are bears, and for two, I'd obviously never find him, no matter how noble or romantic my intentions. Also, I have class.

As I walk away from his house, I realize his car isn't in the driveway.

Duh, I think to myself.

And then: *I'll try again tomorrow.*

* * * * * ★ * * * * *

I try again Tuesday. And Wednesday. No car, no Caleb. My roommates tell me to stop being a child and just call him, see when he'll be home, and then talk to him in person, but I don't.

Thursday, I go over again. I knock one million times and wait at least ten minutes, but there's nothing so I finally unlock the door and go inside.

There's mail all over the entryway. I've never seen mail there before. Caleb doesn't leave mail on the floor. He's not a mail-on-the-floor guy.

At last, standing in his house, I call him.

The call goes straight to voicemail. I try again. Same.

Slowly, carefully, I collect the mail from his floor. I sort it into a *looks legit* pile and a *pretty sure this is junk* pile, then put both piles on the kitchen table before heading upstairs, where I stand in the door to his bedroom for a long moment, afternoon light leaking through the curtains.

The bed is made. Everything is in place, though I notice his phone charger isn't there.

And then, despite myself, I go in. I sit on his bed, and I feel half like an intruder and half like I've come home, and for the first time the thought strikes me that this could be the last time I'm in his house.

If he never wanted to speak to me again, the girl who cost him everything, I don't know if I could blame him.

I lie on his bed and put my face right on his pillow, then inhale, and suddenly it feels like he's there, like we're lying naked and sweaty on his bed and we're laughing about something, still casually tangled.

Smell isn't like the other senses. When you see or hear something, those signals get filtered through a part of your brain called the thalamus, which then relays the signals on. Not smell. Our sense of smell is hooked right into the limbic system, the emotional response part of our brain.

I breathe in again, just for good measure, and it's a gut punch.

Then I roll over, onto my back, and call him one more time.

Voicemail.

I lie there for a long time, thinking. I'm thinking that it's probably super weird that I'm in his bed. I'm thinking that he hasn't been here in days and I don't know where he is. I think there's a possibility he's never coming back, though it seems remote.

And then, finally, I think of someone who'll know. I pull out my phone. I do a single google search, take a deep breath, and hit the phone number.

"Loveless Brewing," says a friendly female voice. "Tammy speaking."

I did not have a plan for this.

"Hi, Tammy," I say after a quick, awkward silence. "Would it be possible to speak with Seth Loveless?"

"I can check, sweetheart," she says. "What's this concerning?"

She sounds so nice that I don't even mind being called *sweetheart*.

"It's a whole long thing, really," I say. "Can you just tell him it's Thalia?"

"Of course, hon," she says, and if I didn't know better I'd say there was pity in her voice. "But he might be busy right now so chances are he'll have to call you back."

"That's fine," I say.

"One sec," she says, and then the hold music starts, some instrumental version of the John Denver song *Country Roads*.

I start pacing, fully prepared to wait a while, but instead the music clicks off after about thirty seconds.

"Thalia?" a familiar-ish voice says. "Oh, thank fuck. I'm nearly out of room for bookshelves."

CHAPTER FIFTY-ONE
CALEB

I stand back and survey my work, folding my arms over my chest as I do.

Not bad. They still need to be painted, and I don't think Seth's walls are perfectly even because the very top of the right side has about a half-inch gap between the wood and the wall, but it'll do.

I should ask Seth if he still has any of the paint he used to paint that wall, I think. *That would be the easiest way to match it and make them look like built-ins —*

The key turns in the front door, and out of habit, I glance at the clock.

Then I frown, because Seth is hardly ever home before six and it's four-thirty.

" — That every bag had one single poison M&M in it, but you couldn't learn how to tell the poison M&M until you were ten," Seth is saying, and I frown harder because whoever he's telling the story about Eli's M&M lie to, it's not one of my brothers.

We all know the story. We all *lived* the story.

"That seems like it would only work until the first time

you decided you wanted M&Ms so much that you'd risk it," Thalia's voice says. "And it's not like kids have good judgement."

"No, they do *not*," Seth says, though I can hardly hear him over the sudden pounding of my heart, and several thoughts crash into each other, all at once.

Did I shower today?

He didn't warn me.

What day is it?

She's here. She's here. She's here and I'm not ready. I haven't figured anything out, I don't know what to say, all I've done is build a really big bookcase.

Then they both come around the corner, into Seth's living room, and Thalia stops.

"Oh," she says.

"I thought you were at Levi's," Seth says, walking past her and toward his kitchen. "Do either of you want anything to drink?"

"No, thank you," calls Thalia.

"Same," I say.

"Well, I'm just *parched*," Seth says, his voice echoing from the next room over the sound of his fridge opening. "It's been a whole Friday, you know?"

"Is it really Friday?" I ask Thalia, *sotto voce*.

"It really is," she confirms. "What day did you think it was?"

I sigh, run a hand through my hair, because I'm very much not the kind of person who loses track of days, though apparently I am right now.

"Maybe like... Wednesday?" I say.

Seth comes back out of the kitchen, drinking a glass of water, and looks from me to Thalia and back.

"Right," he says. "Let me just grab something from upstairs and text Levi that we're not coming over, and I'll go... somewhere that isn't here."

Thalia's already blushing.

"We could go —"

"Nope," he calls, already heading up the stairs of his townhouse.

" — somewhere less intrusive," she finishes, even though Seth's long gone.

"It's fine, he once stabbed me in the hand hard enough to draw blood because I tried to take one of his french fries," I say. "He owes me."

"How are any of you alive?" Thalia says, half-laughing and half-horrified. "On the way over here he was telling me about Levi convincing Eli that eating dandelions made you capable of flight."

"That ER trip is one of my earliest memories," I tell her.

"All right, I'm out," Seth says, coming back down the stairs, putting something in his pocket, then grabbing his coat and swinging it onto one arm. "Getting drinks and then seeing a movie with, uh, a friend. I'll call before I come back."

"Have fun!" Thalia says.

"Thanks," he says, and then turns and walks backward, pointing at me. "Don't fuck this up. I like her and I'd like for us to keep her."

"Bye," I call, and then he's gone and his door opens, closes, and suddenly it's very, very still in this living room, the smell of freshly cut wood permeating the air and Thalia and I looking at each other.

There are a thousand things I want to say to her, but I can't find words for any of them. I missed her and I love her and I spent nights roaming the darkness of Seth's living room, feeling like a thousand tiny cactus spines were working their way into my skin, too agitated to sleep and too tired to do anything but pace.

Sometimes I feel like I'm staring into the void, the sudden blankness that's the rest of my life. Sometimes I feel like I'm staring into the blue sky, endless possibilities. Which it is depends on the day.

"I didn't mean to stay here a week," I finally say. "I guess I got really involved in making Seth the bookshelves I promised him a couple years ago when he moved in here."

"They look good," Thalia says, her gaze roving over them, then coming back to me. "I was afraid you'd gone off to hike the Appalachian Trail again when you weren't home by yesterday."

"It's the dead of winter," I point out.

I did a deep dive into what equipment I'd need and how feasible it would be, what my route would look like, whether I could make it if I started in Georgia now.

"That's why you didn't go?" she asks.

"No," I say. "I didn't go because I don't want to escape you. I didn't go because it's a long time and I'd miss the hell out of you."

I pause. We look at each other, something tense and unspoken between us, something that needs words I can't find. I've spent the last week mostly silent, mostly alone: making these bookshelves, hiking solo through the forest, doing a thousand chores at my mom's house.

I spent the week trying to untangle the sudden mess of my life, trying to find the right words to take back to Thalia, but I still haven't.

"I miss the hell out of you now," I say.

She looks at me steadily, unblinking, and then she takes a deep breath and closes the distance between us. She looks up at me, her hands in the back pocket of her jeans, her elbows splayed.

"Are you pure of heart?" she asks.

"No," I say. It's instant, the word bypassing my brain and going directly to my mouth, a truth spoken straight from the heart.

It's not the answer she was expecting.

"Of course I'm not," I say, going on even though I know I'm giving the wrong answer to this question. "I slept with you while you were a student. I wanted what I shouldn't have. I took what wasn't mine to take. I lusted after you before I even knew your name and if you gave me half a chance I'd do it all again. No, I'm not pure of heart."

Now she's got her eyes closed, one hand to her forehead, and I think she might be smiling.

"I'm not pure of anything," I say.

"That was a really weird question, wasn't it?" she says.

"A little," I admit.

"Can I try again?"

"Always."

"Why'd you write the letter?"

I wonder, for a moment, if this question also has a right answer that I don't know, if I've wandered into a labyrinth with a sphinx at the center, and to get past it to Thalia I've got to outsmart it.

But then, I open my mouth and the truth pours out.

"It'll be easier for me to start over than for you," I say, simply. "Because I already have a post-graduate degree and I can find some other job. Because I didn't want to throw your life off track."

I hold out one hand, palm up. Slowly, she takes it, and I fold her small hand into mine, hold on tight.

"And because it was my responsibility and I fucked up," I go on, just as she looks up at me.

"Caleb —" she starts, exasperated.

"It was literally my job not to sleep with students," I remind her. "I'm older, I'm allegedly wiser, I was in charge. It was my job to be in control and do what was right and I didn't. You can say what you want, but it was my job and I fucked it up, and that means I should be the one to take the fall."

Her hand is a fist inside mine and I squeeze it, fit my fingers to her knuckles.

"I'm sorry," she says.

"Don't be."

"It doesn't feel right," she admits, her eyes on our hands, and she swallows hard, takes a deep breath. "This wasn't something that you did to me. We did this together. I knew what I was doing when I kissed you in the hospital, and when I gave you that bottle of wine, and when I saw you at the organ concert and went over to flirt with you —"

"And I understood the consequences," I tell her. "I knew precisely what I was risking when I invited you over for dinner, and I was in full possession of my faculties when I did it anyway."

"Still," she whispers.

"I wanted to be with you more than I wanted to be a professor," I say. "That's all. In the end, it was that simple. There are other jobs but there's no one else like you."

Thalia just sighs quietly, looking down at our hands and I look at her and finally, finally, the words I've been searching for this past week start pouring out.

"I thought I had what I wanted," I tell her, slowly, blindly. I speak like I'm cutting myself open and words are coming out instead of blood. "But then, there you were, hiding in the men's bathroom."

"God," she mutters, but I think she's laughing.

"Until then I thought I wanted to teach and publish papers and go on coffee dates with women who wore flannel, but I was done before you were out the window," I tell her. "Because it turns out that none of that can hold a candle to you telling me that you like believing in magic for the space of a second, or that sea monsters were really just oarfish, or that you suspect werewolves want to howl at the moon even when they're human. I want to live my life next to you. That's all."

"I was really sure you thought I was a lunatic," she says.

"I should have told you about the letter," I say, and I close my eyes, lean my head down to hers, her hair warm and smooth against my forehead. "I'm sorry. I was afraid you'd try to do something and wouldn't let me."

"I probably would have," she admits.

She breathes. She offers me her other hand as well.

"I'm sorry I got so angry," she says. "But I really want — I mean, you're — "

Thalia takes a deep breath, pulls away, looks up at me.

"I want to be next to you too," she says, simply. "That's all. This is once-in-a-lifetime, and I know it, and you know it, and I don't want it to be *me* and *you*. I want it to be *us*. Always."

"Always," I echo. "Whatever we face, we face together."

"Promise?" she asks, whispering.

I take my hand from hers, graze my fingers along her chin, tilt her face up toward mine, hold her eyes with mine.

"I promise," I tell her.

I touch my lips to hers slowly, softly, so gently I almost don't feel it because I want this kiss to last forever. I pull back, push forward, run my thumb along her cheekbone. She steps forward, into me, suddenly on her toes, her arm slung around me and I kiss her deeper, harder.

I can't help myself. I never could, not with her, and now I want to fall into this girl, drown in her and never come up for air.

At last, I make myself pull away. I want to pull her onto the couch, brace her against the back of it, wrap her legs around me. I want to give her that promise, skin to skin as we intertwine, but I don't.

We're in Seth's apartment, and it's Seth's couch, and I have a better idea than I'd like of what that couch has been through.

So instead I drop kisses on her fingertips and say, "Thank you for finding me," and she laughs.

"I'm the one who stormed out, so it only seemed right," she says. "You did enough."

She tilts her head, looks at me.

"Also, I was afraid you were on some incredibly long hike and I'd never find you," she says.

"That was only if you didn't take me back," I admit.

"You know what we should do?" she says, leaning into me.

Before I can say anything, there's the sound of keys in the front door, and then it opens.

"Is anyone naked or crying?" Seth calls out.

"Yes. Both," Thalia says instantly. "It's really cathartic. Come try!"

There's a very, very long pause. We're both laughing silently when, at last, Seth peeks one eye around a corner, quickly followed by the rest of his body.

"I was being *polite*," he says, quickly walking through the living room, toward his stairs. "Sorry, I forgot something. One second and you can go back to your orgy of tears."

"An orgy requires more than two people," Thalia points out as Seth disappears.

"Oh, he knows," I tell her.

"Is he the slutty one?" she whispers.

I almost say *yes* instantly, but then I stop.

"He was," I say. "It's... I don't know."

I doubt that Seth would appreciate me taking it upon myself to lay out his entire love life and recent lack thereof to Thalia, so I don't.

"All right," he says, coming back down, though he doesn't seem to be carrying anything else. "Sorry about that, please go back to groping each other or whatever you were doing."

"We were exchanging haikus," Thalia volunteers.

"Is that what they call it?"

"Bye!" I say, and Seth just laughs as the door shuts behind him.

I look back at Thalia.

"We can't stay here," I tell her. "We'll get lulled into thinking we have privacy, but we'll only get caught in a compromising position."

She raises one eyebrow.

"Which one?"

Several possibilities present themselves, and I push them all away.

"Don't," I say, bending toward her, my voice dipping lower.

It's been two weeks. I'm pretty sure that if Thalia said *eggs Benedict* in the right way it would set me off.

"All I said was —"

I put my thumb over her lips, silencing her. She smirks, her eyes wicked.

"No," I tell her. "We're going on a date. In public. Dinner and a movie. We're gonna hold hands and everything."

"What's every —"

"*No*," I say again, pressing my thumb to her lips again. Now she's laughing but my pulse is racing and I'm quickly flipping through a mental catalog of available beds in Sprucevale.

Scratch that. Available private spaces. I don't care if there's a bed, but I'm coming up blank: not here, not my mom's house or Levi's, not Daniel's spare bedroom or Eli's couch.

Okay, I think. *What if we just took a tent into the woods —*

Then, I think of the obvious answer, and I start grinning.

"What?" she asks, suspicious, the word still slightly blurred by my thumb.

"A date," I tell her. "We're going on a date, that's all. Let me go change."

She starts to say something else but I lean forward, kiss her, then practically run upstairs to Seth's study where the pull-out sofa is currently functioning as my bed. I put on clothes that aren't covered in sawdust, run a hand through my hair, make sure there's nothing weird on my face.

Then I pull out my phone. I do a quick search. I find what I'm looking for.

And I place a quick phone call.

CHAPTER FIFTY-TWO
CALEB

I take her to the only Thai restaurant in Spucevale, which is uncreatively named *Taste of Thailand*, but it's slightly better than the Thai place closest to campus in Marysburg, so I can't complain.

It's still odd to be with her in public, and it's even odder to know that it doesn't matter if we're seen. We hold hands over the table like we're in a cheesy movie. I lean over and kiss her more than once.

And we talk. I tell her about all the irritating things my brothers have done this week, about Thomas and Rusty, about preparations for Levi's wedding, and she laughs.

She tells me that Javier is doing well in rehab, that he's making ceramics in arts and crafts class, that he's painting again, that he's made friends with a barn kitten named Eustace, that he's seeing a PTSD specialist every day.

Thalia tells me that Margaret was the one sending the emails to me. She tells me about the huge fight they got into in the middle of the night, and even though I think she downplays it, I can tell she's rattled by the whole thing.

Then she heaps more sticky rice on her plate and scoops ginger stir fry on top, and pauses.

And she says, "My dad reported us."

"I saw the pictures," I say, and Thalia just nods.

"It was probably stupid of me to introduce you," she says, shaking her head. "Not that I've ever introduced him to a boyfriend before, but I didn't need a crystal ball to know how he'd react. Or that he'd find out you weren't a grad student with a one-second Google."

"You had other things on your mind," I point out, eating one more spoonful of soup.

"I should have known," she says.

"You should have done no such thing," I tell her, and I reach out, across the table, capture her hand in mine again.

"I can't believe he didn't even talk to me first," she says, and a pang of guilt works its way between my ribs, but then it's gone. "He didn't even ask what was going on. No, 'Are you okay with this? No, 'Are you happy?' Because *yes*, and *I am*, and that's not what mattered to him."

"We can't choose our parents and we can't account for what they do," I tell her, running my thumb over her knuckles.

She watches my hand for a long moment, then looks up at me.

"We're no longer speaking," she says. "I called him when I found out and told him he wasn't welcome in my life any more."

"Are you okay?" I ask, and she just nods, pushing her hair out of her face.

"Yeah," she says, thoughtfully. "Yeah, I'm very okay."

· · · · ★ ★ ★ ★ ★ · · ·

"THE MOVIE THEATER'S DOWNTOWN?" Thalia asks, looking around Main Street, her hand in mine. "It must be a really small theater."

"It is," I confirm, trying to hide a smile. "One more block."

We cross a street, pass two antique stores, and then I stop, open a door, hold it for her.

"This is a movie theater?" she says, frowning, reading the sign. "It says it's the Martha Johnson Inn and —"

The moment she says it out loud, she stops and gives me an *I see what you did there* look, like she's trying not to laugh.

"Seth's sofa bed squeaks," I murmur into her ear as we walk for the front desk.

"What, when you sleep on it?" she teases.

"Well, it squeaks every time I roll over, so I can only imagine the symphony it's capable of producing when people fuck on it," I tell her.

She's faintly pink from the cold, but I swear the look she gives me glows.

"And here I was hoping for a dark parking lot and the back seat of your car," she says.

"Never say never," I tell her, and she laughs.

Check in feels like it takes hours. I went to high school with the owner's daughters, of course, so I have to get updates on what Amanda and Bethany are doing these days while all I want is to take Thalia upstairs and listen to the way she says my name when I'm inside her.

After all, it's one of my very favorite sounds.

At last, I've got the key to the Lafayette room, and when I turn, Thalia stands from her overstuffed armchair, tosses *Rural Equestrienne* onto the coffee table, and saunters over to me.

"After you," I tell her, and nod at the stairs.

I've never been inside the Martha Johnson Inn before, but it's pretty clear that it caters to the ten tourists that Sprucevale gets every year, most of whom are drawn by some obscure point of early American history.

Fittingly, the Inn looks like it was plucked straight out of Monticello or Mount Vernon — everything is hand-turned wood and thick, lushly patterned carpet, including the stairs. The place has a severe, buttoned-up feeling, as if someone in a waistcoat is about to bid me good day and maybe also refer to me as a rake.

After all, I'm about to be rakish as *fuck*.

Just for fun, I grab Thalia's ass as she mounts the stairs. I'm pretty sure that my hand is in full view of everyone and anyone in the lobby, and I couldn't care less.

"Don't you know half the people watching us right now?" Thalia asks, looking at me over her shoulder.

I don't unhand her ass. In fact, I squeeze it harder, sliding one finger into the crevice between her legs, and I can hear her breath hitch when I do.

"Probably," I say. "And I don't think they're used to their upscale inn being used like a cheap hourly motel."

"You never know," she teases, looking around, then glancing back at me. "Early Americana gets some people pretty hot."

"Some people?" I ask, as we reach the first floor and I spin the key around one finger, looking for room 104, my other hand still on her ass. "It's working, then?"

"Sure," she says as we walk up to the door. "A hand-turned bannister really gets me going, you know."

"I knew we were in the right place," I tease, looking down at the key in my hand, then at the door.

It's an old-fashioned, heavy skeleton key, because of course it is. I shrug and shove it into the keyhole, but it doesn't turn.

"Come on," I mutter.

"Maybe you need to be gentle with it," Thalia suggests, her voice dipping low, her words sending an electric tingle up my spine. She's leaning against the wall by the door, winter coat open, hips cocked, the curve of her body a tantalizing suggestion.

"You think that's it?" I ask, pushing a little harder, twisting both directions.

"I'm just saying, make sure it's good and ready for you," she says. "Go nice and slow."

I glance down at her, eyes dancing, a laugh tugging at her lips.

"And how exactly should I go about doing that?" I ask, matching her tone. "Do you want me to talk dirty to a door, Thalia?"

"Only if you think you might get it open that way."

Now she's definitely laughing at me, her voice husky, tantalizing, and there's a moment where I think I might lose my mind. Then I take a deep breath, focus, take the key out, put it back into the lock slowly, carefully.

"Ooh, just like that," she whispers. "Fill it up nice and deep. Mmm."

"Do you imagine you're helping?" I tease.

"No," she laughs.

I reach out, grab her by the waistband of her jeans, her hip hot against my cool fingers, pull her in toward me.

"Well, you're not," I tell her.

"Try turning it real hard and slow," she murmurs. "Make it beg."

I let her go but her body is still pressed against mine, still standing outside this stupid shut door. I run my thumb across her bottom lip, and all at once I'm trying not to laugh and also trying to get this door open before I give up and tear her clothes off in this hallway.

"Quit it," I growl, twisting the key again and motherfucking hellfire bitch-ass fuck, it still doesn't turn.

Thalia grins, and now she's got one hand underneath my shirt, slowly tracing shapes along my skin.

"Have you tried," she murmurs. "Jiggling it?"

I jiggle the key, ever so slightly.

It turns the tiniest bit, and Thalia gasps. It's the same way she gasps when I do something she likes, and the noise goes straight to my already-painfully-hard cock.

"Don't stop," she murmurs, looking up at me, teasing me even as her face flushes a shade of pink I've come to know well. "It's so close, Caleb. Don't stop. *Please* don't stop."

I jiggle it again and the lock turns, slowly, then all at once and the bolt slides back.

I swear Thalia makes the quietest of moans as it does.

I shove the door open so fast it slams into the doorstop on the other side, the *crack* echoing through the hall so loudly I'm certain someone will come investigate.

I grab Thalia, laughing. I push her inside, slam the door, bolt it again, take her by the hips and walk her backward.

"Tomorrow everyone's going to be talking about how the youngest Loveless brother tried to fuck a door, and it's all going to be your fault," I tease her.

"Oops," she says, her arms already around my neck, her fingers in my hair, clearly not sorry. "But it worked, didn't it?"

She backs up against a table and without thinking I grab her, lift her onto it. It protests slightly under her weight, and it's probably hand-made from expensive wood, and I couldn't care less as I grab her hand and press it against my cock, still straining at my zipper.

"Did it?" I ask, capturing her mouth with mine, her

bottom lip between my teeth. "Did it work like you wanted, Thalia?"

I shrug my coat off as she wraps her legs around me, kiss her again, harder, groaning into her mouth as she slides her hand from tip to root.

"Because this is what happens when you suggest that I do anything *slower* and *deeper* and *harder*," I go on. "But you knew that."

"Well, I was hoping," she admits, a smile in her voice.

"Liar," I say, grinning. "You know exactly the effect you have on me and you enjoy every second of it. Get this off," I tell her, pushing her coat over her shoulders.

She sits back, pulls it over her arms, and it slides off the table.

"And this," I say, tugging at her sweater. She pulls it off and I get my own shirt over my head just as she reveals a long-sleeved shirt.

"That too," I say, planting my hands on the wooden table, her thighs between my hips and forearms. "Anything else you've got on, get it off. You're done teasing me for today."

"It was cold," she says, revealing a tank top, pulling that over her head.

"But it's warm *now*, and I like it when you're wearing nothing," I tell her.

She unhooks her bra and I practically rip it off her body, pull her to me, kiss her feverishly. Her skin against mine is molten, electric, and I think I growl as I run my hands up her stomach, let her breasts fill my hands, pinch her dark nipples between my fingers.

Thalia groans into my mouth, her legs tightening around my hips and I press myself against her, cock throbbing like I might explode.

She opens her mouth under mine, and I find her

tongue with mine, tangle them together as I roll her nipples again between my fingers, feel the tremor move through her body and into mine.

I do it again, feel the tremble, the aftershock and I record every motion, every noise, a seismograph to her earth. She makes me believe in magic, it's true, but I still want to map her bit by bit, know precisely what causes which reaction.

It's by far the most fascinating data I've ever compiled, and I pinch her nipples again, harder and this time she gasps, bites my lower lip.

"I did miss you," she murmurs, her mouth on mine, and I take her nipples between my fingers, brush my thumbs over the pads.

"Tell me again," I say, and I feel her smile against me.

"I missed you," she says, and she sits forward. "When I couldn't find you I went to your house and laid in your bed."

I move my hand, run them down her back, along her spine, feel the way she arches. I grab her ass, pull her into me, imagining her naked and spread on my bed, one hand between her legs as her eyes drift closed.

"And what did you do?" I ask, my voice rough.

"What do you think?" she murmurs.

I pull open the button on her jeans, practically rip the zipper open, splay them open around her hips. She leans back, on her elbows, and she lifts her hips and I pull her jeans off, throw them on the floor behind myself, drop to my knees.

"I think I should probably be concerned that you went to my house when I wasn't there and got yourself off on my bed," I tell her, pushing her legs apart.

I press my mouth against the inside of one thigh, then suck her soft skin into my mouth, just hard enough to leave a welt for the next day or so. She makes a soft noise that's half gasp, half moan, and I breathe in her scent: heady and musky and so, so sweet.

"I have a key," she says, her breath coming faster, teasing. "I didn't break in."

I laugh softly and mark her again, harder this time, leaving a bruise that'll last a few days on the inside of her golden thigh. I like thinking of her finding these later, in the shower, when she's getting dressed, and blushes as she remembers what left them.

I look up at her. She's propped herself up on one elbow, her eyelids low, and as she watches me she slides a hand through my hair, one knee thrown over my shoulder, her other foot on a chair.

"Are you marking me?" she asks, and I run a thumb over two small splotches on the inside of her golden thigh, my heart beating so hard I can feel it in my fingertips.

"Yes," I admit. "It's so I can come back here tomorrow and remember right now."

"Good," she says. "I like the reminder."

"Good," I say, and finally slide my hand up the inside of one now-marked thigh until my fingers reach her wetness, skimming across her lips, and her hips jerk. "I like giving you something to think about."

Thalia makes a noise in her throat that's partly a strangled groan, partly a sharp gasp, and her fingers tighten in my hair, then instantly release, like she's afraid of hurting me.

She can't. Not when she's so wet for me that my fingers are soaked from a single touch. Not when her lips are swollen with desire, not when her hips move ever so slightly toward me.

I'm lost, giddy. I want to fall into her and never come out. I want to possess her. I want her to never say another name that isn't mine. I want to be the last person to ever spread her legs and find out just how wet she is, the last person to feel her shudder at the first lick, the last person to feel her come.

Thalia says my name, barely a whisper. I slide my fingers along her slit and revel in her one last time, and I push them inside her and find her clit with my tongue and God, she moans. I lick her harder, sink myself in her to my knuckles, and I swear she tastes like honey on my tongue.

I take her right to the edge. I wait for the tremor that says she's holding her breath, that she's almost there. I wait for her toes to curl and I wait for that sound, that high-pitched gasp, and then I stop. I lick her one last time and I pull my fingers out of her, turn my head, mark her one last time as she releases me.

I stand and she's already sitting up, mouth on mine, tasting herself as she practically tears my jeans open.

"Tease," she gasps, pulling down the zipper.

"Just greedy," I say, pressing my body to hers, my mouth to hers, and she wraps her hand around my length, strokes me. "I like when you come in my mouth, but Thalia, I *really* like when you come on my cock."

"What else do you *really* like?" she murmurs, stroking me again.

"Raindrops on roses," I say, and she bites my lower lip, stopping me.

I grab a condom from my pocket and I get my pants off, my cock still in her in hands. I reach between her legs again just because I can, strum her clit again, feel the wave move through her body.

"I like that out there, you're a polite good girl, and in here you're my own personal sex goddess," I tell her. "I like the list you made of ways you want to fuck me. I like that you took notes when we tried them."

I didn't care that she was a virgin when she told me. I still don't, but there's something about knowing she's never said this to anyone else that makes my heart beat like a drum.

There's something about *first* that, despite everything, makes me flutter.

There's something about *only* that makes me feel like I own the universe.

I step back, find the chair, sit and pull her after me.

"And I like that being with you feels like the solution to a problem I didn't know I had," I say. "You're strangely like coming home, Thalia. Truth is, I just like *you*."

She straddles my lap and the chair creaks below our combined weight as she moves forward, pressing my length along herself.

"I like you too," she says, simply. I put my thumb on her lower lip, slide it over her chin, down her neck.

"But what do you *really* like?" I murmur. "Come on, Thalia."

She smiles and leans forward, her face against mine, and without looking she takes the condom out of my hand.

"I like looking across a room filled with people and knowing that I'm the one who gets to go home with you," she says, pulls back slightly. She rips the condom open with her teeth, and my cock jumps against her.

"What else do you like?" I ask, holding onto her hips as she grabs my cock, rolls the condom down it, pumping me slowly, a slow, wicked smile spreading across her face.

"I like the way you look on the very first stroke," she murmurs, breathless. "I like the way you feel inside me. I like the sound you make when you realize you're not going to hurt me and you start fucking me as hard as you can."

For a moment, I'm speechless, because I've never heard Thalia say anything like that before.

Speechless and utterly, completely desperate for her.

I grab her, pull her up until she's half-standing and half kneeling, her forehead still against mine, and I slide the tip of my cock against her clit, between her lips, against her tight, hot entrance.

"Are you teasing me?" I whisper.

"No," she murmurs. "I'm savoring the moment right before you make me lose my mind."

With that, she sinks onto me. Her eyes slide closed and she groans, her fingernails digging into my shoulders as she takes me all in one stroke and my vision goes black, then gray.

I have her by the hips, holding her so tight I think I might leave bruises but I can't stop myself, pulling her down, pushing as deep as I can as she moans, her hips rolling, her whole body a single movement that begs me for more.

"That look," she whispers.

"The one I make because you feel so fucking good I'm afraid I'm going to come instantly?" I ask, voice rough and low.

She leans forward and kisses me. It's a soft kiss, a delicate kiss, careful and gentle, even as she rolls her hips against me and moves my cock inside her and I can't help but growl, can't help but grab her and move her and push myself harder and deeper and feel the quiver that moves through her body.

I want her. I *need* her like I didn't know I could need someone else. I want her to belong to me in a way that transcends possession, that transcends everything. I want to burn her into my skin just so everyone who sees me knows whose I am.

We kiss again and then she leans away, just slightly. She reaches behind herself and anchors her hands on my thighs. She rocks back and forth and I drag her into me, over and over again, as hard and deep as I can.

I watch her face, feel the way she shakes and I hit that spot over and over again. She whimpers, moans, bites her lip. Her breasts bounce, her nipples tracing circles in the air and she's gloriously beautiful, flushed and rapturous and, unbelievably, *mine*.

"Caleb," she whispers, and she reaches one hand for my face, darts a thumb across my lips.

"Thalia," I answer, the only word I have right now.

"You're not gonna hurt me," she says.

I pull her onto my cock as hard as I can. Every muscle in my body tenses and Thalia cries out, gasps, digs her nails into my thighs so I do it again and she whimpers, moans, pulls me forward.

"Please," she says, the words hardly audible. "Caleb, please."

"I love you," I say, and she trembles and I sink as hard and deep as I can, like maybe I can meld our bodies into one.

"I love you back," she says.

"Come," I tell her, the word a growl, a command, a foretelling as she flutters, clenches, her foreshocks rocking through me. "Let me feel you come, please let me feel you —"

"Caleb," she whimpers, and she does.

I feel like the earth shakes, like the timber of my bones might crack apart. Thalia is a cataclysm, a force of nature, unstoppable and perfect as she says my name again and again and clenches like a fist around me, still somehow begging for more.

I follow her instantly, helplessly. Everything I have is hers, and I offer it over and over until she finally stops moving, warm and supple against me. I kiss her on the neck and on the cheek and then, finally, on the mouth, my arms around her as she curls herself around me.

We stay like that for a long time, my face pressed into the crook of her neck, her chin atop my head as I run my fingers up and down her spine and she traces idle circles on one shoulder.

Finally she shifts, just enough that I slide out of her, and she moves and sits on me sidesaddle, one arm slung around my shoulders as I lean back against the chair that we've probably just sullied.

"I have a confession," she says, playing with my hair again.

"Go on," I say, and can't help but smile.

"I lied about what I was doing on your bed when I went to your house."

I pause for a moment, looking at her.

"Were you really on my bed?" I ask, tapping my fingers against her back.

"I was," she says. "I really did miss you. I just didn't lie there and think of you and masturbate."

Damn.

"You just laid there and missed me, then?" I ask.

"Not exactly."

"Thalia," I say, and I'm trying to scold her just a little, but my voice comes out slow and lazy. "The hell did you do on my bed?"

"I called your brother," she says, her eyes dancing with laughter. "To see if he knew where you were."

I can't help but smile, start laughing myself.

"Thank you for lying earlier," I say. "That's the least erotic thing you could have said."

"I'm sure it's not the *least* erotic," she says, then gives me a quick kiss and hops off my lap, heading for the bathroom.

"It is," I call. "Seth's a total bonerkiller."

"Be nice, he's letting us stay with him," she calls back, then shuts the door.

· · · · ★ ★ ★ ★ ★ · · · ·

THE ROOM HAS A FOUR-POSTER BED, a plush couch, and a fireplace, not to mention a very fancy shower and fluffy, luxe bathrobes.

We sit on the couch in bathrobes and debate which founding father was the coolest, though we quickly settle on Benjamin Franklin. We talk about my future and our future and then my future again, though it's not much of a distinction because it's obvious they're the same thing. We talk about a month from now and six months from now and a year from now and we both assume that we'll still be together so easily that it's completely unremarkable.

Then she takes a shower and obviously, I interrupt it and it turns out I like the way she moans my name when her voice is bouncing off tile.

We fall asleep together in the huge bed, and I don't dream about a single thing.

CHAPTER FIFTY-THREE
CALEB

I hear the door shut downstairs and the sound jerks me from half-awake to fully awake, the springs of Seth's sofa bed sighing underneath me. I lie there, Thalia sleeping next to me, her arm draped over my chest, and I listen.

Footsteps: a creak on that floorboard in Seth's living room, then quickly, quietly, up the stairs.

I glance at the clock: six-thirty in the morning, and a dark shadow flickers across my heart because I know, I *know*, that he's just now coming home. I haven't seen him since Friday afternoon, and now it's Sunday morning, and I have a sinking feeling about where he's been.

I move Thalia's arm as gently as I can, roll off the sofa bed. I find my pants in the dark and pull them on, glance back at her one more time, open the door of Seth's office and close it quietly behind myself.

Two doors down, the outline of my brother pauses.

"Did you just get home?" I ask.

"I went out for a run," he says, his voice quiet, hushed.

"In jeans?"

Seth sighs, rocks back on his heels. He turns and faces

me, arms folded over his chest, and looks me dead in the eye.

"What?" he says.

"Don't do this," I say, softly.

"Do what?" he says, his voice low, quiet, deadly.

"Don't go back to her again," I say, nearly whispering. "Do you remember the last time? You *swore* —"

"I was lying," he says, and I close my eyes, take a deep breath.

"Please?" I ask.

My eyes are adjusting, and now I can see his face, light eyes and dark hair, cheeks and jaw and chin all variations on my own.

"I'm fine," he says, answering the question that I didn't even have to ask.

"Are you?" I say, and the words drop like a stone into the floor, lie there between us.

"Of course I am," he says, and turns away, opens his bedroom door. "I'm totally fucking fine, just like always. I'm gonna take a shower, see you in a few."

Seth closes the door behind himself and I stand there, glaring at it, wishing that I knew black magic so I could curse her name.

Then I take a deep breath, shake it off, and go back into a sleeping Thalia.

CHAPTER FIFTY-FOUR
THALIA

"All right," says Caleb, looking at his phone and swiping a few times. "So far, so good. Next."

He holds his phone screen out to me and I lean forward, studying the face that he's zoomed in on: bearded, brown-eyed, very obviously one of his brothers.

"Levi," I say instantly. "I met him yesterday. Oldest brother, engaged to June, lives in the cabin he built, Chief Arborist for the National Forest, has a dog named Hedwig and a rug named Jedediah."

"Excellent," says Caleb, taking the phone back and swiping more, then holding it out again.

"Violet," I say. "Married to Eli, the middle brother —"

"Second oldest," Caleb corrects.

"Damn. Married to Eli, the second oldest, lives in the house on the lake, manages operations at the Folk Art museum."

"You're on fire," Caleb says, grinning, looking at his phone and swiping some more. "Okay, who's this?"

He holds out a picture of a man who's handsome and

smiling, but who doesn't look related to him. For a moment, I'm stumped.

Then I snap my fingers.

"June's brother," I say. "Levi's friend. Lawyer, former Marine..."

"And his name is...?"

I squeeze my eyes shut in concentration.

"Rhymes with... guileless, sort of?"

"Guileless?" I repeat, baffled.

Then, it hits me.

"Silas?" I say.

"Correct!" Caleb says.

We're sitting on Seth's couch in his living room, both drinking coffee while Caleb quizzes me on the people I'll probably meet this afternoon.

"That doesn't rhyme at all," Seth's voice says from the staircase, and half a second later, he appears.

"Seth," I say to Caleb, pointing. "Fourth oldest, owns the brewery with Daniel."

"Don't forget coolest, handsomest, and smartest," Seth says, walking in front of us and to the kitchen.

"He's not that cool," Caleb says, flipping through pictures again as he sips his coffee. "Or that smart," he mutters, mostly to himself.

"Did you make flashcards?" Seth calls.

"Not technically," Caleb calls back.

"Dork," Seth says.

"Dweeb," says Caleb.

Seth comes out of the kitchen with his own steaming mug, looks from me to Caleb and back, then takes a seat in the leather armchair opposite us as Caleb holds his phone out toward me again.

"Daniel," I say. "Married to Charlie, owns the brewery with Seth, has a nine-year-old named Rusty and a baby named Thomas. Will give you a hard time if you curse in front of his kids."

"He's relaxed about that a little," Seth offers. "I think Rusty's finally learned about context and doesn't call the lunch line at school a *total clusterfuck* any more."

"Charlie's also a calming influence," Caleb says, flipping through pictures again. "I think that's pretty much everyone."

"And if you get a name wrong, don't panic," Seth offers. "Mom still doesn't get my name right on the first try half the time, and she gave birth to me."

"I'm Levi or Daniel a lot," Caleb says. "Even though I'm way better looking."

"I get Javier sometimes, and we're not even the same gender," I offer.

"Last week Mom called me Thomas, and he's been dead for almost twenty years," Seth says. "Unless she meant the baby, I guess."

Caleb and I exchange a quick, half-second glance, and then it's over. I wonder if he'll ever tell his brothers. I wonder if he *should*.

"You and Eli do look a lot like Dad," Caleb says.

"So I hear," Seth says, then finishes his mug, stands, stretches. "Anyone else need more coffee? I'm gonna make another pot."

· · · * * ★ * * · · ·

"YOU'RE NOT NERVOUS, ARE YOU?" he asks, taking my hand as we walk up the gravel driveway to the big, old farmhouse.

We're back in the woods, probably a quarter mile from the road, the naked trees waving overhead in the breeze.

It's cold but clear, the air so crisp I swear it smells like leaves and granite.

"Of course I'm nervous," I say. "I'm about to meet your entire family for the first time and I just cost you your job."

"No, *I* cost me my —"

"You know what I mean," I say, my other hand tugging at the scarf around my neck. It's the same one he lent me a few months ago, and even though I keep offering to give it back, he never takes it.

"I do," he says, slowly. "But I prefer to think of you as the girl so amazing that I didn't mind giving up my job, and that's definitely how I've been pitching this."

"Thanks," I say, and I try to sound light, but I'm nervous. Of course I'm nervous. I'm sure it would be easy to see me as some wicked seductress who led to their youngest brother's downfall, not to mention I'm younger than Caleb and *way* younger than his brothers.

That said, I did do the math, and I'm technically closer in age to Levi than to Rusty, so hopefully they still let me sit at the grownups' table.

We head up the stairs to the front porch, but before Caleb opens the screen door, he turns to me, takes my shoulder in the hand that isn't holding several baguettes.

"I love you, and so will they," he says, quietly, then gives me a quick, soft kiss.

"Thanks," I say again, trying to quell the beating of my heart.

Then Caleb glances at the door, and for the first time, he looks a little apprehensive.

"That said, their love can be kind of a lot, so steel yourself," he says, and pulls the door open.

" — tell pine from oak just by looking at it," someone is already shouting. "It all looks wooden."

"The heavier one is oak," a voice calls from the next room.

"Hey, Caleb," says a woman's voice as we step inside, and I look around. "Oh! Shit! Hey, Thalia!"

"Hey, Charlie," Caleb says, already laughing. "This is —"

She's already practically scooped me up in a hug, her wild curly hair all over the place.

"We're so glad you could make it!" she says, cutting Caleb off. "Seriously, it's been nothing but 'Thalia this' and 'Thalia that,' so thank God you're finally here!"

"It's nice to meet you too," I say when she releases me, slightly stunned.

"Hey, Thalia," calls a man who's kneeling in front of the fireplace. "Can you tell pine from oak?"

"One's got needles," I point out, and Charlie laughs.

"I mean in log form," says Eli, standing and brushing his hands off. "Hi, it's nice to meet you in person."

He also gives me a hug. Apparently we're all huggers here.

"Here, I've got your name tag," a woman says as he lets me go, and I turn to see Violet holding up a large sticker that says:

HELLO
My name is
THALIA

- Caleb's girlfriend
- Psych major
- Navy brat

"Wow," I say, because for a moment, words truly fail me, but Violet just laughs.

"I tried to include at least one conversation starter," she says. "Oh, here's Caleb's."

"I'm literally the one person here who everyone knows," he points out, accepting the sticker anyway.

"Let me have my fun," Violet says, and he dutifully puts the sticker on his chest.

"This was fun?" he teases her.

"You have no idea," she says.

· · · · · ★ ★ ★ ★ ★ · · · ·

CALEB WAS RIGHT, and everyone is wonderful. For a little while I feel guilty about how nice they are, just welcoming me into their lives like they've been waiting this whole time, especially when my own family has been somewhat less than kind to Caleb.

Okay, a lot less than kind.

But still, I remember what Caleb told me when I was crying on the floor of his bedroom, when I called his family perfect and he laughed and told me everyone's flaws, the ways they'd fucked up.

Finally, meeting most of his family for the first time, I realize his point: flaws are just flaws, not the entirety of a person. They matter, but what really matters is learning to look past them.

I meet Eli (whose name tag says *older brother / married to Violet / chef*), who tries to get me on his side in some argument he's having with Levi about wood, and Violet (*married to Eli / knows a lot about quilts*), who laughs and pokes holes in his logic.

There's Levi (*oldest brother / engaged to June / likes trees*), and June (*engaged to Levi / ask me anything about old-timey outlaws*), who I met yesterday at dinner, and I talk to them for a while about the checkered history of firearms in national parks. It turns out that June has a deep and broad knowledge of everyone who's been murdered in a national park, and we talk for a *while*.

I meet Rusty (*Daniel and Charlie's daughter / knows skateboarding tricks*), who very quickly tells me that technically, Charlie is her stepmom but since Charlie is her legal guardian, she and Violet decided to simplify the name tag. She also asks me if I know anything about an Olympic sport called *skeleton*.

I do not. She tells me. It's like the luge, but you go head first.

I hold Thomas (*Daniel and Charlie's son / hates socks*). I meet Clara (*mom / astronomer / baker of pies*), and we talk for a long time about grad school, about academia, and then finally about why we can send people to the moon but not make high heels that don't suck.

We have dinner, then pie, and by the time that I'm practically quizzing Daniel (*middle brother / married to Charlie / Rusty and Thomas's dad / co-owns the brewery*) about yeast behavior at various temperatures during the fermentation process, I've completely forgotten that I was ever nervous to meet them in the first place.

· · · · ★ ★ ★ ★ ★ · · · ·

AFTER DESSERT I use the bathroom upstairs, and when I come out, Caleb is on the landing, alone.

"I'm allowed to be in there," I tell him, and he just laughs.

"I didn't come to bust you for using the wrong bathroom, I came to see how you were doing," he says, keeping his voice low, glancing at the stairs. "Like I said, I know they can be a lot."

At the bottom of the stairs, someone — Silas? — is

asking loudly about some kind of event permit, Thomas is starting to fuss, and I can hear Daniel very patiently explaining that something or other is dangerous. I don't know what's dangerous, but I'm pretty sure I know who he's talking to.

Caleb casts a suspicious glance at the downstairs, then nods his head and pulls me into one of the bedrooms.

"Was this one yours?" I ask, looking around. Right now it's just a guest room: bed, dresser, curtains, all perfectly nice but nothing that suggests who slept here.

"They were all mine at some point," he says. "I think we changed who slept where every six months or so. There were a lot of shifting alliances."

"Sounds tricky," I say, still glancing around.

"It wasn't really," Caleb says, laughing. "If nothing else, we're all pretty straightforward so it was pretty much a matter of me telling Daniel that I was annoyed with him and I'd like to sleep in Levi's room now, please, or Levi getting tired of sleeping with a middle-schooler and swapping me for Eli, or... you get the idea."

"I don't. I'm the only girl, I always had my own room," I say.

"Aren't you fancy?"

"Yes."

"You doing okay?" he asks, pushing a strand of hair from my face.

"With your family?"

He nods.

"I am," I say, a little surprised at how easily the words come. "They're really nice. And actually interesting."

"That's one way to put it," he says, and I laugh.

"I like them," I say. "I like you, and I like them. Deal with it."

"If you insist," he says, bends down, and kisses me.

I very, very briefly consider the guest bed that we're standing next to, but it's clearly the worst idea in the history of bad ideas.

"Thanks for calling Seth from my bed and tracking me down," he says when the kiss is over. "I was a little out of sorts."

The corner of his name tag sticks to me slightly, and I pull it from my shirt, anchor it back to him.

"You like it?" he asks, looking down.

HELLO
my name is
CALEB

- Youngest brother
- Thalia's boyfriend
- Good at math

"I guess it's only fair," I point out. "Though I'm not really sure who it's for."

"It's for Violet and June, who made these and thought it was funny," he says, smiling.

"They were right."

"I kind of like having a label that says I'm your boyfriend," he says, running his finger across the handwritten name tag one more time.

"It does look good on you," I tease. "Should we head back out there? I should head back to Marysburg soon, I've got class in the morning."

"Probably," he says, but as I turn he catches my hand.

"Hey, Thalia."

I just raise one eyebrow.

"Love you," he says.

I twist his hand around in mine, bring his knuckles to my lips.

"Love you too," I say. "And for the record, I love them. Flaws and all."

"I wouldn't say that until you know their flaws," he murmurs.

"I know yours and I love you anyway," I point out, and he leans in again, rests his forehead against mine.

"I have no idea what I'm going to do," he admits, his voice low, quiet. "To be totally honest, I only know one thing."

The base of my neck tingles, and I close my eyes, lean into him.

"What's that?"

"I'll be doing it next to you," he says. "And I'm pretty sure I can handle anything if you're with me."

"Anything?"

"Anything."

I put a hand around his neck, draw him in, kiss him. He tastes a little like cinnamon, smells a little bit of pine and just-fallen leaves and I wonder again, for the thousandth time, at my luck in finding him.

Then the kiss ends. Caleb squeezes my hand, reaches for the door, pulls it open and the cacophony floods in.

And it sounds just like home.

EPILOGUE

THALIA

SIX MONTHS LATER

I ignore the sweat pouring down my back and crouch in front of the box, bending my legs and keeping my back straight. The corners firmly in my hands, I take a deep breath, plant my heels, and lift.

"Ollie, for fuck's sake," a voice behind me says.

"I got it," I gasp out, fingers already slipping.

"You don't," Javier says, hurrying around the other side of the box I'm attempting to lift. "What happened to *I'll get the smaller boxes*?"

He wraps his arms around it and takes it from me, lifting it like it weighs nothing.

"I can get that one!" I protest, but Javier ignores me and walks down the ramp of the moving truck, then into the open front door of our apartment.

"Do you think you're Rosie the Riveter again?" Bastien asks, hopping up into the moving truck.

"I've been taking a weightlifting class at the gym," I

protest, eyeing the rest of the boxes, because I think Javier just took the last one I had even half a chance of lifting.

The rest all seem to be labeled *BOOKS*.

Turns out that between Caleb and I, we have a whole lot of books. That's actually one of the reasons we picked this apartment in Ochreville, the town that contains the Virginia Institute of Technology: the living room is lined with bookshelves.

"Has that made you taller than five-foot-two or infused your body with testosterone?" Bastien asks, casually lifting a box and hoisting it onto his shoulder.

"I'm five four," I tell him, and finally grab a floor lamp that's sitting next to a box. It's very light, and I carry it into our new living room, then plant it on the floor and look around.

Boxes. Boxes everywhere, interspersed with furniture that mostly came from Caleb's old apartment, because it's not like I fought to keep the coffee table that Harper, Victoria, Margaret and I found on a curb our sophomore year.

"Which room is green?" asks a voice, followed moments later by Silas, bringing another box in.

"Green is the study, purple is the bedroom, blue is the living room," Levi says with the patience of someone who's explained something a thousand times. "It's on the chart on the wall."

"You know, Thalia," Silas calls, walking down the hall. "Some people just label their boxes with words."

"Every system has flaws," I call after him and Levi.

I didn't even know Silas was coming until he showed up this morning at Levi's house, where Caleb and I had spent the night. He claimed that he just wanted the free donuts and pizza, but as we were driving, Caleb told me his suspicions.

It's early August, and the two months since I've graduated have been a whirlwind. My lease with my roommates ended in June, so I moved in with Caleb for a little while. Dr. Castellano offered me a summer job continuing my research for her before I started graduate school this fall, and Caleb got a freelance gig writing problems for a mathematics textbook.

Slowly but surely, things are working themselves out. I kept my scholarship and graduated Magna Cum Laude; Caleb has been tutoring and working on textbooks and generally figuring out what to do with his life, now that he can do anything.

I was worried he'd hate it. I was worried that he'd resent me for losing his job, that he'd feel like he'd wasted years of his life in graduate school only spend one semester as a professor, but he's been fine.

Happy, even. Almost giddy. Once a week he comes home with some new harebrained scheme, and even though he never acts on any of them — an audio tour of the Appalachian Trail? An app that will instantly tell you if a number is prime or not? — he's got a verve and energy just talking about them, about all the possibilities that he's got now.

"You're not just standing around, are you?" he says, and speak of the devil, Caleb comes into the living room through the sliding glass door that leads to the back yard we share with the other two apartments in this building.

"I'm strategizing," I say, my hands on my hips.

"Sure," he says, grinning. "Looks exhausting."

"Well, every time I try to move a box someone else comes along and does it for me," I point out.

"Poor thing," he teases.

"I've accepted that my fate is to direct the lot of you," I say. "Someone's gotta be the project manager."

"And someone's gotta be the workhorse?" he asks, raising his eyebrows.

I just shrug, laughing, and he heads back outside to get some more boxes.

Twenty minutes later, it's done. Or, at least, everything that was once in the moving truck is now in our apartment, so Silas, Levi, Javier, and Bastien are done.

Our unpacking adventure, on the other hand, is just beginning. Or it will be, soon. Not today.

Today, the six of us flop on the floor, couch, and kitchen chairs, drinking cold lemonade that I had the foresight to bring. I'm on the couch between Bastien and Caleb, Levi is on a kitchen chair flipping through my paperback of *One Hundred Years of Solitude*, and Silas and Javier are on the floor while Silas digs through a box of my old textbooks.

"That's also the golden ratio," Javier is saying, lifting lemonade to his lips. "Everything is the golden ratio. It's golden. Humans just like it."

"What about the *Mona Lisa*?" Silas asks.

Javier leans back on his hands, sighing and looking thoughtful. He's still wearing long sleeves, despite the heat, but his skin is back to being the right color. There's life in his eyes again. He's been out of rehab for a little over three months, and so far, I think it's working.

"Probably," he says. "Da Vinci was all about using math in art."

Caleb leans back, puts one arm around me.

One second later, he takes it back.

"Sorry," he says. "Too hot."

"Also, you're sticky," I say, laughing.

On the floor, Silas pulls out my Abnormal Psychology textbook.

"Well, you're also sticky," Caleb says, resting his hands on top of his head. "We should unpack the shower first."

"Pretty sure the shower's already there," I say, and Caleb just laughs.

"I'm not the one who has a specific conditioner for each day of the week," he teases. "Just hand me some dish soap and I'm good."

"I didn't just hear that," I tell him. "Are you *trying* to decimate your moisture barrier?"

"Yes?" he asks, quizzically. "No? Which one's the right answer?"

"No," offers Levi, still reading *One Hundred Years of Solitude*. "You need your moisture barrier."

I point at Caleb's oldest brother.

"He knows," I say.

"Fine," Caleb concedes. "We'll unpack the shower accoutrement before bathing."

We go quiet again. Silas and Javier are still talking, leaning against boxes, as Silas asks Javier why my textbook is so ugly and Javier explains all the design problems with the cover.

He's been taking graphic design courses at night and working in a hardware store during the day, still living with my parents, and I admit, that last part worries me. I wish I could get him out of Norfolk, away from the same people who were there last time he slipped, but I haven't been able to yet.

On my other side, Bastien leans in toward me.

"You know," he confesses, quietly, "I thought there would be fewer shirts."

I look around the room, and then at him.

"Is that why you helped?" I ask, giving him a look.

"No, I helped because you're my favorite sister and you asked very nicely," he says. "But…"

"You *know* they're all straight," I point out. "And also one is your brother."

"I wasn't excited for *him* taking his shirt off," he says. "And I know they're straight. Doesn't mean I can't look."

Caleb leans toward me again.

"What are you two talking about?" he murmurs. "Are you talking about Silas and your brother?"

"Sort of," I say.

"It's not important," Bastien says.

"Wait, what about them?" I ask.

They're still talking, animatedly, sitting on the floor. Now Silas is just pulling random books from boxes, and they're flipping through them, talking, laughing.

"I think this is why Silas came," Caleb says.

"To meet Javier?" I say, quietly, as my brother and my boyfriend both lean in toward me.

"Wait, what?" Bastien asks. "Hold on."

"Silas heard that you had a brother in rehab who'd come out of the Marines with some pretty bad problems," Caleb says, shrugging. "He asked me a ton of questions last time we were both at my mom's for dinner, probably because he's also a former Marine."

Bastien and I just stare at Silas and Javier, on the floor, chatting away.

"Huh," we say, exactly in unison, then look at each other.

"Jinx, you owe me a coke," Bastien says.

"Put it on my tab," I tell him, then lean back, into the couch.

"Okay," I say, raising my voice enough that the whole room can hear me. "What kind of pizza do you guys want?"

· · · · ★ ★ ★ ★ · · · ·

AFTER WE EAT, Silas and Levi both leave for Sprucevale again, though Silas gives Javier his card before heading out. I unearth a trash bag, throw away pizza boxes and paper plates, and then take a good, long look around at the apartment.

At *our* apartment.

It still feels a little surreal. I've wondered a couple times if this is a good idea, if moving in with my older boyfriend at twenty-three is the right move. From the outside, it looks weird, like I'm settling down too fast when I should be sowing my wild oats and living a wild life and… whatever you're supposed to do in your twenties.

But I don't feel any of that. I know I'm supposed to wonder what it's like to have sex with other people, but the truth is, I don't really care. I found my person. What does it matter if anyone else is out there?

I'm still standing there, looking at the living room, when Caleb comes up behind me and wraps an arm around my waist, slings the other over my shoulder, rests his chin on top of my head.

"We should probably get rid of some books before the next time we move," he says, contemplating boxes.

"I can't think about moving again right now," I admit.

"I thought it went pretty well."

"It did," I say, hooking my hands over his arms and leaning back. "Though I think I lifted, like, two things, so of course it went well for me."

It also went well because I got to watch Caleb lift a lot of heavy things, which is one of my favorite sights, even if he didn't take his shirt off.

Down the hall, in the room that's destined to be the study, I can hear Bastien and Javier talking, the sound of an air mattress being inflated. They're spending the night and heading back to the Tidewater tomorrow.

"You're not going to surprise me by being one of those people who organizes her bookshelf by color, are you?" he asks, his arms still around me.

"What if I am?" I say, still leaning back.

"Well, I'd point out that there are far better ways to organize a bookshelf," he says, his voice dipping. "And I, for one, value efficiency over looks."

"I'm gonna make a heart," I tell him, and point at the bookshelves. "Right there. In the middle."

He just sighs.

"And I'm gonna mix all your nerdy sci-fi books with my Jane Austen, and your number theory stuff with my neurology stuff, and you know what else?"

"I can't bear to listen," he says, laughing quietly.

"I'm not even going to separate fiction from nonfiction," I whisper dramatically. "It'll be chaos. You'll rue the day you decided to live with me."

"I doubt *that*," he says. "Chaos, yes, obviously. Rue the day, never."

"Textbooks and poetry, side by side," I threaten.

"You're gonna have to try way harder than that to get rid of me," he says, arms still tight. "Thalia, I'll love you even if you start using bookshelves for non-book items. Like plants, or knickknacks."

"Even knickknacks?" I tease.

"Even knickknacks," he confirms. "Even if they're creepy porcelain dolls."

I just laugh.

"I won't," I promise. "I love you too much for that."

"Thank you," he says, and plants a kiss on top of my head, and we stand there for a long moment, just looking at the living room together.

"I like this place," I say, finally. "I like that it's ours."

"I like that too," he says, softly. "And I like that the next place we live will also be ours, and the next one, and the next one."

I turn my head so that I fit perfectly under his chin, speak to his shoulder. It's been a long, hot, hard day, and my whole body feels slightly fuzzy, like I'm out of focus. Like I'm fading into him.

"Promise?" I ask.

"Absolutely," he says. "You're gonna have to grow old listening to my opinions about bookshelf organization."

"Only if you agree to grow old watching me rearrange books to be prettier," I tease.

"I can't think of a better way to live," he says, and I laugh, and I raise his hand to my lips and kiss his knuckles.

"Love you," I say, softly.

"Love you back," Caleb says.

I close my eyes. I relax, sinking into him. I try to crystallize this moment in my mind, this second where everything is perfect, because I know it won't always be. There will be rough times and fights and we'll get angry with each other, and I might need this moment then.

We'll get through it. I have complete and utter faith in that, in our love for each other, in the unbreakable chain that binds my heart to his.

I still don't believe in magic.

But this, I know, is magical.

The End

ABOUT ROXIE

Roxie is a romance author by day, and also a romance author by night. She lives in Los Angeles with one husband, two cats, far too many books, and a truly alarming pile of used notebooks that she refuses to throw away.

www.roxienoir.com
roxie@roxienoir.com

Made in United States
North Haven, CT
23 June 2024